Prais

"This is a fast-paced novel in which several apparently disparate threads converge in a potentially catastrophic conclusion. Along the way, it is a medical novel, a romance novel, and an international terrorism intrigue novel. It is also a great learning experience for people unfamiliar with toxicology and practical epidemiology as well as the foibles of academic medicine."

- Phil Harber, MD,
Adjunct Professor of Public Health,
University of Arizona
Professor Emeritus,
UCLA School of Medicine

'I found this first novel by Bob McCunney to be a thrilling and informative read, not a combination you often find. The plot involves a Boston physician, Dan Murphy, who starts to receive patients with unusual symptoms who work in one particular chemical business in South Boston, which uses unofficial Irish labour. The other plot that twists around this one concerns a revenge-seeking British intelligence officer who strives to exact revenge for losing his wife and one limb in an IRA bombing in London. McCunney is extremely knowledgeable on both the Irish republican question, as seen from the American side, as well as the business of getting to the bottom of an environmental disease; the result is both an exhilarating and instructive read. The main characters are expertly drawn, especially the physician Dan Murphy and also the one-legged British spy, whose psychological state is menacingly revealed. The developing romance between Murphy and a student is well-judged and together they form a team that cracks open the mystery of the link between the illness in the chemical factory workers and the IRA, in a nail-biting conclusion. The lesser characters are expertly drawn and generally the atmosphere of Boston's Irish community, as well as its medical community, give credence and background to a well-constructed story that has a satisfying and explosive conclusion.'

- Ken Donaldson, PhD,
Research Fellow, Royal College of
Surgeons Museum, Edinburgh
Former Professor
University of Edinburgh Medical School,
Edinburgh, Scotland.

"Cluster will keep you gripped and intrigued throughout the story. Dr. McCunney deftly employs his experience in occupational and environmental medicine to create a realistic storyline with everyday characters to which that anyone can relate. He uses the backdrop of Boston, a lively city bustling with academia, culture, and history to create a realistic perspective. For readers familiar with the city, it is easy to place yourself among its streets, cafes and neighborhoods. The imagery is geniusly crafted and places the reader in real time throughout the story. The characters are each uniquely bonded in ways that one only learns as the story unfolds. Several subplots bring the characters together in unexpected ways. Psychological drama, terrorism, a deadly illness, a gambling addiction, medicine, a tantalizing romance, and international viewpoints are all intensely intertwined. McCunney does an excellent job of building climax both in the story and in the bedroom as romance heightens this thriller. As the story nears its resolution, an unexpected turn of events and a psychological twist bring you to another level of perspicacity. The human element leaves you to ponder in ways you may not have otherwise considered. Simply brilliant!

- Jacqueline LaSalle, MAT,
Educator

"In this his first novel, Dr. Robert McCunney brings together three seemingly unrelated stories: an academic investigation of a "cluster" of obscure disease; the role of the IRA in Brexit and contemporary politics; and the burgeoning romance between a graduate student and her mentor. McCunney deftly weaves these stories into an explosive conclusion (actually several explosions!) while illustrating the process by which public health experts explore the causes of diseases in our increasingly complex world. A fast-moving read!!"

- Jonathan Borak, MD
Clinical Professor
Yale University School of Medicine

Aplastic anemia, the Irish Troubles, Brexit, Boston, terrorism, hazardous exposures, occupational medicine, epidemiology, and love. What do they have in common? You'll have to read Cluster, a new novel that blends all these together into a compelling story that's both entertaining and educational.

- Paul Brandt-Rauf, ScD. MD, DrPH.
Dean and Distinguished University Professor,
School of Biomedical Engineering, Science and Health Systems
at Drexel University. Editor, Journal of Occupational and
Environmental Medicine

Cluster

Cluster

A potentially fatal disease, a tantalizing romance and international terrorism converge with explosive consequences in this medical thriller.

Robert J. McCunney

Archway Publishing books may be ordered through booksellers or by contacting:

Archway Publishing
1663 Liberty Drive
Bloomington, IN 47403
www.archwaypublishing.com
844-669-3957

ISBN: 978-1-6657-4396-9 (sc)
ISBN: 978-1-6657-4397-6 (hc)
ISBN: 978-1-6657-4398-3 (e)

Library of Congress Control Number: 2023908896

Print information available on the last page.

Archway Publishing rev. date: 08/07/2023

To my parents, who inspired in me at a
young age the love of reading and writing.
To them, I will be forever grateful.

Acknowledgements

Writing this book, in addition to considerable patience and persistence, has required the advice of numerous people, who have provided support, inspiration and encouragement. Attending writers' workshops and participation in an invigorating creative writing course at Harvard, along with reading books too numerous to mention, have been instrumental in helping me understand the principles of developing plot and characters and the critical importance of researching topics in depth to make the story realistic and scientifically accurate.

The following friends, family and colleagues have kindly reviewed various drafts: Dr. Phil Harber, Dr. Ken Donaldson, Dr. Jonathan Borak, Dr. Jon O'Neal, Jacqueline LaSalle, Ruthie Nelson, my brother Jim McCunney, Doreen O'Brien and Mary Beth Hardy. An earlier version of the book was also reviewed by my deceased father, an avid reader of novels. Dr. Ken Miller, a noted hematologist, provided me an on-site review of a Bone Marrow Transplant Unit and helped me understand the challenges of a bone marrow transplant and the corresponding risks of serious consequences. And finally, I'd like to add a special thanks to Ellie Eckhoff, my partner and love who provided support, guidance and motivation to complete the seemingly unending challenge in bringing the book to completion.

I wrote the book to both entertain and provide a glimpse into how to pursue the cause of a disease with no acknowledged cause. Too often in my medical career, I have tried to address the concerns of patients bewildered and frustrated about being told the cause of their disease was idiopathic-in medical parlance- of unknown cause. Hopefully, this book will offer readers a glimpse into one aspect of this challenge-evaluating a potential occupational and environmental cause of a disease.

Prologue

As he departed the rooftop restaurant after lunch with an old college friend, Parker Barrows looked out the window and down onto the street activity he so often associated with the flavor of London. A few minutes later, he descended in the elevator and strolled through the hotel lobby en route to the Hyde Park station. A short ride on London's Underground rail system brought him to Piccadilly Circus, where he took the elevator to street level. Crowds milled about and people hurried in all directions. He feared being knocked over in the flurry of activity but was able to successfully navigate his way to Trafalgar Square.

With a few hours to spare until he met his wife of a year for dinner to celebrate their wedding anniversary, Barrows thought a few hours at the National Gallery of Art would be a welcome diversion. In the mood for reflection, he hoped that a leisurely stroll among the famous Dutch, French, and English masters of the past few centuries would smoothen the edge he'd acquired from the pressure and tension of his work for the British secret service.

After savoring his time at the art gallery, Barrows walked to Leicester Square and past the ticket office for the half-price theater. He continued to wander through the West End and passed through Covent Garden and Chinatown, en route to the restaurant where he planned to meet his wife, Susan. After years of being single, he had never imagined that he would fall in love in his late thirties.

A few blocks later, he entered the Albertina Restaurant and was met by the alluring smile of the woman who had helped make his life so much more interesting and stimulating than it had been before he'd met her.

Seated at a table by the window overlooking the chaotic street scene of West End London, she reached out to him with open arms.

"How wonderful to see you, darling," Barrows said as he drew up a chair. "Happy anniversary."

Susan kissed him on the lips in response, enhancing the mood with her smile, which Barrows considered magical.

A waiter approached and handed each of them a menu. "Good evening. Can I offer you a drink?" he asked.

"Yes. Of course," Barrows replied. "I'll have a Glenfiddich, and my beautiful wife will have a glass of the best chardonnay you have."

"How was your day?" Barrows asked, his smile hinting at his love to even the most casual observer.

"Crazy—and stressful. People are selling everything," answered Susan, a financial analyst for a major international investment firm.

Within minutes, the waiter obliged them with their drinks.

"To us," they said in unison as they tapped their glasses together. Once they began to sip their drinks, a thunderous blast rocketed throughout the restaurant. Screams of frightened people filled the air. Chairs tumbled in the background, and breaking glass flew in all directions. Barrows and his wife were knocked to the floor and lost consciousness. Soon the wail of sirens from ambulances filled the air, along with the relentless and horrifying cries of the injured.

Momentarily, Barrows regained consciousness, but he was still dazed as he looked around. He began calling out in fear, "Susan! Susan!"

Hearing no reply, he tried to stand but fell over, looking down at his crushed right leg, which was bleeding profusely. He fought the urge to pass out and crawled in Susan's direction. When he reached her, she was lying on her side, unresponsive, with blood covering her pale blue dress. Barrows cried in agony when he saw a large sliver of glass stuck in her neck with blood exiting without restraint. He frantically tried to stop the bleeding until he passed out again from the trauma and blood loss.

Faintly, Barrows heard the arrival of the emergency medical team, who lifted him onto a gurney for the ride to the hospital. The techs quickly wrapped his leg in a tourniquet to prevent further bleeding. Susan and Parker, along with other injured people, were promptly whisked away in ambulances to the hospital.

—

Barrows finally regained consciousness in the surgical intensive care unit. He looked over to a nurse and motioned to her to get her attention. "What happened?" he inquired, his mind still blurred from the anesthesia.

"You needed emergency surgery, Mr. Barrows. I'm sorry to have to tell you this, but your leg was so crushed that it couldn't be saved."

"My God!" he exclaimed, turning to his side in disbelief of the news. "Where's my wife?" The fear in his voice was palpable as he expected a sad reply.

"I'm sorry, sir, Susan didn't make it. Her carotid artery was so damaged from the impaled glass that she hemorrhaged to death."

"How did this happen?" Barrows asked in a raised voice, anger and fear overwhelming him.

"There was an explosion at the restaurant where you were eating."

"Who's responsible for this madness?"

"No one seems to know."

Chapter 1

Patrick Murphy was petrified. For the first time in his life, he actually thought he was going to die. The monitors, the IV bottles, and the steely silence of the hospital room amplified his fear.

Why was he drifting in and out of a dreamlike trance? He had never had a fever as high as 104°, the level it had reached last night, when his wife dragged him into the hospital.

It had been a few weeks since he felt well. Lost was his energetic zeal for activity, whether tending bar or working construction projects down at the pier. His work suffered. He didn't want the overtime despite being paid a hundred dollars an hour for driving a truck.

Patrick's sense of monotony was broken by a woman in her early forties dressed in a white nursing uniform. "How are you feeling today, Patrick?" she inquired with a warmth that begged an optimistic reply.

"Why am I so drenched? These sheets are disgusting."

"Oh, don't worry about things we can take care of. Your temperature is down to a hundred and one. The antibiotics are starting to work."

"What's wrong with me?" His voice displayed the fear that he could no longer camouflage.

The nurse paused before responding, having no idea what to say. "Dr. Allen will be in later. You should talk with him."

"I don't understand what the secret is. Why can't I know?"

"Patrick, we don't know yet."

"When will you know?"

"You really should talk with Dr. Allen."

Leaving with a haste that mirrored her discomfort in continuing the conversation, the nurse fueled Pat's fears about his fate. As he gazed up at the ceiling, the medication she had injected began to burn inside his arm, reminding him of high school when he broke his hip playing football. *What is it about IV injections?* he thought. *It's like battery acid running through your veins.* Tempted to ask for more pain medication, he decided against it, hoping to be alert when Dr. Allen came. Already, the haziness from the fever was making him feel disconnected from his surroundings, a sensation he had not experienced since using PCP as a teenager at rock concerts. In the past two years, however, he had cleaned up his act—no drugs, and alcohol only rarely. Even his gambling habits seemed mostly under control. Now, he and his wife of a year were expecting their first child.

Pat shivered and pulled the blankets up to his neck. *The fever must be coming back,* he thought. *What did the nurse say? My fever might "spike" again?* He shook uncontrollably and felt the room whirling in all directions—clockwise, counterclockwise—so chaotically that his stomach churned, threatening to release its contents. *Not again,* he thought. *There's nothing left.* Seconds later, he was leaning over his bed, directing what little remained in his stomach into a small blue bowl that the nurse euphemistically called an "emesis basin." He wiped his face then put some ice chips in his mouth. "Don't drink anything," they had told him, "not even water." But as he rinsed his mouth, he noticed blood in the basin. *What now!* He was afraid. *What's happening to me?!*

He pressed a button to lower his bed, then turned off the television. He wanted to sleep, then awake with the nightmare over. Unfortunately, his problems were only beginning.

—

When Patrick next opened his eyes, he had no idea how long he had slept. It could have been fifteen minutes or three hours. The combined effects of the medication and his fever had caused him to lose perspective on time. His spirits were buoyed, however, when into his room came a physician dressed in a long white coat with a stethoscope draped around his neck, accompanied by a short young man in his late twenties, also in a white jacket. *Probably an intern,* Pat thought, recalling that his older brother once told him never to get sick in July, when medical students officially become interns. Dan, Pat's brother, had completed his own internship four years earlier.

"How are you feeling, Patrick? I'm Dr. Allen," the doctor said with confidence, extending his hand.

"Lousy," Pat answered, the tension in his voice palpable.

"Your chest x-ray was abnormal. It looks like pneumonia."

"How would I get pneumonia?"

"Many different ways," Allen replied, as though about to embark on a short discourse designed to impress medical students. "From people, usually, the way a cold is spread through coughing and sneezing, but there are other ways, such as from microbes that contaminate air-conditioning systems and cause Legionnaire's disease."

"What type do I have?"

"Pneumocystis."

"What's that mean?" Pat asked, his deep frown telegraphing his apprehension.

"It's the name of the organism that causes the pneumonia."

"Am I gonna be all right?"

Allen hesitated before replying. "We need to do more tests. But let me ask you a few questions first. How long have you been feeling ill?"

"About a month or two."

"What has most troubled you?"

"I haven't been myself. I have no energy."

"Anything else unusual?"

"Just the tiredness. I don't wanna do anything."

"Tell me a little bit about your medical history. Have you ever had surgery or been hospitalized before?"

"In high school. I broke my hip playing football."

"Were there any complications? Did you lose any blood?" Allen methodically inquired without raising his head from the chart.

"I think they gave me some blood. I'm not sure though."

"Have you been in the hospital any other time?"

"No, I've been pretty healthy."

"The ER note says something about an eye injury."

"Oh yeah! I forgot. I hurt my eye—I think they said it was the retina—playing basketball."

"Does anyone in your family have any medical problems?"

"I think my mom has high blood pressure, but I'm not sure."

"Any history of cancer, leukemia, or any blood disorders?"

"No."

"Is your father living?"

"No."

"How did he die?"

"He was shot."

"I'm sorry," Allen replied with genuine sincerity. "How'd it happen?"

"He was a police officer in Boston."

"How about your mother?"

"Like I said, she's got a problem with her blood pressure. What's this have to do with me? Why do I feel this way?"

"It's the pneumonia, but the blood tests will help us get a better idea."

"What happened to all that blood they took last night?"

"The results aren't back yet," Allen replied. Dr. Allen reviewed the chart as Patrick gazed at the television, watching the last quarter of the Patriots football game.

"Would you talk with my brother, Doc?"

"I'll try, but I have to make rounds on another twenty patients."

"Look, my brother's a doctor too," Pat said. "I want you to talk to him."

"Ask him to page me. Hopefully, the labs will be done by then even though it's Sunday."

As Dr. Allen left the room, Pat turned back to the game, rubbing his hip and thinking back to high school. One simple dive into the end zone and his dreams of college football were gone. Despite the disappointment of his failed dream to play college football, Pat's life wasn't at risk from the bad hip. The outcome of his current illness was less clear.

Chapter 2

It was almost eight o'clock at night when Dan Murphy heard his brother Pat's message on his phone: "Call me at Boston Hospital. I need to talk with you." Five years older than Pat, Dan had just returned from a weekend of skiing in New England, with the slopes lined with enough ice to force the most reckless to stay in control. After accepting an invitation from a nursing colleague to join friends for a weekend in Vermont, Dan was supposed to meet the woman of his dreams, the nurse's cousin from New York. With the absence of any spark, Dan returned home disappointed, a common reaction since leaving Washington after his divorce.

Another message waited for him on his phone, this one from Pat's wife, Maryann. "Danny! Call me as soon as you get in. Patrick is in the hospital. He has some kind of pneumonia, and it's serious. I'll be at Mom's all day."

Dan Murphy, the third of four children in an Irish Catholic family from South Boston, had recently returned to his hometown after spending four years in Washington, DC. Following medical school in Boston, he finished three years of an orthopedic surgery residency, which he left prematurely because he lost the drive, then worked for a year in an emergency department. The breakup of his marriage prompted his decision to leave town and start afresh, both socially and professionally. Although he loved medicine, he had lost heart for orthopedic surgery and was drawn to a preventive medicine specialty. He dialed the hospital.

"Pat, this is Dan. What's going on? What are you doing in the hospital?"

Pat described the events that had led to his hospitalization the previous night.

"Did they tell you what type of pneumonia you have?"

"Yeah, something called 'new-mo-sistis,'" Pat replied.

"You mean pneumocystis jiroveci?"

"That's it."

"Pneumocystis? Why would you have pneumocystis pneumonia?"

"That's what the nurse told me. You know I'm not gay. And you know I don't use drugs anymore."

Dan listened intently, aware that his younger brother had abused ecstasy and cocaine in his early twenties and lost a job because of a urine drug test coming back positive. Although reasonably confident that Pat never ventured into IV drug abuse with heroin, morphine, or amphetamines, Dan recognized that blood transfusions and illicit encounters with prostitutes could also lead to AIDS. Dan then recalled his brother's hip surgery, during which Pat received three transfusions of whole blood. Although the risks were remote, Dan wondered whether his brother could have contracted HIV then and the disease was only appearing now. Or was it some other illness that had its own effect on the immune system leading to the pneumonia?

"Did they do an HIV test?" Dan asked.

"Yeah. Would ya call this doctor and find out what's going on so I can get outta here?"

"What's his name?"

"Dr. Allen. Mark Allen."

"I'll track him down and let you know. Talk to you later, Pat. Hang in there."

Dan Murphy tracked down a fatigued Dr. Allen later that night.

"Dr. Allen, I'm Dan Murphy, the brother of your patient Pat Murphy. I don't mean to intrude, especially so late, but he's asked me to talk with you. I'm an occupational physician at South Boston General."

"I understand," Allen said. "I know how physicians often serve as intermediaries between their families and the medical profession. Your brother has pneumocystis pneumonia—at least according to the sputum stain. We're still waiting for the blood cultures."

"Do you think he has AIDS?"

"I'm not sure. There are some peculiarities to your brother's case."

"What do you mean?" Dan asked.

"Well, for one, he doesn't have an elevated white count, which is hard to fathom in light of how sick he was last night."

"How about the rest of the results?"

"It looks like a bone marrow disorder, especially if the HIV test is negative."

"Why?"

"The combination of his symptoms and lab results. He's shown evidence of bleeding, both in his gums and in his eye. That eye injury from basketball that bled so much is probably a result of his low platelet count. He's also anemic."

"How's he doing today?" Dan queried.

"Improving, but I think we should pursue the heme problem," Allen answered, indicating his concern about the abnormal blood studies. "If the HIV test is negative, we should ask Marty Novich from hematology to look at him. A bone marrow biopsy may be helpful."

Dan paused before responding. "Thanks. If you don't mind, I'd like to keep in touch."

"No problem. Call me tomorrow. I'll let you know how things are going."

Patrick lay on his side, covered with sheets and blankets, as a nurse brought both encouraging and disheartening news. His HIV test had come back negative—again—but the blood studies suggested a serious problem with his bone marrow.

"What's the bone marrow?" Patrick asked the nurse who had advised him of the probable diagnosis.

"It's here." She pointed to her breastbone and then to her hip. "And here."

"What's it do?"

"It makes all your blood cells—the ones that fight infection, control bleeding, and carry oxygen," she answered, her pleasure in educating patients obvious to the casual observer.

"How do you know I have a problem with my bone marrow?"

"The test results. Your blood count is down in all categories."

"What are they going to do?"

"I'm not sure, but you'll need a bone marrow biopsy."

"What's that?"

"They put a needle into your hip for a sample. It's not too bad."

"That's easy for you to say."

Just then, Dr. Novich, a physician whose practice focused on all sorts of blood disorders, entered the room. After brief introductions, the hematologist casually walked over to a metal tray on which a variety of medical instruments had been placed. Without any hesitation, in the event that Pat might refuse to undergo the procedure, he said, "Don't worry, it only causes minor discomfort."

"I don't believe it," Pat quipped. "Discomfort—that's what you doctors tell everybody. 'It'll cause some discomfort.'"

"It'll be over before you know it," Dr. Novich replied matter-of-factly.

"I want to talk with my brother about this," Pat said with an air of authority.

At the end of his bed stood his wife, Maryann. Bright, alert, and smartly dressed in a blue dress, she looked to her husband. "Pat, I've talked with Danny. He says it's OK."

"When did you talk with him?"

"This morning. He talked with Dr. Novich." She nodded toward the physician, who was now anxious to obtain Pat's signature on the consent form.

The hematologist looked through his black-rimmed glasses at Patrick. "We're only going to take a piece of the marrow. It may cause some discomfort, but we'll give you a local anesthetic to help numb the pain."

"Discomfort! I'd like to give discomfort to some of you doctors."

Novich, without acknowledging Pat's worry about the pain, responded, "We'll take the sample, then look at it under the microscope."

Maryann, whose expanded girth from the pregnancy had rounded her customarily trim physique, said, "Pat, you can handle this. Come on now!"

Dr. Novich, dressed in green surgical garb and outfitted with two pairs of latex gloves, nodded in agreement. "We should get going."

Patrick hastily signed the consent form, then passed it to the nurse, who prepared a table with a local anesthetic, sterile gauze pads, sutures, and a biopsy needle. She then arranged some small glass jars designed to house the marrow for its trip to the pathology lab.

"Patrick, roll over on your side, please," the nurse requested, her youth belying her self-confidence.

Pat did as instructed, then the nurse draped green cotton sheets over his lower back and upper legs. After marking an area over his left hip, she said, "Patrick, don't touch the drapes. They're sterile. I'm going to prepare an area for Dr. Novich to do the biopsy."

After methodically attending to his task of the biopsy, Novich removed his surgical gloves, then said to the nurse, "Send some tissue for culture as well." She nodded in agreement, then prepared the specimens and the inevitable paperwork designed to ensure that the biopsy made it to the right lab and was analyzed properly.

"What's your date of birth?" she asked Patrick.

"March 17, 1975, Saint Patrick's Day," he said. "My father said any Irish son born on Saint Patrick's Day had to be called Patrick."

Chapter 3

Freezing rain made Dan Murphy's drive through Boston's rush-hour traffic more arduous than customary. En route to Harvard's Countway Library, a medical library, Murphy navigated through absentminded pedestrians, randomly stopping cabs, and cars running red lights. Traffic had become much more exasperating since he had left Boston four years ago. *Now,* he thought, *if you stop at a yellow light, you risk getting hit in the rear.* Drivers used their directional signals so infrequently before switching lanes or turning that when any of them did use their signals, he wondered if the driver's electrical system was working properly. The early dusk associated with mid-December added to the driving challenge as he patiently made his way to one of the world's best medical libraries.

Murphy pulled into a metered spot on Huntington Avenue, the lower end of Harvard's medical area, which also included the medical school and its major teaching hospitals. After dodging a streetcar, he climbed the steps to the Countway Library, where as a member of the Massachusetts Medical Society he had privileges. None of Dan's medical training had focused on aplastic anemia, the illness from which Pat was suffering. Late that afternoon, a pathologist had called him: the bone marrow was hypocellular, typical of a disease known as aplastic anemia. The results reflected a deficiency in Pat's bone marrow, which explained why all his blood cell counts had shown a decrease.

Having never treated a patient with aplastic anemia, and not terribly knowledgeable about an illness first described in 1888, Murphy decided to conduct a literature search of medical articles written on the topic. After reaching the library, he went to the computer bank on the lower level to access the National Library of Medicine's database.

He entered the keywords *aplastic anemia*, *treatment*, and *prognosis*. Numerous articles appeared on the screen, some of which motivated Dan to review their abstracts. He continued his review of the references in the hopes of finding additional studies related to the cause of aplastic anemia. Then, armed with his list, he ambled through stacks of journals to retrieve the articles that were not readily available online without paying a fee.

After reading half a dozen reports, he realized that his brother's condition was more serious than he imagined and that the disease could actually kill him within months, if not sooner. Only half the people with aplastic anemia lived more than two years after being diagnosed.

The cause of aplastic anemia, Murphy learned, was often difficult to determine, although drugs, toxins, and radiation were accountable at times. In fact, the author of one article claimed that searching for drug or toxin exposure was probably the most appropriate action to take in finding the cause. *Could Pat's work as a truck driver have anything to do with this?* Dan wondered.

Dan spent the rest of the evening poring over medical articles related to aplastic anemia. The stress he felt because of his brother's illness, however, intruded on a restful night's sleep. He reflected on how Pat had recovered from drug abuse and a gambling habit that had kept him constantly in debt. During that time, he and his younger brother had become closer. Pat had finally allowed an opening in his tough-guy exterior to permit Dan and Maryann, Pat's future wife, access. Still drawing a substantial part of his self-image from his life as a jock, Pat found it difficult to display what he and his buddies might consider to be any sign of weakness, such as seeing a counselor for help. As was the case for most people trapped in the whirlwind of dysfunctional behavior, a crisis had forced him to change. In Pat Murphy's case, being arrested for driving while intoxicated, followed by falling in love, is what had prompted the alteration in his lifestyle.

Finding it difficult to fall asleep, Dan Murphy surfed the TV channels while paging through weekly newsmagazines, neither of which distracted him from the spiral of insomnia. Surrendering to his tension, he got out of bed and read the remaining articles, learning that the immune system plays a major role in the development of aplastic anemia. Amid the dismal reading material were hopeful remarks referring to spontaneous recoveries from a disease whose outcome depends upon the extent of bone marrow failure.

Murphy's thoughts bounced randomly about in both uncertainty and hope. Could the official reading of the bone marrow biopsy be more encouraging than the aspirate that the pathologist interpreted? Perhaps his brother's results were confused with those of someone else.

Chapter 4

As Pat's wife, Maryann, finished the interminable hospital paperwork, an ambulance awaited them for the transfer to Boston Medical Center. Only a week earlier, they had been house-hunting in South Boston. Now, Pat was en route to a major teaching hospital for a bone marrow transplant. He wondered how he could have become ill so quickly and whether a bone marrow transplant would cure him.

As the ambulance made its way through traffic, Pat turned to the side and closed his eyes. Maryann reflected on comments made by the hematologist who had performed the bone marrow biopsy. Her husband probably had developed aplastic anemia a few weeks ago but was just beginning to feel ill, the physician told her. When the marrow is injured, he advised, it takes a few weeks thereafter before serious symptoms occur.

Shortly, the ambulance pulled up to the emergency department at Boston Medical Center. With military efficiency, two attendants welcomed the driver, then moved Pat from the gurney to a wheelchair. Within minutes, he was wheeled onto an elevator that took him to the Hematology Unit and his isolation room.

"Pat, look." Maryann pointed to her waist as Pat lay in bed with a thermometer perched in his mouth. "How's the temperature?" she asked the nurse.

"It's been down since last night. It's a good sign."

Maryann smiled hopefully, just as a bearded physician of average height confidently entered the room and reached for the chart.

Moments later, Pat's brother, Dan Murphy, appeared.

"Danny," Maryann said, rising from her chair to greet him.

"Hi," Dan replied. "How are you making out?"

"A lot better. I'm so glad you're here."

The bearded physician approached the side of Pat's bed and spoke with the assurance of a man well versed in his own discipline. "Patrick, I'm Dr. Harrington. I'm the physician to whom Dr. Novich referred you. I direct the Bone Marrow Transplant Unit here. We treat all sorts of blood-related disorders such as leukemia and the illness you have."

Pat nodded. "While you're here, you'll have some more tests. We'll take another look at the slides from your biopsy and recommend the best option for you."

"A transplant?" Pat asked.

"Most likely, but we want to look at other alternatives too."

"What do you mean?"

"Well, a medication has been effective for certain types of patients."

"Do you mean ATG?" Dan asked, fresh from his review of the articles. His younger brother looked on approvingly.

"Yes, as a matter of fact. But first, we should do some genetic tests on your family members."

"What do they have to do?" Maryann asked.

"Not much," Harrington replied. "Just a blood test."

"They can handle it," Pat said, looking over at Maryann as though she were a candidate.

"No, actually only direct family members can be bone marrow donors," Harrington added.

"Not wives?" Maryann asked.

"No. Not even aunts, uncles, or cousins."

"What do you think the chances are of finding a match?" Dan asked.

"The usual odds are one in four," Harrington answered. "But many factors are involved. Transplant rejection rates are down considerably."

"What happens if there's no match?" Pat asked.

"Well, there are other alternatives. For example, there are about half a million people in the country who have been HLA tested."

"What's that mean?" Pat asked.

"They've had their genetic blueprints determined. And they've volunteered to be bone marrow donors."

"That's marvelous," Maryann said. "What are the chances of Pat getting a transplant that way?"

"Again, it varies," Harrington said. "But there's a 10 percent to 15 percent chance of getting a match through that route."

"Why do I need this transplant?" Pat asked. "I'm feeling better."

"Unless your bone marrow is rejuvenated, you're susceptible to major infections and other serious medical problems. At the risk of being too blunt, you could die from it. Your bone marrow has shut down. It's not making the cells you need to live."

Stunned by the sobering news, Pat looked on in silence as Maryann asked, "What does he have to do, Doctor?"

"If he qualifies for a transplant, we give him medication first, then he'll have radiation treatment. We need to completely destroy any remaining marrow."

"Why?" Pat asked.

"We destroy your marrow to prevent what's known as graft-versus-host reaction," Harrington replied.

"What?" Pat asked, clearly upset about another potential problem.

"Pat, I'll work with Dr. Harrington," Dan said encouragingly.

"Your brother and I will keep you informed about what to expect here." Dr. Harrington extended his hand to Pat and said, "I'm confident we can help you." Then he turned to leave the room.

Once the doctor was gone, Pat looked up at his brother, Dan. "What's all this mean?"

"Harrington's one of the best in his field. He's written book chapters and articles on aplastic anemia and has done lots of research. We're fortunate to have him."

"Danny, when does your family have to do the genetic tests?" Maryann asked.

"As soon as possible. I'm going to have my blood drawn while I'm here today."

"How will I know if I can get the transplant?" Pat asked.

"First, everyone in the family needs to have their blood tested."

"What do they test for?" Maryann asked.

"They try to find someone with as similar a genetic makeup as possible to make sure the transplant works."

"What difference does it make? Why don't they just give me some of your marrow?"

"It's not that simple. You might reject the graft or get graft-versus-host disease."

"What's that?" Pat asked.

"It's when the body fights the transplant. We can discuss that later. Let's get a genetic match first."

"How long do you think he'll be here, Dan?" Maryann inquired, her face reflecting the worry that she couldn't conceal. *Counseling patients with serious illnesses when it's your job as a social worker is expected,* she thought. *It's quite another matter to counsel your husband about an illness that may prevent him from seeing your first child.* Biting down on her quivering lip, she looked to Dan for an answer.

"It's hard to say, but probably a few weeks."

"You're crazy. There's no way I'm staying here a couple of weeks," Pat said, not yet grasping the severity of his illness. With essentially destroyed bone marrow, he lacked enough red cells to carry oxygen, enough white cells to fight infections, and enough platelets to control bleeding. Had his brother or Dr. Harrington apprised him of the prognosis—at best, a fifty-fifty chance of living for two years—Pat may not have shown such panache.

Chapter 5

Dan Murphy guided the young woman into his medical office.

"Thank you for meeting me," she said with a gracious smile. "I know how busy you are."

"Not at all," Murphy replied. "It's a pleasure. My mother said you might call."

"Oh yes, she's a sweetheart." The woman blushed. "We play bingo together, and she gets me babysitting work."

Dan immediately recognized the Irish accent and the ready charm.

"Dr. Murphy, I'm very worried about Liam. You know he has aplastic anemia too. Your mother told me that your brother has the same disease. Do you think it is from something in the environment—air pollution, water pollution?"

"Frankly, Theresa, I don't know," Dan answered.

Theresa continued, saying, "I saw this movie on TV where the wells were polluted and some of the children died. I think it was a blood disease—leukemia maybe? Does it make any sense? You know we have a little boy. He's two, and I don't want anything to happen to him."

Dan, recognizing a chance to interject, responded, "Theresa, I'm not sure."

Before he could continue, she said, "Your mother said you

specialize in this now. Is that right? She said something about illnesses and injuries at work. That's what you do—and you try to prevent environmental hazards."

"Sort of," Dan answered, content to allow Theresa to guide their conversation.

"Well, don't you treat people with environmental problems?"

"At times. It depends on the circumstances. But my experience is limited. I'm just getting started in the field."

"Can you help me?"

"I'm not sure. These things get very complicated."

"But why would your brother and Liam each have the same disease? Doesn't it seem strange to you?"

"I see your point, Theresa, but there's so many coincidences in medicine."

"How could you know if aplastic anemia is caused by something in the environment?" Theresa asked.

"It would be very difficult," Murphy answered.

"What do you do here?" she asked, her appetite for learning obvious.

"We treat people who get sick or hurt at work or need special exams because of the type of work they do.

"Why don't you ask your husband to come see me?"

"I don't think he'll come."

"Why not?"

"He doesn't like going to doctors. He was sick for a few weeks before he agreed to go to the hospital, and even then he was a problem. You know we don't have health insurance, so we had to go to Boston City Hospital."

"I didn't know that."

"We can't get insurance. We don't have our green cards. I hate to say it, but you know what people call us—illegal immigrants."

Murphy thought back to his reading on aplastic anemia. Although he was most concerned about the proper treatment of the disease, his attention was also drawn to its causes, including chemicals such as benzene and pesticides. Pinpointing precipitating factors, however, was a daunting task since the bone marrow looked similar regardless of what caused the disease.

"Do you have any records, Theresa?"

"Yes." She handed over a large manila folder.

Murphy opened the file containing her husband Liam's hospital discharge report and associated laboratory results.

"I'm worried about my son. He's only two years old. Suppose the water is contaminated. What'll happen?" Tears welled in her eyes. "We should have never come here. We should have stayed in Ireland. I loved Cork."

"Let me look over the records, Theresa. We can get the water tested if necessary. Don't worry."

"OK," she answered hopefully.

"But why don't we wait until I have a chance to look over these records? Do you think Liam would mind if I talked with his doctor?" Murphy asked, showing his sensitivity to the confidentiality of medical information.

Since he'd been practicing occupational medicine, medical confidentiality had become increasingly important to him. Workers required to undergo medical exams as part of their jobs often raised concerns about the fate of the results: "What information is sent to the company? Where is it stored? Can my family doctor get a copy of the results?"

"I don't think he'll do it."

"Why?"

"I don't know. He doesn't want to talk about it."

"What do you mean?"

"Well, his doctor asked him about his work, but he didn't say much other than he drives a truck. I know he does other work. He comes home some days with a horrible odor on his clothes, and his hands get red and tender. But he just shrugs and says it's a job and that we shouldn't complain. He says he can't risk his job."

"You seem convinced that Liam's work made him sick. Where does he work?"

"At a factory by the pier."

"What do they do there?"

"I'm not sure."

As Murphy was about to respond, his attention was drawn to the intercom on his telephone.

"Dr. Murphy, you have three patients waiting."

"OK," he responded. "I'll finish up."

"Theresa, I wish we could speak longer, but I have to get going."

"I understand."

"Let me look over the records. But it would help if you would ask Liam if I could speak with his doctor."

"I'll do my best, Dr. Murphy. How's your brother?"

"We're hoping that someone in the family has similar genes so he can get a bone marrow transplant. Otherwise, as you know, there's no cure."

"How's it look for him?" she asked.

"We'll know soon."

Chapter 6

"Dr. Murphy," the head of hematology said in greeting him. Accomplished academically and with the savoir faire to raise funds from the snootiest of clients, Dr. Harrington was at the pinnacle of his distinguished career.

"Dan's fine, please."

"Your brother is fortunate. You look like a compatible donor."

"Excellent," Dan replied.

"He also continues to improve from the pneumonia. I think we should prepare him for the transplant. Let's tell him the good news." Moments later, Harrington and Murphy reached Pat's room, where his wife was sitting. After explaining the process of preparing Pat for the transplant, Harrington asked, "Do you have any questions?"

"Yes, Doctor. Do you know how Pat got this disease?" his wife, Maryann, asked.

"We're not sure. We're still waiting for some test results."

"Sounds familiar," Patrick chimed in, not disguising his frustration.

"What causes it?" she persisted.

"Most of the time, we don't know, but in some cases, it can be the result of hepatitis."

"What's that?" she asked.

"It's a viral infection of the liver. Some people with aplastic anemia develop hepatitis before they become ill."

"Does Patrick have hepatitis?" Maryann asked, looking to her husband, who was pale and washed out, appearing to be older than twenty-eight.

"I don't think so," Harrington replied. "But some of his lab tests suggest liver damage."

"Why?" Pat asked. "I don't drink anymore."

"I'm not sure," Harrington answered. "But we'll find out."

"What else can cause this disease?" Maryann asked, starting to show her frustration.

"Pesticides, chemicals, radiation. Lots of things."

"What do you think caused Patrick's disease?" she queried.

"I don't know."

Despite his confidence in Dr. Harrington, Dan Murphy doubted that a cause for Pat's disease would ever be determined. Among two hundred seventy-five patients described in a *New England Journal of Medicine* article, nearly two hundred had no known cause for developing aplastic anemia. Murphy wondered whether the figures represented lack of cause or lack of pursuit of the cause. Determining the cause of the aplastic anemia, he recognized, was a luxurious use of time in contrast to the immediate need to find a compatible donor for the transplant. Disconcerting to Murphy, however, was his recognition that continued exposure to a hazard, if a hazard was what had caused the condition in the first place, would affect the outcome of the transplant. If contaminated drinking water were the cause of the problem, would Patrick suffer a relapse if he were exposed to a similar hazard at work, even after a successful transplant? Murphy, while avoiding hasty conclusions, was intrigued about his meeting with Patrick's neighbor Theresa O'Malley. *Maybe she's onto something,* he thought.

"Look," Dr. Harrington said to Pat, "try not to worry. After all, your brother has matched genetically. Bear with us and you'll be back at work before you know it." Harrington smiled confidently, then turned and left the room as Pat allowed a smile to overtake his frown.

"Oh, Danny, Theresa gave me these records," Maryann said, handing him a manila folder about three inches thick. Her husband had allowed the doctor to give her the records.

"Thanks, Maryann," Dan said. "I'll look these over. I wonder if there's any connection to this guy?" he said, pointing to his brother.

Chapter 7

He strode with confidence and purpose. Wearing blue jeans and a black leather jacket over a black turtleneck, the stocky dark-haired man of average height walked through the revolving doors of the hospital lobby. Now showing the effects of managed care's reduced funding for upkeep, the lobby was filled with furniture long past any respectful life span. Sporting a scruffy black beard like the one made famous by Yasser Arafat, the man approached the receptionist.

"I'd like to see Patrick Murphy. Which room is he in?" The possibility that Pat might be limited to the type and number of visitors never occurred to him.

"I'm sorry, sir, but Mr. Murphy's in a special unit. He can't have visitors now."

"Why not?"

"I can't tell you, sir."

"Why not?"

Just then, the phone rang. As she answered the call, the receptionist walked away from the man. He remained at the counter, unsatisfied with her response. Annoyed by her inattention to his concerns, he walked toward her.

"Ma'am, I need to see Mr. Murphy."

"Excuse me?" the receptionist replied, striding toward the man, who was now leaning on the counter.

With a facial expression intended to intimidate, he said, "Look. I'm busy. You're busy. I'll be short." Then he began to walk to the elevator.

"Sir, I'm sorry," she called after him. The man then turned around to return to the receptionist.

"I suppose you're right," he said in a tone that an acquaintances would immediately recognize as insincere. He had just realized that charm would likely work to his advantage. In his late thirties and in fine physical condition from work on a stationary bike and weight lifting, he presented an attractive figure to the plain young woman.

"You must have a tough job," he began, changing his tone from demanding to flattering.

"Yes. It can be."

"You can imagine that I'm upset—just anxious to see my friend."

"Oh yes." She warmed while fumbling through a pile of paper.

"You must get lonely working here alone," he continued.

"Oh. It's not too bad."

"Look, do you have any idea why I can't see my friend?"

"I'm not sure. It just says access is limited."

"But why? Could you help me? He's my best friend, and I haven't talked to him since he came in here," he lied.

"Just a moment." The receptionist then clicked away at the computer as the man surveyed the lobby. Visitors had left, leaving behind only patients and those who tended their needs. As the receptionist gazed at the computer screen, the man noticed an emergency exit adjacent to a stairwell that led to a parking lot.

"Oh. Here it is," she said. "Infection control. Patrick Murphy. Need special permission to visit."

"Who's his physician?"

"Dr. Harrington, hematology."

"What floor?"

"Medical. That's 6 South," she willingly offered.

The man winked and replied, "Thank you. Maybe I'll call his physician tomorrow."

"Would you like me to tell him you stopped by?" she offered.

"No. But thank you," he answered, turning to leave.

He then pushed through the revolving doors to the parking lot and strode to an old Ford pickup truck. A short ride around the hospital gave him time to calculate his next move. He had to see Murphy tonight. A phone call might not get the message through to him as well as a face-to-face encounter would.

His cell phone had enough battery power for a quick call to the hospital. He asked for 6 South, and within minutes had convinced the ward secretary that he would be visiting Pat Murphy with the approval of Dr. Harrington. The man lost no time in returning to the hospital parking lot, where he left his truck, then walked to the emergency exit that he had spotted while in the lobby.

Sure enough, the door was open, allowing him entry to a stairwell that took him to the sixth floor. On entering the quiet, dim hallway, the man, whose name was Wilson, heard the steady chatter of nurses and assistants in the background. Eventually, he noticed a sign that directed him to 6 South.

—

Moments later, the intrusive tones of a ringing telephone captured Pat Murphy's attention.

"Mr. Murphy, you have a visitor."

Patrick, after pulling the phone away from his ear, replied in a daze, "Wilson?"

"I'm at the nurses' station."

"Whaddya want, Wilson?"

"Just a friendly visit," he answered sarcastically.

"I don't have time for this."

"I'll be right there. Don't go anywhere," he said in mock acknowledgment of Murphy's confinement in the hospital. Pat Murphy rolled onto his side and looked out the window into the black, cold winter night. Moments later, he heard three crisp, loud knocks on his door. Wilson, dressed in protective clothing, entered the hospital room. "Murphy, you look like a mannequin," he said, referring to Pat's pale and waxy complexion. He then walked over to Pat.

"So, what's wrong with you?" he nonchalantly asked.

"I'm tired all the time. I pee blood. I can't eat."

"What'd your doctor say?"

"My bone marrow has shut down."

"What's that mean?"

"It's a long story. Why do you need to know?"

Wilson responded condescendingly, "A little feisty, Murphy, especially for a guy in a hospital bed. When you gettin' out of here?"

"I don't know!"

"Don't you think you oughta find out? I thought we had a deal."

"I'll help—if and when I get out of here."

"What do you mean? Just leave!"

"It's not that simple."

"Well, make it simple."

"Get someone else to take my place."

"That won't work," Wilson replied.

"Why not?"

"Because of the money you owe me, that's why."

"If I can do it, I'll help, but don't count on me."

"You will do it, and I will count on it. Don't make it difficult, Murphy. There's too much at stake here."

"I'll help if I can," Pat said.

"No, Murphy. You will help. Figure out how to do it. I don't care about your fuckin' bone marrow. You owe me too much money, and I need your help to get it back." Wilson confidently left the room. As he carefully made his way along the hallway to the stairwell, he wondered whether he could count on Murphy. He also worried whether Murphy would keep his mouth shut.

Over the years, Jake Wilson, a Philadelphia native, had developed a reputation for being a half step beyond the reach of the law. Through street smarts and a savvy for sensing trouble, he had stopped dealing cocaine a few months before a sting operation had gone through pockets of Boston and nabbed some kingpins. Smelling the end of the quick big bucks from dealing, he entered into more respectable business ventures with the cash he had accumulated. Among a circle of Irish immigrants to South Boston, Wilson was known as the person to contact for jobs for carpenters, electricians, and plumbers, among others. He had gained a reputation for providing work and not asking questions about green cards.

Jake Wilson left the parking lot and drove to the site of one of his favorite passions, a bar with a girlie show. After grabbing a seat, he quickly put a dollar bill into the bra of the woman who was dancing near his table. Alone, but not lonely, Wilson gulped down the rest of his beer, then made his way to the exit. It was getting late. He was growing tired, and the striptease dancers had begun to bore him with their routine, especially the redhead with the ample rear whose breasts spilled out of her skimpy bra.

On leaving the Silky Dolly, one of Boston's most popular gentleman's clubs, Wilson braced for the cold weather, which shocked his senses. The frigid temperatures, coupled with the blustery wind, made him think fondly of his native Philadelphia, three hundred miles to the South. He began to walk along the dimly lit street in search of his pickup, which was parked near the Boston Common, a large park in the center of the city. The empty streets didn't surprise him, as it was about two o'clock in the morning. The eerie silence and absence of the ubiquitous Boston traffic, however, seemed disconcerting to him. As he walked along the park, his mind wandered aimlessly, until he focused on his work planned with Pat Murphy and a few of his other pals. Would he need more help? Would Murphy pull through?

As he reached his three-year-old pickup truck, he fumbled through his pockets for the keys. Thinking he heard a strange noise that he couldn't categorize, he paused and looked about.

Calmly, Wilson got into his truck and placed the keys into the ignition. Just as he was about to start the engine, he felt something tight being wrapped around his mouth. Then, someone grabbed his arms and pulled them behind his back. No slouch in fighting, Wilson struggled to gain control, but he felt powerless without the use of his voice or his arms. Vainly, he tried leaning back to kick the thug, then felt a needle pricking the back of his neck. Within seconds, his mind clouded as though he were in a dreamlike trance.

The two assailants, a burly man in his early thirties and a tall muscular guy who looked like a professional football player, tied Wilson's feet together. They then drove onto the Storrow Drive ramp and out to Boston's western suburbs. En route, the football star took out a razor and shaved Wilson's beard off. When he was finished, he leafed through his wallet, taking out a few hundred dollars.

On reaching a high school athletic field, the two thugs removed the unconscious Wilson and dragged him about one hundred yards onto the center of the field, where they left him.

Chapter 8

After arriving late because of a traffic jam on the Southeast Expressway, Dan Murphy sat in the back of the auditorium at the Harvard School of Public Health as Dr. Richardson lectured on environmental health. It was Murphy's preferred place to sit during lectures since from there he could quietly depart if the presentation fell short of his expectations. That morning, his brother, Pat, had received his first treatment in preparation for the bone marrow transplant.

The professor stated, "We will continue to see clusters of diseases that prompt people to suggest an environmental cause. Given strong public demand and wider recognition of environmental health hazards, you, as health-care professionals, can expect to be called upon to address these challenges. I remain convinced that such efforts are worthy of our attention, especially when they occur in work settings. Inevitably, statistical flukes occur. Simply because there's an apparent excess of an illness doesn't mean that an environmental cause is responsible. One has to be discriminate in determining cause-and-effect relationships."

Murphy listened to the concluding remarks of Dr. Richardson, one of the nation's authorities on environmental health. Throughout the lecture, his attention had been repeatedly distracted by the profile of a woman who sat a few rows in front of him as she threw her hair back over her shoulders.

"It's been a pleasure speaking today," the professor continued. "If you have any questions, I'll try to answer them."

The students clapped politely as Dr. David Becker rose from his chair and extended his hand to Richardson. "Any questions?"

A male student in the front row raised his hand. "What are the most common illnesses recognized in cluster investigations?"

Richardson approached the microphone. "Most efforts have been directed to geographic outbreaks of leukemias or lymphomas. When these illnesses affect children, especially in a certain geographical area, they attract attention and raise suspicions as to the possibility of an environmental cause. In general, cluster investigations have most commonly uncovered cancer, respiratory diseases, neurotoxic disorders, chemical hepatitis, and the aplasias." Murphy's attention was piqued upon hearing the word *aplasia*, while gazing at the woman below.

"Yes?" Richardson pointed to another student.

"How many cases do you need for a cluster?"

"That's a good question," Richardson responded. "The answer, however, is arbitrary. Some authorities suggest that at least two cases of a rare disease might be acceptable to launch a preliminary investigation."

Two cases are a cluster? Murphy asked himself. *Could Liam O'Malley and Pat Murphy have something in common?*

"One final question," Dr. Becker said, standing next to the guest speaker.

"What has been your experience with illness clusters near hazardous waste sites?"

Richardson nodded, indicating he was ready to respond. "Despite the wide attention given to hazardous waste sites as threats to health, few investigations have uncovered new types of disease or serious illness."

Becker began to clap, hoping to cue the students, who responded by offering the guest speaker another round of applause.

Murphy was relieved that the lecture was over. Although the topic fascinated him, especially since he thought it may have some pertinence to his brother's case, he was tired. *Lectures in late afternoon are deadly,* he thought. *They should serve coffee.*

Dr. Becker approached the microphone. "Don't forget, Dr. Richardson will be joining us for a reception. We hope to see you there."

Murphy, unsure about attending the reception, stared at the back of the young woman who had sat in front of him during the lecture. Throughout the presentation, he wondered what she might look like as he admired her shoulder-length light brown hair, which bounced off her red sweater. As she rose from her chair and turned to leave, Murphy met her eyes. She returned the glance with an unhurried, relaxed smile. Murphy, a bit off-balance, smiled in return, embarrassed, as though she had known he was staring at her during the lecture. As he reached to the floor to retrieve his notes, he turned to look at the woman as she walked up the stairs of the auditorium. Impulsively, he rose to follow her. As she approached the reception hall, he felt nervous. *Is this gauche?* he asked himself, feeling a strange nervousness about wanting to meet her, but at the same time fearing rejection. He certainly did not want to appear inappropriate. *After all, this is a professional meeting,* he thought, *not a singles bar in Back Bay.*

The reception hall was filled with people. Richardson entered, accompanied by students peppering him with questions. The young woman with the shoulder-length hair stood off to the side talking with two other women. Murphy made his way to the food tables, at which were vegetables, dips, and crackers—nothing fancy, simply a way to be gracious and help students get to know one another.

Murphy had never seen this woman before. At least she wasn't in the occupational medicine seminar he had been taking for the past two months on Tuesday afternoons.

As students milled about, Dr. Becker approached a microphone.

"May I have your attention?" The din of the conversation persisted, so Becker interceded. "May I have a moment, please?"

The noise dimmed. Becker continued, saying, "There are some handouts from the NIEHS and information on fellowships over here." He pointed to the information from the National Institute of Environmental Health Sciences. Murphy, meanwhile, went over to the side of the room where the dip and crackers were placed, which was near the young woman he wanted to meet. Walking by her and her friends, he caught a glimpse of her tall, slender physique, then waited in line for the hors d'oeuvres. It was easy to overhear the women's conversation.

"What do you think of Dr. Becker?"

"Becker's a bit much."

"What do you mean?"

"I think he's arrogant."

"Why?"

"Just listen to him. He acts as though he's never wrong. It's his way or no way."

"He's the chief, isn't he? No wonder."

"That's no excuse."

David Becker, a dermatologist, served as acting chief of occupational medicine at the School of Public Health. Considered by many to be an opportunist who routinely stepped on and over others to advance his career, he had made quite a few enemies along the academic pathway. With a reputation for demeaning subordinates, he gave the repeated impression that he was too busy for students. They would often suffer through his indifference as he talked on the phone or looked through his mail when he was supposed to be listening to discussions about their projects.

With a plateful of vegetables and crackers, Murphy ambled to a corner of the room like a cat in pursuit of a mouse. Sitting down and munching a carrot, he felt embarrassed about hesitating to initiate a conversation. He stole periodic glimpses and hoped the young woman wouldn't notice. By wearing a skirt and an attractive sweater, especially among public health students, where jeans, L.L. Bean boots, and a flannel shirt were the rule, she showed an independence that appealed to him. Trying to meet a woman surrounded by two others, however, was an intimidating prospect for all but the most socially adept of men. When she walked over to the hors d'oeuvres again, Murphy rose from his seat.

"I see you like broccoli," he said with a grin, which he hoped would stimulate a repartee.

"What is it? Beta-carotene, the former magic ingredient?" she responded, referring to a compound that was once touted as having the ability to prevent lung cancer.

"Did you enjoy the presentation?" Murphy asked.

"Yes, he's a captivating speaker. I've been intrigued by this topic for a while," she said.

"No kidding," Murphy replied, still embarrassed and feeling like a teenage boy asking a girl to the prom. "Are you a grad student here?" he asked,

"Yes, I'm in the general MPH program," she answered, referring to her pursuit of a master's degree in public health.

"How do you like it?" he asked.

"Great, so far—although Boston's a challenge."

"Where are you from?"

"Minneapolis. How about you?"

"Boston. Went to high school, college, and even medical school here. But I just moved back from Washington, DC."

How trivial my conversation sounds, Murphy thought, encouraged by her easy smile.

"I'm Anna Carlson," she said with pride.

"Dan Murphy," he said. "I'd shake your hand, but I ought to keep the food on the plate and not drop it on the floor."

"I understand," she replied, adding a smile to her response.

"Why's Boston a challenge?" Murphy asked, hoping to pick up on her earlier comment.

"Oh. It's probably just the change. After living in the Midwest for thirty years, I find the pace of the Northeast to be pretty fast."

"But Minneapolis is no slouch," Murphy said.

"That's true."

"What do you want to do after you finish here?"

"Oh, I don't know. Maybe get a job in journalism or write for a newspaper," she said, nodding to a friend passing by. "How about you?"

"I'm working at a clinic in South Boston. Trying to practice occupational medicine."

"What do you do?" Anna asked.

"Primarily treat people who get hurt or sick from work. I also go to factories and businesses to look for health hazards."

"That sounds interesting."

"Oh, it is, but there's a tremendous amount of paperwork and reports. At least it's helping me learn how to write, which is not my strongest suit."

Anna smiled but was again distracted by one of her classmates. "Anna, nice to see you. You're looking well as always."

The fellow student, a prematurely balding man a few inches shorter than Anna, rudely stepped between her and Murphy to reach for some dip. "We're going to Chinatown tonight. You want to join us?" he asked Anna, ignoring Murphy.

"Oh, thank you, Alvin, but not tonight."

"Come on, Anna. Ron, Susan, and George are going. You can prepare your presentation later."

"No, but thanks. Maybe next time."

"You gotta give me a chance, Anna," Alvin said, then walked away.

"You're giving a presentation tomorrow?" Murphy asked.

"Oh, it's not much. A little talk for a public health class."

"What's your paper about?"

"How a community deals with having a waste incinerator brought into their town. I attended two town meetings and reviewed the town's newspaper articles."

"What did you find?"

"All sorts of things. For one, there's a big difference in how scientists and the public view health risks. Lots of emotions come into play."

"What got you interested in the media?" Dan asked.

"After nursing school, I worked as a floor nurse at the University of Minnesota Hospital for about five years. Then I took courses in writing and communications. Eventually, I got a job at a local newspaper doing health stories, while I did coursework for a master's in journalism at night."

Dan nodded in acknowledgment of her academic accomplishments and professional direction. "That's great." Then he switched the topic to her presentation. "What's the focus of your topic tomorrow?"

"Communicating health risks to the community."

Another female student approached Anna. "Hello, Anna. Nice to see you," said the petite, dark-haired woman in rumpled pants and a T-shirt. "Hi, I'm Rachel Lang," she said to Murphy. "Are you a student here also?"

"Well, sort of—part time. I'm taking one course right now. I wish I had the luxury of going full time."

"Yes, it is nice. Like a refuge from the real world," she replied while glancing at Anna, then walked away.

"What risks are you going to talk about?" Dan asked, trying to keep the conversation alive.

"Pollution associated with an incinerator."

"Are their decent studies available?"

"Some. But a lot of the information is difficult to get. It's often buried in government reports and obscure animal studies," Anna replied.

Just then, a small, red-haired woman approached Anna. "Anna, are you ready to leave yet? Why don't you come with Rodney and me? We're going over to Our House for a drink."

"I don't think so, Melissa."

"Come on, Anna, you need to socialize more," she countered. "How about your friend?" Melissa pointed to Dan.

"I'd be delighted," Dan said. Turning to Anna, he added, "You can use me as a sounding board. I'll be your critic."

"Anna?" Melissa said. "Let's go."

Murphy looked directly into Anna's bright blue eyes. In a moment, they engaged, and he sensed a spark. *This is silly and giddy,* he thought, but in that brief moment, he knew her response before she even answered.

"OK, why not?"

—

Our House, as the name implied, was an early twentieth-century house in Boston that had been converted into a social club. Popular among young professionals and graduate students, it offered a variety of sitting areas and also a dance floor in the old dining room. Dancing was done to contemporary music, but the sounds of Beethoven, Mozart, and other classical composers filled the small sitting areas.

Melissa and her friend Rodney, bounding with energy, wasted no time in getting out on the dance floor.

"Cheers," Dan said, raising his bottle of beer to Anna's glass of chardonnay.

"Good luck," Anna said, referring to Dan's operation the next day. In their short ride from the reception and their walk to the restaurant, Dan had told Anna about his brother's bone marrow transplant. In that brief period of time, he sensed a spark with Anna that he hoped was mutual and that reminded him of the excitement he had felt in college when meeting someone new.

"How long will you be in the hospital?" she asked.

"Only a night. I go in tomorrow morning, then have the procedure in the afternoon."

"What'll they do?"

"A hematologist essentially bores a hole into my hip somewhere between eighty and a hundred times to get enough bone marrow to transplant into my brother."

"What!" she asked in surprise. "That sounds crude—and painful."

"Right on both counts. Most people have hip pain for a while afterward."

"Are there any other risks?"

"Not really. It's relatively safe. The major risk is from the general anesthesia—which doesn't excite me either."

"Why?"

"Well, I've never undergone general anesthesia. You're completely out. Your life is literally out of your control."

"It's very safe though, isn't it?" Anna asked encouragingly.

"In general, but you never know. Strange and unexpected complications can arise from anesthesia."

"But aren't the risks remote for someone healthy?"

"Usually," Dan replied. "But I hate to admit how much I don't want to be a patient."

"All doctors should be patients once in a while," she said.

"I suppose it can be humbling to be a patient, but I'm anxious to get this over with."

"It's impressive that you would go through all this."

"I never really doubted whether I should do it, especially to help my brother. But allow me to switch channels. Why did you decide to come to Boston?"

"Because Harvard foolishly accepted me into their master's program in public health," Anna replied. "It wasn't part of any grand plan, just luck and timing—essential ingredients to any good fortune. At first, I wasn't sure about leaving Minneapolis, but eventually I realized the change would be stimulating."

"How did you earn the fellowship?"

"Knowing the right people," she answered in jest. "I did an exposé on the EPA's Superfund program in Minnesota for the *Minneapolis Tribune*."

"Do you think there's much of a health risk with these sites? It seems there may be more hype than fact."

"Some people feel that way, but there are enough studies suggesting problems—with polluted water, polluted air, and so forth—that I'm convinced that it needs serious attention."

"Come on, you two, stop the talking and start dancing," Melissa chimed, as energetic as always. "Anna, don't let this handsome guy stay in that chair. Get him on the dance floor," she said, pulling Anna by the arm.

"She's right," Dan said. "We need to lighten up. Let's go."

He grabbed Anna's hand to lead her onto the small dance floor. As they moved to the rhythm of contemporary rock music, Murphy was struck by Anna's lightness and grace. The warmth and ease of her smile belied the seriousness of her earlier conversation with him. Even though he knew his reaction to her was premature, albeit intense, there was an ease to the attraction he felt.

Shortly thereafter, Dan drove Anna to her Brookline apartment. Murphy then returned home, but he couldn't fall asleep, a problem he rarely faced until recently. In fact, one of his lasting memories about his internship was his uncanny ability to sleep at virtually a moment's notice. Long nights on call had taught him to treasure quiet times when he could get some rest.

Tonight, his mind was racing in different directions, preventing him from feeling the peace he needed to drift into sleep. Although he had participated in hundreds of operations as a resident in orthopedic surgery, he was apprehensive about the risks of the general anesthesia that he would receive in the morning. Ruminating over side effects such as his heart stopping or his breathing failing, he felt embarrassed about being so self-absorbed in his own worries in light of the consequences his brother could face without the transplant.

Dan still found Pat's illness difficult to grasp. So much had happened in only a flash of time. How could his bone marrow have completely shut down? Was it worth pursuing a cause? Dan kept thinking of Anna's confident suggestion to try to find out how Pat had become ill. After tossing about for a while, he got up and tried to distract himself with reading—first, the newspaper, then newsmagazines, and finally a novel he had stopped reading a few months ago. Since he had no urge to sleep, he thought the television seemed a hopeful prospect. Surfing the channels, he stopped to watch a woman reporter appearing in front of the White House talking about the president's new budget proposals. *How closely she resembles Anna,* he thought, *in appearance and demeanor.*

Dan Murphy thought about Washington, the city he had left more than a year and a half ago. He recalled his four years in the nation's capital, when he shared an apartment and his life with a woman he had married two years earlier. They were each so busy with their respective careers, though—his wife an assertive young attorney, and Murphy a fatigued orthopedic surgery resident—that they had little time to nurture their marriage. The distractions and their professional demands eventually led to a distance that set the stage for his wife's affair. The inherent duplicity associated with the episode destroyed the trust so essential in marriage that they grew progressively apart. Despite a casual effort at counseling, Dan grew bored and became unenthused, until finally Susan took the initiative and moved out. Murphy then left to live on his own in a large apartment in DC, but soon he became weary of his surroundings and of his position at Washington General Hospital.

Now he wondered whether he had made the right decision. Should he have stayed and made more of an effort with Susan and the residency program? Although he had dated a variety of women he had met through friends, the health club, and the hospital, none had struck the proper chord. *Could Anna be different?* His thoughts reverted to tomorrow's operation. *It'll be routine,* he assured himself. *Nothing will happen.*

Insomnia drove Murphy to reach for the file that he had thought he wouldn't open until after he'd left the hospital. Impressed by Anna's points in favor of pursuing the cause of Pat's disease, he paged through Liam's medical records. Having recently emigrated from

Ireland, Liam O'Malley, a neighbor of Pat, was considered illegal, and as a result could not find work with any reputable company. Taking jobs wherever and whenever available, he barely earned enough money to support his wife and family. Although he preferred to remain in Ireland, good job opportunities in his native country were limited. Many of his acquaintances and friends had come to Boston, so it seemed natural for him to live in the city that had hosted Irish immigrants since the mid-nineteenth century.

Dan carefully leafed through Liam O'Malley's medical records, but nothing unusual surfaced in his review. The lab tests, biopsy results, and referral to Boston City Hospital were all typical for aplastic anemia. No mention was made of the type of work Liam did or whether he had any hobbies that involved the use of chemicals. On completing the survey, Murphy reflected on both his brother, Pat, and Liam. Could they have been exposed to some toxin, or was it just a coincidence that two healthy men from the same street, who drove trucks for a living, had each contracted a rare fatal illness within a short period of time of one another?

Dan knew that his brother's trucking firm delivered warehouse goods and other materials to distribution centers. Liam also drove a truck, but because of his illegal immigrant status, he took whatever came his way in terms of job assignments, so naturally he lacked health benefits. Could it have been the absence of health insurance that caused Liam not to follow the physician's recommendations for further testing?

No longer able to think as alertly as he preferred, Murphy turned off his light and tried to sleep. As his thoughts turned to Anna, he felt a physical rush, then fell asleep.

Chapter 9

"That wasn't bad, Carlson," said David Becker, a dermatologist and the acting chief of occupational health at the School of Public Health.

"Thank you," Anna replied, with the satisfaction that comes from having pleased a demanding professor.

"Questions or comments?" Becker said to the class.

Anna had just completed her presentation on the community response to the proposed waste incinerator. As part of her graduate seminar requirements, she interviewed representatives from state and local government, and industry and community leaders in a town north of Boston. Her goal was to understand the process of gaining government approval and the necessary permits to site a facility with implications for the environment. Earning a master's degree in public health required a fair amount of independent and creative work, but Anna was up to the task. After having spent the past three years as a health reporter for the *Minneapolis Tribune*, she recognized the need to doggedly pursue a topic. Her energetic approach had helped her to learn of the enormous difference between actual and perceived health risks, especially when it came to siting an incinerator in a community.

A student raised his hand. "How did the town's politicians react to the incinerator?"

"They actually encouraged bids to construct a facility because the incinerator offers the promise of jobs and taxes to help the school district," Anna answered. "The hospital agreed to provide a continuous source of material that could be processed at an economical rate. Some community members actually welcomed the potential for new taxes, but others resisted even the concept of bringing someone else's waste into their own backyard."

"What do you think people were most afraid of?"

"A combination of factors," Anna replied. "On one hand, I sensed a threat to their pride in needing something they might consider unsavory, such as an incinerator, as an embarrassing way to raise taxes or provide jobs. On the other hand, I also sensed an anxiety, if that's the right word, about the potential health risks."

"What do you mean?" the same student asked.

"Well, people get conflicting information. For example, they hear about an EPA report on the dioxin that's generated from incinerators. They hear that releases cannot be controlled. Then, they hear the battle of the experts, some of whom say the risks of dioxin are overstated, that problems have only been theorized, not proven, with others saying that caution is warranted because of animal studies."

"Don't you think animal results have value?" Dr. Becker asked Anna in his trademark condescending tone.

"Well, of course," Anna said, Becker's stridency having taken her by surprise. "It's a matter of how they are interpreted when evaluating risks to people," she replied confidently.

"Any other comments?" Becker asked. It was another of his trademarks to disingenuously interrupt a discussion to pursue his own agenda.

Another student raised her hand. "Do you know whether there may be any risks to children in the school nearby?"

"I doubt it," Anna replied, "but a number of residents are very concerned about the proximity of the incinerator to the school."

Becker chimed in with the pedagogical flare for which he was noted for exhibiting on the hospital floor. "A number of studies have suggested links between particulates and other forms of air pollution and childhood asthma. See the recent issue of *Archives of Environmental Health.* There's also a review article published recently in the *American Journal of Public Health.* I suggest that all of you get the articles and be prepared to discuss them next week."

When Becker suggested that his students review an article for a class, they failed to do so only at great peril to themselves. If Becker were to find one of them unprepared, he would embarrass the student mercilessly. His intent was to rule by fear. In fact, he was proud to admit that he was an academic totalitarian. His professional reputation from publishing books and numerous articles, coupled with substantial grant money and research support, enabled him to get away with behavior that would be unacceptable in other settings.

As the students left, Becker approached Anna.

"Carlson, have you decided on your project yet?" He was referring to the yearlong publishable effort he required of all the students in his department. Anna, unlike most of the students in his program, was not a physician. Nonetheless, she had been assigned to him, a physician adviser, because of his interest in the media. Becker loved to work with media relations people. Described as a gadfly by some, he used the media to advance his own interests, whether appearing on television or being described in the newspaper as an expert. "Exposure" was good for his referral practice and grant endeavors, he told his associates. Now with Anna as his student, he had a chance to mold a reporter to his own view and develop future contacts.

"Dr. Becker, I have a number of ideas, but I haven't formed a final decision yet," Anna replied. Becker, despite the relative informality of the School of Public Health, where ties and suits were a rarity, insisted on being addressed as Doctor. He also had a penchant for wearing bow ties.

"You don't have much time, you know. I expect an outline within the week. You're the last of my students to deliver." Becker turned to retrieve his briefcase, then unceremoniously left the room without waiting for Anna to answer.

Taken aback by his abrupt but typical behavior, Anna was spurred to action. She went to the student center, where she hoped to get an idea or two while working on her laptop. Gaining access to the health-related literature was becoming so much more convenient with more reliable and expansive medical search engines such as PubMed and Web of Science, among other sources that tabulated peer-reviewed publications. Like a medical Google, these search engines could readily identify articles and abstracts based on the use of key terms. Staring at the screen after accessing PubMed, the National Library of Medicine's database of more than six thousand health and medical journals, Anna hoped to identify a challenging issue in environmental health that might prompt an idea for a project and please the demanding Professor Becker, her academic adviser.

The first topic that came to mind was aplastic anemia, the rare disease for which Dan Murphy's brother was undergoing a bone marrow transplant. Her thoughts then took her to Dan, who at the same time was in surgery donating bone marrow that would be used later for his brother. Anna typed "aplastic anemia" into the PubMed search box. Within seconds, the titles of upward of a hundred articles appeared. One particular article caught her attention: "Aplastic Anemia and Pesticides, an Etiologic Association." Recalling Dan's comment about the unknown cause of his brother's ailment, she noted the reference, reviewed the abstract, and downloaded the full article for careful review. *Perhaps there's an environmental cause for Patrick's disease,* she thought. *Didn't Dan mention that a neighbor had a similar problem?*

Chapter 10

Anna was struck by some of the similarities between the cases described in the studies and the experience of Dan's brother. Their clinical patterns were similar—that is, otherwise healthy people, primarily men in their late twenties and early thirties, suddenly had become ill. Many died within a short time after the diagnosis.

The article that most attracted Anna's interest referred to two hundred eighty cases of aplastic anemia that were thought to be associated with exposure to some type of pesticide. The average age of the people with the disease was twenty-eight—the same as Patrick. Although Dan seemed to think that there was no specific cause for his brother's condition, Anna wondered whether he could he have overlooked something. She began to realize how often she thought of Dan Murphy, even though they had only met the night before. Not particularly interested in becoming involved with anyone during her education in Boston, Anna was content with the frequency of the phone calls and messages she received from Roger, the man with whom she had been living for the past two years back home in Minneapolis.

Prior to leaving Minneapolis, Anna refused Roger Bresman's offer of marriage. "It's not as if I won't marry him," she had mentioned to one of her friends. "I'm just not ready." It was a difficult decision for Anna to leave Roger to pursue her fellowship. *I can't believe I'm thirty-two. Am I putting my biological clock at risk by putting off Roger?* she had fretted.

Thus, it was with a bit of hesitation and some guilt that Anna called Dan Murphy in the hospital room where he was resting after donating the bone marrow for his brother's transplant.

"Dan, I hope you're feeling OK. I was doing work for a project and was distracted thinking about your brother's illness. So, I found an article that I'm sure you'll find interesting."

"Where do you get all this energy? Didn't you have a presentation today? Incidentally, how did it go?"

"Fine, I suppose. My adviser is difficult to read and hard to please. But I think OK."

"Great."

"Dan, do you need a visitor? You must be sore and groggy. But if you're not, I can be over in an hour."

"I'll rouse my forces. Come right over."

"See you in a bit," she replied.

—

Anna felt a little silly as she dressed to visit Murphy in the hospital. She put on a skirt and a turtleneck, then added a touch of makeup. Being enthused about meeting another man, however, made her feel a bit guilty because of Roger back in Minneapolis.

Don't make too much of this, she reminded herself. *You're going to marry Roger when you finish the master's.*

Shortly thereafter, Anna entered Dan's hospital room after a few knocks on the door. About five-foot-nine in height with shoulder-length light brown hair, her slender appearance exuded fitness. In her view, however, she always had room to lose four or five pounds from her agile frame. Despite the winter coat she was wearing, she still appeared lean and slender. On seeing Dan, she smiled in a way that said, *I'm glad to be here, but I feel a little pushy.*

"What a pleasant surprise." Murphy greeted her in a tone that quickly helped her feel at ease.

"How are you?" she asked.

"Not as bad as I thought I would be. The nausea from the anesthesia is tough to take."

"How's your hip?"

"Sore. Now I know how a quarterback feels when he's sacked."

"Can you take anything for the pain?"

"Sure. But the strong types make me too light-headed."

"Have you heard anything about your brother?"

Dan nodded. "He had the marrow transfusion just a few hours ago. He's in a special room now to minimize the risk of infection."

"That's nice to hear. When are you going home?"

"Probably tomorrow. People can't lounge in hospitals anymore. Managed-care programs get you out as soon as possible. But I need Dr. Harrington to give his OK. He should be here shortly."

"He's impressive. Heading the transplant unit, and a full professor at the medical school," Anna said.

"A gentleman as well," Dan added.

"Did he mention anything about the cause of your brother's aplastic anemia?"

"No," Murphy answered. "It's difficult to pinpoint a cause. In nearly half the cases, a cause is never determined."

"Maybe it's because people don't bother to look for a cause," Anna suggested.

"I suppose, but it's probably academic, don't you think? Most important is curing the disease."

"Yes, but according to some articles I've read, if the disease is the result of certain hazards, whatever they may be, then further exposure can cause relapses. Plus, Dan, who knows in this crazy world of biological and chemical weapons? Anything is possible." She reached into her book bag. "Here, an article from the *Journal of Occupational Medicine*. Just published last year." She read to Dan: "'A history of chemical exposure is often not sought by the clinician or recorded in the record. The average age of this group of over two hundred eighty cases was twenty-eight'—the same as your brother."

The last comment attracted Dan's attention.

"Look." Anna pointed to the page as she handed Dan the article, well marked from her own review.

Dan looked over the ten-page report and was struck by how little attention was usually directed to determining the cause—especially environmental—of aplastic anemia. The article reported that causes are usually described as unknown, although the disease may have been provoked by chemical exposure of some sort or another. But no one bothered to pursue the issue.

"A provocative article, isn't it?" Dan replied. "But I don't know what chemicals would have to do with my brother. He's been working as a truck driver, and I don't think he delivers hazardous materials. He goes from warehouses to distributors to retail outlets."

Murphy stared ahead with an expression that suggested doubt about his brother's outside work activities. He and his brother never discussed his work in any great depth, and usually they didn't say anything about it at all. Their social affairs consisted largely of family gatherings. At times, the two of them would share a beer and watch the Red Sox, Celtics, or Patriots on television. Occasionally, one of them would bring up a political topic, but the discussion rarely went too far because of the family's allegiance to the Democrats. Murphy's grandfather, at the age of eighteen, emigrated from the Republic of Ireland and became a naturalized citizen a few years thereafter. As a result, political discussions at the dinner table were limited to two sound bites: "All politicians are crooked" (except, of course, Congressman Daley, who helped Grandfather Murphy become a citizen) and "The Republicans are for the rich."

"Does the article describe the average interval between exposure to the chemical and diagnosis?" Anna asked.

"You mean the latency?" Dan responded, looking over the article.

"Yes."

"Five months." Dan continued, "That means you'd have to explore virtually any hazardous exposure Pat may have had for the previous five months! That's nearly impossible."

"Why?" Anna asked. "There aren't that many substances that have been found to cause aplastic anemia—at least according to what I read."

"But these chemicals are all over the place. Benzene's in gasoline. Does that mean if you pump your own gas, you'll get aplastic anemia?"

"Of course not. But it might be worth looking into possible causes, Dan. You'll never forgive yourself if there's a preventable cause."

"Anna, of course I'm concerned, but these scientific issues are so complicated."

Just then, Dr. Harrington knocked on the door and entered. "Excuse me," he said respectfully. "I hope I'm not interrupting anything important."

Anna looked sheepishly toward Dan, who replied, "Not at all. Please come in." He immediately asked Harrington, "How'd it go with Pat?"

"Your brother's doing well. A bit washed out, as you might imagine, but quite well overall."

"Are you allowing visitors?" Dan asked.

"No, not for now. I'd like to reduce the risk of infection as much as possible. The next few days are critical. Then if he can get by the next few months in particular, the outcome is even more favorable. The biggest risk is acute graft-versus-host reaction."

"How much of a risk do you think my brother faces?" Murphy asked.

"Each case is unique, but in general, younger patients do better. Your brother is about the right age to ensure a favorable prognosis," Harrington said encouragingly.

"Is there any way to prevent the graft-versus-host reaction?"

"No approach is widely accepted, but there are some acceptable alternatives," Harrington replied, his having developed the transplant unit more than twelve years ago. Despite rapid advances in bone marrow transplantation, however, numerous uncertainties remained. Harrington, considered to be on the cutting edge of his field, recently received a grant from the National Institutes of Health to conduct a clinical trial of protocols designed to prevent one of life's most nasty illnesses, graft-versus-host reaction.

"One promising approach," Harrington said, "is the use of thalidomide posttransplant."

"Thalidomide?" Dan asked with piqued curiosity. "Isn't that the medication that caused those birth defects? Babies having deformed arms?"

"Yes," Harrington answered. "It was used about forty years ago to prevent miscarriages, but it's making a comeback. A number of studies have demonstrated that it has anti-immune functions," he emphasized. "It's helpful in treating both acute and chronic graft-versus-host reaction."

Harrington, who could graciously launch into a variety of discussions about his life's passion—hematology—paused upon recognizing Anna. "I'm sorry. I didn't mean to sound so clinical."

"Oh. I trained in nursing, so it's not too much over my head," she said with self-deprecating charm.

"Well then, I'm sure you'd appreciate the essential biological struggle that'll take place between Patrick's immune system and Dan's bone marrow," Harrington said. "If Pat's immune system overwhelms Dan's marrow, the graft will be rejected. On the other hand, if Dan's marrow wages war against Pat's organs, it can cause a debilitating illness and in some cases death."

Dr. Harrington adjusted his plaid tie and fidgeted with the stethoscope that he always carried in his side pocket.

"Are there ways of knowing Patrick's outlook?" Anna asked, looking to break the silence.

"Some," Harrington replied. "But not enough to be definitive."

"Do you have any idea how Pat got the aplastic anemia?" the graduate student from Minneapolis asked.

"No. I'm sorry, I don't. I hardly ever do with this disease. It's so rare that it is hard to conduct major studies on the causes."

"How rare is it?" Dan asked.

"Well, it depends," Harrington replied. "Different geographical areas have different rates. We see about fifteen cases per year here, but then again, we're a referral center for Boston and New England. In this area, five to ten cases occur per million population. That translates to about twenty to thirty people in the Boston area each year."

Anna recognized a chance to probe Harrington for knowledge and his natural tendency to lecture in a most respectful way. He enjoyed sharing information about his field, especially with patients and their families. Having educated four clinical fellows in hematology each year for the past ten years, he had established his own legacy throughout the country.

"Dr. Harrington," Anna said, "have you any experience with pesticides or any other chemicals that cause aplastic anemia?"

"I've read about it in a number of articles here and there, but I don't know of any definitive studies."

"Is there any way blood or urine could be tested to determine a cause?"

Harrington thought for a moment before answering. "Probably not. In my experience, the bone marrow tends to look the same regardless of the cause."

"But how about a blood test?"

"I doubt it. We don't routinely do toxicologic testing here."

Anna continued, saying, "I was reading this article on pesticides and aplastic anemia." She handed the article to Harrington. "It seems that some cases are linked to lindane, a wood preservative. Radiation's another cause. I don't mean to be an alarmist, but I've been reading about terrorists and dirty bombs. Do you think it may be worth considering some environmental cause? Two cases of a rare disease in two healthy men in their late twenties living on the same street—that sounds too coincidental to me." Harrington noted the points Anna had made.

"A public health graduate student," Murphy said to Harrington.

"Anna, you make a good case for digging deeper. But I'm sure you realize that we need to focus on curing the disease. Determining its cause is a luxury at this stage."

"Why don't we do both?" Dan suggested.

"What do you have in mind?" Harrington asked.

"Is there any way of determining whether your aplastic anemia patients live in a certain geographical area more so than in other areas?" Anna asked.

Harrington paused for a moment.

"An increase might indicate an environmental cause," Dan offered.

"Not exactly," Harrington chimed.

"But it's a nice start," Anna said.

"It's a bit more complicated than that," Harrington said. "We'd need a control group to which we could compare our patient group."

Harrington got up to leave, but he turned toward Anna as Murphy watched from his hospital bed. "Are you willing to explore, but with no guarantees of success?" the hematologist asked.

"I'd be delighted," Anna responded, taken aback, but nonetheless pleased with his overture.

"I just finished a study of our leukemia patients and I have the original data on the control group. Perhaps we could use some of the information to study aplastic anemia."

"When can I come to your office?" Anna asked enthusiastically.

"Call my administrative assistant," Harrington replied. "Tell him I want to see you for about a half hour. In fact, you should both come. Dan, perhaps you could help Anna answer these questions on toxicology testing."

"I don't have a clue," Dan answered.

"Maybe you ought to try. At the very least, you'll learn something." Despite Harrington's grace and savoir fare, he was also a creature of pedagogical habit.

"You're quite the charmer," Dan said to Anna as she walked toward him.

"Was I too much?"

"Not at all," Dan replied. "I'm envious of your energy, especially, since I don't feel like getting out of bed."

"You've had a demanding day. You'll feel great in a day or two and be back on your skis next week."

"Are you sure you're not a motivational trainer or a salesperson on the Home Shopping Network?"

"Aren't you pithy!" she responded.

"I should have had you as a basketball coach. I could have played every minute of every game with your inspiration."

"Basketball?" she asked.

"My favorite sport. At least until I hit thirty-five and my knees went sour."

"You sound like a good match for me now."

"For basketball?"

"No, tennis. We should play sometime." Anna found the naturalness of her overture to Murphy surprising. Although attracted to him, she wasn't sure why or to what extent. It was the middle of December, so she doubted he'd take her up on the offer, unless they were to use an indoor court.

"You're on," Murphy said, staring directly into her soft-blue eyes.

"I'd better go. You need your rest," Anna said.

"Anna, thanks for coming. It was a great surprise. Even if you undercut my relationship with Harrington," he said in jest.

Anna smiled. "I suppose I'll see you at his office. Are you sure you want to do this?"

"Oh yes," Murphy answered, convinced he wanted to see Anna again, but unsure of walking down blind alleys in trying to find the cause of his brother's illness. He knew, or at least he thought he knew, that the exercise was bound to be futile.

"Why don't I call you," Murphy said, "when I get out of here and feel myself again."

"That's great! I'll sit by the phone," she replied with a wry grin as she turned to leave. "Hope you feel better."

—

After a few hours of rest, Dan's aching hip woke him. A dull, relentless pain bore through to his back, the pain medication barely dousing its intensity.

Dan Murphy looked blankly at the television news program while in the neverland between full alertness and the dreamy peace brought on by the analgesics. Moments later, the phone rang. Quickly picking up the receiver, he hoped to avoid waking the man adjacent to him in the semiprivate room.

"Oh, hello, Theresa," he answered, addressing Theresa O'Malley. Hoping to conceal his overwhelming tiredness, he continued with an effort at being friendly. "How are you?"

"Dr. Murphy, Liam died." The bluntness of the words clobbered Murphy's sensibilities and roused his attention.

"What?" he answered, unable to conceal his shock at the news.

"My husband. Liam. We talked about him. You looked at his records." She sobbed uncontrollably.

Murphy, from his experience as an emergency physician, recognized that little could be done to comfort the woman in light of the inevitable pain and sorrow that had only just begun. All he could muster in reply was, "I'm so sorry, Theresa." She cried. Murphy let her continue uninterrupted.

"He was doing OK," she said, "but then, I don't know, something went wrong."

Murphy felt the foggy sensation from the pain medication rapidly disappear as the stress of the moment jolted him into a level of alertness that he often experienced in the middle of the night when treating people who had been injured in car accidents, falls, or alcohol-fueled brawls. Even a full cup of Colombian coffee didn't have the ability to rouse him as much as responding to a medical emergency did. "What happened?" he asked.

"He got some kind of infection two days ago, and it kept getting worse. The doctors gave him medicine, but nothing worked. He kept getting worse and worse! Oh, I can't believe it!" she sobbed.

"Did he get the bone marrow transplant?" Dan asked.

"Yeah! A few days ago. But what good did it do? He's dead, Dr. Murphy. I don't know what I'm going to do."

"Did he have a good match?" Dan asked, referring to the genetic blood testing done prior to transplants to ensure success.

"I think so, but I'm not sure. The doctors were so busy that I could hardly talk to them."

"Where did he have the transplant?"

"At the city hospital."

"Why there?"

"We have no health insurance. Don't you remember, Dr. Murphy? We don't have our green cards, so we can't get insurance with the type of work Liam does."

"What did he do?"

"Whatever he could find—construction, odd jobs, driving a truck." She sobbed again. "I can't believe it. I don't know what I'm going to do!"

"Theresa, I wish I could help."

"You can. Find out why he got sick. Why this happened. Why I lost my husband."

Chapter 11

That afternoon, Dan had no trouble convincing Dr. Harrington to discharge him from the hospital. Despite the achy hip and his lust for more sleep, he was anxious to get back to work.

Liam's wife, Maryann, and Dan's mother, Beth, were waiting for him in the visitors' lounge.

"Did you talk with Dr. Harrington?" Dan's mother asked, her five-foot-four frame covered by a wool overcoat that had seen many winters. Dan functioned as the intermediary between the medical community and his family. It wasn't that his family members weren't capable, but his mother, in particular, held physicians in a certain awe, a trait that has long since diminished among most of the public. As a result, his family rarely probed or questioned a physician's recommendations, an approach that necessitated Dan's involvement.

"Yes, last night," Dan said. "Harrington was pleased with how well Pat did."

"When can he come home?" Maryann asked. Her eyes mirrored her emotions, bloodshot with swollen lids. The surprise and uncertainty of her husband's illness was a burden she didn't need while being pregnant. Her face grimaced in a hopeful but frightened way when she asked Dan, "What do you think? Is he going to be all right?"

"I'm confident," Dan replied. "Our genetic match was similar. There's a lot in Pat's favor."

"But how will you know?" Dan's mother asked. "How will you know if this transplant takes? Are you sure it was the right thing to do?" The rapid firing of her questions reflected her own anxiety. Her youngest son was special to her. She always denied it, however, claiming that she loved all four children equally.

"Mom, no one knows for sure," Dan answered, then quickly regretted being so blunt in front of Maryann, to whom he wanted to be encouraging. *It's a difficult challenge,* he thought, *to convey medical information that is realistic, is honest, and inspires hope.*

"Why don't you go see him, Maryann!" Murphy's mother, Beth, said. "Danny and I will wait here."

"Are you sure? Would you like to go first?"

"No, you should," Beth replied with motherly concern.

Maryann rose from her chair a bit off-balance. In her sixth month of pregnancy, her mobility had lost its customary grace.

"This is going to be hard on her," Dan said to his mother.

"How about your mother? He's my son too, you know."

Despite how much she and her daughter-in-law liked one another, there was an underlying competitiveness between them that became obvious in certain family affairs. Maryann tended to acquiesce, but occasionally she stood firm, at the risk of incurring the wrath of her mother-in-law.

"What's all this treatment and radiation going to do to Patrick?" Dan's mother asked. "Tell me, Danny. Don't keep anything from your mother." Dan Murphy may have been a thirty-five-year-old professional, but his mother still knew how to command his allegiance.

"Radiation can cause problems."

"What type of problems?" she asked.

"Well, it may be difficult for him to have kids in the future," Dan said with obvious sadness.

"Why?"

"Radiation can kill the cells that produce sperm."

"Why do they do it then?" Beth asked.

"They needed to destroy Pat's own bone marrow since it wasn't working right, in order to have the transplant marrow from me take hold."

The news of her son's potential sterility caught Beth off guard. She wanted lots of grandchildren, but it didn't look as though she would have more than the two she already had from her daughter. *Who knows whether Danny will get married again!* she thought.

"Mom, let's trust Dr. Harrington's judgment," Dan suggested.

"How did this happen, Danny? You should know, you're a doctor. Why don't you know why your brother got this crazy disease?"

"I don't know, Mom. I don't know. I don't know if anyone does."

"If you really cared about him, you'd do something about it."

"What do you mean?" Dan asked, trying to conceal his frustration and also satisfy his mother's insatiable requests.

"Find out why he got sick. I can't believe this happens out of the blue!"

—

Dan walked toward his brother's room and began to dress in the special hospital gown required.

His brother lay on the hospital bed with his head propped up at an angle. Pat's customary élan had been blunted by the demanding medical treatment. An intravenous pole stood adjacent to his bed with the tubing entering the back of his hand. On the television was a college football game, while the radio blared hard rock music. The cacophony of sounds jarred Dan, but he quickly dismissed his own concerns upon recognizing the isolation Pat must have felt.

Dan Murphy hesitated on entering the room of his brother, now dancing with death in a way that made his friends and family question their own mortality. *So much of life is unpredictable and unfair,* Dan thought as he knocked on his brother's door. *This could be me.*

"Hey, dude, come in. I don't bite," Pat said upon recognizing his brother. "Do you have a sore ass?" he asked, referring to Dan's biopsy site. Even in a state of fear, Pat showed a sense of humor and hubris that made people, including his family, feel at ease. It was a trait that should have served him well as a salesman, but after a brief period hustling life insurance, he had left the job. Although getting along with other people was one of his strengths, he had tired of the need to sell things for a paycheck.

"When am I getting out of here?" Pat asked. "These doctors act as though it's classified information."

"Pat," Dan replied, "you've just undergone a major procedure."

"Major?" his brother said. "Are you kidding? It was like getting blood drawn."

Pat accurately described the relatively simple process of a bone marrow transplant. After bone marrow had been withdrawn earlier from Dan, it was simply infused though an intravenous catheter into his younger brother, an uncomplicated procedure, especially in light of the detailed preparation required for the transplant.

"Relax, Pat. There's more to come!" Dan said.

"What? I thought all I had to do was wait this out for a while—that as long as I don't reject your graft, I should fly clean."

"That would be great, wouldn't it? How do you feel?" Dan said.

"What do you think, amigo? I'm scared as hell. But don't tell anyone or I'll kick your ass."

"How's Maryann?"

"She's fine; her ultrasound was normal."

"That's terrific," Dan said. "Have you decided on any names yet?"

"Scheherazade if it's a girl. Jefferson if it's a boy."

Dan laughed quietly, his response making it clear that he neither believed his brother nor was ready to challenge him.

"That's what I tell Mom. She wants me to call it Patrick if it's a boy."

Just then an orderly entered the room. "Will you be eating this evening, Mr. Murphy?"

"Whaddya got?" Pat asked.

"Chicken."

"Bring it in."

"Pat, a lot of people are wondering how you got this disease," Dan said.

"No kidding."

"Have you thought about it?"

"Thought about it! I've thought about it. I'm pissed off. What did I do to deserve this?!"

"Does your work have anything to do with hazardous materials?" asked Dan.

"Like what?"

"Benzene, chemicals, whatever."

"No. None of that shit."

"Have you done anything different lately, like stripping furniture?" Dan asked, hoping that he might uncover an association with benzene, a component of furniture stripper and gasoline, the same benzene that can cause leukemia and aplastic anemia.

"What are you getting at with work and chemicals?"

"Aplastic anemia can be caused by certain chemicals."

"Such as?" Pat asked.

"As I just said, benzene, pesticides, radiation, some medications."

"But those things have nothing to do with me!"

"Are you sure? Apparently, it doesn't take much exposure to cause a problem in some people. You may not have been aware of contact with a hazard."

"I'm no Einstein, but I know when I'm working with nasty stuff."

"I'm only bringing it up because if a chemical caused this disease, you may be more susceptible to a relapse, especially if you're reexposed."

"Great, but why don't you tell me something practical, like when I'm going to get out of here?" Pat said.

"I'm not sure."

The orderly knocked on the door again.

"Coffee, sir?"

"This is better than a hotel," Pat answered. "Not now, but I'll have a Sam Adams—with a chilled glass."

"Sorry, sir. You'll need your doctor's permission," the young Hispanic male replied.

"That's something you can arrange, isn't it, Dan?"

"You ought to talk with Dr. Harrington, Pat."

"Great. I'll never be able to enjoy a football game again. What's football without beer and pizza?"

Dan smiled then looked down at his watch. "Pat, I have to go. I'm going to see someone."

"Someone?" Pat asked. "You mean a great-looking chick, I hope?"

Dan smiled, trying to conceal his enthusiasm at having met Anna.

"Aha. That's great. It's about time you got over that old wife of yours. She deserves to stay in Washington with all those slick politicians," said Patrick, who rarely had a kind word for Dan's ex-wife.

Chapter 12

Jake Wilson's shoulder ached constantly; it was even more painful when he tried to comb his hair. Overcome with anger about the previous night's events, he threw the brush against the wall, then ignored the pain as he readied himself for an evening in which he hoped to be entertained by the right woman.

He had no idea who had accosted him the evening before. Determining who was responsible, however, would not be an easy task since Wilson had managed to create a few enemies in his past.

Getting back to Boston after being dumped by thugs in a suburban football field was no easy task either, but his cleverness and nerve provided the fuel to overcome the cold, his injuries, and the lack of money he needed to get home.

Jake Wilson viewed his meetings with Tony Mesa with mixed emotions. On one hand, Wilson admired the charm and self-effacing style of the man with whom he had been working for the past few months. On the other hand, Wilson's street-smart intelligence prompted him to wonder whether Mesa always gave him the full story. Although Wilson doubted Mesa, he needed him.

Over the past few years, Wilson had developed a reputation for arranging jobs—small nonunion construction projects. Whenever a business needed renovation, trucking, or disposal services, Jake could find people ready and willing for the task. Working for him, however, had its limitations, such as no benefits like health insurance, vacation pay, or even workers' compensation coverage. Wilson essentially provided a job paid in cash. Anyone hurt in the process was at the mercy of the hospital providing treatment. Although the state required employers to cover insurance for work-related ailments, Wilson considered the premiums too high. They cut too much into his profits.

Although Wilson occasionally thought about seeking a proverbial real job, he felt invigorated when orchestrating his under-the-table work projects. He also enjoyed the influence he accrued in having people become indebted to him. The independence and income that his work style and skills afforded him were added benefits.

On entering the bar, the atmosphere of which brimmed with the din of scattered conversations, Wilson searched the faces for Tony Mesa. Suddenly, he felt a thump on his back and turned to see a tall, broad-shouldered man sporting a goatee.

"Wilson, my man. You're here," Mesa said with a sarcastic flare.

"At your service, as always," he replied, also with a hint of sarcasm.

"You're gonna get your boys to finish up for us now, aren't you?"

"You know I deliver. You have some money, I hope?"

"How could I forget!"

"Man, the women are lookin' good tonight, aren't they?" Mesa asked with a satanic grin.

As though responding to a mating call, three women, each sporting an ear-to-ear smile, approached Mesa.

"Hi, Tony," they said in unison, as Wilson dodged people cruising the bar, which was wall-to-wall with people who had just finished work for the day.

"Hello, ladies," Mesa responded. "Do you know Jake?"

They looked at Wilson, who offered his hand to one of them in response.

"Jake Wilson. It's a pleasure," he said, then turned to Mesa. "You're king of the jungle here, Mesa. What's your secret?"

"Brawn. Sheer masculine brawn backed with a lot of testosterone," he answered jokingly as he thrust out the chest that had taken a pounding—along with his chin—in his last professional boxing match.

After polite introductions, one woman said to Wilson, "What happened to your hand?" pointing to the splint on his middle finger.

Unsure how to respond, Wilson replied, "Working out. I'm lifting too many weights. One of the bars fell on my hand." Hoping the answer satisfied them, he glanced at Mesa, who sported a blank expression.

"Oh. You'll just have to be more careful," she responded encouragingly.

"Tony, we have to go, but nice to see you," the young woman said. Then she and her friends navigated through the crowds to the exit.

"Mesa, you should spread some of your friends around," Wilson said in reference to the women.

"Hey. You got it or you don't," Mesa replied with palpable self-confidence. He then quickly changed the topic to his own agenda. "Look, man, we need to talk." He led Wilson to a corner of the pub, where they found an empty table and some chairs. Mesa continued. "Look, we need to get this done as soon as possible."

"Why the rush?"

"We need it. Just do it. And we can't take any risks on leaks. Use the same people, and make sure they keep their mouths shut."

"When am I getting paid?"

Mesa reached into the pocket of his black leather jacket to withdraw an envelope, which he handed to Wilson.

"How much is here?"

"Enough."

Wilson searched through the crumpled envelope filled with bills. After a quick count, he said, "This isn't enough."

"There'll be more later."

"That's bullshit."

"This is it for now."

"When do I get the rest?"

"I'll see if I can arrange for more after the next trip."

"And when's that planned?"

"Soon."

"When?"

"I'm not sure, but as soon as I learn from Barrows, I'll let you know."

"I don't understand why this Barrows asshole has to be so mysterious. Why can't I meet him?"

"It's not necessary."

"I don't care if it's necessary or not," Wilson replied.

"Get over it. Security's too important."

"What if something goes sour?" Wilson probed.

"Don't worry. It won't. Just do what you're supposed to do."

Chapter 13

Dr. Harrington's office, located in a three-story building adjacent to the hospital, housed a conference room and administrative suites. As Dan walked through the corridors of the building, he couldn't stop thinking of Anna. Captivated by an emotional fervor he had never before experienced, even with his ex-wife, he hoped that the feeling was mutual. *A dangerous dance of emotion,* he mused. Moments later, a familiar voice jarred him out of the reverie.

"Dan," she said. "Hi. I'm glad to see you're on time."

"Anna." Dan extended his hand.

"We may be on time, but I think we're lost. Do you know where Harrington's office is?" Dan asked.

"It's supposed to be on this floor," Anna replied, surveying the hallway looking for a sign. "Oh. There it is. Hematology."

Harrington's office, conspicuous with its lack of pretension, included a modest waiting area with walls lined with books, periodicals, and hospital photographs.

A secretary politely addressed Anna: "Can I help you?"

"We're here to see Dr. Harrington."

"Are you Anna Carlson and Dr. Murphy?" she asked.

"Yes."

"Oh, please come in. He's in the office."

Harrington's administrator, secretary, and confidant for the past fifteen years guided them to the professor of medicine and chief of the Bone Marrow Unit.

"Welcome," Harrington said, his head full of gray hair that showed no sign of thinning. He walked toward a conference table, to which he directed Anna and Murphy to sit.

"Please," he pointed at the seats. "Would you like coffee or a soft drink?"

"Coffee would be great," Anna answered.

"I'll have the same," Dan said.

Toward the end of the room was a small sink where Harrington kept coffee and other refreshments to help him through the long hours he often worked.

Dan wasted no time in inquiring about his brother's outlook. "What do you think of Pat's chances?"

"So far, so good, but it's much too early to be certain. It's difficult predicting who will do the best, although your brother has a lot in his favor," Dr. Harrington answered, showing compassion, which helped soothe Dan's uncertainty in much the same way that Harrington had helped motivate many patients throughout his long career.

"The transplant essentially prompts a battle between the host, which is your brother's immune system, and the graft, which is your marrow. There has to be a delicate balance so that one does not overpower the other. Either the host will reject the graft or the graft will cause acute and chronic illness in the host."

"What's the outlook for Patrick?" Anna asked.

"It's difficult to predict. Patrick's chances, however, are better than fifty-fifty. He's young and otherwise healthy, and your genetic match was very similar."

"Have you learned anything more about the causes of aplastic anemia?" Harrington asked Anna.

"A bit. It seems that many types of chemicals, especially pesticides, are associated with aplastic anemia."

"Have you ever tested any of your patients for toxic substances?" Dan asked Harrington.

"Some, but the results have not been encouraging."

"Why?" Dan asked.

"For one, the exposure to the chemical usually occurs many months earlier. Blood tests don't help much because there are so many different compounds that can be detected. Just because a chemical is present in the body doesn't mean it caused the disease you're investigating."

"What did your study on leukemia show?" Anna asked.

"Risk factors associated with the disease," Harrington answered. After a momentary pause, he said, "In fact, some of the data might be of value in a review of aplastic anemia." After publishing more than one hundred fifty papers, rising to full professor at the medical school, and receiving numerous grants from the National Institutes of Health, Harrington still loved a new project.

He pushed his chair away from the table. "Come over here," he said, then directed Anna and Murphy into an adjacent office lined with books and journals. At the far end of the room was a computer with a printer at its side. "I'll pull up the control group that we used in the leukemia study. Then you can then look at the demographic data we have on the aplastic anemia cases."

"How many people do you treat a year with aplastic anemia?" Murphy asked.

"About fifteen."

"I think there's an environmental cause," Anna said.

"Why?" Harrington asked.

"Just a hunch," the graduate student in public health replied. "It seems too much of a coincidence that two healthy men in their late twenties get a rare, life-threatening disease in the space of a few months."

"Coincidences like this are common in medicine," Harrington replied.

"But how could you rule out an environmental factor?" Anna persisted.

"I'm not sure," answered Harrington. "Maybe we could get some help from the health department."

"But isn't it premature to contact a health department?" Dan asked.

"Maybe we don't need a health department," Anna interjected.

"You might evaluate if certain residents, perhaps by zip code, had a higher rate of disease than the control group," Harrington suggested. "Perhaps an environmental cause can be raised. Then you could study other factors in more detail."

"How would you do that?" asked Dan.

"We have demographic data on all our patients for the past five years. You could survey certain risk factors."

"What would the survey tell you?" asked Dan.

"It would give you some idea as to whether your hypothesis, in this case, that an environmental chemical caused the disease, is plausible. If so, a more detailed analysis can be performed. I'm happy to work with you, assuming you get approval from your adviser."

"Thank you, Dr. Harrington. I'd love the opportunity to work with you."

"My pleasure," replied Harrington. He then said to Murphy, "Dan, you're welcome as well."

"Thanks. I'm happy to carry Anna's books," he said, which prompted a smile from Anna that stimulated him to grin in return.

Chapter 14

After spending the afternoon with Harrington's administrator, Anna had learned how to use the epidemiology program that the professor had developed for his study on adult leukemia. She compared information from the patients with aplastic anemia to that of a group of other patients from the same hospital who did not have blood disorders. Unsure of what to do next, she wanted to see Dan despite her ambivalence about her attraction to him.

So excited that she couldn't wait for the elevator, she bounded down the stairwell, convinced of the need to talk with Dan Murphy. She had uncovered a potential environmental link to Pat Murphy's illness.

Anna hoped that Dan would not be offended by her enthusiastic interest in pursuing the cause of his brother's ailment. Needing a project for Becker, she wanted to show her adviser that she should be taken seriously. She had an innate sense that she was on to something, perhaps from her experience as a journalist. *Pursue your leads,* she thought. *You never know where they'll take you.*

Murphy, dictating a chart in his office, was alerted by Anna's knock on the door.

"Dan," she said. Immersed in his work, Murphy looked up,

startled at the pleasant interruption. "I hope you're not too surprised," she added.

"Anna. It is a surprise, but a terrific one. To what do I owe the pleasure of this visit?" he asked.

"I think I found an environmental link to your brother's disease," she continued, taking off her maroon overcoat and black leather gloves. Boston in December could be quite inhospitable to those unprepared for the snow, ice, and windchill, which could sour the best of spirits.

"What happened?" Dan asked, turning his chair in her direction, anxious to hear good news.

"You know that Harrington did this study on leukemia, right?"

Dan nodded in agreement, remaining in rapt attention.

Anna continued, saying, "Well, he has tons of data. The patients in his leukemia study all completed extensive questionnaires about their medical history, job situation, children, and so forth. He also had a control group with the same information. Since he already had a control group, I compared them to his aplastic anemia patients."

"Are you sure you can do that? Scientifically, is it a valid approach?" Murphy asked.

"I'm not sure, but nonetheless, I was struck by the results, especially after I noticed another case of aplastic anemia in South Boston, a man within the same age range as Patrick and Liam, whose records you reviewed."

"How old?" Dan asked, his interest in learning of another person with this rare disease of the bone marrow piqued.

"Thirty-three," answered Anna.

"Where's he live?" Dan asked.

"I'm not sure. But they all have the same zip code, which suggests an environmental factor."

"Anna, isn't that a stretch—just because they live in the same zip code? Don't zip codes cover large areas?"

"It's only a start, like a lead in a crime investigation. You've got to start somewhere," Anna replied, her enthusiasm both palpable and infectious.

"What did you do?" Dan asked.

"I compared features that were different between the aplastic anemia cases and the people without the disease."

"And?"

"The area of South Boston where your brother lives had about a tenfold higher rate of aplastic anemia. I think it would be worthwhile to keep digging into environmental and work issues, especially among the men in your brother's age group."

"How many cases did you find?" asked Dan.

"Harrington has treated about twenty-eight people over the past two years. One of the cases that we didn't know about was diagnosed a few months ago. It'd be interesting to see if your brother has heard of anyone else," said Anna.

"What's the name of the new person you learned about?"

"I don't know," Anna answered. "The records were coded to protect confidentiality.

"Dan, where do you think we should go from here?"

"I have no idea. What do you think?"

"Well, I feel a little funny. Here I am barging into your life with some phantom possibility of helping your brother, while at the same time getting a decent project for my degree."

"Anna, go ahead," Dan said, pleased to be able to spend more time with her, even though she seemed more interested in the project than in him. He'd bide his time, he thought. Eventually he could win her over.

"What I'd like to do is present this review to my adviser to see what he says."

"It sounds like an interesting project."

"Thanks," she said, rising from her chair. As she put on her coat, she turned to Murphy. "Can we keep in touch?" she asked, surprised at how easily the words came out.

"I'd love to," Dan answered.

"Great," Anna answered, walking to the door. "It'll be a challenge to find out if something caused your brother's illness."

"Yes it will," Murphy answered hopefully just as she left the office.

Chapter 15

As he turned the corner toward the Albertina Restaurant, his heart pounded ferociously as though it were trying to bound out of his chest. He walked slowly and carefully as though walking on an unsafe surface. He stopped, then became startled by a loud noise. He looked around in all directions, but nothing seemed to have happened. His eyes ached and his leg screamed in pain. Street life swirled around in chaotic patterns. Black hackney cabs drove sideways, and people seemed to fly by.

Reaching into his jacket for the pint of scotch that he kept readily available, he stared blankly ahead in silence, unable to take his eyes off the bright red sign that advertised the Albertina. As his gaze drifted to the windows of the restaurant and the diners within, he heard screams and sirens. Chairs tumbled in the background as police barked orders to help the injured. Curious onlookers peeked into the restaurant as he heard the shrill, fearful cries of his dying wife. Then, like a videotape on fast-forward, Parker Barrows witnessed a litany of events that followed the explosion: his wife's funeral, the media accounts of the attack, and the relentless interviews.

Shortly, he awakened from the nightmare, just another one of many in a long string of nightmares he had been experiencing since the explosion. With his hands moist and his heart racing from the nightmare, Parker Barrows looked with disgust and anger at the irregularly shaped stump—what remained of his thigh. The scar, a deep maroon for the most part, reminded him of the endless hours of rehabilitation in which he learned to adapt to his injury. *Adapt.* That was the term his health-care providers used when trying to motivate him out of the waves of depression he encountered in adjusting to his new life. To Barrows, however, losing a leg required more than adaptation. It demanded an abrupt alteration of every aspect of his life, from hobbling out of the shower to enduring the frustration of not being able to play tennis.

It was a slide, one that led him to a rehabilitation hospital in Boston, where months and months of physical therapy, exercise, and training helped ease the burden of simple acts, preventing them from becoming complicated. Providers skilled in psychiatry, nutrition, and medicine pooled their talents to help Parker adapt. To his good fortune, price was no object as only the best-quality medical care could satisfy the British citizen. The beneficiary of a generous package from his former employer, the British secret service, Parker Barrows thought little about the costs and whether his care would be managed like that of an anonymous client of a health maintenance organization.

Throughout his recovery, Barrows experienced excruciating pain in the foot he no longer had. The sharp relentless pain bolted up his leg unexpectedly like a lightning flash. After all sorts of tests, he was advised that he was suffering from phantom pain, an odd way to describe unprovoked and unbearably painful sensations that can occur after amputation of a limb. Hardly phantom to him, the arresting pain drove him into a tailspin of narcotic abuse, accompanied by flagrant indiscretion with alcohol. Although for many years a fan of the world's best scotch, Barrows saw his affection grow into an addiction in a relatively short period of time.

Free from the worry of supporting himself thanks to a combination of inherited wealth, fortunate investments, and his disability pension, he had the luxury of not working. Without the drive to achieve professionally, he spent his time searching for the person responsible for the loss of his right leg. It was a frustrating, arduous process that took him through three countries and eventually led him to South Boston.

Barrows reached over to strap on the artificial leg that he hated wearing. He also hated how his life had changed so dramatically since the accident, but he knew there was little he could do to reverse the tragedy. About all he could do was to avenge his misfortune.

He walked into the spacious bathroom of his condominium on Commonwealth Avenue, where he combed his hair, splashed on some aftershave, and brushed his teeth. The image in the mirror, however, displeased him considerably. He saw a man in his fifties who was losing his physical agility, gaining weight, and growing gray hair. His appearance mirrored the emotional slide that he was taking into middle age, a descent hastened by the consequences of his amputated leg and his dependence on alcohol.

He could sense his heartbeat more quickly. Just the thought of encountering the man responsible for his injury caused Barrows to feel agitated. Sweaty palms and an inability to relax were common reactions whenever he contemplated contact with the man he had spent years tracking down. That prosecutors had yet to pin the cause of the explosion onto anyone failed to sway Barrows's conviction that he, himself, had tracked down the criminal in Boston, more than three thousand miles away from London, where the event occurred.

Although it made no sense to his ultimate plan to exact retribution from Wilson, Barrows was overcome with a compulsive desire to see the man he held responsible for his misery. Unwilling and uninterested in forcing a confrontation, he only hoped to catch a glimpse of his enemy.

As he drove off in his Land Rover, Barrows glanced at his watch. His hands shook, so he gripped the steering wheel more tightly. His heart pounded as though it were about to leap out of his chest. He tried to distract himself by tuning into his favorite piece by Wagner, "The Ride of the Valkyries," hoping to find the courage to continue.

—

Dan Murphy's mother and her friend Theresa O'Malley checked their coats, then entered the auditorium to find seats in the front. Despite her hearing difficulty, Mrs. Murphy refused to see a physician to be evaluated. Clear recollections of her father fidgeting with his hearing aid made it impossible for anyone to convince her of the value of a hearing test. Any discussion of a possible hearing aid was simply out of the question.

Saint Brigid's welcomed guests to bingo, followed by a Christmas reception sponsored by the Ladies Auxiliary. The evening's event had been designed to raise money and goods for relatives in Northern Ireland, as well as spread holiday cheer.

South Boston, well-known for its sympathies toward Ireland, was suspected by the British government of providing a safe haven for IRA members on the run and for fostering IRA terrorist activities through fundraising. In the mid-1980s, for example, a boat filled with weapons departed New England and was eventually intercepted off the Irish coast. A pamphlet was left on each seat with the first lines reading, "Will Brexit kill the peace established with the Good Friday Agreement?" referring to the political, military, and social strife in the six northern countries of Ireland under British rule.

While waiting for the evening's event to begin, Theresa and Mrs. Murphy paged through the material. Mrs. Murphy leaned over to Theresa. "Can you believe this, Theresa? Listen," she said in surprise at what she was reading. "'The majority in the six counties was artificially created.'" She placed emphasis on the following: "The British government effectively ensured that the Protestants would rule in Northern Ireland after the civil war in the 1920s.'"

"Oh yes," Theresa replied.

"I didn't know that. Serves me right for leaving high school early," she said self-deprecatingly.

Most South Boston Irish people were well aware of the discrimination faced by Catholics in Northern Ireland. Although British authorities viewed the American perspective as idealized and unrealistic, the Boston Irish had great political influence at both the state and federal level.

"'Great Britain sent in its army in 1969,'" Mrs. Murphy said, continuing to read to her bingo partner. "'The British army was initially welcomed by the Catholics when the Troubles began in 1969, but soon they were considered more supportive of the Protestants, or Unionists as they like to be called.'"

"I thought people knew that," Theresa responded.

"Maybe in Ireland, sweetie, but not here." Mrs. Murphy read aloud, "'Northern Ireland costs the British taxpayers upward of four billion dollars per year in support.'"

"That's a lot of money," Theresa added.

"'Catholics are two and a half times more likely to be unemployed than Protestants,'" Mrs. Murphy continued, reading from another pamphlet. "'Although discrimination is officially illegal,'" she continued, "'it has been widely practiced in subtle ways. In accepting an application for a job, one only needs to ask where a person lives or went to school to know his or her religion.'"

"That's well-known in Ireland."

"I never liked those limeys," Mrs. Murphy responded, using the pejorative term first used to describe British sailors who recognized how to prevent scurvy on long sea journeys by eating certain types of fruit high in vitamin C such as limes.

"Only 5 percent of the police force is Catholic," Theresa replied. "There's no way that Catholics consider the police fair."

People continued to fill the auditorium, until clapping began. A tall, middle-aged man wearing a dark blue suit and blue tie entered and approached the podium.

"Who's that?" Maryann heard a voice behind her.

"That's our state senator."

"Good evening, ladies and gentlemen," the man began. "I'm so glad you can be here. It's the Christmas spirit to be so gracious to our friends and family, especially to those not as fortunate as we are."

The crowd responded by applauding.

The politician, accustomed to his speeches being punctuated with applause, allowed the crowd to show their approval.

"You people are special citizens. Your care and attention to the plight of our Irish brothers and sisters, both here and back in Ireland, is truly remarkable. Only through your efforts have the lives of many of our compatriots been improved. And that's not easy in today's political climate, where people call undocumented immigrants 'illegal aliens.'"

The audience acknowledged what he'd said by clapping. The senator continued, "Our countrymen are hardly lazy and interested in going on welfare. They work—and very hard at that. Our 'new Irish,' as they've been described, are well educated. Some have law degrees and college educations in business and engineering. And they'll do what they need to do to get a chance at the American dream." More applause.

"Just the other day, I spoke with an older woman who came here from County Cork right after World War II. She's lived in South Boston since then and has seen lots of changes—some good, some bad. But none, she said, was as bad as this nasty attitude that's developed against people described as illegal, these hardworking people who slave sixty to seventy hours a week at the jobs no one else wants. And we all know how well the Irish do when given a chance. The best professions in the United States today, including medicine, law, science, business, and the arts, all are well represented by the talents of Irish Americans. So, I appeal again to the generosity of your hearts, especially at this special time of year. Give what you can to help your neighbors here in Boston and our fellow Irish in Northern Ireland. Thank you for coming. It's a pleasure to see you all."

The crowd clapped in agreement. The state senator acknowledged their support by waving an Irish flag.

The senator continued, saying, "Your director has asked me to make a few comments about Brexit and how it may affect Northern Ireland and the Good Friday Agreement, which as you undoubtedly know has had a favorable effect in terms of reducing violence and other troubles in Northern Ireland. As you know, we have all been pleased with the favorable effects of the Good Friday Agreement on peace in Northern Ireland. Unfortunately, according to an article in the *New York Times* by Mark Landler, 'A leader of the Irish nationalist Sinn Fein party, Ms. O'Neill vacated her office as deputy first minister of Northern Ireland's government after the first minister, Paul Givan, a member of the main Unionist Party—that is, the main party supporting Northern Ireland's current status as part of the United Kingdom—abruptly resigned. Under the power-sharing agreement that governs the territory, she automatically lost her post as well.' There appears to be a momentous political shift in Northern Ireland. Assuming that current poll numbers hold, Sinn Fein, with its historical ties to the Irish Republican Army and fervent commitment to Irish unification, will become the largest party in the Northern Ireland Assembly after the coming elections."

The senator went on to read more from the *New York Times* article: "'The Democratic Unionist Party, which represents the Protestants, is desperate to rally its voters before the election.' Its most emotional issue of all is the North's trade status after Brexit. The Unionists, who represent the Protestant interests, complain that the protocol, which requires border checks on goods passing between Northern Ireland and mainland Britain, has driven a wedge between the North and the rest of the United Kingdom. It's as though there is a border through the Irish Sea that separates Ireland from the UK.

"Mr. Landler in his article notes that by pulling their leader out of the Stormont parliament, the Democratic Unionists are trying to put pressure on the British government, which is in the process of renegotiating the final protocol with the European Union. Unless the trade rules are radically overhauled, Unionists say, they will not return to the government and Northern Ireland's on-again, off-again experiment, and the power-sharing principles will collapse."

The senator continued, saying, "Another Unionist minister, Edwin Poots, declared that the government would stop inspecting agricultural goods coming in from Britain, which is a violation of the

Brexit protocol. A judge ruled that the checks must continue until the issue is decided in court. This dispute has become a potentially deadly contest for the future of Northern Ireland, one that could destabilize not just the island but also Britain's relations with the European Union and the United States.

"In my view, this is a critical juncture in the Brexit negotiations," the senator emphasized. "A hundred years after its creation, Northern Ireland has fundamentally changed. If Sinn Fein wins the largest number of seats, the most likely scenario would be a prolonged negotiation as the two parties tried to figure out how to live with each other. But some experts said they doubted the Democratic Unionists could ever take part in a government with a Sinn Fein representative as first minister.

"The Northern Ireland Protocol for Brexit is an arrangement that grew out of a deal between London and Brussels to avoid resurrecting a hard border between Ireland, an EU member state, and Northern Ireland, which left the European Union as part of the United Kingdom. The Brexit terms require checks on goods flowing across the Irish Sea from mainland Britain to the North.

"This is clearly a complicated political matter. We will need to continue to keep abreast of developments. I hope these brief remarks have provided some background to a topic that we will undoubtedly hear more about. Any questions?" the senator said after completing his remarks.

"What do you think the British prime minister will do?" a young woman asked, using a microphone placed among the audience.

"The least difficult option for the UK is to sacrifice Northern Ireland," the senator responded. People clapped in agreement, recognizing that the ultimate solution may be a united Ireland.

An older woman with a full head of white hair raised her hand. The assistant acknowledged her request to speak. In switching topics to more practical concerns affecting her, the woman asked, "Senator, what can you do about getting workers' compensation for our boys? My neighbor hurt his back, and the poor fellow has no income. And he has a wife and a cute little two-year-old boy." Implied was that the family was undocumented immigrants.

"That's a good question," the politician answered, showing his ability to gain rapport with his constituents, "but the answer is, not much. You know that some employers won't process claims on their undocumented workers. And some of the recent immigrants to our country do not want to risk being noticed. After all, most only have six-month tourist visas, and when that runs out, they're at risk of being deported. I think the answer to your question is that we all have to help out." His political support for the undocumented workers from Ireland was well-known to the press and to his colleagues.

"Good luck at bingo," he hollered into the microphone as he left the podium. The audience left the auditorium to enter the large room where the game was played.

"What do you think of that Brexit plan, Theresa?"

"Oh, I don't know. I don't think anything will work."

"That's not too encouraging."

"It's realistic. The Brits will never let go of Northern Ireland."

"Why not?"

"Pride. Superiority. They think they're better than the Irish."

"But they're not. They're just limeys, and they talk funny. They think they're so sophisticated with that English accent, but it makes the men sound swishy," said Mrs. Murphy, who was known for her blunt candor. She knew she could be outrageous and get away with it. Smiling in return, Theresa hoped for more colorful commentary.

"They should just leave Ireland, the Brits. I don't know why they're there anyway. What's wrong with England?"

"You should go to the peace talks," Theresa said with a wan grin.

"They'd throw me out, I'm sure."

"But you would add flavor and spontaneity."

Mrs. Murphy's natural gifts of warmth, humor, and sensitivity helped Theresa momentarily forget the trauma of losing her husband, Liam, to aplastic anemia.

"Theresa, how are you doing?" Mrs. Murphy asked, the tone of her voice mirroring the concern only a mother could show.

"I don't know," Theresa answered flatly, barely holding back tears. "I just don't know why he died." She began to sob. Her husband had been buried only a week ago; her senses remained numb.

"Did Danny help?" Mrs. Murphy asked, referring to her physician son, who had reviewed Liam's medical records.

"He was nice and helpful, but he said he wasn't sure why Liam got sick."

"Did the doctors tell you?"

"No."

—

As bingo continued inside the church auditorium, Parker Barrows drove by, looking for a parking spot. His legs trembled, and his hands perspired so heavily that he nearly lost his grip on the steering wheel. Suddenly, he doubted whether he could confront his prey and wondered whether the man would even be at the church fundraiser. Finding it difficult to locate a spot to park, Barrows continued driving around, hoping to get relief from his vise like headache and the wrenching pain in his abdomen. His lips began to feel numb, and his chest felt as though a brick were lying on it. Unable to stand the discomfort any longer, he pulled to the side of the road, stopped the car, and reached into the back seat for a pint of scotch. He gulped the remains of the bottle. Slowly and deeply, he breathed, then leaned back against the seat and closed his eyes.

Immersed in a haze from the quick jot of alcohol, Barrows visualized a red double-decker bus passing through London's Piccadilly Circus. He felt as though he were walking toward Covent Garden and finding his way through the backstreets of Central London. Suddenly, the smell of gunpowder awakened him. On opening his eyes, he looked about in fear, but saw only an empty, quiet residential street in South Boston.

Barrows leaned back against the seat again as the scotch glided him back into mental oblivion. Shortly, his mind took him off to London again, where he walked toward an Italian restaurant. It seemed natural to have both his legs. In a flash, he heard sirens and a cacophony of screams filled with fear. His leg hurt, and the phantom pain shot up the remains of his leg, rudely awakening him from the anxious reverie. Momentarily disoriented and unaware of how he had gotten to where he was parked, Barrows reached for a cigarette, but his hands shook so much that he had to light four matches just to get it lit. As he inhaled the last of his second pack of the day, he felt defeated. *If this psychiatrist doesn't help me, I will go crazy,* he thought.

Chapter 16

Most graduate students avoided a meeting with Dr. David Becker, dermatologist and acting director of the Occupational Health Department at the Harvard School of Public Health. Located across town from the Boston Medical Center, where Dr. Harrington practiced, the School of Public Health attracted a wide sampling of students, diverse in both professional background and geographical origin. It was not uncommon for students to come from far-flung areas of the world, including sub-Saharan Africa, Australia, and the Middle East.

Becker relished his role in academic medicine. With a knack for achieving the power and influence needed to thrive in the academic world, he worked the angles to make his efforts profitable in terms of money. A master of politics, he knew the right committees to be on, the best journals in which to publish his research, and the ideal conferences at which to present his papers. His students quickly realized how much of their work he extracted for use as his own and how infrequently he acknowledged their efforts. In many ways, he acted as though the stature he had achieved because of his accomplishments justified his arrogance. Although his success was well acknowledged, he had sacrificed much on his route to achieve it, especially friendships. The fact was, Becker had no real friends, except perhaps his wife, primarily because he had no time for friends. His work was his life—he spent at least eighty to ninety hours a week at his career, despite having enough wealth to retire in affluence. Bright and energetic because of having achieved both academic excellence and great wealth, Becker paid a serious price, including the estrangement of his son, with whom he hadn't spoken in more than three years. He could never overcome his frustration with his son, who not only rebuffed his urgings to become a physician but also had become a lawyer and moved to Chicago.

Anna entered the main building on campus and proceeded to the elevator, which took her to the seventh floor. Down the hall on the right was the suite of Dr. David Becker. Anna entered, then with reserve approached a receptionist.

"I'm here to see Dr. Becker," she said to the young redhead filling in for a secretary who had unexpectedly resigned.

"Oh. Let me get him," she said, then rose from her chair to guide Anna to the master suite.

"He's not free yet," said a short, plump, dark-haired woman in her midthirties who rose from her desk to intercept the secretary and Anna en route to Becker's office.

"Sorry," said the redhead, who sheepishly turned to Anna. "Would you like to have a seat? Can I get you some coffee?" she continued, anxious to please.

"No, but thank you," said Anna, who walked to a chair in the waiting area. Looking at her watch, she noticed that she was five minutes late. While waiting, she reviewed the notes of her presentation and tried to ignore the distractions of office workers pecking away at their computers. In the background, she could overhear Becker's loud voice as he spoke on the phone.

—

Becker sat at his large mahogany desk, which was cluttered with stacks of papers, books, and reports. With his feet propped on the desk, he talked to the director of one of his psoriasis clinics.

"You should get the safety data sheets," Becker said, in reference to determining the cause of a skin disease in a painter. "You can then decide whether to do patch testing." Here he was referring to the application of minute amounts of material onto the skin to detect allergic reactions.

"My pleasure," Becker said. "Refer him to us if you want a thorough workup." After a pause to hear an expression of thanks from his subordinate, he said, "Goodbye," then replaced the receiver.

Similar telephone conversations went on throughout the next hour as Anna waited to see Becker. She understood how matters more important than a graduate student might occupy a director's attention, but nonetheless she was struck by his profound lack of courtesy. *Will he keep me here the rest of the day?* she thought.

"Miz Carlson," Becker called, adding a snide affectation to the formality.

Anna rose from her chair. Becker directed her into his office without further comment.

"Please." He pointed to a chair next to a large conference table that could easily accommodate a party of ten. "Shoot," he said impatiently, showing no interest in the social lubrication of small talk.

"I think I have a project," Anna began, handing Becker an outline of her proposal.

"Let's hear it," Becker replied, looking at his wristwatch.

"I'd like to study possible environmental causes of aplastic anemia."

"What makes you interested in that topic?"

"Well, I've had a strong interest in health and the environment since I worked at the *Minneapolis Tribune*," Anna answered, trying not to appear frustrated with Becker, whose reputation motivated her to work with him. She felt privileged to be the only student in the program who lacked a doctorate or a medical degree.

Becker's style as a hard-driving professor with a "take no prisoners" attitude toward students was widely known. Tenure and access to senior leadership, however, preserved his stature and allowed him to perpetuate his ways.

Anna continued, saying, "Some studies suggest that pesticides, benzene, and ionizing radiation may be involved—as you know." She was pandering to him. "But aplastic anemia is a relatively rare disease and difficult to study."

"Oh, come now, it's not a difficult disease to study, Miz Carlson. It's just a challenge to identify the risk factors."

"Yes," she answered, feeling like an unwilling sycophant.

"What do you plan to do?"

"I'd like to write a case series of eight patients with aplastic anemia."

"What makes you think you can handle the clinical information?"

"Dr. Harrington, from Boston Medical Center, said he would help." Anna relished dropping Harrington's name because she knew Becker would pay attention. The hematologist was well-known in Boston because of his skills in bone marrow transplantation. He had learned his techniques under the direction of Dr. Thomas from Seattle, who won the Nobel Prize in 1990 for his pioneering efforts in terms of the procedure.

"Clifford Harrington?" Becker asked, having taken the bait. "From Boston Medical Center?"

"Yes," Anna answered.

"Well, that's good. How did you do that?"

"A friend of mine's brother just underwent a bone marrow transplant."

"By Harrington?" Becker asked.

"Yes."

"I see. Well, what do you have?"

"I made a crude attempt at determining whether there might be an environmental cause of some of the aplastic anemia cases." Anna stopped, expecting Becker to interrupt, but to her surprise, he seemed to be listening. "Dr. Harrington has compiled a lot of information about his patients who have undergone bone marrow transplants. It's coded to preserve confidentiality."

"How did that help?"

"I compared the aplastic anemia cases to other patients."

"What other patients? You mean people with other types of blood diseases? That would skew your results."

"No. Harrington developed a control group of orthopedic patients for another study."

"Why would they be helpful?" Becker asked in a pedagogical tone.

"Well," Anna confidently replied, "they would most likely be similar in age to the aplastic anemia cases."

"OK. That's appropriate, but what were you looking for?"

"To see if there was some link between the environment and people with aplastic anemia."

"What did you find?" Becker quizzed.

"A certain area of South Boston was more likely to have patients with aplastic anemia."

"Clever, Carlson, but how did you determine the *rates* of the disease? This is a typical problem with these cluster studies. You can make the rates as high as you want just by drawing a tight boundary around the cases," Becker said, referring to the Texas sharpshooter phenomenon. The visiting professor at the Harvard seminar, where Dan met Anna, had offered the same cautions.

"Do you have good data on the prevalence of aplastic anemia? Do you even know what the expected number of cases might be?" Becker, showing his academic teeth, displayed the intimidating manner that both inspired and irritated his students.

"You're right," Anna answered respectfully. "The rates for aplastic anemia vary and good data are difficult to obtain, but Dr. Harrington thinks a small survey would still be interesting."

"Interesting, but of any value?" countered Becker.

Anna recognized the biting repartee that Becker seemed to relish. Ignoring his off-putting style, she replied, "Some case reports suggest environmental causes. I'm willing to take it on, if you'll give me some guidance." The pandering had worked, she thought, as Becker softened in his response.

"What are you planning to use for the occupational and environmental history?" he asked.

"I'm not sure yet. I need to do more reading to make sure I don't overlook something."

"You should use the one I developed," Becker said, rising from the table. He opened a door to call his assistant. "Would you get the history form we use?" he said, then walked back to the conference table at which Anna remained seated.

"When are you going to do this?" he asked her.

"I'd like to get started right away. I have some time before I go home for Christmas. I can work on it now and be prepared at the beginning of the year."

"Pursue the environmental causes first," Becker interjected. "That's your strength. And it will add value to the study."

Anna took the unexpected encouragement with aplomb. Following a knock on the door, an assistant entered and handed Becker a twelve-page form, which he passed onto Anna. "Keep me informed. I don't like surprises," he said.

Anna left Becker's office, smiled at the young secretary who had helped her earlier, then readied her coat, gloves, and hat for the gusts of winter wind brewing outside.

Chapter 17

Following her session with Dr. Becker, Anna was motivated to start her project of reviewing possible environmental causes for the cluster of aplastic anemia cases in South Boston. She recalled that as a result of federal legislation that allowed public access to air and water pollution data, she could get valuable information. *I'll probably face a morass of bureaucratic roadblocks,* she thought. Despite the challenges, she thought it was worth the effort to navigate through information assembled by government agencies to get a firsthand glimpse of environmental regulations in action.

At the top of her list of environmental concerns was the domestic water supply, especially since it was first raised as an issue by Liam's wife, whose husband had just died of aplastic anemia. Media attention about lead and chemical contamination of the water supply had also roused Anna's interest. The Environmental Protection Agency recently established a lower limit for lead and some chemicals in the drinking water since animal studies suggested a number of chemicals in drinking water might cause cancer.

In South Boston, where the cases of aplastic anemia occurred, Anna learned that people received their drinking water from a municipal source overseen by the Massachusetts Water Resource

Authority (MWRA). It seemed a logical place for Anna to initiate her fact-finding mission.

"I'd like to speak to someone about testing my water," Anna said to the young woman who answered the phone at the MWRA.

"Call your water company."

"But doesn't your office oversee water quality?"

"Wait a minute," the receptionist said in exasperation. Anna heard a click, followed by another ringing sound.

"Bacteriology lab," a gruff male voice said.

"I'm trying to find out how to have my drinking water tested."

"For bacteria?" he asked.

"Yes, but I'm also interested in overall water quality, including chemicals and other contaminants."

"We don't do that here."

"You mean the MWRA doesn't check for chemical content of the water?"

"Some other office does that. I thought you were asking about this lab."

"How often do you test for bacteria?" Anna asked, hoping to learn in piecemeal fashion.

"Every day," he answered. "It's to prevent infections through the water supply. Remember Rwanda, when refugees went into neighboring countries?" he asked, anxious to give Anna a minilecture, referring to the bacteria-borne illnesses that killed thousands of people in the poor African country.

"Yes," Anna answered.

"Well, a lot of them died from typhoid fever because of bacteria in the drinking water."

"But can you help me find the department responsible for overall water quality—chemicals, bacteria, whatever?"

"Just a minute," he said. "Call extension 4654."

"Thank you. Would you connect me, please?"

"Sure."

Anna then heard the connection sever. After dialing again, she asked for extension 4654, but it was busy and she was advised to call later. Three more attempts led to three more busy signals, so she went to the website and searched for "water analysis."

Anna then contacted four different laboratories, each of which provided information about what is tested in drinking water. She quickly learned that all water quality tests are not the same.

"Do you want a lead test?" one clerk asked her.

"Actually, I'd like to know if there's a standard test to see if a water supply conforms with government standards. For example, is there a test to see if all the EPA guidelines are met?" she asked, referring to the Environmental Protection Agency.

"We do have a sample for eighteen different items, for example, lead, copper, fluoride, and bacteria."

"How much is that?" Anna inquired.

"Let me see. Seventy-five dollars, which includes the sample bottle."

"How long does it take to get the results once I give you the sample?"

"Two to three working days," he answered, "depending on how busy we are."

"I hope you'll excuse me for the next question," Anna said, "but isn't the water company supposed to give that information on request?"

"Yes, I believe so."

"How often do they test?"

"I'm not sure, but it's not as often as you'd think. Bacteria levels are checked regularly, but the chemicals are another matter—that may only be annually," he said.

"Annually?" Anna asked, incredulous. "You mean a major municipal water department only checks concentrations of various chemicals annually?"

"Yes, but if you decide to use us," he said, hoping to attract the business, "we can give you recommendations on how to fix any problems you find. For example, there are ways you can control lead levels with special filters."

Private enterprise in action, Anna thought. *What a contrast to the government agency.* "Thank you. I appreciate your help."

"My pleasure," he replied. "Let us know if we can help further."

Anna decided to call the municipal water department again. This time, she reached a government employee.

"Bacteria, lead, and copper levels go to our headquarters," answered a young man at the water department.

Anna persisted in her quest for information. Eventually, she reached an office that sent her water sampling results from the drinking water reservoir. About forty different items, ranging from metals such as arsenic and nickel to water quality measures such as alkalinity, dissolved oxygen concentration, and residue, were noted. Of the four columns on the report, one was completely blank, described as "out of service." The other three columns noted concentrations of lead, sodium, and chlorinated hydrocarbons. The report did not indicate whether the levels were within EPA guidelines.

Anna then reached for the questionnaire that Dr. David Becker had given her to use for interviewing the people with aplastic anemia. She coded the questionnaire to facilitate a comparison with her control group—orthopedic surgery patients who were similar in age, sex, and race—and the people with aplastic anemia.

Anna left the School of Public Health with no particular destination in mind. As she walked down the stairs and into the courtyard, she thought of Dan Murphy. *It's only three o'clock. He's probably at work.*

She fumbled through her purse for her cell phone, then dialed the South Boston Health Center. She was greeted by a pleasant voice, still fresh and unruffled by the rigors of dealing with a demanding public.

"Occupational Health Center."

"May I speak with Dr. Murphy, please?"

"Just a moment. May I ask who's calling?"

"Anna Carlson."

"Hold on, please."

"Hi, Dr. Murphy, this is Anna. I thought I'd test your capacity for spontaneity and ask you to meet me later."

"Anna," Dan Murphy said in a tone that telegraphed his pleasure at being interrupted by her. "Sure. Is anything wrong?"

"No. Not at all. But it'd be nice to talk. Can I come to your office?"

"It'd be a pleasure."

"So, you don't mind if I intrude?" Anna bantered.

"How's six o'clock?"

"Perfect," she answered.

"Drive safely," Dan advised. "Traffic is crazy this time of the day."

On leaving the campus, Anna, with three hours to spend before meeting Dan, decided to drive through South Boston. From her background reading for the project, she had learned that many environmental regulations require public reports on water and air pollution and chemical releases from factories. How to get that information, however, was another story. If her experience in finding water quality data augured the outcome of future efforts, then optimism was not warranted. Anna found it perplexing that hazards like pesticides, wood preservatives, herbicides, and even gasoline may be in drinking water and that safe levels of these materials had actually been proposed. *How do you determine what's safe?* she wondered.

Anna, immersed in thought about her efforts to date, turned off the Southeast Expressway to reach South Boston. Winding her way through narrow streets crowded with holiday shoppers, her attention was drawn to the diversity of the buildings, which ranged from triple-decker houses to restaurants and small factories. The proximity of warehouses and business facilities to residential areas seemed unsafe to her. One block might include a huge warehouse across the street from a string of row houses. Her aimless drive eventually brought her to the Boston Harbor and L Street beach. En route, she passed churches, playgrounds, baseball fields, and hockey rinks. Along the beachfront, people walked, jogged, and strolled. As she reached Castle Island, large oil and gas tanks of a shipping terminal loomed menacingly in the background.

Warehouses, a bus depot, and a hazardous waste company came

into view as she drove by a huge electric power plant. Trucking firms, auto body repair shops, and dry-cleaning storefronts occupied the same neighborhood with triple-decker houses. Bars, sandwich shops, and variety stores added to the eclectic mix.

As in most areas of Boston, finding a parking spot in South Boston was a daunting task. Eventually, Anna noticed an older woman pulling out of a spot by a parking meter. *It'll be nice to walk around the shopping area,* Anna thought. She considered it important to get a feel for the place she was studying. In writing her exposé about hazardous waste sites in the Minneapolis–St. Paul area, she had learned the importance of speaking with the people affected. Although she had no idea whether her efforts would uncover an environmental cause for aplastic anemia, she wanted to prepare for the inevitable scrutiny of her adviser, David Becker. She would know the local environmental situation and would pursue plausible explanations for the cluster of blood diseases in South Boston.

Barely two blocks from her parked car, Anna smelled the aroma of fresh bread and entered a pastry shop, carrying a folder full of notes and articles about her project. Within minutes, she was sipping a large mug of coffee, nibbling a cranberry muffin, and watching a collage of people pass by the storefront window at which she sat. *The pleasure of unstructured time,* she mused, then her thoughts were drawn to Dan Murphy. She marveled at his ease amid the inevitable stress of a brother facing death at a young age. With schoolgirl enthusiasm, she craved to know more about him and his robust spirit, but then she quickly admonished herself for idealizing a man she barely knew. Guilt about Roger slowly crept over her.

Soon, Anna would visit Minneapolis and see Roger, who was now struggling to develop his bookstore. Thoughts about him and her future raced through her head. She wondered whether she should return to Minneapolis after earning her master's degree. *Should I take that position the* Minneapolis Tribune *offered and marry Roger? Or should I risk it all by getting more involved with Dan?*

Hoping to control the diversion of her attraction to Dan, she thought of her project. *Maybe Dan can help me with the medical issues?* she thought.

After paging through her notes, Anna concluded that a case series, that is, a description of symptoms, abnormalities, and other features of the people with aplastic anemia, would be the best approach for her project. This information may lead to clues for more sophisticated analyses.

A case series would be much more manageable, Anna thought. *At least it's something I can finish by the end of the academic year, and it's a great topic for the seminar Environmental Data: What to Get and How to Get It. Oh, how I wished I knew!* Avoiding the natural progression of the title, that is, "What Do the Results Actually Mean?" she decided to leave the question to another student or for a different time. Risk assessment, an art of science that attempts to establish levels of safety for hazards, bewildered her. The assumptions and safety factors built into the calculations made the process seem both arcane and uncertain.

Having gained a sense of direction for her project and a boost of confidence for approaching Dan, she paid her check and made her way through the streets of South Boston, which were now dark at four o'clock on the first day of winter.

Anna pulled into the parking lot, entered a two-story brick building, then followed the signs to Occupational Health. On reaching the reception area, she found no one to greet her, so she looked around, hoping to spot someone who might direct her to Dan Murphy.

Within minutes, Anna noticed Dan.

"Ms. Carlson, please," he called to her in a tone, suggesting that she was his next patient.

Anna smiled, then walked toward the desk. "Are you sure I'm not intruding? You look busy."

"Stop being so deferential. Come on, I'll show you around." Dan guided Anna to a small lab, the x-ray area, and some examining rooms. Along the way, he showed her some of the equipment.

"What do you use that for?" Anna asked, pointing to a circular rubber tube attached to a microprocessor.

"That's a spirometer. It measures lung capacity," he answered, "and helps to determine if a person has asthma or some other lung problem."

"Can I try?"

"Adventurous, I see," Dan said. He turned on the unit. "Take a deep breath when I tell you, then blow out as hard as you can for six seconds."

"What's this, an endurance challenge?"

"You'll do fine after all your aerobics classes!"

Anna smiled then reached for the tubing through which she would exhale.

"Blow. ... Blow. ... Blow," Dan coached as she exhaled through the rubber tubing. "Great. Now one more time."

"Are you kidding?" Anna asked. "What's wrong with this test?"

"Nothing. You need to do it three times."

"Do all your patients come back?"

Dan smiled. "Come on. You can do it."

"Don't send the results to my aerobics teacher," Anna said. "She'll want me to lose five more pounds."

"You don't need to lose an ounce," Dan quipped.

"Flattery goes far. Don't stop."

"Enough with the diversionary tactics. Try it again."

Anna finished her second attempt without difficulty, then did her third and looked to Dan for the results.

"Excellent," he said. "The aerobics are working."

"But I still need to take off a few pounds."

"Please," Dan replied, "worry about other things, like your project and joining me for a concert sometime."

Anna smiled. "What kind of patients do you treat here?"

"Almost anything related to work—injuries, exams for people who work with lead or asbestos, and exams trying to determine if a certain disease is caused by the job."

"Sounds interesting. Do you go to court a lot?"

"I try to avoid it, but some of it's inevitable."

"I imagine you treat a relatively young group of patients," she said.

"Yes, and many of the conditions are preventable, so it's satisfying from that perspective."

"Where do your patients come from?"

"Different places—employers, other physicians, insurance companies."

"Aren't you pressured to do what the companies want?"

"Sometimes," Dan answered. "But you need to be consistent and fair. Otherwise, you'd go crazy."

Anna smiled. "Do you mind if we discuss my project? I'd like to get your impressions."

"You know I'm no academic scholar," Dan said.

"Here it is," Anna said enthusiastically. "I'll review the environmental information that's available to the public. Then, I'll get results of the water testing at Pat's house. We need to compare those results with EPA guidelines." She recognized Dan staring at her legs.

"Dan, would you look over the charts from Dr. Harrington's eight patients?" she asked, referring to the people in South Boston who had contracted aplastic anemia in the past two years and were treated at Boston Medical Center. Harrington did not know, however, if other people from South Boston with aplastic anemia may have been treated at other Boston hospitals.

"What would you like me to do?" Dan asked. "You know I'm no star at getting grants or publishing papers. I've never conducted a research project."

"We'll fumble together."

"That I'll enjoy. But what should I do for your project?"

"Why don't you look over the medical and occupational histories in the records?"

"That information is hard to find, though," Murphy answered, referring to the difficulty in making sense of unstructured comments in a hospital medical record about a person's work or environmental history, especially at teaching hospitals, where the major emphasis is on the treatment of the disease, not determining its cause.

"I saw a table that might help us," Anna said. She reached into her sack to withdraw an article from a file. "You might want to evaluate the quality of the information from each record. That way, you'll be consistent and apply the same scrutiny to all the records," she said.

"They teach you well," he said. "I'm sold. How do I get the records?"

"They're at Dr. Harrington's office. He has approval to use the data as long as personally identifiable information is not used."

Dan nodded just as his beeper sounded. Two short beeps alerted him to an outside call, so he reached for his phone.

"Dr. Murphy, just a minute," the voice said methodically.

"Danny. This is Maryann. I'm leaving the hospital, but I need to talk with you," Dan's sister-in-law said in an anxious tone.

"What's up?" Dan asked.

"It's Patrick. He has a really high fever, and I'm worried. Do you think it's a bad sign?"

"I don't know. Did Dr. Harrington see him?"

"Not yet. He's supposed to come over later. Could you go over to see him? I need to pick up Mother," she said, referring to Dan's mother and her mother-in-law, who was scheduled to play bingo that night at Saint Brigid's Parish.

Dan paused and looked at Anna, who was observing the framed degrees and certificates on his office walls.

Maryann continued the conversation, which Anna overheard as Dan listened on his phone with the speaker app. "Dan, would you go over to see Patrick? He's been acting strange today, saying he's tired of being in the hospital and that he's going to leave. I'm not sure whether it's the medication, that isolation room, or something else. But I know you can help."

"I'll go over as soon as I finish up."

They bade farewell, then Dan turned to Anna.

"I'm sorry, but we should probably finish our talk on the study. My brother has a high fever and is acting strange, and my sister-in-law asked if I'd go over to the hospital."

"I'm sorry to hear that," Anna said. "Can I help?"

"I ought to go on my own. But let's meet tomorrow. How about dinner? Doyle's is only a few blocks from here. We can compare notes. I'll review the charts, and you can tell me about your environmental pursuits."

"Sounds great," Anna said, concealing her disappointment that Dan wanted to go alone to the hospital.

"Well," Dan continued, "thanks for the serendipitous visit."

"Did you study that word for your College Boards?" Anna asked in jest.

"It's a wonderful word, isn't it?" He put on his down jacket, wool hat, and gloves to brace himself against the bite of the December wind. "Serendipity actually sounds like a pleasant event that occurs by chance, doesn't it?"

Anna smiled in return. "The next article I write, I should use you as a thesaurus," she quipped, wrapping a red and black wool scarf around her neck.

"Let's go," Dan said, directing Anna out of the office and into the Boston night.

Chapter 18

The last meeting with Tony Mesa had convinced Wilson of the importance of responding to his every whim. Although Mesa could appear self-effacing and easygoing, beneath the surface lay a core of rock-solid strength that ensured his views would prevail. Wilson knew that he would need to limit the number of people involved in his current work with Mesa. They simply could not afford the risk of anyone asking probing questions or leaking any information, which might result if too many people were to participate. As a result of this thinking, he needed guys like Pat Murphy, whom he could trust to do his job and keep his mouth shut. Wilson wondered, though, about the amount of pressure he should exert on Pat in light of his hospitalization. Whatever was affecting Murphy, however, was not Wilson's concern. Finishing the work and getting paid was the priority. Somehow he would have to convince, cajole, and even threaten Murphy to stay involved, regardless of the risks to his health.

Since arriving a few years ago in Boston, Wilson had insinuated himself into the activities of the area of South Boston in which he lived. In many ways, Boston resembled his native Philadelphia, especially the section immediately south of center city that had long been the province of Irish and Italian immigrants. In South Boston, Wilson quickly adapted to the community that for decades had spawned cops, politicians, and clergy. Recently, however, many of its brightest had gone on to be educated at prestigious universities and move to the suburbs. The tight-knit working-class communities of South Boston had seen much of their influence wane as populations became mobile, educated, and motivated to pursue other options in life.

Wilson, soon after finding an apartment on his arrival to South Boston, quickly learned about the local network of Irish immigrants, some of whom had official entry visas and work permits. Others had taken a gamble, hoping that luck would prevail in obtaining a job, a home, and a life free from harassment by the Immigration and Naturalization Service. It was the so-called "illegals," those without entry visas, for whom Wilson's efforts proved most helpful. Without an immigrant's visa, these folks were at the mercy of employers who risked major fines by federal and state authorities for hiring undocumented immigrants. As a result, these assertive people, anxious to gain a foothold in a new life, took work when and where available. Women found jobs as nannies, housekeepers, and shop assistants, while the men tended to work on minor construction projects, including ventures initiated by Jake Wilson.

Wilson, having seen too many of his buddies die or be maimed in military operations, found that the antiseptic smell of the modern hospital provoked riveting memories that had long lain dormant. His surprise visit to Liam Murphy a few days earlier had been an exception to his rule against entering any hospitals, but it was necessary to demonstrate to Murphy how seriously he was about engaging him in the project to pay off the gambling debts. A phone call loomed as the more attractive alternative for reaching Murphy.

"Hey, Murphy, what's up? You gonna come out of there horizontal or on your own two feet?"

"Wilson, an unexpected pleasure," Pat responded wryly.

"Life's full of surprises. How's your transplant going? Any news?"

"I'm not dead yet."

"When ya gettin' outta there?"

"I don't know."

"Can you find out?"

"What's the rush? I'm stuck in here like a fool, not knowing what'll happen next."

"I need your help, and you know it."

"Get someone else, or wait until I leave this place."

"I need you, Murphy. You owe me too much money. You gotta get your act together. We don't have much time."

"I don't understand the rush."

"The money guy wants the project to move. If we wanna get paid, we gotta go."

"I still don't know when I'll get out of here."

"Leave early. Look, Murphy, you gotta help. Get your sweet ass out of there."

"I'll try."

"You need to do more than try. You owe me the fuckin' money, remember? I didn't put a gun to your head and force you to bet on horses, football, basketball, and everything else you blew your money on."

"Buy me time."

"There's no time. Look, a few nights ago, someone jabbed me with a needle. I don't remember anything after that, until I woke up on a football field. It made no sense. My feet were freezing, and I can't feel my hand because they broke it. It took me forever to get home. You're probably next."

Pat was silent a moment. Maybe he was scared, or maybe he was just really tired. "Sounds crazy."

"I walked around trying to find a gas station, a store, or anything that might be open. I must have walked for an hour or so, then it started to get light, which was when I found a Store24, about twenty miles west of Boston."

"What did you do?"

"With no money and no credit cards, nothin', I got a hold of a friend downtown who picked me up, then I went to this health clinic where they told me I had a broken finger."

"Who do you think did it?"

"I don't know, but I don't want to take any chances with our project."

"Why?"

"Just get the hell out of there and you'll learn all you need to know. Look, Murphy, I'll catch you later."

Jake Wilson hung up the receiver and thought about whether he should tell Murphy any details of his plans. It wasn't worth the risk, he decided.

—

As Pat Murphy stared out the window in fear of Wilson's potential for violence and what he might do to him if he couldn't repay the gambling debts, he heard a knock on his door, followed by the entry of his older brother, Dan.

"Hey, dude," Pat called out, trying to overcome his fatigue, and now his fear provoked by the conversation with Wilson.

"How are you feeling, big guy?" Dan asked.

"I feel like shit. I shake. My head hurts."

"Has Dr. Harrington come yet?"

"No. One of his lackey medical students came. He looked me over and poked and probed, but he didn't say much."

"Are you coughing?"

"A little."

"Are you drinking?"

"Yeah, right. I had a six-pack of Sam Adams."

"Water?" Dan asked.

"No. I don't feel like eating or drinking."

"Let me look over your chart. I'll be back in a few minutes." Murphy left the room and approached the nurses' station.

Dan Murphy knew his younger brother didn't look well. He recalled all the reasons a person might develop a fever following surgery. *But most of the reasons are no big deal—at least in people with healthy immune systems,* he thought. He then recalled that Pat had undergone both chemotherapy and radiation treatment and that his immune system was so impaired that he could develop serious illnesses from common infections that would not affect a healthy person. *I can't believe he can die from this.* Dan was afraid.

As Dan Murphy reached the nurses' station that oversaw his brother's care, he created his own differential diagnosis, that is, a list of possible causes for his brother's fever. He reached for his brother's chart and considered the major possibilities: urinary or wound infection, pneumonia, or dehydration. The wild card, however, was that rare infections could occur in a patient who has just undergone a bone marrow transplant. He read the recommendations of the senior medical resident, which included the standard approach to evaluating a fever in a hospitalized patient. No mention was made of whether the fever was the result of the body's rejection of the transplant. He placed the chart back into its slot.

As Murphy was walking toward a kitchenette to get coffee, he heard a woman's voice in the background saying, "Hello, Dr. Harrington." Putting the coffee aside, Dan went out into the hall to greet the hematology chief.

"Dr. Murphy. How are you?" Harrington said, pleased at the surprise encounter. Having practiced at a teaching hospital for more than twenty years, he was accustomed to being observed, questioned, and inundated by medical students and house staff. In both age and demeanor, Murphy seemed like one of his hematology fellows.

"Very well, Dr. Harrington. I hope you don't feel I'm intruding. My sister-in-law called and—"

"Please," Harrington interrupted. "I understand. The young lady is entitled to worry about her husband. Let's go see your brother." Dan accompanied Dr. Harrington to Pat's hospital room.

Dr. Harrington then reviewed Pat's chart. "Has he been getting enough fluids?" he asked.

"We've been encouraging him," a tall, dark-haired nurse replied, "but he doesn't seem to follow through."

"Why don't I go see him," Harrington said. He began walking toward Patrick Murphy's hospital room. "Patrick, how are you, young man?" he asked upon walking in.

"I feel like shit—pardon my French."

"Let me listen to your lungs," Harrington said, moving toward Patrick. "Take deep breaths." Harrington placed the stethoscope over numerous areas of Patrick's chest, then completed his examination as he looked for signs of infection.

"Mr. Murphy," Harrington said in a benevolent but authoritative tone, "you've got to help yourself. I think your fever's due to dehydration. You're not drinking enough fluids. Water, juice, or whatever you like is fine, but you need to drink more and take slow deep breaths to keep your lungs open."

"That's the first time anybody told me to drink more. Can you send up some Sam Adams?"

Harrington grinned but changed the course of the conversation. "I understand your wife's worried about you. I know this is difficult, but try not to get yourself too down. I'm confident that you'll do well."

"Right! How about this?" Pat quipped. He pulled off a baseball cap, threw it across the room, and exposed his bald head.

"That's from the radiation. Most of it should grow back," Harrington replied.

"Are you sure?" The lightness that was typical of Pat's disposition was gone.

Harrington nodded.

"What's this I hear about being sterile?" Pat asked. "Am I gonna be able to"—he paused—"you know, be with my wife, have kids and all that?"

"Pat, there's a difference between being sterile and having sexual relations with your wife."

"What's the difference?" Pat asked, the edge of his voice obvious to Harrington.

"A person who is sterile can function perfectly normally even though unable to have a child."

"So, I can still get it on with my wife?"

"Most definitely," said Harrington in an upbeat tone. "It's also not guaranteed that you'll be sterile."

Patrick's hospital room, although specially designed to prevent infections, had created for him an isolation that began to unnerve him. Coupled with the realization of the seriousness of his illness, the baldness, and the possible sterility, he had started to feel that the room was like a prison cell. Harrington, however, was not surprised by Pat's emotional dive since he had observed similar reactions in other people who had contracted life-threatening illnesses. Harrington, in turn, recognized early signs of depression in Patrick, who, like many Irish Catholic youths from South Boston, had difficulty expressing his feelings.

"Patrick," Harrington said, "take it a day at a time."

"When can I get out of here?"

"Be patient. As soon as it's safe. But I like your attitude. It'll help you get better," Harrington said as he left the room.

At the end of the hall, he was greeted by Dan Murphy, who was anxious to hear the assessment.

"How's he doing?"

"He'll be fine. Just a little dehydrated and despondent—problems we can handle," Harrington said confidently. "Why don't you come back to my office. I thought you might want to see some charts."

Dan looked a bit puzzled, then asked, "You mean for Anna Carlson's study?"

"Yes."

Chapter 19

With no classes scheduled, Anna didn't rush to get out of the jogging suit in which she had slept. Paging through her notes, she thought of Dan Murphy and wondered whether his brother was improving. *He would have called me if there was anything serious,* she thought hopefully. Restraining her urge to call, she did not want to appear more assertive than she had already been with Dan. On the other hand, she recognized Murphy's self-confidence and realized that he would not be intimidated by, but likely attracted to, the overtures of a strong woman.

Back to work, she urged herself.

With limited success in obtaining information on water pollution, Anna pursued results of tests related to air pollution. Her first call was to the Air Quality Division of the State of Massachusetts's Department of Environmental Protection, or the DEP as it was known to many.

"What type of air pollutants are monitored?" Anna asked.

"Primarily particulates," the DEP officer explained.

"Nothing else?"

"No, but the electric utility in South Boston monitors other materials. I think they look at oxides of nitrogen, sulfur dioxide, and sulfates in addition to particulates."

"That's interesting," Anna said. "Is there any attempt to compare the results?"

"No, because the state DEP measures respirable particulates. The utility measures total particulates, some of which may not be inhalable."

"How about those other materials, oxides of nitrogen and sulfur dioxide?"

"They're typical products of combustion, especially from an oil-fired power plant. They use a low-sulfur fuel to keep the emissions down."

Anna recalled from her course in environmental health that the major cause of acid rain was the release of sulfur and nitrogen compounds, which, when coming into contact with the moisture in the atmosphere, become acidic. She vaguely remembered a discussion about the health effects of these compounds, especially the sulfur dioxide, on children with asthma.

"You know there's an air pollution monitoring station right there in South Boston," the DEP engineer said.

"Where?"

"East First Street, in the northeast corner of South Boston."

"How often are measurements conducted?" Anna asked, pleased to have encountered a knowledgeable and accommodating government official.

"They're measured for twenty-four hours every sixth day."

"How are the results usually?"

"Actually, quite good. They average about thirty micrograms per cubic meter," the official answered in the customary way for describing the concentration of a pollutant in the atmosphere.

"What's the recommended level?" Anna asked.

"The EPA annual average is thirty-five, so their results are in compliance."

"Can I get the results from the electric utility? Doesn't the public have access to certain types of environmental data?"

"Yes. The electric utility submits the information to the state

DEP, and then it's maintained in the National Archives by the EPA. You might want to call Frank Rivers here at the DEP. He oversees that program, but he's not in today. Our website has the results of our air monitoring for the past few years."

Anna had one more question. "You've been a great help to me, but I want to push my luck. Do you know how I can get information on the types of chemicals used at certain factories?"

"You'll need to search the Emergency Planning and Community Right-to-Know. It's sponsored by the EPA."

"Thank you so much," Anna said, who immediately dialed the number and was greeted with a recorded response that described a range of EPA activities. Hazardous waste, underground storage tanks, and chemical releases from factories were discussed as Anna waited to speak to a person described as an information specialist.

Soon, she was welcomed by a cheery voice, anxious to help. Anna explained that she wanted to understand how the public could gain access to certain environmental reports. The EPA representative gave her some background on the Emergency Planning and Community Right-to-Know Act, which requires companies to submit information to government authorities about chemicals used at their facilities, especially if the quantities are above a certain volume. The regulation, designed to aid in pollution control and toxin use reduction efforts, also supports firefighters and other emergency personnel in preparing for an accidental release.

Anna asked, "How do I get that information? Are there any hazardous waste sites in South Boston on the Superfund list?"

"I don't know, but I can check," the federal employee answered.

Anna waited for the response, pleasantly surprised at her good fortune.

"There's a new EPA-designated Superfund site—the Neponset River. There are ten or so waste sites in Massachusetts."

"Thank you for looking," Anna said. "You've been very helpful. Goodbye now."

Anna was pleased with her progress in navigating through

government channels to learn more about publicly available environmental reports. The ultimate question, she realized, was how to make sense of the information once she got it. Nonetheless, her success motivated her to consider the questionnaire she needed to develop for her study of the aplastic anemia cases.

As part of her project, Anna planned to interview the people with aplastic anemia who had been treated by Dr. Harrington. Only residents of South Boston who had been diagnosed within the past two years would be included in the study. Since the interval from exposure to a chemical and the onset of aplastic anemia was usually less than six months, and often much shorter, she saw no point in pursuing cases diagnosed more than two years ago. Moreover, the increase in cases in South Boston had not become apparent until the past year.

Anna knew that her questionnaire would need to focus on occupational and environmental health risks. *I'm sure there's a logical way of constructing a questionnaire that gets the right information and keeps Becker happy.*

David Becker, her adviser, would have to approve the questionnaire she intended to use for the study. *Undoubtedly,* she thought, *he'll notice some problems.* Confident that she had covered all the possible causes of aplastic anemia, however, she realized that it would be necessary to phrase the questions to avoid biasing the answers. Becker had warned her about not leading a person with a major disease down the interviewer's path. The tendency to ascribe the cause of a serious illness to some external factor overwhelmed most people. This understandable response, however, could create an artificially elevated risk of disease due to a certain risk factor, such as an environmental hazard, if people without the illness were not as vigorously questioned.

Anna, tired of her detailed work with the study, yearned for an hour to work out, ideally in an aerobic session at the health club. The intensity of the physical activity always served as the perfect antidote to mental fatigue. Preferring the camaraderie of exercising in a group, she headed to one of the university's numerous fitness facilities.

Chapter 20

Anna and Dan Murphy agreed to have dinner at Amrhein's Restaurant on West Broadway in South Boston. Although they planned to meet at six o'clock, it was twenty minutes after the hour before Dan finally appeared. Anna's experience as a journalist instilled in her a compulsive sense of punctuality since many of the people whom she interviewed were busy and often inaccessible.

"Sorry I'm late," Dan said, extending his hand to Anna, who was sitting by the window at a table cluttered with her papers, some notepads, and coffee. Removing his jacket, he said, "It's so nice to see you. You look as energetic as ever."

Anna smiled as she collected her papers into an organized pile. Dan caught notice of the blush and eye makeup amplifying her icy-blue eyes. Anna's attention to her appearance encouraged Dan as a sign of her attraction to him. Dressed in a wool pleated skirt and a maroon turtleneck, she seemed relaxed and confidently attractive.

"Have you been able to track down any more environmental information?" he asked.

"Oh, better than I expected, but tell me about your brother first."

"He's doing well. It seems that his fever last night was due to dehydration and some pulmonary atelectasis."

"He has a collapsed lung?" Anna asked with obvious concern.

"No, but it's similar. The small air sacs in the lungs retain fluid if people don't breathe deeply after surgery. He'll be OK. Part of the problem was his mood. Dr. Harrington sensed a mild depression, which is not surprising."

"Wouldn't you have noticed that, Dan?"

"Not really. Patrick's never been expressive, but Harrington seems to have gotten him back on track."

"It must have your worried."

"I try not to let it bother me," he said.

"You know, I read an interesting report today about contaminated drinking water," Anna said.

"Not before lunch, I hope," quipped Murphy.

Anna smiled. "A report from the National Resource Defense Council said that nearly half the country's water systems had some type of EPA violation over the past two years."

"What kind of problems were there?"

"I haven't gone through the full report yet, but all kinds of violations were described, like too many bacteria or pesticides, even contamination from underground storage tanks."

"Underground storage tanks? You mean from gas stations?"

"Yes. When they leak, they can contaminate the groundwater." She then asked, "Did you have a chance to review the medical charts?"

"Yes."

"Anything interesting?"

"Oh, definitely, but information in the histories was limited. Most charts only listed the person's job without describing what the job actually entailed, including whether the person worked with any chemicals or other hazards."

"Why?"

"Good question. Most physicians focus on diagnosis and treatment. Little attention is given to understanding the cause of a disease or its prevention—at least outside of research studies. The environmental histories were even scanter. No mention of whether there might have been lead, asbestos, or radon in the home, or whether any home remodeling efforts were recently performed, or whether the occupants had certain hobbies, especially in the arts."

"Arts?" Anna asked incredulously.

"Some materials used by artists, especially painters and sculptors, are just as hazardous as chemicals used in factories. Sometimes, they actually pose a greater danger because the control measures are less effective."

"That shouldn't be a problem with our group, do you think?" Anna asked.

"I don't know. People could have hobbies ranging from radiator repair, to stained glass work, to shooting their guns at firing ranges—and be exposed to lead."

"You've learned a lot at those courses," Anna interjected. "Why do you think information that can be so important could have been overlooked in the medical records?"

"The focus of hospital care is usually on treatment, but another reason is that few physicians have had training in occupational or environmental health, so they don't think about it. There simply aren't very many physicians certified in occupational medicine. Look at me, for example."

"I love to." She grinned in return.

"I'm directing a clinic that focuses on injuries and illnesses at work, but I'm not board certified and I haven't gone through a residency program in occupational medicine."

"So, the record review didn't help much?" Anna stated.

"I don't mean to suggest that it was worthless. I tried to follow that form you gave me."

"You mean Becker's ten-item questionnaire?" Anna asked.

"Yes. I also looked over the bone marrow biopsy results of Harrington's patients. I couldn't find any obvious differences, but we should ask him for an opinion." Dan hoped to find peculiarities in the bone marrow analyses of the people with aplastic anemia. Perhaps slight differences may lead to clues about the cause.

"I developed a questionnaire, or at least a draft," Anna said encouragingly, "that I'd like to use in interviewing the patients. But I could use some help." She opened a manila folder to withdraw her creation.

A waiter approached their table. "Good evening, folks. What can I get you?"

Dan looked to Anna.

"Chardonnay."

"OK. And you, sir?" the robust mustachioed man asked Dan.

"A draft, please."

"Are you eating, folks?"

Anna and Murphy nodded and said yes in unison.

"Then you'll need our menu. You came on a good night. We're having an Irish band later."

"Excellent. That sounds like fun," Anna said. The waiter nodded, then left the table.

Dan paged through the seven-page document that Anna proposed to use when interviewing the patients with aplastic anemia. "How did you develop this?" he asked her.

"I looked at a number of review articles and did a PubMed search," she answered, referring to the computer-based index of medical journals, a program developed by the National Library of Medicine.

"Impressive. You've done your homework."

"There are loose ends, though," Anna countered.

"Such as what?"

"I'm not sure if I've phrased all the questions in a way that people will understand if they've ever been exposed to certain hazards."

"What do you mean?"

"Well, take glycol ethers for example. Now excuse me for sounding like a chemistry major, but I just looked it up. These materials are in so many different products. Does using a product that contains these compounds mean exposure? Is that exposure significant?"

"Anna, they're great questions, but I think you can wait until later to deal with them. Just collect the information and analyze it later."

The waiter returned. "Are you ready to order?"

Dan looked to Anna.

"Why don't we wait a bit? I'm in no hurry. How about you, Dan?"

"That sounds fine to me. I'm off tomorrow," he said, referring to the first day of the long Christmas weekend.

The waiter left the table.

"Dan, an area I'm not sure about is how far back to go in looking at environmental exposure. Do you know what I'm referring to—the latency?"

"Oh yes, the interval from the first contact with the chemical until the time when the person is diagnosed with the disease."

"Looks as though you've been attending all your classes," Anna said with a grin.

Dan and Anna were discussing a common feature associated with many occupational and environmental illnesses, that is, the damage to a person's health that may occur a substantial period of time after coming into contact with a hazard. Some diseases, such as a tumor on the lining of the lung, known as mesothelioma, can result from exposure to asbestos as much as twenty to thirty years earlier. With blood disorders resulting from hazardous agents, that interval can be much shorter, at times only a few months.

"I'm not sure, Anna, about the latency with aplastic anemia, but some articles suggest that exposure occurred only a few months before the disease."

"I know."

"I'd assume that even a few weeks may be a sufficient interval."

"This project is very interesting. I hope it can help your brother," she said.

"That would be great."

"You're not drinking your beer," she said, changing the topic. "Enjoy yourself, Dr. Murphy. Moderate drinking can be beneficial to your health."

"Right, to some extent," he answered, bringing the bottle of beer to his mouth.

Anna reached for her glass of wine and said, "If you'll indulge me just a bit, I'd like to tell you the environmental plan for the study, then I'd like to forget about it and learn more about you." She couldn't believe the assertiveness in her tone, especially since she was planning to fly to Minneapolis the next morning. There, waiting for her at the airport, would be Roger Anderson, that is, if he could wrestle himself away from the bookstore he owned.

"I'll indulge you, Anna. It'll be a pleasure."

"Well, thank you. You're quite the gentleman to allow a young lady who's had two glasses of wine to ramble on about a study for which she's corralled your participation."

"Two glasses of wine, but oh so glib."

Anna grinned, then looked out into the restaurant, hoping to spot the waiter. "Maybe we should order," she said.

"After I hear your plans."

"My plans?" Anna answered, the wine having momentarily distracted her as she thought of her visit with Roger tomorrow evening. "Oh, you mean for the study," she said, trying to hide her embarrassment at being temporarily disconnected from the conversation. "I see two components to the environmental review—the personal and the area," she said, then sipped the remainder of her wine. "By personal, I mean the home, the water, and so forth."

"OK," Dan answered, encouraging her to continue.

"By area, I mean publicly available information on water test results, air pollution data, and so forth."

"That makes sense," Dan responded.

"We'll still do the standard review of demographics—where people live, how old they are, and so forth."

"Sounds good."

The waiter appeared again. "Ready, folks? The beef stew is great tonight."

"Beef stew," Anna said. "How Irish. I'll have some."

"More wine, madam?" the waiter asked.

"Why not? One more! I don't have to drive tonight," she said, then sheepishly looked in Dan's direction, concerned about his reaction.

The waiter again left the table.

"Dan," Anna said with a hint of affection, "I hope I'm not interfering with any lady friends of yours. I wouldn't want you to be seen in public with another woman."

"Oh no," Dan answered quickly.

"You mean you don't go out with anyone right now?"

Dan hesitated. "Well, no one regularly at the moment.

"How about you?" he asked, hitting the ball back into her court.

"What about me?"

"Are you seeing anyone in Boston?" he asked.

"I'm looking at you," she responded with a grin.

"Is there a man in Boston who occupies your attention?" Murphy asked in a guarded tone, hoping the answer would be no.

"No," Anna said, avoiding discussion of Roger back in Minneapolis, but Murphy wouldn't let her off the hook that easily.

"But how about Minneapolis?" he asked. "Surely someone's recognized your charm, brain, and wit."

"How well stated," Anna replied with a smile that accentuated her eyes. She sipped the wine, then looked around the restaurant for the waiter. "Do you eat here often?"

"You're adept at changing course in a discussion, young lady. I bet those techniques work well in journalism."

"Oh yes. You need to keep the people you interview on track. People love anecdotes and digressions. They relish telling stories."

"Well then, I should follow your advice and continue to ask about the man who has your interest back in Minneapolis."

What should I tell him? she thought, sipping her third glass of wine. *If I say too much, he may get discouraged. On the other hand, I'm not sure that I want to encourage him.*

"I've been seeing someone for a number of years back home."

Dan's heart sank momentarily, but he continued, hoping not to show his disappointment. "I couldn't imagine that you'd be a free agent," he said, using the sports metaphor. "How's he feel about you being here in Boston?"

"He understands."

"But doesn't he fear someone like me pursuing the woman of his dreams?"

"My, you can be charming."

"Just another technique of the journalist—how to get information from the subject," Dan responded.

"You learn quickly. Getting information painlessly and easily is an art."

"So," Dan said. "Have I pinned you down?"

"Oh, I can always squirm a bit," she answered, "and only tell you precise answers to precise questions."

"Of course," Dan answered. "But this isn't a dance with lawyers at a deposition."

"No, but our repartee is presenting me with a challenge in avoiding a direct response."

Just then the waiter appeared with the beef stew that each had ordered. "Bon appétit. Would you like some more wine, madam?" the waiter asked.

"Oh no. I'd better not," Anna answered. "I'm already getting into trouble."

"And you, sir?" the waiter asked Dan. "Another beer?"

"Yes, please."

As the waiter departed, Anna and Dan began to sample the beef stew, the restaurant's major specialty.

Anna continued. "Tell me about yourself, Dan. Why aren't you married, living with someone, or pursuing three different women at once?"

"There's a shotgun question. Just take a shot and see what you hit."

"I'm confident we could play verbal ping-pong all night," Anna said. "Are you threatened by a woman who's halfway intelligent?"

"No. I love the challenge. This intellectual sparring is good for the brain. After dinner, I'll have to push another wine or two onto you so I can take advantage of you."

"That would be nice," Anna answered, tongue-in-cheek and with a demure smile as she looked down at the stew.

"I hope to get the chance," Murphy said.

As the Irish band warmed up, the waitstaff began to clear tables and chairs from the dance floor.

"How do you like the stew?" Dan asked.

"Great. I don't think I can eat it all, though."

"Stop worrying about those few pounds," Dan added. "I've never met a woman who's totally satisfied with her weight."

"Oh, there are a few beauty queens, some models, and those who just don't care," she answered.

"So, are you going to tell me about your true love?" Dan asked.

"What do you want to know? Remember, you're talking with a journalist who recognizes when the net's been thrown at her."

"How's this?" he said. "Anything you want to tell me."

"Well, then. Roger runs a bookstore. He works hard; he's reliable; and he loves me," Anna said.

"Are you planning to get married?" Dan asked, zeroing in on the target.

Anna reached for more of the stew. "Perhaps, but not at the moment." *What an astute answer,* she complimented herself. *Maybe I have potential for a career in politics.*

"Not tonight, then?" Dan asked.

"No. No plans right now," she replied, feeling as though she may have said too much.

The waiter returned to their table. "How was it, folks?"

"Delicious," Anna answered.

"Yes, very good," Dan said.

"Would you like coffee?" the waiter asked.

"No. Not for me," said Anna.

The waiter looked toward Dan. "No, thank you. I'll pass. We'll have the check, please."

"OK." The waiter added up a column of numbers, then handed Dan the check.

"Let me pay my share," Anna interjected. "After all, I asked you out tonight, didn't I?"

"I wouldn't think of asking you to pay anything," Dan said. "You're a poor student, and I work for a living."

"Well. Thank you."

"My pleasure," he answered. "But let's go out somewhere. Would you like to dance?"

"That sounds great," Anna answered.

"Are you sure Roger doesn't have any spies, thugs, or unsavory characters willing to mow me down for taking out his girlfriend?"

"Hardly," Anna answered. "Roger's a quiet, unassuming guy who loves his books and his business. You know, I think you might like him."

"Not as much as I like you," he replied.

"This repartee is wonderful. I have to stay alert, though, to keep up with you."

"Let's go," Dan said. They put on their coats to prepare for going back out into the Boston winter.

At a dance club in downtown Boston, Dan Murphy and Anna Carlson mingled with other people in their twenties through their forties. The loud music impeded conversation, so they communicated their affection through the subtleties of touch. An extra embrace during a slow dance, a grasp of the hand, or a stroking of the hair helped express the growing attraction they felt for one another. Although Dan thought he was more attracted to Anna than she to him, it didn't matter to him. Sensing a unique attraction to her, he was willing to buy time and be patient.

As the night drew to a close, Murphy drove Anna back to her apartment in Brookline. Feeling awkward and adolescent, he pulled the car into a parking space outside her building, then reached his arm around her shoulders to pull her lean body toward him. Anna responded immediately to the gesture, and within seconds they were locked in a kiss that neither wanted to end.

"This will get us into trouble, you know," Anna said.

"I don't see how," Dan responded, then drew her toward him and kissed her again. They embraced with a passion that neither had felt in a while.

"I'd better go," said Anna.

"Have a great trip," Dan chimed. "Give me a call when you return. I'm anxious to hear how the study goes."

"Is that all?" she asked with a grin that appeared both coquettish and alluring.

Dan smiled in return.

Anna closed the car door and turned to walk to her apartment. Dan paused before driving away to gaze at her from behind. Struck by her athletic agility, he marveled at the grace and confidence with which she carried herself. How uncertain he felt about her! Should he follow his instincts and pursue Anna with abandon? Since being dumped by his ex-wife, he had carefully guarded the keys to his emotions.

As Anna entered the door to her apartment, she turned to wave to Dan, who drove off with his mind racing in all directions.

Chapter 21

It was another difficult night of sleep—frequent interruptions because of terrifying explosions, wailing sirens, and the shouts of injured people. For the past few evenings, ever since attempting to drive by Saint Brigid's Parish during the fundraiser, Parker Barrows's sleep had been marred by intrusive nightmares, all of which contained some element of the London blast in which he had lost his leg. Like a news program that flashed short segments of a major event, the nightmares breezed from scene to scene of the tragedy and eventually roused him from his troubled sleep. On awakening, his heart raced, skipped, and pounded. His legs felt so weak that he felt he couldn't rise out of bed.

Increasingly frustrated about the nightmares, Barrows contemplated canceling his trip to Washington so he could remain in Boston and see his psychiatrist, who had advised him that his symptoms could be from posttraumatic stress disorder, PTSD in psychiatric parlance. Barrows learned that the condition, which became more recognized as a result of the Vietnam War, occurs following a tragic event such as his own accident in London. He thought the psychiatrist had a point. He poured a scotch and thought about his day. *Ugh. I just don't care about people the way I used to,* he thought. It was hard to get going. *But that IRA runaway will pay. I want him to suffer before he dies.* These thoughts buoyed his spirits immensely.

The psychiatrist had explained that the nightmares and his avoidance of confronting the alleged perpetrator also supported the diagnosis of PTSD. Unpredictable behavior, in particular, was a feature that, if not properly recognized, could lead to dire consequences.

Barrows's spirits became invariably buoyed, however, whenever he contemplated getting his retribution. Eventually, he felt, he would prevail with the IRA runaway and demolish the demons of the night. His life would again be free, at least from the perils of the past.

He showed his ticket to the agent, then boarded the plane for Washington. Riding in first class, Barrows became optimistic as he felt in control of his destiny. "What type of scotch do you have?" he asked the flight attendant. After being served two drinks, Barrows leaned back against the headrest for a nap. About an hour later, he arrived at Washington's National Airport, then boarded a taxi to his favorite hotel in the northwest section of the city. Along with a health club and indoor pool, the hotel featured a four-star restaurant in which Barrows could indulge his appreciation of fine food. It was also closely located to a club in Georgetown where he met his contacts.

A swim, sauna, and shower invigorated Barrows for his evening tryst. A short taxi ride took him to the Upriver Club, where he was greeted by a bushy-headed man sitting alone at a table by the dance floor. Although only a few people had arrived, the bar would later be filled with politicians, consultants, attorneys, and other Beltway professionals.

"Barrows, you old salt. How the hell are you?"

"Miserable, you ugly cuss," he replied in his typically abrasive but good-natured tone.

"Have a seat. Can I get you a beer?"

"How about a scotch? Can you afford it?"

A waiter, dressed in a red jacket with black trousers, approached. After receiving their orders, he departed.

"Tell me, Parker, how's it been?"

"Could be better. The leg's driving me crazy. It wakes me up at night with this horrible pain."

"What's your doctor think?"

"He says it's phantom pain. Even though most of my leg is gone, some of the nerves that controlled feeling in it are still there. They go all the way to the brain."

"Can't they do anything about it?"

"Pain medication. There's no cure."

"Just take the medication then. Why be a hero?"

"Mark, I didn't come here to regale you with my health problems. I need information."

"I have information that I'm sure you'll like," his contact responded.

"What's that?"

Barrows's friend handed over a blank white envelope.

"People in Defense confirm the information. The sources are solid."

"What's in here?"

"Names, addresses, and phone numbers of people from a plant in upstate New York. It's being decommissioned, and the local community's upset. Two people in the waste disposal section are about to be laid off. They frequent a country-and-western bar where they play pool a few nights a week. Both are divorced. Their wives have custody of the kids. They'd be easily influenced by money."

"Why this plant?"

"They're casual in how they monitor waste disposal."

"How certain are you?"

"Very. Now that the plant is closing, people's attitudes about their jobs are changing. People are bitter."

"How about security?"

"Also casual."

"What do you suggest?"

"Have your people get up there and ingratiate themselves with the two at the plant. We'll get into other details later."

The bar began to fill up, with well-dressed professional men and women occupying the remaining seats. When the three-piece band warmed up, Barrows's attention was drawn to a tall, dark-haired woman standing alone by the bar. His friend, noting the gaze, commented, "Parker, help yourself to one of life's great pleasures—beautiful women. Ask her to dance."

"Nice idea, but not for this wooden-legged sailor," Barrows responded. Despite having had extraordinary athletic skills before his injury, he had gained weight and lost his zeal for most forms of physical activity, including dancing.

"Buy her a drink then."

"You've convinced me," he answered with confidence, then rose from his chair to approach the bar.

Chapter 22

Anna began to resent Dr. David Becker. Although her academic adviser offered her an unusual opportunity to pursue a master's degree in public health, his authoritative style struck her as inappropriate and counterproductive. Students were well aware that it was ill-advised to incur Becker's wrath by submitting a tardy or inadequate report. A meeting, a semiformal affair, required both an appointment and an agenda since Becker carefully guarded his all-important time. His rudeness, in returning phone calls and reviewing mail while meeting and talking with graduate students, was well-known. Not known for his patience, Becker would quickly end a meeting if a student was unprepared.

"Anna Carlson," Becker's secretary called out. Becker rarely invited an underling into his office, a task delegated to a subordinate, who would usher the cautious student into his "inner sanctum." Becker, standing at the door as Anna appeared, said, "Sit down." He then directed her to the long table positioned at the center of his office. At one end of the room sat a brown desk that was cluttered with assorted piles of papers, manuscripts, and books. Behind his desk chair, a window provided a glimpse of Huntington Avenue and the Green Line trolleys that passed by throughout the day.

Three walls of shelves filled with books from floor to ceiling surrounded him. Just about any book published in dermatology was represented. Noticeably absent from the office were pictures of Becker's family—a wife, a son, a daughter—about whom people knew or had heard little.

Based on a new treatment he had developed for psoriasis, Becker established clinics at three community hospitals. His efforts profited him handsomely, both academically and financially. With a tremendous capacity for work, he spent his professional time at any one of three hospitals, in addition to lecturing to medical students and conducting clinical research. The one reward he allowed himself for the eighty-hour workweek was an August vacation at Cape Cod. Within a few days of his vacation, however, he would start writing research papers, calling the office, and sending overnight mail. His all-consuming energy for success proved highly effective as he published papers, received grants, and reached the rank of clinical professor.

"Tell me what you want to do," Becker said, initiating the meeting with Anna.

She handed him a one-page sheet on which she had outlined her plans.

"A case series?" he asked incredulously. "I thought I told you to do a case-control study?"

Anna, taken aback by Becker's abrupt critique—made before even reading her summary—paused before answering. "I thought a case series would determine if there were any common features among the patients with aplastic anemia, especially since I've been able to get some information on possible air and water pollution."

"Haven't you taken epidemiology?" Becker asked, referring to a basic course in public health that focuses on the determination of risk factors for diseases.

"Yes," Anna answered tentatively.

"Didn't they tell you that a case-control series is the best way to study rare diseases?"

Sheepishly, Anna responded, "Yes."

"Then, that's what you should do. Correct?" Becker asked.

Anna knew there was no option for a negative reply. "OK." She nodded.

"What kind of a control group will you use?" Becker seemed to derive pleasure from causing her discomfort.

Anna began a bit hesitantly, but nonetheless was confident. "A control group would consist of people who resemble the patients with aplastic anemia but who do not have the disease. They should resemble the cases in age, occupation, income, and gender so they can be fairly compared to people with the disease."

"Why?"

"To determine whether any differences between the two groups might hold clues to the cause of the disease."

"You've learned something this semester. Let me see the questionnaire," Becker said. Becker, very old school and not computer-savvy, wanted paper copies. A PDF file sent by email would not suffice.

"I gave it to your secretary," Anna said. *This guy is over-the-top exasperating,* she thought, maintaining eye contact with Becker.

"Well, I don't have it." As Becker thumbed through a manila folder, he mumbled, "I don't see it. Are you sure you gave it to her? Sarah doesn't make mistakes."

Anna knew she had handed the questionnaire to Sarah yesterday. Although she recognized Becker's reaction as clear theatrics, she began to resent, as well as fear, his antics.

"Oh. Here it is," he said, having reached the last pages of the file. Without a hint of apology, he scanned the four-page questionnaire. "Where's the work history?"

"Page two, at the bottom."

Becker thumbed to the page. "Where do you ask about exposures?"

"On the top of three," she replied.

"No. I don't mean the list of chemicals. Exposure monitoring. Air sampling results. What was actually there—not what somebody tells you."

Exasperated, Anna answered, "Do you think we really need that?"

"Need that? Where have you been for the past three months?"

Becker's belittlement struck Anna like a punch to the stomach. If alone, she would have teared up, but her pride would never allow her to lose control in front of him.

"I'll add it to the questionnaire."

"What are you going to ask?" Becker continued.

"Well, first we should ask if any exposure monitoring has been performed. If so, when and for what substances? Was it done for routine purposes or because of a chemical spill and so forth?" Anna replied.

"You're moving in the right direction," Becker said, showing the first signs of encouraging her since the meeting began.

"Thank you."

"Look," Becker said authoritatively, "get two controls for every case. Harrington probably has controls from his hematology studies like the orthopedic surgery patients we talked about at our last meeting."

Anna, pleased that Becker had softened his bite a bit and now appeared poised to offer some help, ended the meeting on a high note.

"I'll look forward to your presentation," Becker continued. "When's it scheduled?"

"The third week of January, I think."

"You think? When?"

"The twenty-third," Anna answered.

"I'll be away that week—in San Francisco," he replied with self-importance, then called to his secretary. "Get her a new date for the research seminar!"

Sarah opened the appointment book. "The twenty-ninth?"

"No. Earlier. This young lady needs some motivation," he said with a condescending air.

"The tenth?" the secretary asked.

"That'll do," Becker replied. Turning to Anna, he said, "Show me you're capable of decent work."

Anna left Becker's office and felt as though she had been mugged in a dark alley. As she rode down the elevator, she vowed that this would be the last time she would suffer his condescension.

Chapter 23

Anna leaned back in her seat as the plane took off from Boston's Logan Airport. On the way home to Minneapolis for Christmas break, she reflected on the events of the past few weeks. Recognizing a need to make sense of what had happened, including with her project and in meeting Dan Murphy, she reached for a pad of paper. It was a habit she had developed in her days as a journalist. A few notes here and there helped her sort out her thoughts.

So far, her study suggested that South Boston had a relatively high rate of aplastic anemia. Eight people had become ill within the past year, when, according to rates expected for South Boston, only one case should have occurred.

Motivated to succeed, Anna began to summarize her efforts to date. She wrote as follows:

1. The environmental results, including the drinking water supplied to Pat's house, were normal, at least according to EPA limits.

Since the drinking water results were unknown, Anna wondered whether it was worth the expense of testing the local water. She recalled her environmental health professor emphasizing that lead in drinking water was often overlooked and that even modern houses may contain lead solder around pipes that transport water to the kitchen and bathroom. *Even so,* Anna thought, *lead is not known as a cause of aplastic anemia. Nor, for that matter, has any water pollutant been linked with the disease.* She decided to refer the question to Becker. *If he advises me,* she mused, *I won't have to take the blame for chasing a red herring.*

She continued her note-taking:

2. The Boston area air pollution results met federal standards, at least last year's measurements did. Information from private companies and the power plant in South Boston was similar.

Anna had obtained the air pollution results through the Clean Air Act, which requires monitoring of six types of air pollutants. These pollutants, which arise primarily from car exhaust, power plants, and industrial processes, include ozone, carbon monoxide, sulfur dioxide, nitrogen dioxide, particulates, and lead. With no training in chemistry aside from courses taken for her undergraduate nursing degree, Anna was unaware of the health implications of these pollutants. Nonetheless, she recognized no serious elevations and no hazards known to cause aplastic anemia.

Unable to find any obvious violations to either water or air pollution control laws, Anna recognized that the chance of linking the aplastic anemia cases to an environmental cause was remote. In addition to the lack of EPA violations, Anna also learned from the Agency for Toxic Substances and Disease Registry (ATSDR) that South Boston had no hazardous waste sites on its priorities list. The ATSDR tabulates waste sites according to their potential to affect people's health.

Perhaps the questionnaire will give me some direction, she thought hopefully. Despite her initial disappointment about not having found a clue to the aplastic anemia cases, she recognized the limitations of the available information. Many pollution monitoring results were based, at times, only on *one* test per year! How accurately the one measurement reflected typical situations was unknown.

Anna also noted that area monitoring results might not reflect the amount of a hazardous compound a person may actually breathe. As her frustrations with the study mounted, she closed the files and reached for the airline magazine.

Thumbing through the index, her train of thought took her to Dan Murphy and their last evening together. In a moment of bliss, she sensed his presence, as though he were with her in the plane. Savoring the feeling, she drifted off into sleep, until she was jolted back to reality by air turbulence. Now, her blissful ruminations about Dan turned to guilt as she imagined Roger waiting for her to land in Minneapolis.

Back and forth like the tennis volleys she loved, Anna thought of Murphy and Roger, whom she had dated now for nearly eight years. Steady and reliable to the point of being boring, Roger had settled into a comfortable pattern after starting his bookstore on the West Bank of the University of Minnesota's campus. While liking Roger's stability and faithfulness, Anna disliked his lack of enthusiasm for travel, athletics, and music, interests that inspired her. *I think Roger would be content to buy a house and commute to his bookstore for the next fifty years,* she thought.

Anna reflected on her first semester at Harvard, during which she met students from around the world. Ranging in age from twenty to fifty, her classmates included some who served in the Peace Corps, conducted research at universities, or served at the highest levels of world health organizations. Contact with people of such disparate backgrounds caused Anna to anticipate a range of professional options that had never occurred to her when she lived in Minneapolis.

She thought about her last night with Dan Murphy again, when he embraced her on the way back to the car. Feeling silly about being enamored by a sign of affection that teenage girls would take for granted, she appreciated the unexpected pleasure of his gentle touch. *Silly,* she reflected. *So silly of me.*

"Ladies and gentlemen, fasten your seat belts, please. We're about to begin our descent to the Minneapolis–St. Paul Airport." Anna looked out the window at the flat landscape of southern Minnesota, where snow blanketed farms, lakes, and towns. The sight of pickup trucks parked on frozen lakes made her recall the hearty souls who fished through Minnesota's bone-chilling winters.

Chapter 24

Parker Barrows loved the musty odor of the health club. Situated in South Boston, the facility appealed to him because of the weight lifting equipment and the boxing ring. Although his days of boxing prowess were long gone, he remained interested in the sport, which he had learned in the British military. Despite being limited to the punching bag because of his amputated leg, and despite the prosthesis, he enjoyed watching the amateur sparring matches that took place on Monday evenings. The skills of a tall, burly former football player with an uncanny ability to withstand a punch and land a left hook impressed him a great deal. Eventually, the two of them had become acquainted, to the point that Tony Mesa gained part-time work as Barrows's virtual bodyguard.

"Parker, buddy. How the hell are ya?" Mesa yelled upon entering the weight room with a towel tossed over his shoulder.

"Glad to see ya, Tony," Barrows replied with obvious pleasure. "Are you finished?"

"Yeah. Let's get going. I'm ready for the steam," Mesa said, referring to the club's steam room, where the two discussed all sorts of private matters well out of earshot and well beyond email.

Mesa turned on the valve that allowed a gush of fresh steam to enter the small room in which they usually ended a workout.

"Did you take care of our boy?" Barrows asked.

"And then some, my man. We left his sweet little ass out in the middle of a football field in the suburbs."

"Anything else? You didn't let him off that easy, I trust."

"He got a souvenir bruise on his head and a broken finger."

"Does he know what happened?"

"He was drugged, gagged, and dumped. He has no clue what went on or who did it."

Barrows adjusted the steam valve to lower the intensity of the heat. "You've got to keep a close eye on Wilson. He's dangerous," Barrows advised.

"He won't mess with me, my man, if he knows what's good for him."

"Don't take him lightly."

"Parker, you seem to forget who I am. I've been in the ring with the best. I've had my head knocked around."

"That's what worries me."

"What do you want me to do with him now?"

"You've got to get him into action at another plant."

"Where?"

"Upstate New York. North of Albany. Keep on top of him."

"He's not going anywhere. Plus, he's got to be spooked after his escapade in the middle of the night."

"But don't let him know what happened. Keep him guessing. Maybe we'll do it again just to make him a little crazy."

"Your call, my man," Mesa answered, sounding like a faithful employee.

"Have you had enough?" Barrows asked, referring to the steam.

"Yeah! I need a beer."

"Don't forget about Wilson's cronies. Make sure he keeps them in check."

"What do you have in mind?"

"The same crew. And only people you can lean on for some reason."

"Gotcha."

Shortly, Barrows and Mesa were sitting at a bar across the street from the health club.

"Johnnie Walker Black on the rocks with a twist," Barrows said to the bartender.

"And you, sir?"

"Guinness."

"You like your scotch, Park."

"Soothes the pain, Mesa. You could never know."

"Getting punched in the face by Wendell Richards was no picnic," Mesa replied, referring to a heavyweight boxer he had fought toward the end of his career.

"Here you are, gentlemen," the bartender said, presenting the drinks.

"Not many women here yet," Mesa quipped.

"Drink up," Barrows countered. "Cheers."

They each lifted their glasses in unison.

"You've got to keep on top of Wilson," Barrows reiterated.

"I know, man. We've been through this before."

Barrows gulped down the scotch and motioned to the bartender for another one, as two women in their early thirties, each wearing warm-up gear from their workout at the health club, appeared.

"Tony," a petite blonde-headed woman called to Mesa.

"Kathleen, always a pleasure," Mesa responded with surprise.

"Hi, Tony," said her companion, a short-haired woman sporting a gray jacket with "Harvard" emblazoned in maroon letters across the front.

"Who's your friend?" the blonde asked, pointing to Barrows.

"Mr. Parker Barrows," Mesa answered with flair.

"This is Kathleen and her friend in crime, Susan."

"How do you do?" Barrows extended his hand to each of them. "It's a pleasure to meet such fine young ladies."

"Where you from with that accent?" Susan asked. "Are you English or Irish?"

"Irish," Barrows quickly responded, hoping they would not

recognize that he had never incorporated the Irish dialect into his speech despite three years at University College in Dublin.

"The English are assholes," Kathleen abruptly said, her words jarring Barrows to respond condescendingly.

"My, my, such language from a lady."

"What do you do?" Kathleen asked.

"I'm in business," Barrows answered. "I work at an economic consulting firm."

"Sounds important," the blonde responded.

"He's a big shot," Mesa quipped. "If you're nice to us, he'll buy you a drink."

"How honored!" Kathleen answered in jest.

"How about a rain check? We're meeting some friends." She pointed to a group of rowdy guys at a table off in a corner of the bar.

"Enjoy," Mesa said, then turned to Barrows as the women walked away. "You look like you need a refill, my man."

"Right," answered Barrows.

"I order. You pay. We're a great combination."

Barrows, buoyed by the momentary boost from the alcohol, smiled as though he were a content man, but in reality he was merely concealing his internal turmoil.

Chapter 25

Christmas Day at the Murphy house was the most festive time of the year. Friends, relatives, and neighbors felt at ease dropping over to visit. At any one time, as many as twelve to fifteen people would crowd into the living room of the small three-bedroom house. Laughter, music, and scattered conversations distracted anyone from complaining about the lack of seats or the wait time for a drink.

Off to the side sat Dan Murphy, sipping on a bottle of beer and nibbling some peanuts. For the moment unengaged in conversation, he enjoyed playing the role of observer. Some people, such as his sister's friends, seemed so much different from his childhood image of them as they dragged along with them two or three children with or without the husbands he had never met.

"Danny. Oh, I mean Dr. Murphy," a small, dark-haired woman in her early sixties said.

"Mrs. Johnson. Merry Christmas. It's nice to see you," Dan said to his mother's friend.

"You look wonderful. Your mother's so glad you came back to Boston. I see her every Tuesday night, you know. We play bingo down at the church. It gives us old ladies a chance to go out and gossip and talk about our kids," she said in spirited animation. Hardly pausing for a breath, she continued, saying, "You know, I'm sorry to hear about your divorce."

Dan nodded politely, but Mrs. Johnson quickly put her hand over her mouth as though her comment were inappropriate.

"Oh. I'm sorry, Danny. Oh, I mean Dr. Murphy. You know your mother calls you Danny all the time. I hope you don't mind. You know I mean no disrespect."

Dan nodded in agreement.

Not having a clue about Mrs. Johnson's life other than her love of bingo, Dan tried his hand at cocktail conversation. "Are you enjoying the party?"

"Oh yes. You have such a nice family. I keep telling your mother how lucky she is. My husband, bless his soul. I lost him six years ago. Christmas was always his favorite time. He'd put up the Christmas tree and lights around the house. And he'd even help me cook. And I know you men don't like to cook."

Dan nodded, not so much in agreement, but to acknowledge that he was listening. Mrs. Johnson could talk for hours. If there were a talking marathon, something akin to a senate filibuster, Mrs. Johnson would surely qualify for the finals. She could be a relief or deadly as a passenger on a long plane ride. Dan, however, knew that her heart was warm and, more important, that she was his mother's friend. For that reason alone, he patiently followed Mrs. Johnson's conversation as it took off in all sorts of directions, until she blurted out, "Danny, you must get all kinds of medical questions at parties. Do people ask you about their gallbladder?"

"What's worse," he replied, "is when they want to discuss their hemorrhoids," he said in jest, hoping to discourage a medical discussion. *Why do people think doctors only want to talk about medicine?* he thought. *Do we appear that one-dimensional?*

"Oh really!" Mrs. Johnson exclaimed. "Well, let me ask you about my problem then?"

"Sure," Dan responded.

"You're probably going to think I'm a little nuts."

"Now, why would I think that, Mrs. Johnson?"

"Oh, I don't know."

"I think there's something strange going on at work."

"What do you mean?"

"Oh well, it's probably nothing, but do you know anything about sick building syndrome? Is that crazy? A building that's sick. I read about it in a women's magazine. The article said that people can get sick at work—not factories, but at office buildings. Can you believe it?"

Dan, with a chance to answer as Mrs. Johnson caught her breath, recalled a discussion at a conference related to indoor air pollution. "Yes, Mrs. Johnson, some buildings, usually those with inadequate ventilation, can cause people to experience all sorts of symptoms."

"Can headaches be caused by sick buildings?" she asked, captivated by Dan's interest in her concerns.

"At times."

"Dry skin?"

"Sure."

"Tiredness?"

"Yes. It sounds as though you read the article very carefully. What makes you think your work is the cause?" Dan asked.

"Oh, I'm not sure. Maybe it's just in my head. I take these medical articles on the internet too seriously. It can make you worried about everything—what you eat, where you live, where you work." Without pausing for air, she launched off in another direction. "Your mother said you were some type of occupational doctor. What does that mean? Do you need to know about sick building syndrome?"

"Yes, definitely," he answered.

"How would you know if the building was sick? Do you take its pulse or temperature?" She laughed. "Just kidding. You know, your mother says you have a great sense of humor. Doctors should have a sense of humor. How else could they put up with all those nutty patients—people like me who don't shut up?"

Dan smiled. "Mrs. Johnson, your verbosity is part of your charm."

"Verbosity? I hope you're being nice to me."

"It means you have a lot to say," Dan answered politely. "Mrs. Johnson, your work could have an effect on your health. It depends on a number of factors, but I can't do your concerns justice here. Besides, you should have some more eggnog," he said kiddingly.

"Do you think I make any sense?"

"Yes, but perhaps we should do it right and talk later."

"When?" Mrs. Johnson asked.

On recognizing her persistence, Dan replied, "Call me tomorrow. In the afternoon will be good."

—

At the same time in Minneapolis, Anna Carlson was getting into her father's new Oldsmobile for a ride to the convenience store. She and her parents, along with Roger, had finished dinner earlier after having exchanged Christmas gifts. As the house filled with neighbors from their suburban Minneapolis town, Anna felt comfortable leaving for the short trip to the store. Although she hinted to her mother that her menstrual cycle was early this month and that, as a result, she was unprepared, she actually wanted to go to a quiet place to call Dan Murphy.

As she drove by frozen lakes on which children skated and dogs chased sleds, her emotions tumbled, ranging from guilt about Roger to longing for Dan. Although Roger wanted to leave the house with her, she discouraged him and, in the process, caused him to wonder about her intentions. Her compulsion for talking with Murphy overpowered her, but not because of the study. She just wanted to hear his voice. The intense urge to call him was inscrutable and prevented her from relaxing and enjoying her family and friends.

After Anna pulled into the parking lot of the convenience store, she dialed.

"Hello. This is Dan Murphy. I'm unable to answer your call, but if you don't mind leaving a message, I'll call back as soon as I can." After a brief pause, Anna heard a beep and recognized her chance to speak.

"Dan, this is Anna. I'm sorry I missed you, but I wanted to wish you a Merry Christmas." As she returned to the car for the drive back to her parents' house, she wondered where Dan might be, then quickly returned to the moment as she reflected on Roger and the ambiguity of their relationship.

Chapter 26

Dan Murphy, refreshed from a four-day vacation over the Christmas break, returned to his responsibilities at the Occupational Health Center. He enjoyed his work and was stimulated by the challenge of a new endeavor after his abbreviated residency in orthopedic surgery. It seemed that he finally had found a specialty that he could pursue with vigor and enthusiasm.

After a holiday, the clinic was usually busy since people tended to put off their medical appointments because of numerous other demands, such as parties and other social distractions. At the health center, a part-time physician and a nurse practitioner assisted Murphy in taking care of people presenting with routine conditions. Brenda, the nurse practitioner, conducted physical examinations and initial evaluations of people who had both occupational and nonoccupational ailments. Since many workers who were treated at the Occupational Health Center lacked personal physicians, some returned for treatment of other illnesses. People with colds, sore throats, and urinary tract infections were first evaluated by Brenda, who reviewed the medical history, performed an examination, and ordered blood tests and other necessary studies. At that time, she would recommend the initial treatment. Her familiarity with Dan Murphy's protocols, coupled with his supervision, enabled her to work well with him as a team. After their having spent almost a year together, a synergy had developed to the point that Dan listened to her requests for advice with rapt attention. She sought his counsel when stumped, which wasn't often.

Finishing a call to a pharmacist, Murphy heard Brenda at his door.

"I know you're really busy, Dr. Murphy, but could you take a look at a patient for me?"

"What's the trouble?"

Unless it was an emergency, Murphy preferred to have Brenda describe the case up to the same standards expected of medical students. Dan felt that the academic rigor improved the quality of their patient care; it also motivated Brenda to improve her clinical skills.

"I think this man has hepatitis, but I don't know why. All his serologies are negative."

"Why don't you tell me about it?"

"He came in about a week ago," Brenda said, thumbing through the patient's record. "He's a fifty-seven-year-old man who wasn't feeling well for a few days. No appetite, lots of headaches, general discomfort." Brenda continued in her customary manner as Dan took notes. "On exam, I found a tender liver. It wasn't enlarged, but he was very sore in the right upper quadrant."

"Any other physical findings?" Dan asked.

"Not really. His eyes seemed a bit yellow, but nothing dramatic. No adenopathy or lung or heart findings either. His temperature was only slightly elevated."

"What did the lab tests show?" Dan asked.

"Bilirubin in the urine and elevated liver enzymes."

"Sounds like hepatitis."

"I agree, but I'm not sure why. I saw him before Christmas to review his serologies," she said, referring to tests that determine the type of virus responsible for hepatitis.

"You know that hepatitis, strictly speaking, is just an inflammation of the liver that can arise from many different causes," Dan advised her.

"I know, but he's negative for hepatitis A, B, and C—the three major types that cause liver infection," Brenda answered.

"Any alcohol history?"

"No, he doesn't drink."

"How about medications? Is he taking anything?"

"No. Not even aspirin."

"How about Tylenol?" Dan asked, referring to the pain reliever that has been associated with liver disease.

"No."

"Does he have any other illnesses, such as psoriasis or rheumatoid arthritis?"

"I don't think so."

"Certain medical disorders," he said, trying not to be pedagogic, but wanting to share information with an eager student, "are linked with hepatitis."

"I know. I thought about ordering a mono spot test."

"For infectious mononucleosis?"

"Yes."

"Were the lymphocytes elevated?"

"No."

"It won't hurt to run the mono spot, but I wouldn't be optimistic."

Brenda looked at him for advice.

"How about his work?" Dan continued, saying, "What does he do?"

"He retired from the fire department last year and now works as a custodian and maintenance man—sort of a handyman."

"Did he retire from the fire department on disability?"

"No. He's pretty healthy. Runs about ten miles a week. Takes his grandchildren to the park, downtown, and so forth."

"Why don't we see him?" Dan asked as he rose from his chair.

As he entered the examining room, Dan was introduced to Mr. Shaw by Brenda.

"Hi, Mr. Shaw. I understand you haven't been feeling too well lately."

"No, Doc. Your nurse tells me I have hepatitis, but I don't know where I got it. No one in my family has it, and I don't know anybody with it. What do you think?"

"I'm not sure, but I'd like to ask you a few questions. You don't drink, I understand."

"Don't touch the stuff," Mr. Shaw said emphatically. "I've seen too many guys screw up their lives, Doc. I don't need that."

"What do you do at work?"

"I'm a custodian—jack-of-all-trades type. I clean the place, repair equipment, run deliveries."

"Where do you work?"

"At a plating shop in South Boston, by the power plant."

This is a bit too coincidental, Dan thought, recalling the conversation he had had with his mother's bingo friend. "How long have you worked there?"

"About a year. Since I retired from the fire department."

"Is there anything new about your work? Do you use any different chemicals or do anything you haven't done before?"

"Nah. Not really. Just the same old routine."

"Tell me about your routine. What's a typical day like?"

"I go in, have my coffee. Only one cup, Doc; it gets me going." Dan smiled in acknowledgment. "I wouldn't start a day without it."

Dan responded, "One of the lasting benefits of my internship was learning how to both drink and appreciate all types of coffee."

"So, after my coffee, I usually empty the trash, then I accept deliveries or repair equipment—whatever needs to be done."

"Do you work with any chemicals?"

"Not unless you call Windex and bleach chemicals."

"Actually, they are," Dan said, a bit tongue-in-cheek.

"Once in a while, I change the filters on the HVAC system."

As Dan paused, he observed Shaw's physical appearance. Despite his fifty-seven years, his skin resembled that of a man much younger. Not carrying much weight, Shaw appeared to be in excellent physical condition.

"I'm not sure why you contracted hepatitis, Mr. Shaw, but we'll run a few more tests." Murphy turned in Brenda's direction. "We ought to repeat the hepatitis panel, and let's get a sed rate, an arthritic profile, and the mono spot test."

"Good idea," Brenda said, diligently making notes of Murphy's recommendations.

To Mr. Shaw, Dan said, "I'd like you to review all the materials you work with so we can go over it next time."

"Everything, Doc? I work at a plating shop. They use all kinds of acids and plating solutions and degreasers."

"Yes, it may be important."

"OK."

"Now, I'd like to examine you, Mr. Shaw," Dan said. "Would you lie on your back, please?"

Murphy approached the side of the examining table, then looked into his patient's eyes to observe the yellow discoloration of his conjunctiva, the outer layer of the eye that is normally white. He listened to Shaw's heartbeat and palpated his abdomen, especially the area beneath his lower-right ribs. Shaw jumped back reflexively in pain.

"Sorry, Doc, you caught me by surprise."

"I didn't mean to startle you," Murphy said. He turned to Brenda. "We should see him in a couple of days to go over the lab results." Then to Shaw, he said, "It would be helpful if you could get the safety data sheets for the chemicals at your work. Do you know what I mean?"

"I think so. We had some hazmat training in the fire department, Doc. Part of emergency response," he said, referring to the education firefighters receive in preparing to fight fires and attend to other emergency situations involving hazardous materials, hence the term *hazmat*.

"I'm not sure what caused your hepatitis, but it seems to be stabilizing," Murphy said. "The liver enzymes have started to drop, so you should continue to improve."

"Thanks, Doc. I'll get that stuff for you."

"That would help. See you soon," Murphy said. He extended his hand to Shaw, who shook it, then turned to leave the room.

As he entered the hallway, Murphy's receptionist called to him: "Dr. Murphy, you have a call on line one."

"Thank you," he answered, walking back to his office.

"Hello. This is Dr. Murphy."

"Danny. Oh, I mean Dr. Murphy. This is your mother's bingo friend. Remember me from your Christmas party yesterday?"

"Of course I do. How are you today?"

"Well for now, but I'm worried about going back to work tomorrow."

"Why?"

"Remember I told you about the sick building?"

"Yes."

"I think my symptoms are from the building where I work. I know people think I'm flighty, but I only get headaches at work—and I never used to get headaches."

"Where do you work?"

"Boston Plating," she answered.

Dan paused in reflection as he recalled his other patient who worked at the plating shop. "What kind of work does the company do?"

"It's a plating shop." It seemed coincidental that the patient whom he had just evaluated, Mr. Shaw, worked at the same place.

"I'd like to see you," she continued. "Can I make an appointment? I have my own insurance, you know."

Murphy readily agreed. "Of course. Let me put you through to the receptionist."

Chapter 27

Jake Wilson, hardly a fool in recognizing a legitimate threat, especially from the ex–heavyweight boxer Tony Mesa, who worked for Barrows, wasted no time in getting down to business in a small community in upstate New York about a four-hour drive north of Manhattan. His travels brought him, along with the now ever-present Tony Mesa, to a run-down hotel on the outskirts of town. There, they shared an adjoining set of rooms and mapped out the plans aided by Parker Barrows's information.

Barrows, however, remained anonymous to Wilson. According to Mesa, it was a wealthy benefactor supporting their efforts, but because of the sensitive nature of their work, he chose to stay out of view.

Spartan in amenities, the most deluxe of which was cable television, the motel offered a spot to be unnoticed. Its worn-out, tired atmosphere, however, motivated Wilson and Mesa to spend their evenings in local bars and at other nightspots. Tonight, they were watching the Buffalo Bills play the Dallas Cowboys.

Wilson stood behind the blue line and aimed a dart at the board. With the precision of a painter's stroke, he threw the dart toward the target.

"Not bad for a clown," Mesa offered, who followed his quip with uproarious laughter, which encouraged others to join him.

"How about I aim at your nose next time?" Wilson rebutted.

Before Mesa could respond, he was greeted by a tall, lean man with thinning blond hair who appeared to be in his midfifties.

"Hey, dude. What's up?"

"Hey, Struck. How the hell are you? Ready for a decent game tonight? My buddy Wilson here couldn't hit a chick's ass if she sat on him."

Struck laughed.

Wilson had long since learned to tolerate Mesa's humor at his own expense. The benefits of working with him and the excellent pay in cash well outweighed the annoyance of being the brunt of Tony Mesa's corny jokes.

"Here," Wilson said, handing over three darts to Al Struck. "See what you can do."

"How much money you got to lose?" asked Mesa, whose blunder Struck seemed to appreciate.

"Twenty bucks."

"Easy pickin's."

"How about some beers, you guys?" Wilson asked, turning to walk to the bar.

Mesa answered, "Yeah. Get us a couple."

Wilson ambled through the dimly lit bar, which was crowded with casually dressed men and women in their twenties and thirties. Behind a dance floor, a country-and-western band was preparing to play at halftime of the football game. Wilson fondly noted the women who appeared available, but turned his attention to the mission at hand, namely, manipulating Al Struck into agreeing to participate in their ploy at the local production plant. As he waited his turn at the bar, Wilson gazed about at the crowd. At the same time, Mesa seemed in control of the dart game. "You'd better get your wallet ready," Mesa said as he aimed at the dartboard.

"I can't believe it," Struck said. "You beat me again."

"Ready to go again, pardner?"

"It might be easier to pick my pocket."

"I could do that too, but I like to see you sweat."

Wilson returned with the beers.

"He took me again," Struck said to Wilson. Struck's attitude seemed nonchalant, as though he were flattered simply to be playing with Mesa, the former professional heavyweight boxer. For the past few days, Wilson and Mesa had been visiting the Blue Marlin, where Struck liked to hang out. Information that Parker Barrows had given Mesa helped them track down the plant worker, who would soon learn that he was about to be laid off.

"Wanna play again?" Mesa asked Struck as he good-naturedly punched him on the shoulder. "I could use some more of your money."

"I think I'll pass."

"How about some poker?" Wilson suggested. "I'm tired of this stuff. Let's play a man's game. Besides, I want to do some serious drinking. After all, Mr. Struck here doesn't need to get up in the morning and probably won't have to at all pretty soon."

Struck looked back at Wilson, then to Mesa.

"Show him what you got," Mesa said to Wilson.

"What are ya talking about?" Struck asked, his eyes wide with apprehension.

"Everything's back at the room."

"Let's go back, then," Mesa said. "We can drink, play poker, and tell Al about all the wonderful opportunities he'll have to work with us."

"What are you talking about?" Struck asked, his hands shaking noticeably.

"Life's full of surprises, Al," Wilson said. "Just be patient."

As Wilson drove the Ford rental car back to the hotel, Mesa said to Struck, "Jake tells me your ex-wife's been pretty tough on you lately. What's she want, more money?"

"Yeah! She wants more money. Don't they all?"

"No. Some just want me," Mesa quipped, erupting into his signature laugh.

"She's got your kids too, doesn't she?" Wilson offered.

"Yeah," Struck answered, still puzzled as to how Wilson and Mesa knew so much about his personal life. Little did he know that Parker Barrows's intelligence contact in Washington, DC, had obtained information from the human resources department of the military contractor for whom Struck worked.

"Ready for some heavy-duty poker?" Mesa asked.

"Yeah. I need to make some money from you guys," Struck answered.

"For the wife?"

"Fuck the wife. For me."

"That's the spirit," Mesa said. "A man serious about his poker. You're a good poker pal, Al. You know how to drink, lose money, and bitch about your wife."

Soon, Wilson pulled the rental car into the parking lot of the aging one-floor hotel. Moments later, they were all sitting in a room that had been transformed into a living room by the addition of furniture that would embarrass undergraduate students.

"So, what were you talking about?" Struck asked Mesa as Wilson opened the bottles of beer.

"You're getting laid off."

"What?"

"Laid off. You're gonna be out of a job."

"How do you know?"

"Jake, my buddy, give our friend the list."

"It's a memo."

Wilson handed a sheet of paper to Struck, who reviewed it hurriedly.

"How'd you get this?"

"What's it matter, Al? Be pleased to have friends like us. We're here to help you."

"Right. You gonna trust the plant? They don't care about you," Wilson added.

"Work with us, Al. We can help you," Mesa said.

"What are you talking about?" Struck asked.

"Poker, Al. Let's play poker," chimed Wilson, pleased at seeing Al Struck come unglued.

"Drink up, Al," Mesa said. "It'll ease the pain."

"We need a little atmosphere here. Let's get to business—poker, that is," Mesa suggested. "Deal the cards, Jake."

As Wilson shuffled the deck, Struck turned to Mesa. "Is this legitimate, man? Am I really getting laid off?"

"Al, you read the memo. I'd be taking care of myself," said Wilson. "Not too many good jobs around here."

"There's a man who knows the right way to handle stress," Mesa said. "Drink up, Al!"

They each reviewed the poker hand Wilson had dealt, and bet accordingly. After each drew additional cards, Wilson called the action. His four kings won the pot.

Throughout the next hour, they drank beer and played poker. Before long, Al Struck was feeling the effects of the alcohol. Almost magically, his demeanor changed from nervousness and insecurity to joviality and confidence.

"So, what kind of work do you do, Tony?" Struck asked Mesa, looking over his own hand of cards.

"We're contractors."

"What are you doing here?"

"We've got a big project."

Struck looked at Mesa for more information.

"We're gonna build a shopping area on the far side of the plant near where you work," Wilson responded with a straight face, giving Struck no indication that he and Mesa had absolutely no intentions of doing anything but taking advantage of Struck and the plant.

"The plant's gonna shut down eventually, Al. You're lucky we're clueing you in early, before you get your sorry ass laid off," Mesa added.

"We're gonna give you a chance to work with us. Clean, easy work. The pay's great—in cash. You won't even have to tell your wife," Wilson said.

"What do you want me to do?"

"Later, Al," Mesa answered.

"First, you need to get your buddy Healy to come along. Just the four of us."

"Healy? You mean Drew Healy—in security?"

"You got it."

Chapter 28

The plane landed uneventfully at Boston's Logan Airport. Anna withdrew her hand luggage from the overhead rack and walked through the terminal to a bus that took her to the Blue Line. En route to her apartment in Brookline, her thoughts bounced in different directions. *Will Roger think that I left Minneapolis too early? Will Dan think I'm too eager? Will Becker approve my project?*

Anna's feelings about Roger troubled her because she found herself drifting away from him. Her visit to Minneapolis had been both unexciting and predictable, a metaphor for her relationship with him. While Anna was at home, her mother used the most subtle methods to encourage her to marry the history teacher turned bookseller. "It's time to have children," her father had advised.

Now, excited about the career opportunities when finished with her public health degree, Anna anticipated newspaper columns, feature articles, and even books. Perhaps a syndicated health column or a feature series in a magazine was on the horizon. At the same time, the proverbial biological urge to have children surfaced periodically, especially after she visited an old college roommate and her three-year-old son. The charm, cleverness, and warmth of the little boy struck a part of Anna's heart that had lain dormant. *Not now, but definitely later,* she told herself.

As the trolley jolted to an abrupt stop, she looked out the window to the snow that had accumulated since she left four days ago. As they passed a medical office building, she reflected on Dan Murphy. How anxious she was to see him, although she was cautious not to appear too available. *Is Dan simply a decoy to divert my attention from Roger?* As her mind raced, she decided to let life take its course.

Soon, she arrived at her three-room apartment. On opening the door, she heard her black and white cat scamper across the kitchen floor. Anna enjoyed the affectionate but fiercely independent personality of her cat. Now, Schubert wanted to be fed since Anna's neighbor had left him hungry while she was away.

Anna's phone rang. "Hello, Anna. This is Marci from Dr. Harrington's office. All of the letters have been sent out. We can schedule the interviews. Hope you had a nice Christmas at home. Bye."

Anna, relieved to have the support of Dr. Harrington's staff, planned to complete the interviews and compile the results prior to Becker's January 10 deadline. With limited time, her determination to gain her adviser's respect by delivering a quality project gave her the energy for the work ahead.

With the help of Dr. Harrington's secretary, all the patients whom Anna was to interview were sent a letter encouraging their participation in the study. The invitation described the investigation, ensured confidentiality, and promised a report for all who participated. Marci also called the patients to inform them of the study, to introduce Anna, and to make appointments for the interviews. Anna estimated each review would take about sixty minutes. Allowing for travel between the houses, she hoped to visit about four people per day.

Anna entered the main hospital lobby, then rode the elevator to Harrington's floor. As usual, Marci greeted her with a receptive smile. "Anna, nice to see you."

Anna, a bit embarrassed about Marci's overly gracious greeting, responded similarly. "Hi, Marci. How are you?"

"Fine. Although I'd rather be off this week," she said with a mischievous smile. Born in Iowa, Marci's midwestern roots were visible when she acknowledged acquaintances and business relations as though they were her long-lost friends. Although some New Englanders considered such behavior naive and disingenuous, Anna appreciated the warmth that Marci's attitude emitted. Marci's disposition created an atmosphere that made work at Harrington's office considerably more pleasant than the tension-laden suite of David Becker.

"Dr. Harrington left you a package. Let me get it for you," Marci said, rising from a chair. "He said to call him if you have any questions."

"Thank you," Anna replied, then opened a large manila envelope that contained Harrington's critique of the study, with suggestions for the control group. Typical of Harrington's fastidiousness, his comments were clearly typed in an organized report. *What a contrast to the hostile environment at David Becker's office,* Anna thought. *How could two similarly distinguished physicians have such distinctly different personalities and work styles?* With Becker, Anna felt on edge, as though at any moment a trapdoor would open into his wrath and displeasure. Harrington, on the other hand, seemed to value her role and respect her abilities. Anna sensed that Becker wanted her to fail or, at best, was trying to motivate her by causing her to fear his disapproval.

"Why don't you use this office?" Marci suggested, pointing to a room adjacent to the waiting area.

"Thank you, Marci. You've been very kind."

"Oh, you're welcome. Enjoy. I have to get some of Dr. Harrington's dictations done, but let me know if you need any help. And don't forget, let me know if those times are good for your schedule."

"Times?" Anna asked.

"For the interviews."

Anna looked through the file that Marci had given her.

"Oh. Did I forget? Let me get it for you." Marci returned to her workstation and tapped a few keys on the computer. Moments later, a two-page document emerged from the printer. "I called the patients and scheduled interviews for you. There are a few I haven't reached yet, but I'll get them tomorrow. Oh, I meant to remind you. Dr.

Harrington selected the controls for you. I made appointments for some of them too."

"Marci, that's very nice of you. Thank you," Anna said. She looked over the schedule. "I need to interview twenty-four people—eight cases and sixteen controls. With any luck, I might get done in a couple of weeks."

"I'm sure you'll do well," Marci said encouragingly.

"Analyzing the information's a different matter though."

"Don't worry. You can use the same program Dr. Harrington used for his leukemia study."

The phone rang in the background.

"Hematology. This is Marci. May I help you?" Marci's voice projected warmth and an ease with people. *How frequently such marvelous qualities are overlooked in establishing an ambience in a work group,* Anna thought.

"Hello, Dr. Harrington."

Anna heard Marci pause, obviously listening to her boss. "Only one message. From the admissions office, but they'll call back. Anna Carlson is here.

"Would you like to speak with her?" Harrington's secretary asked.

"Just a minute." Marci depressed the hold button on the telephone, then called Anna. "He'd like to speak with you," she said in a tone suggesting it was a privilege to speak to the chair of hematology.

"Hello, Dr. Harrington. Thank you for your help with the study."

"Oh, it's a pleasure. I like to encourage young investigators. Plus, more attention should be given to a patient's environment as a risk factor for illness."

"I found your suggestion of the orthopedic patients as controls interesting," Anna responded.

"Do you know why I selected people admitted to the hospital for orthopedic surgery?" Harrington asked.

Anna paused as though being quizzed by a pedagogical intern, but she knew Harrington was too stylish to resort to condescension in order to educate.

"Well, they might be more closely related to the age of the cases," Anna answered.

"Right. Isn't the average age of our cases about thirty-four?"

"Yes," Anna answered, impressed with Harrington's attention to detail.

"As you might imagine," Dr. Harrington said, "the average age of other hospitalized patients would be higher than thirty-four—probably in the late fifties. As a result, patients admitted for elective orthopedic surgery—at least for knee and shoulder repair—are more likely to be similar in age to the aplastic anemia cases."

"Right. The best controls should be very similar to the cases."

"If, as you hypothesize," Harrington said, "an environmental or occupational factor is causing the aplastic anemia, you have to eliminate alternative explanations as much as possible," the physician professor said, enjoying his role as teacher. Despite a thirty-year career in academic medicine, Harrington maintained an enthusiasm for mentoring bright, motivated students.

"How did you decide on the number of controls to use for each patient?" Anna asked.

"Good question. Actually, the more, the better—to a point. Some feel that four controls are ideal for each case, especially when studying rare diseases. But I don't think we need to do that here. This is a survey study."

"Sounds good to me. I'm ready to go," Anna said, trying to contain her cheerleader-like enthusiasm.

"I'm sure you'll do fine," Harrington answered with encouragement. "Let me know how you do. And don't be shy about asking Marci for help."

"Thank you."

"Good luck. Put me back to Marci, would you please?"

Anna depressed the hold button, then called over to the secretary. As Marci picked up the receiver, Anna sat at the desk and reviewed the questionnaire about each person's health, job, and home environment. The answers, coded by numbers to facilitate computer entry, would be used in the preliminary analysis.

Anna reviewed the questions about people's work history, including their job titles and responsibilities, especially for exposures to potentially hazardous materials. She wanted to account for latency, the period of time between exposure to a hazard and time of diagnosis. It seemed complete, but she sensed that Becker would find fault somewhere.

Anna, relieved to see a note with Harrington's approval of the questionnaire, thought, *I'll drop a copy of this note and the questionnaire at Becker's office, then start.* Her renewed confidence after the conversation with Harrington motivated her to plow through the interviews. The methods used by Harrington and Becker to stimulate her performance seemed peculiar to Anna, who sought to gain Harrington's respect, while avoiding the sting of Becker's sarcasm.

Anna reviewed the list of interviews, the first of which was scheduled for nine o'clock tomorrow.

Chapter 29

Phil Shaw walked through the plating shop and watched his fellow workers with an eye toward how they were using the chemicals needed for plating, a process whereby a metal in solution, such as nickel or chromium, is electroplated onto another material. In a process that has been used in industry since the early 1800s, an electric current is passed through the metal in solution, causing it to be deposited onto some other material. Costume jewelry is made this way, usually with a coating of nickel. Plating, however, requires hazardous materials such as cyanides, acid mists, and solvents.

Shaw was worried. Although his hepatitis was improving, no explanation had been offered for why it had occurred. Scheduled to see Dr. Dan Murphy later that day, he hoped to hear good news about the tests for his liver ailment. Suspecting that his work may have been responsible, he was tentative about returning to his job. He also recalled a friend who had died from cirrhosis of the liver but who did not drink alcohol. A few weeks before his friend's death, his work with solvents was implicated as the cause. Shaw heard that his widow had filed a lawsuit, but the insurance company was still contesting the claim.

Observing the plating operation, Shaw saw workers using hand cranks to lower small metal parts into a solvent bath that the workers called a degreaser. He stepped over boarded aisles designed to reduce slips and falls on the inevitable wet floors in plating shops. From the loading dock, he looked out across the work area in which about twenty people were scattered about performing various functions such as rolling drums of material, driving forklifts, or emptying trash.

Shaw walked to a chemical storage area where dangerous materials were separated from other supplies and thought about the training he had received in hazardous materials as a firefighter. He distinctly remembered that the combination of acids and cyanides, essential ingredients in most plating shops, can form hydrogen cyanide gas, the same deadly compound used by the Nazis to kill people in concentration camps during World War II.

Shaw paused before entering the administrative office of the plating shop. At Dan Murphy's suggestion, he planned to request information about the chemicals used by the plant without letting the manager know about it. The plant manager, a hard-nosed guy with more than thirty years' experience in the plating industry, would not look on Shaw's actions lightly. Hired by the private owners of Boston Plating, he thought people had "chemical phobia," the term he liked to use. Despite the manager's reaction to Shaw, he had to release the safety data sheets for the chemicals as required by the Occupational Safety and Health Administration (OSHA).

Entering the office, Shaw deferentially greeted an older woman responsible for numerous clerical functions, including payroll and health insurance claims.

"How can I help you, Mr. Shaw?" Mrs. Johnson, the receptionist, asked.

"Do you remember that hazmat training we had a few months ago and that lecture on the chemicals?"

"Yes. I think so. What about it?"

"Didn't that guy talk about chemical lists that have health information on them?"

"Do you mean the safety data sheets?"

"Yeah, that's it! Do you have it?"

"It?" she asked incredulously. "It's a whole binder full of boring information about chemicals."

"Can I see it?"

"It's right over there." She pointed to a bookshelf in the back of the room. "Take a look at it."

Shaw opened the three-ring binder to find four-to-eight-page descriptions of the chemicals used in the plating shop. Each form had similar information, including how the chemical could affect a person's health.

"Can you email me copies?"

"Why?"

"For my doctor," he answered, annoyed that she would probe into his motives.

Mrs. Johnson paused before returning to her work, recalling her conversation with Dan Murphy on Christmas Day about sick building syndrome. Was it a coincidence that Shaw was concerned about his own health and how it could be affected by work?

"Thank you, Mrs. Johnson. Please don't let him know I took these," he said, referring to the manager.

"Not at all," Mrs. Johnson responded. Shaw knew that she could be trusted.

On reaching the Occupational Health Center later that same day, Shaw was greeted by a receptionist who handed him a questionnaire that addressed his work duties, medical history, and home environment. He sat and answered the questions about the plating firm, his job, and the training he had received.

"Mr. Shaw," the receptionist called out. After rising from his chair, Shaw was directed to an examining room and given a hospital gown.

"You should put this on and hang your coat over there." She pointed to the back of the door. Moments later, Dr. Dan Murphy appeared.

"Hello, Mr. Shaw. How are you feeling?"

"Better, Doc. Much better."

"I see you brought the safety data sheets. Let me take a look at them." As Murphy thumbed through the stack of papers, he said aloud, "A number of acids."

Shaw watched Murphy anxiously.

Murphy noted, "Cyanide solutions," then continued reviewing the materials. "Any solvents?"

"Sure, Doc. We have a degreasing machine."

"Oh. I see," Murphy said. "It's trichloroethane. Do you use that very much?"

"I don't think so. Three guys do the degreasing work."

"Did you fill out your questionnaire?" Dr. Murphy asked.

"Yeah. Here it is, Doc."

Shaw watched Murphy reviewing his work history. "I was in the air force for four years," Shaw said. "I then spent thirty-four years as a firefighter for the City of Boston before I retired and took on this work at the plating shop."

"What kind of work do you do?" Murphy asked.

"Shipping and receiving, trash disposal, minor errands, maintenance."

"Have you done anything different lately?" Murphy asked.

"Like what?"

"Well, jobs you might not otherwise do. Any maintenance work, for example. Any machinery need to be repaired?"

"Come to think of it, I did some work on the ventilation system a couple of weeks ago."

"What type of work?"

"One of the fans broke and we weren't getting enough air circulating."

"How did you know about it?"

"The fan is right above the main office, and it made a huge banging noise that upset one of the secretaries. It ended up being a broken fan belt."

"Did you spend a lot of time repairing it?"

"A couple of hours. It wasn't the easiest spot to get to."

"Was it dirty?"

"Awful. I convinced the plant manager to have the ducts cleaned. I took all the filters out. They were filthy."

Murphy asked Shaw, "Do you still have the filters?"

"No. All that stuff's been thrown out."

Murphy said to Shaw, "The lab results look good. The liver enzymes are improving."

"How about those other liver tests, Doc? What did they show?"

"The tests for hepatitis A, B, and C are all negative. Everything else is negative."

"Doc, if I got this from work and I go back, will I get it again?"

"I don't know. On the lists you gave me, the only chemical that can cause hepatitis is the degreasing solvent trichloroethane. And you told me you don't work with the degreaser."

"Right."

"Do you know what could have been in the ventilation system?"

"No way. That HVAC system takes care of the whole plant. It could be anything. Doc, what do you think caused my liver problem?"

"I don't know. It's not any of the common reasons, like infections, alcohol, or medications. Your work is a plausible explanation, but nothing is obvious right now. Perhaps I could visit the shop?"

"No. Please don't. That'll create a problem. Don't do anything that would hurt the plant. They're good people. They put a lot of people to work, especially the Irish who can't get jobs—if you know what I mean!"

Murphy looked puzzled.

"The illegals. Our Irish brothers without green cards," Shaw replied.

Chapter 30

Parker Barrows hobbled on his left leg out of the shower and readied himself for another visit to the psychiatrist on the advice of a colleague who had recommended Dr. Steven Reed, a British citizen himself now living in Boston. The nightmares, depression, and chronic headaches had eroded many features of Barrows's personality and were easily recognized by an old friend whom he had not seen since before the accident. Sullen, angry, and prone to unpredictable and self-destructive behavior, Barrows finally admitted that he needed help. Barrows, finding it difficult to vent his fears, approached the psychiatrist with considerable caution and reserve in the first few encounters.

As it became clear to Barrows that a mental ailment was likely the cause of his symptoms, he realized it would be necessary to go into more detail about the London explosion and his life before Boston. Discussion about the circumstances that led to his current state, however, would surely bring his long-term plans into conflict with his psychiatrist's goals for improvement. For it was Barrows's own long-term solution that promised relief. If he could effect his own resolution, he knew he'd succeed. *But why should I tell the shrink about it?* he thought. *Patient confidentiality is fictitious. You can never trust doctors to keep anything secret.*

After a short drive, Barrows arrived at the Harvard medical area on Longwood Avenue, where Dr. Reed kept an office. In the midst of the daily frenetic activity associated with Boston's famous collection of teaching hospitals, Barrows made his way into a modern office building in which his psychiatrist evaluated patients.

Barrows, initially surprised by the elegance of Reed's office, appreciated the photography that adorned the walls. Pictures of people from around the world, attractively framed to enhance their appeal, invited conversation. For Reed, the photos helped people feel at ease and shortened the sense of distance many experienced when dealing with a psychiatrist. The pictures told Dr. Reed's patients that he was a regular guy to whom it was safe to divulge those inner secrets whose captivity often led to all sorts of problems.

Reed's secretary gracefully welcomed Barrows to his appointment. "So nice to see you, Mr. Barrows. Dr. Reed will be with you shortly. How've you been?"

"Oh, taking it day by day," Barrows answered, still unaccustomed to the ingenuousness of many Americans.

"Can I get you some coffee?" she asked.

"Yes, as a matter of fact. That would be nice."

Just as she rose from her chair, Dr. Reed emerged from his office. Dressed in a white shirt, blue slacks, and a red bow tie, the stout, gray-headed man in his early fifties extended his hand.

"Mr. Barrows, please come in."

Barrows entered Dr. Reed's inner sanctum, outfitted with memorabilia from his travels around the world. Chinese wall hangings accompanied African wood carvings and Irish crystal. Tastefully decorated with comfortable antique furniture, the office created an ambiance that encouraged relaxation. People felt at ease on entering Reed's office. The physical surroundings, coupled with the warmth of the renowned psychiatrist, aided many a person in coming to grips with a serious mental disorder.

As Barrows drew up a chair, Dr. Reed reviewed his notes on the computer from the previous visits.

"Tell me, Parker," he began, "how you've been. Is anything new?"

"No. Everything's the same."

"Are you still having the nightmares?"

"Yes."

"How often?"

"It depends."

"On what?"

"I haven't quite figured that out."

"It may help us understand if you try to remember the events of the days when the more vivid nightmares occur."

"Such as?"

"Anything remind you of the accident?"

"Everything reminds me. I'm a cripple, for God's sake. How could I ever forget! I'm with this problem all day, Doctor, every day. It never goes away."

"Parker, the last time you were here, we talked about nightmares, your leg, the rehabilitation, and your frustrations, but we haven't discussed what you were doing when it happened."

"I told you. I was in a restaurant with my wife."

"Your wife? You haven't mentioned her before."

The psychiatrist looked at Barrows, who rose from his chair and walked over to a photograph of a Maasai warrior with "Kenya" labeled on the white matting surrounding the print.

"She died."

"When you lost your leg?"

"Yes."

"Why didn't you mention this before?"

Barrows continued to observe Dr. Reed's photos in silence. "I don't know."

"Did you love her?"

"Of course I did."

"Did you have any children?"

"No."

"Were you married long?"

"A year. She died on our anniversary. My first and probably only wife," he said with palpable sadness. "I should have known!"

"Known what?" Dr. Reed asked.

"That the restaurant was a security risk."

"What do you mean?"

"A risk from terrorism," Barrows replied.

"Can you elaborate, Parker?"

"It's complicated to explain."

"Why don't you try?"

During Barrows's first few visits with Dr. Reed, they focused on the symptoms that troubled Barrow, primarily the nightmares and the headaches. Eventually, they discussed how Barrows had lost his leg in an accident. Unable to describe the events surrounding the explosion without evoking terrifying reactions, Parker elaborated on the surgery, the rehabilitation procedures, and his adaptation to a different life.

Throughout the remainder of the session, Barrows talked about his wife and his work at the time. Reed then leaped back to an earlier part of the session when they discussed the accident.

"Why do you think you should have known about a terrorist risk?"

"I was too casual. I should have recognized some key features about the restaurant. We had advance warning that it was a favorite of the chief negotiator."

"Negotiator?" Dr. Reed asked in puzzlement. "Of what?"

"Of the Good Friday peace process."

"What?" the psychiatrist asked incredulously.

"The peace process in Northern Ireland."

"What did that have to do with you?"

"I was director of security for London."

"Is that where it happened?"

"Yes."

"Why did you come to Boston?"

"It's a long story. Do you really want to hear it?"

"Of course."

"How about if you simply tell me how to get rid of the nightmares? I can't get a decent night's sleep. Should I take Zoloft—or something else?"

"Why don't you let me complete the evaluation?"

"What more do you need to know? There's nothing wrong with me medically according to my internist."

"I don't want to rush. Your situation is complicated."

"What do you think? On my last visit you talked about some type of stress disorder."

"Posttraumatic stress disorder. You seem to have many features of PTSD. For example, you've obviously experienced an abrupt change in your life as a result of the explosion. After all, you've lost your wife, your leg, and your job, but you haven't told me much about it. Or why you came to Boston. Or what happened. Or who was responsible. Or whether the perpetrators were caught."

"I appreciate your interest, Dr. Reed, but what do those details have to do with me improving my life or at least tolerating life better?"

"It's background. It helps me understand more about you."

"What do you think my problem is?" Barrows asked.

"As I said, you have many features of PTSD."

"I'm listening."

"Bear in mind, I may need to alter my opinion, but we should consider PTSD a good working diagnosis so we can move forward. Let's review the first few sessions," the psychiatrist suggested. "You told me about this profound change in your life and personality from the accident and your tendency to drink too much. Tonight, you talked about surviving your wife almost as though you were responsible for her death. The sense you have of your body being permanently disfigured is another feature associated with PTSD."

"Are you sure of the diagnosis?"

"Not entirely, but as I summarize my impressions with you, the diagnosis seems more plausible."

"Why?"

"A number of criteria must be met for a reliable PTSD diagnosis. For example, one needs to be exposed to a life-threatening event. That's obvious in your case. And the response to the event," Reed said, reading from the text, "involves horror and fear of helplessness.

Now, I've only seen you in a limited number of sessions, but each time you avoided any discussion about the accident. I know it was an explosion, something about terrorism, but beyond that, you've avoided talking about it. I'm not trying to be judgmental, but your response is consistent with the diagnosis."

"Anything else?" Barrows asked as though he were losing interest. As his leg began to bother him, he imagined the pleasure of the double shot of scotch to which he would treat himself after he left Reed's office.

"There are a number of other criteria. Often, people repeatedly reexperience the event, as well as avoid anything associated with the trauma." Reed looked at Barrows for a response, then continued. "You understand, Parker, that you have yet to become comfortable with telling me about the explosion. I do not want to cause you pain, but your avoidance pattern is also consistent with the diagnosis."

Barrows nodded in agreement.

Reed continued. "And clearly, you experience significant distress and panic in certain settings." Reed paused as Barrows thought about what had happened when he drove by the Irish Catholic church during the fundraiser, when he became virtually paralyzed with fear.

"So, what does all this mean?"

"It's too soon to say. I need to know more about you."

"Like what?"

"Why did you come to Boston?"

"Because I wanted to find the bastard who caused this," Barrows said, pointing to his amputated leg. The anger in Barrows's voice alarmed Dr. Reed, who had grown accustomed to a subtle, sullen, and withdrawn middle-aged man.

"Have you been able to find him?"

"I think so."

The buzzer on Reed's telephone jarred them out of the conversation.

"Excuse me," Reed said, rising to pick up the telephone receiver. "I'm sorry, Mr. Barrows, but we've gone beyond the time for today's session."

Chapter 31

Sitting at her computer, Anna entered the results of her interviews, but the monotony of the task necessitated a break, during which she reviewed her mail. A memo from Marci informed her of more scheduled interviews. In a few days, the fieldwork would be finished and the data ready for analysis. After shutting down the computer, she dialed the phone.

"Occupational Health Center, may I help you?"

"I'd like to speak with Dr. Murphy, please."

"Just a moment."

Seconds later, Anna was greeted by the man who attracted her more and more.

"This is Dr. Murphy."

"Hello, Dan. This is Anna."

"Anna! How nice to hear from you. Are you back already?"

"Are you busy?" she asked, hoping for a negative reply.

"No. Just finishing up. Dictating a few letters. Trying to get organized."

"Mind if I exercise one of my New Year's resolutions?" she asked.

"Not at all."

"I'm going to strive to be more assertive. So, you're my first victim. Would you like to meet later for a drink?"

"It'd be a pleasure. Do you have anything in mind?"

"Why don't we try Faneuil Hall? There are some nice restaurants there. How about Crickets?"

"Great. What time?" Dan asked.

"Seven thirty?"

"See you then."

—

Anna applied the finishing touches on her makeup with some guilt and embarrassment. *Is Dan just a distraction from boring Roger?* she thought. She took a good look in the mirror and decided it didn't matter: she was going to meet Dan for dinner, and there was no harm in that. *Right?* she asked, trying to convince herself.

—

Faneuil Hall, decorated for the holiday season, attracted countless visitors to Boston's well-known retail and commercial area. Anna sat at a table in an enclosed courtyard overlooking the main pedestrian walkway, a great vantage point from which to watch the parade of people passing by. As usual, she was early, the curse of her experience as a journalist.

The extra time allowed her mind to wander and think about her brief visit to Minneapolis. Her mother seemed hurt that she had returned to Boston without a leisurely day shopping and a two-hour lunch together.

Soon, Dan Murphy arrived and immediately recognized Anna, dressed in a black turtleneck, red slacks, and black beret. He felt a spark that told him she was special and that there was more to come.

Anna greeted him enthusiastically. "Hello, Dan."

"I hope I'm not too late."

"Only ten minutes. You're getting better."

Anna sipped her beer. "Can I buy you a beer?" she asked.

"No. I can't let a graduate student limping along on a few bucks a week buy me a beer. How was Minneapolis?"

"Fine," Anna answered matter-of-factly, with little interest in discussing her visit.

"Anything interesting happen?"

"No. Not really. How about you? Did you spend Christmas with your family?"

"At my mother's house."

"It's nice to be back, Dan. I have a lot to tell you about the study. I've started the interviews."

"How's it going? Are people being cooperative?"

"Very much so, but it's almost impossible to avoid knowing the cases—the people with the aplastic anemia."

"Why would that matter?"

"Becker thinks the interviewer should be blinded, not knowing whether the person interviewed is a case or a control." Anna recounted an important feature of doing this type of research, that is, if aware of the cases of people with the disease in comparison to controls, the interviewer may be more inclined to ask questions in a way that encourages certain types of answers. If that happens, a bias can occur that artificially elevates the risk of disease.

Just then, a waiter approached. "Can I get you folks anything?" he asked.

"I'll have another beer," Anna said.

"I'll have whatever she's having," Dan responded, then grinned at Anna.

"Have you eaten here before?" Anna asked.

"No. But should we try?"

"Sure. Let's get a menu."

"Sounds like you've been productive," he remarked.

"Becker chewed me out the day before I left. I was so shell-shocked that I went over to Harrington's office to prepare for the interviews this week."

"Why? What's the rush?"

"Becker. He's beating his chest and showing me he's in charge. It's as though he gets a perverse sort of pleasure in seeing his students fear him."

"Why don't you channel that frustration into the project?" Dan suggested.

"Exactly. Becker wants to see if I can deliver. It's strange, but I think he hopes that I'll fail."

"Maybe you're being too sensitive. After all, isn't he supposed to critique your work?"

"Yes, but—"

"But?"

"There are ways of critiquing without demoralizing."

"Why don't you get another adviser?"

"I'd lose face if I dropped out of Becker's group. Becker would crow that only physicians have the academic caliber for his program. I'm the only nonphysician among Becker's eight students, and there's only one other woman."

The waiter appeared with the beers and took their order, then left again.

Anna smiled, then raised her glass of beer. "Happy New Year." She and Dan clicked glasses and exchanged smiles of affection.

"How's your brother?" Anna asked.

"Improving, but still in the hospital."

"When's he getting out?"

"I'm not sure, but Dr. Harrington is pleased with Pat's progress."

"Is there any sign of graft rejection?"

"None. Everything's been relatively uncomplicated. No serious side effects to date, only a skin rash on his back and chest. Otherwise, Pat's getting some of his energy back and grumbling about going home."

"That's nice to hear. His wife must be pleased."

"Yeah! She's been upbeat lately."

"When do you think your brother will know if he's cured?"

"Probably never. The fatality rate is about 50 percent in two years,"

Dan answered. "Half the people with the disease are dead within two years of diagnosis."

"But isn't there a time when it's possible to say that he's cured?"

"Not really," Dan answered soberly.

"Will he be able to lead a normal life?"

"Oh yes. But he'll have to be monitored frequently to make sure he doesn't develop graft-versus-host disease."

"When would that occur?" Anna asked.

"Anytime. Most people have some type of graft-versus-host reaction after a bone marrow transplant. There are all sorts of reactions. Some of them are fatal. The disease, at least the acute form, can occur within a week to a few months after the transplant."

"Does it worry you that no cause has been found for Pat's disease?"

"Not really," Dan replied.

"Why?"

"I'm not sure it would make much difference."

"Suppose Pat got the disease from something at work, then he did the same thing again. Would he have a relapse?"

"I don't know who could answer that question. Aplastic anemia is such a rare disease that most of the medical information is anecdotal. But your point is a plausible one."

The waiter appeared with their orders.

"Bon appétit," Anna said to Dan once the waiter had left.

After making their way through dinner, Anna introduced the project again. "You know I'm going to interview Pat," she said, referring to Dan's brother.

Dan looked at her attentively. "My only concern with Pat is whether he's off the gambling habit. He's been broke a few times in the past, then he gets caught up in shady activities."

"Pat seems to have everything together now, doesn't he? Good job, married. His wife is due to have their first baby. They just bought a house."

"Yes," Dan said, "but Pat has a self-destructive component to his personality. At times, he'll act first and think later."

They finished their meals. Anna commented, "Thank you for dinner, Dan. I hope you didn't think I conned you into picking up the check. After all, I am the one who asked you to meet me."

"My pleasure. Do you need a ride home?"

"That would be nice."

After a short drive, Dan pulled in front of Anna's apartment. He was surprised to find a parking spot.

"Can I be gallant and walk you to the door?" he asked.

"Yes, you may. And may I be assertive and invite you inside?"

"I'm an easy sell." He grinned as he wrapped his arm around her.

Anna opened the door to her three-room apartment. Although her scholarship to the Harvard School of Public Health covered tuition and fees, she was provided with only a small stipend for living expenses. Her small apartment was limited to a moderately appointed chair and couch that, with their current level of wear and tear, would not withstand the test of time. In contrast, the kitchen was highlighted by a new coffee maker to assist in providing fuel for late-night graduate student work. To help her earn some money to add to the limited graduate student stipend she received, Anna had just completed the licensing procedure with the Massachusetts Board of Registration to enable her to do part-time nursing work. Although she had given up her full-time nursing practice eight years ago to pursue her career in journalism, she maintained her nursing license in Minnesota. At times, she worked at a private physician's office or at an outpatient clinic of a local health maintenance organization. The work helped with some of her expenses. Also, she enjoyed the patient contact and the immediacy of her actions.

"Nice place," Dan said, as Anna turned on the lights.

In the center of the large living room was a fireplace, and in a corner, there was a circular table that Anna used as a desk. A square pine coffee table sat in front of the sleep sofa, which served as her bed. Adjacent to the living area was a stand-up kitchen, too small to accommodate a table and chairs.

"I hope you don't mind, but I have a store-bought log for the fireplace. My father would shoot me if he knew. He's always chopping wood out behind the house."

"I won't tell anyone. In fact, I'll even light it," Dan answered.

"Aren't you the charmer?" Anna quipped. "Can I get you anything?"

"Any chance you have a beer?"

Anna opened the refrigerator. "You're a lucky guy, Dr. Murphy. I have four bottles of Sam Adams."

Anna opened a bottle of beer for Dan and did the same for herself. Without forethought or grace, Dan put his arm around Anna's waist and pulled her toward him.

"It's nice to have you back," he said, then pressed his lips against hers. In seconds, their mouths were open and engaged in a passionate kiss that seemed to last minutes. Anna grabbed Dan's hand and led him to her sofa. She then inched toward him and kissed him softly on the cheek. Stroking his hair, she leaned against his chest. The mutual passion drove them to more lengthy and sensuous kisses and embraces. Before long, they were lying on the sofa, embracing, when her telephone rang.

"Great timing," Anna said. She rose from the sofa and shook her shoulder-length hair back into place. "Hello," she said with a cheerfulness that resembled that of Harrington's secretary. "I think you have the wrong number," she said, then hung up the phone.

She then went into the bathroom. As she combed her hair, she thought of Dan, now sitting in her living room. Fiercely attracted to him, she was cautious about getting more involved with him physically, an aspect of their relationship that she was unprepared to address. *How can I avoid getting more involved tonight without hurting his feelings?* she thought. *But I don't want to turn him away.*

Anna entered the living area, where Dan was sitting on the sofa with his beer in hand.

"The phone call came at a great time. It reminds me of a James Bond movie I saw years ago," Dan said. "Bond, Mr. Dapper with the ladies, was in bed with one of his conquests when the phone rang. 'Can't help you,' Bond said. 'Something just came up.'"

"Dan, there's a career for you in stand-up comedy," she replied, then kissed him again. "You know, it's getting kind of late. Maybe we should call it a night."

"Anything wrong?" Dan asked.

"Not at all. I just think it's best that we do it this way."

"Is it Roger?" Dan asked.

"Yes, in part, but no too. Don't I sound definitive?"

Dan drew her head toward him and kissed her gently on the lips. The way she caressed his head and stroked his hair told him that she felt the same magic as he did.

"We shouldn't let emotions get in the way of our work, you know," Anna said.

Dan kissed her again in response, then turned for the door.

"Good night," he said with an impish grin that suggested he knew there would be another time.

Chapter 32

At the Occupational Health Center, Dan Murphy reviewed his patient files. Earlier, he had treated two people from the plating firm: Mr. Shaw and his mother's bingo partner, the company secretary. Mrs. Johnson had told Dan that Mr. Shaw had requested the safety data sheets and that she wanted him to determine whether her own symptoms were the result of sick building syndrome. The older woman, although not sufficiently ill to miss work, described itchy eyes, a stuffy nose, and severe fatigue, all of which she felt were the result of her work.

Aside from minor eye irritation that he noted on examining Mrs. Johnson, Dan considered her to be a typical, healthy fifty-seven-year-old woman. The most striking feature of her account was the strong relationship between her symptoms and her work. At home, she felt well. She was unwavering in emphasizing how the symptoms improved when she was away from the plant.

After winding her way through Massachusetts Avenue and onto the Southeast Expressway, Anna reached Andrews Avenue in South Boston. Before long, she pulled into the parking lot of the health center.

A receptionist greeted her. "Hi. Do you have an appointment?"

"No, actually I don't. But would you let Dr. Murphy know that I'm here? I'm Anna Carlson."

"Just a minute. I think he's with a patient."

"Thank you," Anna said. "I know he must be busy."

"If he has time, I'm sure he'll see you," the receptionist said, her tone acknowledging an admiration of Dr. Murphy.

As Anna waited, she overheard Dan speaking.

"This should help your back," he said. "You may find them most helpful if you take them before you go to sleep."

Then she heard his patient saying, "Thanks. When do I need to come back?"

"Give that form to the receptionist and she'll make an appointment."

"How about work?" the man asked.

"It's on the form," Dan said.

"Light duty?" the man asked incredulously. "There's no light duty, Doc. I work in a warehouse. If I can't lift boxes, I can't work."

Murphy reached into his pocket to withdraw a new form, then changed the recommendations for work.

"Anna Carlson?" Dan said wryly, as though she was waiting for a medical appointment. Exercising restraint in not appearing too familiar with Anna, he introduced her to staff. "Becky, this is Anna Carlson. She and I are working on an environmental study."

"That's right," Becky said. "I hope it works out for you."

Anna smiled graciously and replied, "Thank you."

"Let's go back to the office," Dan interjected.

"Are you sure? Do you have enough time?"

"Yes. I think so." Speaking to the receptionist, Murphy said, "Don't we, Becky?"

"Your next appointment is at four o'clock, so you have about twenty minutes."

Dan directed Anna to his modest office, which was outfitted with a small desk and a solitary guest chair. Two of the walls were lined with books, and another displayed his various diplomas. A window opened onto a school playground.

"Thank you for letting me impose on you. I didn't mean to be so impulsive."

“Everything OK?” Dan asked.

“Oh yes. I’ve been working all the time, either doing interviews or entering data.”

“Does anything look promising?”

“Not yet, but I haven’t tabulated the results or done any of the statistical tests.”

“I’d have no idea where to start with the statistics.”

“It’s not that difficult if you use the right software program.”

Dan Murphy’s phone rang. “Dr. Murphy,” he answered. “Patrick, how are you! What’s going on?” Dan listened to his brother describe his frustration with the lengthy hospitalization. “It won’t be long,” Dan said. After a pause, he continued, saying, “I don’t know. Have you asked Harrington? He told me that your leukocyte count is increasing. That’s a sign the graft is holding.”

As Anna watched in anxious anticipation of knowing the content of their conversation, Pat complained about being hospitalized and wanting to be discharged, whether the doctors agreed or not.

“Pat, we should talk about this later. I’ll call you back about five.”

“How’s your brother?” Anna asked.

“Upset.”

“I’m sorry to hear that. Is there anything I can do?”

“Nothing in particular. Just be yourself during the interview.”

“I’ll do my best.”

“It’s not surprising that a young active person isolated in a hospital room would get depressed, is it?” Dan asked rhetorically.

“Of course,” Anna agreed. “Who wouldn’t get down? I would.”

“But I’m worried about Pat’s tendency to make abrupt decisions. He might sign out of the hospital against medical advice. He’d probably increase his chances of getting a serious infection or rejecting the transplant that way.”

Wanting to change the topic, Dan asked Anna, “What should I do with the study?”

“Dan, help me understand aplastic anemia and bone marrow transplants. How do you know when the graft has taken hold?”

"It takes about three weeks or so for the new bone marrow cells to function properly. As to when he's cured, I have no idea. He could get some type of graft-versus-host disease as long as a year or so after the transplant. Harrington says it's one of the worst diseases anybody can have."

"Can it be prevented?"

"Not very well. As many as one out of three get it, even if the transplant comes from a family member."

"I didn't realize the prognosis was that poor. Do people recover?"

"Some do. Unfortunately, the treatment is steroids and other medication that suppresses the immune system. As a result, people can get very sick from 'opportunistic infections,' organisms that don't affect people with healthy immune systems."

The phone alerted him to a call from within his office. "Your four o'clock appointment is here, Dr. Murphy."

"Thank you," he replied.

"I'd better leave," Anna said, rising from the chair.

"Can we get together later?"

"I'd love to. How about tomorrow?" she asked.

"That'd be great. Pretend I'm Becker. Have your results ready."

"OK," Anna said, suppressing the urge to kiss him.

Dan leaned in toward Anna in response just as the receptionist knocked on the door. "Your patient's waiting."

—

Later that day, Anna made her way to the hospital to interview Dan's brother, Pat.

"Do you want to see Miss Carlson?" the nurse sheepishly asked Pat Murphy, who was lying in bed and watching television.

"Sure. Send her in. Did she bring any beer?" Pat answered.

"Hi, Patrick. I hope I didn't come at a bad time."

"It's always a bad time. How would you like to be stuck here? I'm tired of the white gloves and the white gowns and the blood pressure and the garbage food."

Anna nodded, unsure of the proper response.

"Dan told me you had some questionnaire for me," Pat said. "I hope you find out what the hell caused this. Did you find anything out yet?"

"Not yet, but you're my last interview, so do you want to get started?" Anna, having perfected her approach to the questionnaire, asked Pat about his work in great detail. "Do you ever ship chemicals in your truck?"

"Not that I know of," he answered. "My brother asked me the same thing. The truck I drive handles cargo, boxes, and construction stuff. Special companies handle the hazardous waste and dangerous chemicals."

"Are you sure?"

"About as much as anyone can be sure. You can't trust anybody these days. You know that. Where are you from, Michigan?"

"Minnesota," Anna responded.

"Maybe people are honest there, but there are a lot of shady characters around here."

"What do you mean?"

"Some people'll do anything to make a buck."

"That's not new, though, is it?"

"Right. It's not new, but it means I don't always know what's in my truck."

"Don't you usually drive to the same businesses?"

"Usually, but there are always new runs. And some places I wouldn't drive through at night without a hungry pit bull for protection."

"In South Boston?"

"We deliver all over—not just South Boston."

"Do you load and unload the truck?"

"It depends."

"On what?"

"Whether there's enough people to help at the drop-off or whether the stock is special. Sometimes unions don't want us to unload, so it varies."

"Do you always know what you're shipping?"

"Like I said, you never know the shit—oh, sorry—the stuff that people try to get rid of. So, I don't know."

"Isn't the material packaged?"

"Yeah."

"How about maintenance work? Do truckers ever have to work on the engine or the brakes?"

Pat smiled before responding. "Hey, that's great. A chick who knows cars. I fool around on my own junkers when they break down, but I never wanted to be a grease monkey or change brakes or clutches."

"I don't mean to be a bore. I'm just trying to explore any possible connection between your work and your illness."

Pat looked straight ahead before responding. "I know. Do you have any ideas yet?"

"Some, but I haven't sorted them out. I have to enter lots of information, then do some statistical tests."

"I need to know."

"I can imagine."

"What do you think, Anna? Did my work cause this?"

"I don't know," she answered.

Chapter 33

It was Sunday night, the only reason that Tony Mesa and Jake Wilson were in their motel suite. Since Wilson learned about current events from television, the machine blared constantly, whenever he or Mesa sat in their dank, dark motel unit. The television served as a third partner in stimulating discussion.

Switching the channel to the Super News Network (SNN), Wilson watched highlights of the professional football games played that day. Mesa stood in the bathroom and carefully trimmed his beard.

"Coming up, new violence in Northern Ireland threatens the Brexit peace process," a newscaster announced.

"Any beer left?" Mesa yelled.

Wilson sipped on a can of beer he had just withdrawn from an otherwise barren refrigerator. Mesa and Wilson weren't the type of guys who would push a basket at the supermarket. The only items that resembled food in their suite were beer and peanuts.

"Yeah. I'll give you half of mine," Wilson called back.

"Forget it. I'll get some more."

"Sunday night?"

"I think so. There's a liquor store around here someplace. I'll go look."

Just then, the SNN announcer interjected, "A government facility was bombed in Northern Ireland today."

Scenes of an ambulance with its siren wailing as it pulled away from a crowd of people in shock followed. A policeman feverishly blew a whistle and waved his hands to discourage curious onlookers from getting too close to the smoldering building. While medics and firefighters assisted the injured, a new voice easily recognized as British commented, "The Brexit process was thrown off course again today. There appears to be no end to the violence."

As medics carried the injured on stretchers, the announcer continued, "The number of casualties is unclear, but as many as six people may have died. The number injured, however, likely goes into the thirties. Exact figures are unavailable at this time."

The news announcer, a man with well-coifed hair blown-dry, in his late thirties, reappeared on-screen. "For more on Northern Ireland, the blast, and how it may affect Brexit, we turn to our political commentator in Northern Ireland, Melissa Deaney, now in Belfast. Melissa, welcome."

"Hello, Richard."

"What's going on there?"

Wilson leaned forward and turned the volume up. He barely heard commentary about how Brexit policies exacerbated the situation between the haves and the have-nots, that is, Catholics and Protestants.

"Well, Richard, the full story is yet to be told, but peace has suffered a serious setback."

"What about the average person in Northern Ireland? How do they view Brexit?"

"That's very difficult to answer. Opinions are mixed. It depends to a large degree on the economic stature of the person and whether they are Catholic or Protestant."

"How so?"

"The Catholic middle class has grown considerably since the Troubles, as they're known here, that started in the late 1960s.

Catholics, for example, have made great progress, especially economically, including owning homes in the wealthier areas of Belfast, such as in the Malone Road section. Catholics are also winning a considerable number of antibias suits related to employment. But at the same time, there are those who are left behind. For example, in Northern Ireland it's estimated that two out of every three unemployed persons are Catholic. In other words, Catholics are still twice as likely to be unemployed compared to Protestants—despite the progress."

"So, is the IRA support mostly in the poor and working-class sections?"

"Most definitely."

"What kind of support does the IRA have?"

"Again, mixed. But it also appears to be the only true protection in the minds of many Catholics who are convinced that the police and the RUC [Royal Ulster Constabulary] are controlled by the Protestants. So, for self-protection, these folks tend to sympathize with the IRA, despite misgivings about more violence."

"What is the way out of the mess?"

"Good question. In the short term, cool heads and good intentions, I imagine, but in the long term, a formal end to subtle and overt discrimination. Educational reform is essential."

"But, Melissa, it's my understanding that education reforms have taken place."

"Oh yes, they have. In fact, the Catholics have realized gains in a variety of professions, including engineering, law, and business."

Tony Mesa walked into the modified living room and reached for the remainder of Wilson's beer. "You seem interested in this stuff," he said.

"I am."

"Why are you so curious?"

"I spent some time in Belfast."

"Northern Ireland?"

"Yes."

"How'd you ever end up there? I thought you were from Philadelphia."

"I am."

"Where's Northern Ireland come in?"

"It's a long story."

"We got time."

"But no beer."

"How about later?"

"Fine."

"But don't forget your pals. Have you lined up the team yet? We've got a big game tomorrow."

"We'll be fine."

"Don't rotate your players," Mesa continued, using the sports metaphor. "Stick with the first team."

"Right," Wilson answered, not interested in furthering the discussion.

The weather forecaster appeared on-screen and cheerfully promised a bright and sunny cold day for tomorrow.

"Keep it tight, Jake. I don't want too many people involved." Mesa turned to leave. Wilson thought about Pat Murphy.

As the quintessential wheeler-dealer, Wilson knew how to corral his troops for big projects. Although he had developed a reputation for arranging nonunion construction and service jobs for illegal Irish immigrants, he also danced dangerously close to the edge of the law in other endeavors. Rumors surfaced occasionally about a flair he once had for orchestrating huge cocaine shipments. Never convicted of any criminal activity, however, Wilson combined his street smart savvy with a native intelligence to stay a half step beyond arrest. That same savvy convinced him of the importance of keeping a tight group of people for Mesa's project.

He reached for the phone.

"Murphy. How you doin'? It's Jake."

"No shit. I'd recognize your ugly voice under water."

"You're a pleasant dude, Murphy. Can't you convince any of those good-lookin' nurses to keep you company and not just take your blood pressure?"

"If it were that easy, I'd enjoy hanging out here."

"You seem to be doing a good job of hanging around that hospital. Are you ever goin' to get out?"

"Never. I'm confined here. A life sentence!" Pat answered sarcastically.

"No, man, I'm serious. When you gettin' out?"

"I don't know."

"Find out."

"Yes, sir!" Pat answered in military fashion, albeit while simultaneously showing his annoyance at the command.

"Murphy, you owe me. Don't make me remind you."

"I'm in the fuckin' hospital. What do you want me to do?"

"Get out."

"Like that?"

"Figure it out. That's your problem. I told you there may come a time when I'd lean on you. This is it."

"I don't understand the rush. Why can't we wait until I get out of here?"

"It won't work."

"Why?"

"It's not my decision. The guy who's payin' calls the shots, and he needs our help."

"When?"

"Soon."

"What do you want me to do, just leave the hospital?"

"Murphy, I don't give a fuck how you do what you need to do, just be there. Remember, you're the clown who blew thirty grand gambling. I'm callin' in the chit."

Chapter 34

Seated at her computer, Anna entered the questionnaire data from the twenty-four interviews, including the sixteen orthopedic surgery patients and the eight patients with aplastic anemia; the latter group included Pat Murphy. Since Liam O'Malley, an unregistered immigrant from Ireland, had just died two months prior, she had interviewed his wife.

Anna arranged the results into a number of tables, a tedious process that required exquisite attention to detail. Key items from the medical records, along with results of lab tests, biopsies, and the physical examinations, were noted. She tabulated the initial symptoms that each of the eight cases developed before their diagnosis. Easy bruising, fatigue, and bleeding gums were the most common complaints.

The flurry of activity required to summarize her findings had left Anna little time to consider their significance. Before meeting Dan later that night, she hoped to review the results and catalogue the common features among the cases.

She prepared tables on the patients' environmental histories and the medications they were taking before the diagnosis of aplastic anemia was made. This part of the interview, because of its focus on the chemicals and other hazards to which people had been exposed, held her greatest interest. She knew her academic adviser, David Becker, would also probe her on this aspect of the study.

She developed a graph that contrasted the differences between the patients and controls regarding exposure to glues, paints, pesticides, and other hazards associated with aplastic anemia. Then she performed a variety of statistical analyses to determine corresponding risks of aplastic anemia in the patients and the control group. Growing weary of the number crunching component of the study, she yearned to spend time with Dan.

An hour of aerobics at the health club put her in the right frame of mind for an evening with the man who was making her forget Roger. Invigorated by the exercise and excited about completing a major part of her project, Anna drove to the Back Bay section of Boston, where Dan Murphy owned a condominium.

She rang the buzzer to Dan's unit. Seconds later, the electronic door lock released, allowing her entry to a nineteenth-century brownstone. "Anna, great to see you." He drew her toward him for a kiss that made her feel immediately at ease upon entering his living room. Modestly furnished with a worn-out sofa that served as a bed for guests, two maroon leather chairs, and a wool oriental rug, the room reflected a masculine warmth.

"This is nice," Anna said, gazing about.

"Can I get you anything?" he asked. "Wine, beer, a hug?"

"Chardonnay would be great, and a hug is always welcome," Anna answered, a smile enveloping her face, which was still blushing a rosy red from the brisk Boston winter air. Before opening his refrigerator, Dan reached out to her for an embrace, concluding with a deep kiss that hinted at passion about to be unleashed.

Dan brought her a glass of wine, then poured himself a beer. "How's the study? Any news?"

"Yes. I got through twenty-four questionnaires and had enough energy to get the data into a program."

"Anything interesting?"

"I haven't had much time to review the material, but I'd like to show you." Anna reached into a folder. "The bone marrow biopsy results are all similar. The blood study results look the same as well.

In fact, it doesn't seem as though there is anything unusual about the eight cases," Anna said. "Let me show you another table."

Dan looked it over. Anna commented, "None of them took any medications that might cause aplastic anemia. They were all in good health except for this one patient, who had mononucleosis a few months before the diagnosis."

"Do you think mono is a risk factor for aplastic anemia?" Dan asked, referring to the common viral illness characterized by a sore throat, swollen lymph glands, and profound tiredness.

"I'm not sure," Anna answered. "Most of the information is from case reports, so it's hard to determine the risk of getting aplastic anemia after mono."

"Anything suggestive of an environmental cause?" Dan asked.

"No. I calculated relative risks for about fifteen different variables, including mono, glues, paints, and pesticides. The higher the number, the more likely there's a true association between exposure to a hazard and the disease."

"Thank you, Professor," Dan said wryly, although he was appreciative of the explanation. "So, in this table, the highest relative risk is for truck driving?" he asked.

"Yes. People with aplastic anemia are sixty times more likely to be truck drivers than the control group."

"Are you sure?"

"Yes. I did the 95 percent confidence intervals. The confidence intervals are from 4.2 to 70, which means that there's only a 5 percent chance that the results would be lower than 4.2 or higher than 70."

"I love bright women," Dan said, kissing her on the cheek. "But don't let me distract you."

"Aren't you the charmer! Listen to my lecture, Dr. Murphy," she said with an alluring smile.

"What's different about the truck drivers?"

"That's the next step. What is it about these truck drivers that made them more likely to get sick?"

"Was any nationality or ethnic group a risk factor?" Dan asked.

"I didn't include ethnicity in the analysis, but most of the cases had names that people would consider Irish."

"Would you like another glass of wine?" Dan asked. "I'm getting a headache from all this information."

"Yeah. Why have a headache now if I can get one tomorrow morning by drinking too much wine tonight?" she quipped.

As Dan went to the kitchen to refill their drinks, he said, "I have a surprise. You can savor that parking spot out front, avoid going out in ten-degree weather, and have dinner here with me."

"And to whom do I owe this good fortune?" Anna asked, smiling at Dan.

"Me." Murphy drew her close for an engaging kiss, prompted by a feeling of passion begging for release. Anna responded in kind.

"You'll help me prepare for Becker?" she asked.

"It'll be a pleasure. Use me as a pseudo Becker. I'll criticize everything you say."

"I'm looking forward to it," she said, reaching to him for another kiss.

Chapter 35

Anna flawlessly delivered her presentation and described how the cluster of aplastic anemia was recognized because two people in the same neighborhood had contracted the same serious disease within a short period of time.

David Becker, sitting off to the side of the room, could not resist interjecting. "That's a common feature of occupational and environmental diseases. They look the same and act the same as diseases not the result of chemicals or other hazards." The perpetual pedagogue, Becker wasted no opportunity to flaunt his knowledge.

Anna smiled deferentially, then continued, saying, "Although no particular hazard was associated with aplastic anemia, truckers had a markedly increased risk—almost sixty times greater than the controls."

"Truckers! How interesting!" Becker said. "Would you tell us what's unique about the truckers?"

Reflexively, she turned to the acting department chair. "I'll get to that."

"When?" Becker asked, poised for combat.

Doing her best to maintain her composure, Anna showed another PowerPoint slide. "Truck driving appears to be the greatest risk, but what is it about truck drivers that would lead them to have a higher risk of aplastic anemia, especially truck drivers from South Boston?" she asked rhetorically, beginning her concluding remarks.

She watched Becker carefully. So far, the presentation had gone well, but she could see from his smug expression that he was thoroughly enjoying his latest interruption of her presentation.

Becker strode to the center of the small conference room. At the huge rectangular table sat eighteen graduate students, enrolled in a graduate seminar entitled "Research in Environmental Health."

"What about the methods? Any comments?" he asked, looking at his students. "Is there any bias?" He then turned to Anna, saying, "Tell us about the bias in your study."

"You mean with the methods?" she asked.

"Yes. And elsewhere."

"Ideally, I should have been 'blinded,' so to say, in terms of whether the person I interviewed had aplastic anemia or not."

"You mean you weren't blinded?" Becker asked in disbelief.

"I was originally."

"What do you mean, originally?"

"I didn't know at the outset, but by the nature of my conversations, it wasn't hard to figure who had the disease."

"That is a bias," Becker said, shaking his head in exaggerated disappointment. When bludgeoning a student, he discouraged all but the courageous from interceding.

"Wouldn't the questionnaire eliminate or at least reduce the bias?" a young bearded student asked.

"To some extent, yes, but not entirely."

"Why?" the student asked in earnest. Anna, standing at the end of the long table, breathed a sigh of relief as Becker focused on someone else.

"Since Carlson knew the cases," Becker said, staring at Anna, hoping to intimidate her, "it's conceivable that she was more assertive in asking about chemicals and work histories like truck driving in the people with aplastic anemia, compared to those without the disease."

"But Anna didn't report any chemicals as risks for the disease," the student responded. Anna, pleasantly surprised at the help from a fellow student, vowed to take him to lunch or at least to bail him out later during one of his own presentations. She displayed another PowerPoint slide with results from the study.

"No significant relationship was found with any chemical exposures," she said, pointing at the screen.

Becker, embarrassed and flustered from being caught off guard by an alert student willing to challenge him, responded. "But this extraordinary risk for truckers is overstated. That's where the bias is."

The bearded student watched as Becker asked Anna to display the results again. She showed a table noting the relative risk of sixty for truck drivers.

"What's different about the truck drivers in your study?" Becker asked Anna, having turned away from the bearded student who challenged him.

"I'm not sure, but I have some comments I'd like to make," Anna responded.

"We're anxious to hear," Becker said, showing a hint of sarcasm.

"This study should only be considered preliminary. It was designed to determine whether an environmental factor might be involved in an apparent outbreak of aplastic anemia, but it failed to show any obvious link. In short, this study was unable to pinpoint any environmental parameter such as an air or water pollutant with aplastic anemia. On the other hand, truck drivers had an extraordinarily high risk." Anna continued the presentation.

"Further review should focus on the specific tasks of truck driving, such as the type of materials delivered and to which type of factories. Trucking duties need to be explored in depth, such as loading, unloading, repairing damaged material, or performing maintenance work."

"Is that all?" Becker asked.

"Yes," Anna answered with hesitation, waiting for him to lay his trap.

The students, seated around the table, looked to Becker for the next part of the seminar. "Questions?" the professor asked.

"I have a comment," said the bearded student who had gone toe to toe with Becker a few minutes earlier. He turned to Anna and said with encouragement, "I think you've done an interesting study, but there's more you can do with the truckers. For example, some truckers do odd jobs on the side, not necessarily for their own company. As a result, they may come into contact with hazards off the job that they don't encounter on the job. Also, some interesting studies have been done on truckers who work with certain chemicals. You may want to look into them. In any event, I enjoyed your talk."

"Well, thank you, Professor," Becker said mockingly to the bearded fellow. "Carlson, you've done better than I expected," he then said begrudgingly. Anna nodded in response but remained silent. "But you need to explain the truckers. Find out about the truck drivers. We'll hear from you again when? Next week, perhaps?"

Anna nodded again. It was a waste of time to dispute a date with Becker during the graduate seminar. She'd find out later.

As Anna gathered her books and files and prepared to depart the room, she sighed in relief. Although a presentation at a Becker seminar was invariably a nerve-wracking experience, she felt that the whole event could have been more pleasant and not nearly as hostile. From her perspective, Becker seemed driven to find fault with her work. *Can't he deal with a strong woman?* she mused. *Or is he acting out his own insecurities? After all, why would a dermatologist direct an occupational medicine department?* Despite the frustration, Anna decided that her time and energy were better spent with her work and not on analyzing Becker's behavior. She was encouraged that her work, if it uncovered a cause, may prevent other cases of aplastic anemia and deaths.

Chapter 36

Jake Wilson, recognizing that his pay was contingent on performance, including timing and delivery, was not about to lose the project. He entered the cold, dark, starless winter night and walked toward a white van labeled "Sterling Harbors." He opened the back door and looked in at the empty storage space with ropes scattered about the floor. Then he opened the driver's door, started the engine, and turned on the headlights. After switching on the heater in the hope of minimizing the bite of five-below-zero weather, he went back to the hotel suite, where Mesa lay on the run-down sofa watching a football game. "Let's go, man. It's time," Wilson said, then turned to the truck. Moments later, Mesa joined him in the cabin.

A five-minute drive brought them to the outskirts of a manufacturing plant that was surrounded by metal fencing whose top was adorned with barbed wire. They pulled up to a guard station positioned at the entrance to the facility.

Wilson handed a white envelope to an overweight man in his midthirties whose curly black hair was protected from the cold by a blue woolen cap. A security camera monitored the transaction.

After inspecting the papers that Al Struck, the worker about to be laid off, had pilfered a few days ago, the guard waved Wilson onto the property. "Go straight ahead to the first building on your right, turn into the driveway, then follow it around until you come to the delivery platform. You'll see a big sign. It's lighted, so you can't miss it."

Wilson played along, as though he and Al Struck had never discussed directions to the shipping site. Within minutes, they arrived at a loading platform on which stood Al Struck, waiting for their arrival. Wilson got out of the van, walked up a small set of steps, then handed the shipping papers to Struck, who perused them, then waved Mesa out of the truck.

"Let me get the forklift," Struck said. "I'll help you get it into the van." He opened up a garage-like door to a storage area that contained numerous green fifty-five-gallon drums labeled "Waste." Methodically, he rolled one onto the forklift, then drove it back to the van, where Mesa had lowered the loading ramp. Struck, aided by Wilson and Mesa, filled the van with numerous metal drums. "That's it for now," he said. "I'll catch you later."

"Right," Wilson replied as he walked to the truck. Mesa waved as he entered the passenger side of the vehicle.

Wilson drove to the security hut again and handed papers over to the same guard who had let them in earlier. Just then, a supervisor approached the area. Wilson sensed suspicion on the part of the supervisor, who noted the New York license plate as the van pulled out of the facility and onto the access road. After opening up a large three-ring binder that lay on a shelf, the supervisor, a blond-haired twenty-eight-year-old, paged through the material.

"I don't see that license plate in here."

"It should be," responded the guard who had allowed Wilson and Mesa entry to the plant.

"It's not. I'll check it out with the office."

"Maybe it's a new account. They do a lot of business with us. Sterling Harbors is very good."

"Let's make sure it's Sterling Harbors," the guard said, grabbing his hat. At the same time, Tony Mesa reached over to turn on the radio.

"I need some good ole country music."

"Enough, man. I'm tired of hearing that 'My baby done left me down by the tracks,'" Wilson replied, displeased with Mesa's love of country music.

"Well, get used to it, 'cause we got a long trip back to Boston."

Realizing it was pointless to contest him, Wilson changed the subject. "Al Struck came through."

"Yeah. Just hope he keeps his mouth shut and nobody looks over his shoulder. He seems like the kind of guy who would crack under pressure."

"I don't think so. Not if he wants to get paid and protect his ass from his wife."

"You do well, Wilson, my man. I knew I could count on you. Seems like you want to get paid and you like the adventure, too, don't you?" Mesa asked rhetorically, slapping Wilson's leg and roaring with his trademark laugh.

They continued driving until they reached the interstate highway for the trip to South Boston. As Mesa rocked to the rhythm of a county music piece, he turned to Wilson. "Hey, dude! Tell me about Ireland. You seemed too interested in that TV program last night. What's up?"

Wilson, pumped up about Mesa's apparent interest, responded proudly, "Yeah, I spent time there."

"Doing what?"

"Chasing a chick."

"Did ya catch her?" Mesa laughed.

"I was going out with a sociology student from Penn back in Philadelphia."

"Penn State?"

"No, University of Pennsylvania. They're in the Ivy League, remember? Penn State's the football school."

"Right," Mesa answered. "But what the fuck were you doing there, dude?"

"I was out of the marines, had no job, and got bored. When you're twenty-eight, you chase women anywhere."

Mesa roared with his characteristic laugh.

"She wanted to do a project on the problems in Northern Ireland."

"Why?"

"Her grandmother came from Derry."

"Where's that?"

"Northern Ireland. So, she wanted to understand her roots."

"And you followed?"

"It was an adventure. After a few months over there, we split. She went to Dublin, then moved to Chicago. I haven't seen her in years."

"Why'd you stay in Ireland?"

"That's a longer story."

"Hey, we got a few more hours."

"I met some guys over there who were pretty sick of the Brits."

"IRA dudes?" Mesa interjected.

Wilson nodded. "I started to listen to them about the Brits. Before I knew it, I was going to meetings and learning about Sinn Fein."

"What?"

"A political party. It tries to represent the nationalists."

"The what?" Mesa asked.

"Those who want a united Ireland—primarily the Catholics."

"Hey, Jake, you ain't no politician."

"No shit! But I liked it. I learned how to wheel and deal, and I hated the fuckin' Brits."

"Why?"

"They're assholes. They ought to get the hell out of Ireland. They're the problem."

"Jake, calm down," Mesa said, surprised at Wilson's stridency.

Wilson immersed himself in the furor of his views. "The Brits are the problem. When I first went over there, I didn't care. For me, it was just something to do until I got thrown in jail."

"For what?"

"Minding my own business. Being at the wrong place at the wrong time."

"You're just a lucky guy," Mesa offered good-naturedly.

"Fat chance. Try spending a week in one of the jails over there."

"What were you doing to end up in jail?"

"I was in London when a restaurant exploded. The police grabbed me, threw me in a van, and took me to jail. No charges, just arrested for suspicious activity."

"I don't believe it."

"They have some kind of Prevention of Terrorism Act and they can pick you up if they don't like the way you look. And they're bastards in jail. I was strapped to a chair and questioned for days. They'd make it too cold, then too hot. They wouldn't feed me. They'd leave the room for hours and blindfold me, and never let me sleep without hassling me."

"How'd you get out?"

"After seven days, they let me go."

"What'd they say?"

"What could they say? 'Sorry we've messed with your mind'? I hate the Brits. They really think they're better than the Irish."

"Jake, my man, this is interesting, but let's take a break. There's a truck stop." After pulling off the freeway, Mesa and Wilson entered the diner. Outside were huge tractor trailers with their diesel engines grinding in the background while their drivers kept warm while eating. Tired of the drive, and having made good time, Wilson and Mesa leisurely ate quarter-pound hamburgers and fries.

Shortly, they were back on the interstate heading into Boston with the radio blaring country music. Mesa asked, "So, what'd you do after prison? I didn't realize you were such an adventurer. Here I was thinking you were just a local boy who could wheel and deal real good, and now I hear you've been a highflier in Ireland."

"Thanks, man," Wilson said wryly.

"Anytime, pardner."

"I decided to do something about the Brits."

"Like what?"

"Like I said, I joined Sinn Fein."

"But you're no politician."

Wilson's attention was distracted by a flashing red light on the roof of a car quickly approaching from behind.

"Shit. I'd better put this beer away," Mesa said.

As it became obvious that the flashing light belonged to a police cruiser, Wilson slowed down and pulled to the side of the road.

"What do you think he wants?" Mesa asked.

"What do I know! We weren't speeding."

The state trooper flashed a light onto Wilson and Mesa. Without emotion, he commanded, "License and registration."

"What's up, Officer?"

"Your license and registration, sir."

Wilson fumbled through his wallet, then reached to the glove compartment to get the registration. He handed the papers to the policeman, who turned to walk back to his car.

"Wait here," he said with an authority that ensured respect.

Chapter 37

At the Occupational Health Center, Dan Murphy completed his evaluation of a twenty-four-year-old man who had become short of breath after using a new paint at work. Despite wearing a paper mask, the patient had developed difficulty breathing that forced him to leave work.

Murphy felt challenged in these clashes between a person's job and their health. In this case, something had to yield. Continuing in the job would surely make his patient's asthma worse and more difficult to treat. The painter may even become sensitive to other materials that did not bother him at the moment. Murphy also knew that if he advised the worker against painting, he might be transferred to a job with lower pay or lose his job.

Eventually, Dr. Murphy would also need to decide whether another patient, Mr. Shaw from the plating firm, had developed hepatitis from his work. At the moment, however, Murphy lacked the information to make a decent decision. Unable to gain access to the plant, he was unsure of the next step.

"You should avoid paints and stay out of work until your breathing is better," Murphy said, handing his patient a prescription. "You'll need these for a while."

"Thanks, Doc."

"See you in a week," Murphy said. Departing the exam room, he was met by Brenda, the nurse practitioner.

"Anna Carlson's here," she said with a snide smile and a raised eyebrow. Although Brenda was unmarried, Dan never considered that she might have an interest in him.

"Thank you. Would you tell her I'll be right there?"

"Of course," Brenda replied. "It'll be a pleasure," Her tone of voice suggested to Dan that she had a jealousy that he had not imagined.

Dan walked to the reception area. "Anna Carlson? Here for your lobotomy?" he jibed.

"Aren't you the charmer," Brenda said, as Anna rose from her chair and extended her hand to Murphy.

"Nice to see you." Anna's smile engendered an affection and warmth that Murphy found alluring.

"Where would you like to go for lunch?"

"Your choice."

"How about the hospital cafeteria? It won't win any gourmet awards, but it's close."

After ordering sandwiches, they settled at a table at the far end of the room.

"How's the study going?" Dan asked. "Have you learned anything more about the truckers?"

"I called every one of them."

"How many were there?"

"Five, but only three are alive. And you know that Liam just died recently. Liam's wife called me this morning," Anna offered.

"Why?"

"She wanted me to know more about Liam's work. She thinks a plating firm in South Boston had something to do with his death."

"A plating firm? We have a couple of patients from there, actually. But when I tried to call to get a site visit, the plant manager just blew me off."

"What are their symptoms?" Anna asked.

"Sick building syndrome, mostly."

Anna chewed her sandwich thoughtfully. "You know, the truckers in my study are all Irish. And they all work part time hauling for other clients like that plating firm."

Dan raised his eyebrows. "I think that plant is a problem. Plating shops can be hazardous places to work—lots of acids, solvents, even cyanide solutions. They're usually subject to a lot of regulations."

"Why do you think they are resisting?" Anna asked. "Are the medical services expensive?"

"No. We don't charge for site visits. The whole point of coming to the work site is to become acquainted with the jobs and the type of work people do. That way, we can make better decisions about when people can go back to work after injuries or whether symptoms and illnesses may be related to work."

"Why do you think the plant's been putting you off?"

Dan shook his head. "Who knows! Last week, I called the manager and told him I thought that one of his workers had liver disease and that it may have resulted from work, adding that I needed to visit the plant to get more information."

"What did he say?"

"He blew me off. He said they were undergoing renovations and maintenance and that it was a bad time."

"Maybe he'll relent," Anna said encouragingly.

"I doubt it. I got the same response a couple of weeks ago when I called to introduce our program. Brenda called, but she didn't get anywhere either."

"Do you have any other patients from the plating firm?" Anna asked.

Dan reflected momentarily. "Yes, as a matter of fact." He then thought of Mrs. Johnson, the plant receptionist whom he had evaluated at the clinic and with whom he had spoken at his family's Christmas party. "One of the office staff came to see me also."

"What was the problem?"

"I'm not sure exactly, but the symptoms are typical of sick building syndrome."

"What's sick building syndrome?"

"It refers to nonspecific symptoms such as headache and tiredness that occur in buildings without good ventilation."

"What kind of symptoms did this person have?"

"Headache, eye irritation, and dry skin."

"Hepatitis?" Anna asked.

"No. Nothing like the custodian. So, I'm not sure if their conditions are related just because they work at the same plant."

"They could be," Anna suggested.

Anna and Dan each bit into their sandwiches.

"I think we should look into the plant," Anna said.

"Why?" Dan asked.

"For a number of reasons. First, the two patients you saw from the plant—I don't think it's a coincidence that they work at the same place."

Dan looked straight at Anna and into her crystal-blue eyes, now alive with intellectual energy.

"And finally, I trust my journalistic hunches."

Anna looked at Dan as he thought over her points.

"Plus, I haven't even told you about the truckers, the ones I called over the past few days."

"What did you find out?" Dan asked curiously.

"They're all of Irish descent. They all did local trucking, and they all admitted to doing part-time trucking work."

"Not part of their normal job?" Dan asked.

"Correct."

Dan reflected on her comments, but before he could respond, Anna said, "I think that plant is a problem."

"What do you think we should do?"

"Let's get some information on it."

"Such as? And how?"

"There's all sorts of environmental data available to the public. We could review what they've submitted to the EPA."

"Anna, I love your spirit and optimism. They won't let me or anyone from the hospital visit. What makes you think they would comply with environmental regulations?"

"Isn't it worth finding out?"

"I suppose so."

"Look," Anna said, peering at her watch, "you need to go to your meeting. I'll try to get some information on the plant's environmental reports this afternoon. I'll go to the EPA office in Boston."

Dan smiled, admiring Anna's energy.

"Thanks for lunch, Dr. Murphy."

"Spare the formalities, Ms. Carlson," Dan replied with a grin. "Just let me take you to dinner tomorrow."

"A pleasure," Anna said. She and Dan left the cafeteria.

Chapter 38

Minutes seemed like hours as the policeman checked over Wilson's driver's license and the registration documents for the van.

"What do you think he's doing?" Wilson asked Mesa.

"Hell if I know. The papers are good, aren't they?"

"They're fine."

The sound of a car door shutting alerted them to the policeman walking toward the van. Without emotion, he shined a flashlight onto Wilson and Mesa.

"What are you boys delivering this time of night?"

"Industrial supplies," Wilson answered.

"For what?"

"A machine shop."

"Mind if I take a look?" the cop asked. Wilson's jaw dropped in fear as neither he nor Mesa anticipated an inspection. "What's the problem, Officer? We got a tight deadline. If we don't do the delivery on time, we lose pay."

Ignoring Wilson's comment, the police officer waved him out of the truck. "Let's go."

Wilson got out of the van as Mesa reached into a duffel bag that lay in the front seat to feel for his revolver. As Wilson walked toward the back of the van, he felt blinded by the white light from the patrol car pointing directly at him. The police radio blared in the background as he reached into his pockets for the key to the padlock on the back door of the van. He inserted the key, opened the lock, and grabbed the handle to raise the door.

Suddenly, the wail of a police siren startled Wilson into dropping the door handle. An ambulance sped by, following a patrol car. The cop dashed back to his car to listen to the radio. Wilson hoped the trooper would remain distracted and forget about them. Moments later, the cop emerged from the car and handed Wilson the license and registration.

"You can go."

"Why did you stop us?" Wilson asked.

"Routine."

Wilson walked back to the truck and drove off. To Mesa, he said, "Why do you think he stopped us?"

"I have no idea."

"Do you think someone picked off our license plate back at the plant?"

"Why would they? You gave them all the papers."

"Right."

"Let's hear some music," Mesa said. He turned on the radio, hoping to find a country music station.

"That was close," Wilson said, looking for comfort after the stress of the cop's scrutiny. "Do you think he would have opened the drums?"

"They're all sealed. He'd have to impound the van. But he wouldn't do that."

"Don't be so sure," Wilson countered, recalling the trauma of his arrest and interrogation in Northern Ireland a few years earlier. "You wouldn't believe what the Brits in Northern Ireland would do."

"That's right," Mesa answered. "Jake Wilson, man of the world. Why did you stay over there anyway, after those goons terrorized you?"

"Because I wanted to get their asses. Besides, my grandparents came over to Philadelphia from Ireland. They bitched about the Brits all the time. They never had anything good to say about them."

"Did they come from Northern Ireland?"

"No. County Donnegal. It's in the Republic of Ireland. They came to the States in the 1920s right after the Irish Revolution, when the Irish voted to be independent. Then the Brits shoved a treaty down their throats saying that the northern part of Ireland would be carved out for the Protestants."

"Why did Ireland agree?"

"They didn't agree. A civil war started in Ireland because of the treaty. Some disagreed with splitting off the north. Others thought it was a great step—at least to have most of Ireland independent."

"You sound like a fuckin' history professor, dude. I thought you dropped out of college."

"I learned a lot in Northern Ireland, especially in prison. I got to meet guys in the IRA and in Sinn Fein. When you're in Belfast and Derry, you can feel the pressure."

"Why did you stay there? The marines were probably safer."

"Right," Wilson answered as he drove straight ahead on the interstate. The cold winter night seemed even less inviting because of the pitch-dark sky.

"I stayed to get the Brits. The more I learned about how they treat the Catholics, the more fuckin' pissed off I got."

"Catholics?" Mesa asked incredulously. "Wilson, I didn't think you could tell the difference between a church and a shopping mall."

"Northern Ireland has nothing to do with religion."

"Are you kidding?" Mesa asked. "All you hear is Catholics and Protestants. How is that not religion?"

"It's not about religion. It's about privilege and superiority."

"How long were you in Northern Ireland?"

"About a year. Until I went to London."

"Why did you go to London?"

"After I joined Sinn Fein, I went to London. There are about a quarter of million Irish living there. It's a great network."

"So, what'd you do in London?"

"I worked with the sleepers—college students and other dupes we could stiff-arm into helping us."

"What'd they do?"

"Robberies, primarily. To get money to help the cause. But they did some nasty stuff too."

Wilson felt a recurrent urge to show his self-worth to Mesa, even in discussing matters he had long kept private.

At five feet, nine inches tall, Wilson felt he had a physical disadvantage when confronted with the large six-foot-four frame of Mesa, a former football player and boxer. Wilson tried to compensate for his size with an aggressive weight-lifting program. He wanted Mesa to respect his physical prowess and recognize that he was no one to toy with.

"What kind of nasty stuff, dude? The suspense is killing me."

"Explosions, kidnappings, extortion."

"That's a hefty menu." In Mesa's response was a tone of disbelief. "What did you really do, Jake? Are you telling me the full story, my man?"

Wilson, feeling an urge to demonstrate his virility to Mesa, left out no details. "We helped the IRA pull off bombings and other shit to shake up the Brits."

"Is that why you left?"

"It was getting too hot. The Brits are on to the operations there. When anything suspicious happens, they know right where to go."

"Jake Wilson, IRA operative," Mesa said, again in disbelief. "Why did you come to Boston?"

"I didn't want to live on the run anymore. It was fuckin' dangerous."

"Dude, why'd you come to Boston?"

"Because of the Irish community. It's always been friendly to the cause in Ireland. I knew I could blend in."

Mesa responded, "I'm not sure you're telling me the full story. Are you still part of that … what's it called, Shin Fane?"

"Yeah, you got it. Sinn Fein."

"Were you tossed out?"

"No."

"What do they want from the Brits?"

"To get out of Northern Ireland."

"Hey. Boston, ten miles," Mesa said, having noticed a highway sign. "You're a great storyteller, man. How I spent my summer in the IRA. What's tomorrow? How I tracked down Russian submarines?" Mesa erupted into his trademark laugh, an abrupt change in the tone of their conversation.

"Look, no one else knows this stuff. It isn't bullshit. Don't tell anybody."

"Not even my friends at the *Boston Globe*?"

Wilson laughed, unloading a tension that had begged release. Although he found it comforting to tell his story to Mesa, he also feared the consequences.

"What does Sinn Fein want?" Mesa asked.

"A release of IRA prisoners, an end to the separation of the North from the Republic of Ireland, and the withdrawal of British military forces." As Wilson relayed his views to Mesa, he was struck by how reasonable they sounded—at least from the Irish perspective.

Wilson drove the van through the quiet streets of Boston, which were modestly illuminated by the amber glow of aging streetlamps. He turned down an alley that led to a two-story brick building that was as long as a football field. After parking the truck, he entered through a large black metal door.

"How soon can you get your boys here?" Mesa asked.

"Ten minutes."

"Get working on it."

Chapter 39

At the South Boston Fire Department, Anna easily gained permission to access files containing company reports. Although a lot of information was on the internet, she was advised that it was often incomplete and that, like most situations in life, it would be wise to show up. People can easily disregard emails and phone calls, but it is harder to say no in person.

Anna flipped through the files, looking for South Boston Plating. The firehouse kitchen was a hive of activity this late in the day. Something smelled delicious. The South Boston Fire Department was responsible for storing environmental reports from local companies, as required by the Emergency Planning and Community Right-to-Know Act. From a seminar in environmental health, Anna had learned that the act requires companies that use certain hazardous materials to report such use to the local fire department. Ideally, firefighters used the information to prepare for unexpected chemical releases or fires.

The file for South Boston Plating was fairly straightforward, listing numerous chemicals including acids, alkalis, solvents, and cyanide solutions—all recognized health hazards—as having been used by the plant to make costume jewelry. None of the chemicals Anna reviewed, however, had been recognized as a cause of aplastic anemia or any other type of bone marrow disorder. *Perhaps a previously unrecognized hazard caused the disease,* she mused.

Solvents remove grease, dirt, and other contaminants from metallic materials like the jewelry being made at the plant. Anna was unaware, however, whether one of the solvents used at the plating firm, trichloroethane, posed a risk for aplastic anemia. She nonetheless recognized that its use presented disposal problems for the plant. Since getting rid of hazardous waste can be expensive, Anna wondered how scrupulously the firm was adhering to the environmental regulations. She was well aware that illegal dumping had occurred in various settings, either on business property or through disreputable waste companies paying little heed to regulations.

The plating shop also used cyanide compounds. Hydrogen cyanide, an essential ingredient in many plating operations, can be deadly, a lesson learned by two Illinois businessmen who were charged with the deaths of two immigrant workers who had been overexposed to cyanide gas. During World War II, the Nazis used cyanide in their death camps. Anna knew that plating shops could be hazardous places to work, although none of the chemicals used at South Boston Plating had been reported before as a cause of aplastic anemia. *Could this be a new finding?* she pondered.

As she stared off in thought, the fire chief approached her. "I see you have an interest in our files. Can I help you?"

"No, but thank you," Anna answered. "I'm in the midst of a graduate student project—trying to see how environmental laws really work."

"Do you know we also have reports on the *amount* of chemicals that the plants use?"

"The actual quantities?" Anna asked.

"Estimates. It's a little complicated to explain, but any company that uses ten thousand pounds of certain materials has to report it—to us and to the LEPC."

"LEPC?"

"Local Emergency Planning Committee. And we're the ones

who have to bail 'em out if they get in trouble. What company are you looking for?"

"South Boston Plating."

The fire chief paged through the computer files. "It doesn't look like they reported any significant quantities."

"But they could still use hazardous materials though?" Anna queried.

"Oh yes, of course."

Anna looked puzzled, trying to understand the logic of the regulation. The fire chief then said, "You might want to go over to the EPA. Boston's the headquarters for Region 1."

"That's a good idea. Thanks for your help." Anna put on her light blue ski jacket to brace against the icy wind outside. Her old Honda started without a hitch and soon brought her through South Boston to EPA's Boston office, where she hoped to learn enough about South Boston Plating's activities in order to decide whether the company had caused the unusual string of illnesses, including aplastic anemia and hepatitis. On reaching an information kiosk, she was greeted by a young male clerk.

"Can I help you?" he asked.

"Yes. I'd like to review the Toxic Release Inventory," Anna replied, referring to an annual EPA report.

"Just a moment." The clerk pushed a button on his telephone. "Mr. Morelli, do you have a moment?" he said into the speakerphone. To Anna, he said, "He'll be here shortly. Why don't you wait over there?" He pointed to a small gray chair. Anna was soon greeted by a bearded man in his early twenties.

"Hi. I'm Anthony Morelli. You wanted to see the TRI data?"

"Yes."

"Do you know much about it?"

"Not really."

"Well then, let me give you a minilecture," he said with obvious enthusiasm. To Anna, he looked as though he had just finished college. He projected a youthful zeal, not yet frustrated from working in a government bureaucracy.

"Thank you. Should I take notes?" Anna asked.

"You're quite the charmer." By the tone of his voice, and judging by his grooming and mannerisms, Anna suspected men attracted him more than women.

"You know a lot of this stuff is online."

"What kind of information can I get?"

"Lots. Here, look." The clerk pointed to a booklet entitled *Chemicals in Your Community*, then accessed his computer. "You can find out what chemicals were released into the environment and whether a company recycled or shipped the stuff somewhere else. You can actually determine the emissions of a chemical in a certain area."

"Can I find out what one particular plant emitted?"

"Yes, but you should know about the limitations of our data."

"Limitations?"

"The results are estimates. There are no actual measurements."

"How do you know what was released?"

"You can't be sure. You depend on company reports."

"What other problems are there with the information?" Anna asked.

"Not all chemicals are covered."

"Why?"

"I'm not sure. There's a list of more than three hundred chemicals subject to the regulations. There's a lot of room for improvement." Anna nodded attentively as the agent continued. "Even though the results don't show the extent of how the public could be exposed to the chemicals, the information can pinpoint problem areas."

"How do you know whether the companies are being honest?" Anna asked.

"You don't! But the fines are awfully stiff for noncompliance."

"How much?"

"It depends on the violation, but fines range up to twenty-five thousand dollars a day."

"That's a reasonable incentive," Anna replied. "I think I ought to get to work even though I'd love to talk more. You've been very helpful. Thank you."

"You're quite welcome. What type of project are you doing?"

"It's for a graduate seminar."

"What field?"

"Environmental health."

"That's what I'd like to do. I want to go back to school to get a degree in environmental affairs. I want to get involved in policy."

"That's great. I wish you well." Anna turned to the large book that the clerk had just given her.

"Remember, I'm here if you need help."

"Thank you."

Anna paged through the phone book–sized report, which was titled "Toxic Release Inventory: Public Data Release." *The pleasures of academic life,* she thought. *When will I ever have the luxury of unfettered time again to drift through government documents?*

The introduction to the document included a letter from the EPA administrator, who described how the release of hazardous chemicals into the environment continued to decline and that pollution could be controlled by recycling and substituting with less harmful substances.

The report highlighted leading polluters, such as the chemical, metal, paper, and plastic industries. The top five chemicals released into the US environment included ammonia, hydrochloric acid, methanol, phosphoric acid, and toluene. Although this was interesting to Anna in light of her training in environmental health, she doubted that the information was pertinent to the plating firm and its potential link to the illnesses.

Paging through the document, Anna read that almost 50 percent of the toxic chemicals generated in production were recycled—either on-site or elsewhere. More troubling, however, was her recognition of the sheer volume of chemicals released into the air, into the water, or onto land through underground injections. One Louisiana company actually reported the release of nearly one hundred fifty million pounds of toxic chemicals! Anna reflected, *What effect could this have on people's health? Are people living near the plant?*

Anna thought about the plating firm. Suppose it was emitting hazardous materials. How would she know for sure? Would it matter? There seemed to be more questions than answers. Despite progress in controlling environmental pollution—whether through regulations or industrial efforts, or a combination thereof—numerous uncertainties remained, especially regarding the impact of the hazards on people's health.

Anna pursued her review until she found the entry on South Boston Plating. No unusual releases were reported!

Chapter 40

Dan Murphy finished his coffee and tried to push thoughts of meeting Anna later that night to the side.

"Dr. Murphy, there is a patient in room one."

"I'll be right there." He gulped the coffee, tossed the cup into the trash, and left his office.

Affixed to the door to the examining room was an angular tray holding a manila folder that contained the medical records of his next patient. Murphy recognized the file as belonging to his mother's friend Mrs. Johnson. He opened the door to greet her.

"Hello, Mrs. Johnson."

"Hi, Dr. Murphy. I hope you don't think I'm goofy coming back to you."

"Not at all. How can I help?"

"I'm convinced I have sick building syndrome."

"Why? What is it that troubles you?"

"Headaches, and I'm wicked tired at the end of the day. And sometimes my skin gets really dry and itches. And you know, a couple of other people in my office say the same thing."

"Have you told your boss about it?"

"Are you crazy? And lose my job! I need the money. My husband, bless his soul, passed away two years ago. I need to work."

Mrs. Johnson, well-groomed but charmingly outdated in hairstyle and dress, looked to Dan Murphy.

"Tell me a little more about your symptoms," Murphy said. "How do you feel when you're not at work?"

"I never get headaches. And I take good care of my skin. You probably think us women are crazy with skin creams, but I think they help. Aren't I a shining example?" she asked with a devilish grin.

"Of course," Murphy answered, quick to play along with the repartee. "How's your health otherwise? Are you taking any medications?"

"Only Tylenol, when I get headaches at work."

"Do you have high blood pressure, diabetes, or any other health problems?"

"No. My friends say I can be flaky." She paused, awaiting Murphy's grin. "But I'm usually healthy. That's why this worries me. What could it be? If I tell my boss, he'll say it's in my head."

"What's your work area like?"

"Nothing special. Just an office."

"You work at the plating firm, right?" he asked.

She nodded. "We do the paperwork, order the supplies, pay the bills, and get coffee and doughnuts."

"What does the plant do?"

"All sorts of odd jobs. Everything, but mostly plating. It's a job shop—whatever that means."

"Do you ever go through the plant?"

"No."

"Do you know anyone else sick from work?"

"Just the two women who work in the office with me. One calls in sick all the time."

"Have you had a cough or a fever, Mrs. Johnson?"

"No. Not since I stopped smoking when my husband died. My lungs seem fine. It's just these headaches."

"Have you seen any other doctor about this?"

"No. Just you, Dr. Murphy. What do you think?"

"Let me ask a few more questions, then I'll examine you and decide which tests, if any, might be helpful."

"OK," she answered in earnest.

"Have you ever had surgery?"

"No."

"Do you have any allergies?"

"Just hay fever. Why do you ask?"

"Some people with allergies are more sensitive to buildings with ventilation problems."

"How do you know it's a ventilation problem?"

"I don't, of course, but in many 'sick' buildings, the ventilation is not quite right. And they usually don't find any particular hazard. Something is usually wrong about the amount of fresh air, the humidity, or something else."

"How can you know for sure if it's the ventilation and not something else? I mean, Dr. Murphy, there are so many chemicals they use over there."

"There are ways of checking."

"How?"

"Let me think about it."

Murphy examined her eyes, ears, nose, throat, chest, heart, and abdomen. "Everything looks normal, and your blood pressure is great."

"Then why do I feel so bad?"

"How long has it been since you've had any blood tests?"

"I don't know. I think my gynecologist did some tests, but I can't remember."

"It's reasonable then to get a complete blood count and a blood screen for your liver, kidneys, cholesterol, and so forth. Then I'll see you in a few days and we can go over the results. In the meantime, take the Tylenol. Try to mark down when your symptoms are worse and when they're better. And let me know how your colleagues feel." Murphy, turning to leave, said, "Goodbye, Mrs. Johnson. I hope you feel better."

As he was about to shut the door and enter the hallway of the clinic, she called out to him, "Oh, Dr. Murphy?"

"Yes?"

"I don't know if this matters or not, but the symptoms are worse on Mondays, especially the past three weeks. Then I get better by the end of the week. Do you think that's important?"

"I don't know. It could be. Let's talk it over at your next visit." Murphy gave the list of Mrs. Johnson's blood studies to his medical technologist, then opened the door to another examining room.

"Hi, Doc."

"Mr. Shaw," Murphy replied, surprised at seeing Shaw so soon after the last appointment.

"I'm getting sick again. I went back to work on Monday. It's gotta be something over there at the plant."

"Why did you go back to work?"

"I need the money, Doc. I don't get paid if I don't work. There's no sick leave there. No work, no pay. But I think I screwed up, Doc."

Chapter 41

The ball sailed through the net just as the buzzer sounded to end the first half. Anna and Dan cheered along with the other Boston fans, watching their beloved basketball team, the Celtics. With a boyish enthusiasm for a sport that he had played with boundless energy during high school and college, Dan still found time, at age thirty-five, to play an occasional pickup game at the L Street playground.

"Well. What do you think?" Dan asked. Anna watched the Celtics leave the court for the halftime break.

"Great. The people really get enthused here."

"They love the Celtics."

"Beer here," yelled a vendor, an older man who sported a potbelly and a bushy mustache. "Beer here."

"Would you like something?" Anna asked.

"Sure."

"Sir." Anna motioned to the vendor, who removed the cap to the bottle and handed her a beer.

"Thank you," Dan said. "You're getting into the spirit of a Celtics game." He sipped the beer. Anna did the same. "What did you find out about the plating firm? Any surprises?"

"No. It was actually disappointing. The information is not going to help much. Even though I found a whole list of chemicals like acids, solvents, and cyanides, I have no idea how they're actually used at the plant."

"Have any of them caused aplastic anemia before?"

"No, at least in the articles I reviewed."

"How about plating firms? Are there any special risks of blood disorders or cancer?"

"Yes. Lung cancer from acid mists, but no special risks for aplastic anemia."

Dan drank his beer and looked ahead in thought. "So, even if this plating firm is not the healthiest place to work, there's nothing to suggest it has any connection with the aplastic anemia cases?"

"Right."

"How would you know then if it were something new?"

"A new asbestos, you mean?" Anna asked.

"Not exactly. A new relationship—something unexpected or perhaps just not reported. You know by now with all your courses," he said with playful humor, "that most physicians, including me, until recently at least, rarely consider whether work may have caused a disease."

"That's a good point," Anna acknowledged.

"Did you learn about the plant's environmental emissions?"

"They reported no unusual releases. Apparently, the amount of chemicals they use is not subject to reporting requirements, except for toluene, which has never caused aplastic anemia. The amount the plant uses is barely over the EPA reporting threshold."

"What does that mean?" Dan asked.

"The EPA requires companies to report the amount of hazardous materials they use if it is above a certain quantity. But everything's voluntary and the figures are only estimates. So, who really knows what may be coming from the plant."

The Celtics ran onto the court, and the crowd greeted them with resounding applause. Ahead by twelve points over their Philadelphia rivals, they seemed relaxed. Some took jump shots and others stretched, while the captain stood off to the side and talked with the coach.

"Beer here. Beer here," yelled the same vendor, who looked in Dan's direction, hoping to stimulate another sale.

"My turn?" Dan said to Anna.

"Yes. Of course."

As they tipped their bottles in a mock toast, Anna asked, "Did you learn anything more about your patients?"

"Which ones?"

"The man with hepatitis and the office worker."

"It's either coincidental or just plain strange, but they both came in to see me today. The office worker has a pretty convincing story about getting these terrible headaches only at work. And she says that other people in the office are affected."

"Does she have any other symptoms?"

"Tiredness. And her eyes bother her."

A loud buzzer announced the beginning of the second half of the Celtics–76ers game.

"The man with hepatitis came back too?"

"Yes." Dan sipped the beer. "He seems to have suffered a relapse. His liver enzymes are elevated again. They were normal last week."

"Was he drinking?"

"He doesn't drink. He went back to work, but I didn't know about it. I wasn't even sure whether he should go back to work."

"Why?" Anna asked.

"Because I didn't know whether he developed the hepatitis from work in the first place."

"Why did he go back to work?"

"He needed the money. He was feeling better and didn't want to bother me."

"Great work ethic."

"The Irish have an excellent work ethic. But it may have gotten him into trouble with his health."

The crowd cheered as the Celtics center broke through the foul line for a thundering dunk shot that shook the backboard so hard that the referee called a time-out. The Boston fans roared in appreciation of their team's twenty-point lead.

"Do you think the office worker and the man with hepatitis ..." Anna hesitated.

"Custodian," Dan interjected.

"Custodian, thank you. Do you think they're sick for the same reasons?"

"I'm not sure, but it's plausible."

"How could we find out?"

"Visit the plant."

"Why don't you? That would be interesting. Besides, you could take me. Even Becker would be impressed," Anna said, referring to her academic adviser.

"They're not interested. I called the plant manager again today."

The crowd roared, diverting their attention to the game. The scoreboard signaled the end of the third quarter.

"What could you do, Dan, to get into the plant? Could you call OSHA or the EPA?" Anna asked.

"OSHA, but not EPA."

"What could OSHA do?"

"They could conduct a visit, review records, sample for hazards."

"Why don't you call them?"

"I'm not sure if they'd come."

"Why not? Couldn't you explain that you think there's a health risk?"

"I suppose, but OSHA's overworked and understaffed. Besides, Anna, there doesn't appear to be a life-threatening hazard at the plant, so I doubt if my request would get much attention."

"You really don't know, Dan. Maybe your brother got sick from that plant!"

"He doesn't work there."

"Are you sure? He told me he does all sorts of trucking jobs on the side—waste deliveries and so forth. It's nonunion work, so he doesn't want to advertise it."

"Did he say he worked at the plant?"

"Not the first time I talked with him, but later, when I noticed that truck drivers had the highest rate of aplastic anemia."

"When's he work there?"

"He wouldn't commit himself. Just said he helped out at times."

The crowd cheered so loudly that Anna and Dan were jarred back into watching the game. The six-foot-ten center dunked the ball again.

"Do you think that your brother, the custodian, and the office worker could be sick for the same reason?"

Dan shook his head in reflection. "It seems like a stretch. Do you think your journalistic hunches are degenerating into bad fiction?"

Anna grinned in response. "Why not find out!"

"Any recommendations?"

"Yes, call OSHA," Anna said emphatically. "That plant deserves a visit. They're blowing you off when you have legitimate reasons to be concerned about your patients' health."

"That's tricky business. Why risk getting a reputation as a whistleblower!"

"Can't you do it anonymously?"

"I suppose, but how can you ever guarantee confidentiality?"

"I think you should. You'll be doing the right thing."

"If it were only that simple. I'm not sure those illnesses are the result of work. It's suspicious, but not definite."

"But what better way to find out? Call OSHA! You tried to be reasonable. You called the plant, what, three times! This is America. Three strikes and you're out. I played softball, so I know." Anna smiled.

"All right. You've convinced me. Can I convince you to leave? The Celtics are killing them. Let's go!"

"Where to?"

"Your choice."

"Would you like to come back to my place?" Anna's charm invited a kiss from Dan, who quickly responded to the overture. The crowd bellowed again in appreciation of their favorite center, but not enough to distract Anna and Dan from their passionate embrace.

A short ride later, Anna entered the foyer of her apartment building and led Dan up two flights of stairs to her one-bedroom unit. As she switched on the light, the cat dashed across the living room into the kitchen in anxious anticipation of food.

"Sit down. Can I get you anything?" Anna welcomed Dan.

"How about a beer?"

Anna opened her refrigerator "You're a lucky guy. Will Sam Adams do?"

"Definitely."

"I'll step out and have some bottled water," Anna said, opening a cabinet to take out some chips and salsa.

"How's your brother?"

"He's out of the hospital."

"That's good news."

"I'm not sure it is. He may have left too soon, but he was so restless there."

"How do you think he'll do?"

"He has to get by a few phases. The first is acute graft-versus-host [GVH] disease, which we've talked about with Harrington, where my marrow attacks his immune system."

"Do you think that Pat will get it?"

"It's difficult to predict. It depends on so many factors, like the genetic match we had on the marrow, his age, and whether he received blood transfusions before the transplant."

"Can it be prevented?"

"Not entirely. Medications reduce the risk, and other methods are promising. In Pat's case, they removed most of my T cells before they transplanted the bone marrow. Risk of complications is reduced when the donor's T cells are screened."

"Pat's doing well so far, isn't he?" Anna asked.

"Yes, but he called me today saying that he was really sick, couldn't get out of bed, had no energy, and had a low-grade fever."

"What do you think it is?"

"Hopefully, the flu."

Dan sipped his beer. Anna moved closer to him on her wide, soft sofa, the major piece of furniture in the living room. She reached her hand around his back, then traced up to his neck and rubbed her fingers through his hair. Responding instantly to the affection, Dan drew her head toward him and pressed his lips against hers. Unfettered by thoughts of Roger, Anna thrust her tongue into Dan's mouth and threw her arms around him, percolating with passion. The kiss unmistakably signaled her attraction to Dan, who caressed her ears and neck.

As Dan gazed into her eyes, he no longer saw a partner in an environmental project, but a beautiful woman whose intelligence and character added to the physical allure that he could no longer resist. He hugged her, felt the firmness of her breasts, then thrust his tongue deep into her mouth, a kiss that lasted minutes.

Throwing her hair back in confidence, Anna whispered, "How about some music?" She rose from the sofa to walk to her stereo. "Do you like Linda Ronstadt?"

"Anything's fine, as long as you hurry back to the couch."

Anna, grinning in a response that telegraphed her delight at their sexual energy, turned on the music.

"I notice you don't have a TV," Dan said.

"It's in the bedroom. Out here, I like music. It's better for reading and writing."

Dan drew Anna closer, kissed her again, and roamed his hands over her back, over her chest, and to her breasts, which invited his caress. Anna savored his touch and encouraged more. Dan obliged.

Soon they were rolling over one another in passion. Although Anna's bed would have allowed more room and comfort, the moment's intensity necessitated the sofa as the playing field. Dan slipped his hand under the back of her blouse to release the breasts he yearned to fondle. Piece by piece, they removed each other's clothing, barely allowing any space to come between them.

Fueled by deep, lengthy kisses and gentle touches below, Anna and Dan reached the stage of lovemaking that was bound to affect their relationship. Locked within one another's arms, they thrust and rolled and embraced until their pleasure could no longer be contained.

Anna kissed Dan on the neck while he drew her to his chest. Nestled together, within moments, they drifted off into an inviting sleep. About three hours later, Dan awoke, looked at his watch and then at Anna, who was fast asleep.

Dan's watch displayed five minutes past three o'clock in the morning. He looked at Anna, then he thought, *Now, what have I gotten myself into!* One gaze at her, however, assured him that she was worth the risk of the emotional tumult of another relationship. After being dumped by his wife, Murphy had avoided relationships of any depth. Customarily unwilling to immerse himself in an emotional whirlwind where the outcome was uncertain, he sensed things were different with Anna.

"Anna," he said, gently shaking her shoulder. "Anna." She opened her eyes, momentarily disoriented. "Let's go to bed!" Dan said. Anna, dazed, grabbed his hand to lead him into the bedroom. She drew the blanket and pulled him into bed with her.

"I love having you here," she said, kissing him.

"It's great to be here."

Anna turned off the bedside light then snuggled up to the man who was making her forget Roger.

—

On awakening, Anna went to the kitchen to start the coffee maker. Ever since nursing school, she had had a love affair with all types of coffee, whether Colombian, Jamaican, or Kenyan. She just could not begin her day without the caffeine jolt to which she was accustomed.

The coffee's aroma reached Dan, who began to stir on hearing the unwelcome blaring of the clock radio. As he looked at his watch, he realized he had less than an hour to get dressed, return to his apartment, and get to the clinic. Once he had stumbled into the kitchen, Anna presented him with coffee and a warm embrace.

"Cream or sugar?"

"Black. Cream and sugar masquerade the flavor."

"A connoisseur, I see."

As Dan walked by her into the bathroom, she said, "Help yourself to a shower. There are clean towels in there."

"What a hostess! Do I get breakfast too?"

"Don't push your luck."

After his shower, Dan went into Anna's bedroom, where she was watching a morning news show.

Dan sipped his coffee as Anna sat up in her bed.

"Don't you wish you were a graduate student?" she teased, as Dan scrambled to get dressed.

"I miss the lifestyle, but not the poverty. It's nice to be able to drive a decent car and go to restaurants once in a while."

Anna smiled in return. "Are you going to call OSHA?"

"I'm not sure."

"I think you should," Anna advised. "Aren't there all sorts of hazards at plating firms?"

"Definitely. They put metal coatings on materials like jewelry. Huge tanks of solutions use a metal salt and electric current to get the plating to stick."

"What kind of health risks do workers face?"

"Accidents like slips or falls. People can inhale acids or be overexposed to cyanides. I had a patient who worked at another plating firm who developed asthma from working with nickel salts. He wanted to keep working, but his asthma kept getting worse."

Dan drank the rest of his coffee.

"Would you like another cup?" Anna asked.

"That'd be great."

"I think you should call OSHA."

Dan drank his second cup of coffee as he considered Anna's suggestion.

"I've never had to call OSHA before, but this plating firm is strange. I'm not sure why they're resisting my efforts to come over."

"It's suspicious to me."

"Journalist's hunch again?" Dan asked.

"That and some solid health information. Your patients—and I know you think I'm stretching it, but it wouldn't surprise me if your brother and Liam O'Malley were involved."

"I can't see how."

"You won't unless you get some help—like from OSHA!"

"Let me think about it," Dan replied as he finished off the coffee. "Anna, I'd love to play graduate student for a day, but I have patients scheduled from eight thirty on, plus I have to navigate through Boston rush-hour traffic."

"Don't let me keep you," she said with a wan smile, reflecting her affection for him.

Dan bent over to kiss her. Anna pulled him toward her. He offered no resistance, allowing her embrace to draw him back on to the bed.

"You're going to make it tough, I see."

"Why not!" Anna said, kissing him again.

"I hate to go," Dan said, rising from the bed. "How about tomorrow night?"

"I can't wait."

"I'll call you later. Maybe we can find a decent movie. I need a little escapism."

Dan turned to leave. Anna remained behind in bed, watching *Good Morning America*.

"Don't forget to call OSHA," she called after him.

Chapter 42

Parker Barrows had mixed emotions about returning to London. Despite his having spent many stimulating years in England's capital, the city now served as a reminder of the most painful event in his life. As he walked through Hyde Park, he observed people riding horses on a trail dating back four centuries to King Henry VIII. The joggers, cyclists, and soccer players in the park prompted him to reflect on how the accident had altered his life. Barrows had always considered himself an athlete. In fact, he had played organized sports for most of his life until the explosion.

Rugby, squash, and tennis had sustained Barrows's athletic interests throughout his school, college, and young adult years. Now, as a result of his amputated leg, golf and swimming were the only practical outlets for physical activity. Barrows, however, loved neither. Swimming, he found tedious and boring, while the absence of his right leg limited his ability to hit a golf ball straight or at any distance. His decline in physical activity and the corresponding effect on his self-confidence had led to a tendency to drink alcohol and eat without great discretion. Despite the progress made by people challenged by amputated limbs, Barrows could not accept his infirmity as permanent and adapt to the inevitable change to his self-image and the constant impact on his life. He had struggled through numerous prostheses and hours and hours of physical therapy. His altered self-image, he realized, may lay at the heart of his problems, including the headaches and sleep disturbances, for which he hoped the psychiatrist would provide guidance.

As he ambled along to his hotel, Barrows reflected on the days he had spent living in London. The din of street activity generated by the hackney cabs, the double-decker buses, and the occasional motorcycle evoked fond memories. To Barrows, London represented the quintessence of British society, whose history, culture, and civility distinguished it from other major cities of the world. The theater district, in particular, provided Barrows with a sense of pride for England. Whenever time permitted, he enjoyed the comedies, musicals, and plays that Soho offered. *How could the Irish be so arrogant as to want to rip themselves away from Mother England?* he thought, considering the Northern Ireland situation.

On entering the hotel to meet his colleague, Barrows wondered whether he could mount the strength to visit the site of the explosion in London's theater district. Just the thought of the infamous Italian restaurant caused him to feel faint and light-headed. He sensed his palms being overcome with moisture as he rode the elevator to the rooftop restaurant of the London Hilton.

In typical fashion, Kerry Butler had arrived early and was awaiting Barrows at the bar.

"Parker. How are you?" He extended his hand, greeting his former classmate.

"Could be better," Barrows answered sardonically, "especially after a scotch. I see you've beat me to the punch. Is that tomato juice or a Bloody Mary?"

"You don't think I'd drink tomato juice after noon, do you? Why do you think I agreed to meet you at one o'clock?" he replied with a good-natured grin. Butler nibbled on peanuts as Barrows waved to attract the bartender's attention.

"It's been a long time," Butler began. "What's new?"

"That's what I need to know. What's going on?"

"The PM's position is to stay fast," he said, referring to the British prime minister. "He is not interested in any changes to the Brexit agreement on Northern Ireland. This invisible border through the Irish Sea will eventually kill Northern Ireland and force it to merge with the Republic of Ireland." Barrows was referring to the British agreement on Northern Ireland in which the European Union insisted on no hard border between Northern Ireland and the Republic of Ireland to the south, as stipulated in the Good Friday Agreement of 1998.

"The bloody nationalists," Barrows responded. "They can't be trusted. I don't know why we bother with these peace plans."

"We have to. The political pressure's enormous."

"I know." Barrows nodded.

"Especially since the US president welcomed the Sinn Fein leader to the United States. Now, they've been raising all sorts of money from gullible Irish Americans." Butler continued, saying, "The Protestants feel on the defensive.

A maître d' approached them. "Your table's ready, gentlemen." Barrows followed his former classmate from University College in Dublin, where they had studied Irish history and political science. Few of their fellow students knew that their education had been funded by the British secret service, who hoped their knowledge of Irish affairs would improve their effectiveness in intelligence operations. Both received additional training in Irish-accented English, including idioms and dialect. They also learned the Irish native tongue, Gaelic. Eventually, their appreciation for the nuances of the language helped them determine the origin of suspected terrorists. Barrows, in particular, developed a keen ear for distinguishing the dialect of Belfast from that of Dublin.

After drawing chairs up to the full-length windows that facilitated panoramic views of London, Barrows continued, "Do you think there is any way we can influence these Brexit negotiations?"

"Probably not."

"So, then what?"

"An impasse, sprinkled by outbursts of violence."

"It doesn't sound promising," Barrows remarked.

"It's even more complicated because there may be a change in government soon. The PM is going to call an election, and the Labor Party is more sympathetic to the demands of the Irish nationalists and doesn't think Northern Ireland is worth the trouble. As I see it, it's the start of the eventual merging of the North with the Republic of Ireland."

"That's crazy," Barrows retorted. "We should make sure that never happens."

"How?"

"I have options."

"I'm listening."

"In Boston. But I need more information."

"Like what?"

"When are they coming to Boston?"

"You mean the negotiating team?"

"Yes."

"Next week."

Butler then described the probable location and the participants invited to a diplomatic meeting to promote the final settlement to Brexit and Northern Ireland.

"Boston's a great choice," Barrows offered.

"It's ironic to hold the exchange there in light of all the IRA fundraising that has taken place in Boston. Irish Americans have an idealized view of Ireland. Most have never been there, but they have this fantasy of a united Ireland, as though the British haven't been there for more than three hundred years."

"Is anything going on now in Boston to help the IRA?" Butler asked.

"I think so."

"What?"

"I haven't quite ironed it out, but it may be serious."

"Any threat to the peace delegation?"

"You never know. South Boston has been too receptive to illegal immigrants from Ireland. It's also a pipeline of cash to the Catholics in Northern Ireland."

"Of course."

"Remember in the mid-1980s a boat named *Valhalla*, the one intercepted off the coast of Ireland in the Atlantic? It was carrying a few tons of weapons."

"Right! What happened to those people?"

"You don't want to know."

The waiter approached their table. "Would you like coffee, gentlemen?"

"Yes, that would be quite nice," Barrows answered, showing a civility lacking in his response about the disposition of the *Valhalla* criminals. Moments later, the waiter returned with coffee. Barrows and his colleague completed their plans.

Boston had been chosen. Boston served as a relatively neutral site in comparison to Belfast, Dublin, or London. Ideally, Boston would reduce the likelihood of protests and violent activities.

Butler would get the dates for the meeting of the peace delegates, then inform Barrows of the hotel where the British team would be staying in Boston.

Chapter 43

Dr. Murphy, entering the Occupational Health Clinic about fifteen minutes late, was relieved to hear his receptionist sharing some good news. "You're late again, Dr. Murphy, but you're lucky. Your first two patients called to reschedule. You're free until nine thirty." The unexpected free time gave him an opportunity to get through some paperwork, the least appealing aspect of his medical practice. Reports on patients and reviews of medical tests and hospital policies all required his attention. Murphy doubted that hospital officials understood the extent of the administrative responsibilities assumed by physicians, especially those who directed departments. He sensed that some viewed physicians as "revenue generators" who, if not seeing patients, were not properly "utilized."

Murphy looked to his bookshelf and withdrew a three-ring binder with notes from his course in occupational medicine. He needed to refresh his memory on the physician's role in requesting a work-site visit by OSHA, the Department of Labor agency that enforces occupational health and safety regulations.

After paging through a chapter on the Occupational Safety and Health Administration, he called the number listed for its Boston office.

"Hello. This is Keith Richardson. Can I help you?"

"Yes, I'm an occupational physician. I'm calling because I could use some help in dealing with a health problem that may be related to a local business."

"What type of business?"

"It's a plating firm."

"What makes you think there's a health issue?"

"A combination of factors. First, I've treated two people who work there. One has hepatitis, and I haven't been able to determine the cause. Another has symptoms seemingly related to poor indoor air quality, and her recent blood studies show liver abnormalities. The two cases may be related, but I can't be certain."

"Anything else?"

"Well, yes. Do you have some time?"

"Go ahead."

"A colleague of mine," he said, pausing momentarily to reflect on describing Anna as a colleague, since she had become much more to him, "has been doing a project on aplastic anemia. She's looked into all sorts of environmental possibilities—the air, the water, and even emission reports submitted to the EPA. She didn't find anything definitive about an environmental cause, but her work pointed to truckers having an extraordinarily high risk of the disease—about sixty times higher than normal."

"Interesting," the OSHA official responded, "but what does that have to do with the plating firm?"

"Well, she went back to the truckers to understand their work in more detail—what kind of contact they had with the materials they shipped, whether they loaded and unloaded, and so forth."

"What did she find?"

"Some strong leads to this plating firm."

"Such as?"

"One of the truckers who died of aplastic anemia also worked, sort of off the record, at the plating firm."

"What do you mean?"

"He worked for cash."

"Have you tried to get into the plant?"

"A number of times, but not with any success."

"What did they say when you called?"

"Not much. I can't recite the precise words, but they essentially blew me off. They weren't hostile or suspicious, just indifferent and uncooperative."

"Have you tried anything else?" the OSHA official continued.

"I asked my administrator at the hospital for help, but he couldn't do much either."

"What would you like us to do?"

"How about visiting the plating shop? Find out what's going on."

"On what basis?"

"Health risk. A point can be made for a possible death from aplastic anemia, a case of hepatitis, and now liver dysfunction in an officer worker. Plus, their refusal to allow me entry is suspicious."

Murphy paused. Perhaps the discussion was becoming needlessly complicated. He only wanted OSHA to use its authority to check the company for any health hazards that may have affected his patients and his brother, Pat.

"Your timing couldn't be better," the compliance officer said. "Our director just canceled a staff meeting this morning, so I could probably do something today."

"Excellent," Murphy answered. "I understand my name will be kept confidential."

"If you'd like us to, of course."

"Definitely. As I suggested, there appear to be complicated social issues with the plant, but I'm concerned about the health implications."

"I understand. Thanks for your call. It's not very often that we get a call from a physician."

"My pleasure. I hope it helps." After hanging up the phone, Murphy turned and saw Brenda, the nurse practitioner, standing at the entrance to his office.

"Getting adventurous?" she asked with a devious grin. "What can OSHA do?"

"Conduct an inspection. Look the place over. Write up violations. Fine them," Dan answered.

"Are they effective?"

"It depends, but they have a good reputation for determining whether a company is complying with OSHA regulations."

"Do you think they can help?"

"I hope so. They can review records, walk through the plant, talk with workers, and do air sampling."

"When do you think they'll have any results?"

"Who knows!"

"You have a patient waiting in room one." Murphy's receptionist interjected over the interoffice phone.

"We'll have to leave the suspense of OSHA till later. Time to get back to work," Brenda replied.

—

A few hours later, Keith Richardson, representing OSHA, pulled into a warehouse parking lot in South Boston. He walked in the direction of Boston Harbor until he reached a three-story brick building. In the midst of a howling wind, he dodged a truck to cross a street and reach the entrance to the plant. At the end of the building, which was two football fields in length, a hand-painted sign over a metal door identified South Boston Plating. Richardson was met by a woman in her early sixties who sat inside an enclosed glass booth.

"May I help you?" she asked methodically. A portable TV was set off to the side. A talk show host was interviewing women whose husbands had had affairs with their daughters' college friends.

"Yes. I'd like to see your plant manager."

"You mean Mr. Flannagan?"

"Yes."

"What do you want?" she asked without a hint of grace.

Richardson showed his OSHA identification card.

"What's this mean?"

"I'm from the Occupational Safety and Health Administration. I'm here to talk with the owner or the plant manager."

"What about?"

"That's a matter I'll take up with him. Would you mind calling Mr. Flannagan?" Without responding, she abruptly turned away from the window, then pushed a button on the phone.

"Mildred, there's somebody here to see Mr. Flannagan. Says he's from OSHA or something." She paused for Mildred's response, then turned to the OSHA official. "Wait a minute."

The small waiting area that separated the receptionist's cubicle from the plant lacked furniture, so Richardson patiently waited by standing off to the side. Although accustomed to chilly receptions on his visits to factories, he usually hoped for civility. Moments later, a short, balding man in his late fifties appeared. "What can I do for you?"

"I'm Keith Richardson. From the Occupational Safety and Health Administration. I'd like to talk with you for a few minutes."

"I don't have time."

"I hope you'll reconsider, Mr. Flannagan," Richardson said, showing his identification card. "Is there a place where we can talk?"

Expressionless, Flannagan opened the door to the plant by operating an electronic buzzer. He called to Richardson, "Push the door."

The OSHA rep passed by a clerical area staffed by late-middle-aged women. Mrs. Johnson, Dan's patient with symptoms she thought were the result of poor indoor air quality, sat off in a corner and quietly attended to her work. She stole a glance or two as Flannagan, then led Keith Richardson into his modest office, outfitted in steel-gray military-style furniture. Papers, catalogues, and empty bags from fast-food restaurants were scattered about.

"What do you want?" Flannagan assertively asked. "Don't you guys get tired of regulations? You're killing business."

Richardson, accustomed to comments more acerbic than Flannagan's, moved to the business at hand. "Let me tell you what I'd like to do."

"Shoot." Flannagan snarled.

"I want to take a look at your injury and illness log, the safety data sheets, and records of your training programs. You can put me in an office, and I'll go about my work. We can talk later."

"I'll get the girls to get that stuff for you," Flannagan responded dryly.

"I appreciate it. These things go much more smoothly if we co-operate with one another."

"Mrs. Johnson, get him what he needs. He can use that side office." Flannagan then turned to the OSHA official. "You'll let me know when you're through, I take it?"

"Of course. We usually have a closing conference."

"A conference! Let's not make this a major production."

"Yes, of course," Richardson replied. Moments later, Mrs. Johnson guided Richardson into a small room outfitted with a table and six chairs. Amid the bare white walls and tired linoleum floor, he drew up a chair.

"Would you like some coffee?" she asked.

"Yes. That would be nice," Richardson answered, a bit surprised by her cordialness in comparison to Flannagan's abrupt style.

"Now, what did you want me to get?"

"Here, I've written it down for you." Richardson handed her a standard OSHA form that he used when conducting site visits.

"Just a minute." She walked to a bookshelf, removed three large binders of documents, then placed them on the table. "These are the injury and illness records. I fill them out, so let me know if you need any help."

"Thank you."

"And these are the chemicals—the safety data sheets, I mean." In a hushed voice, she continued, "You know, it's interesting. One of our employees asked for these the other day to take to his doctor. But Mr. Flannagan doesn't know about it. He'd go crazy. Don't tell him I told you."

"Of course not."

Richardson looked through the injury records, most of which noted back ailments caused by lifting. Burns and eye injuries were also reported, along with the occasional laceration. No serious illnesses such as asthma, cancer, or aplastic anemia were reported.

"Who's your insurance carrier?" Richardson asked Mrs. Johnson.

"For workers' compensation?"

"Yes."

"I'm not sure. Mr. Flannagan keeps switching companies."

"Why?"

"I don't know. I suspect to save money. One of the companies wanted him to put in new ventilation over the acid tanks, but he said it cost too much, so he dropped them."

"I see."

"Don't tell him I told you that either."

"Don't worry," he replied with a warmth that suggested he could be trusted. "Do you have the safety data sheets?"

"Yes. These binders," she said, referring to the books in which the chemicals used in the plant were noted. The documents included all sorts of information, such as how to clean up spills, whether workers needed special medical examinations, and whether protective equipment is needed.

Richardson thumbed through the file. On first glance, he found no surprises. Typical materials at plating firms, such as acids, solvents, cyanides, and metal salts, were noted. "Do you have any exposure records?"

"What are exposure records?" Mrs. Johnson asked.

"Do you ever determine whether the air levels for the workers of these acids and solvents are within recommended limits?"

"I don't know. You'll have to ask Mr. Flannagan."

At the same time, Flannagan's name was bellowed over the public address system by the plant operator. The plant manager then walked over to a telephone near the acid tanks.

"Flannagan," he yelled into the phone.

"Flannagan, this is Jake Wilson. Why'd you call? What's up?"

"That's what I want to know. I got some asshole here from OSHA."

"Why the fuck did you let him in?"

"I thought I had to."

"Hell no. Tell him to get a warrant, and throw his ass out."

"Are you sure I can throw him out?"

"Throw him out and don't let him walk through the plant. Call me if he gives you any trouble."

"Fine, I'll take care of it," Flannagan said, annoyed as usual in dealing with Wilson. Flannagan, however, liked the extra work and cash he got from Wilson for storing his materials and felt a kinship from helping his Irish compatriots who were unable to get green cards. He walked into the office in which Richardson was poring over files.

"Hello, Mr. Flannagan," the OSHA official greeted the owner.

"How's it going, pal?"

"Fine, but we don't seem to be able to locate your exposure records."

"What are you talking about?"

"Records of air testing of the chemicals that you use to determine if it's safe for your workers and whether they need respirators or medical exams."

"I don't know where they are," he answered. Mrs. Johnson narrowed her eyes in suspicion. Richardson, the OSHA official, noticed her expression, which he interpreted as indicating that the plant probably never did any monitoring.

"Besides," Flannagan continued, "this place is safe. Look at me and the old-timers around here. There's nothing wrong with us. All these regulations, they just cost money. They don't do anything."

Richardson had heard all these comments before. None of them were new.

"Look, I'd like to walk around your facility, talk to some of the employees, maybe do some air sampling."

"I'm afraid not," Flannagan replied.

"Why? It shouldn't take long." Mrs. Johnson looked at Flannagan as she and the OSHA agent awaited his reply.

"You need a warrant."

"Usually I don't."

"You do here."

"Most companies cooperate."

"We will as long as you do it our way," Flannagan said emphatically. His tone made it clear that he was not poised for debate.

"Are you serious? You really want a warrant?"

"Right. I'd like you to leave. We have work to do."

"Your choice, Mr. Flannagan, but I advise against your approach. It's not difficult for me to get a warrant. Why don't we wrap it up now?"

"Company policy, sir. Goodbye." Then he turned to leave. To Mrs. Johnson, he said, "Show him out, please."

Later that day, after returning to his office, the OSHA official called the South Boston Occupational Health Center.

"Dr. Murphy, this is Keith Richardson from OSHA."

"Hello. I'm surprised to hear from you so soon."

"I don't mean to bother you, but I want to follow up on your call about the plating firm."

"How can I help?"

"How serious of a health risk do you think is present at the plant?"

"What do you mean? And why?"

"Your thoughts have a lot to do with what I do next."

"What do you mean?"

"The plant manager or owner, whatever he is—he never quite identified himself—told me to get a warrant to review the plant."

"You're kidding! What do you think is going on?"

"I'm not sure. The whole encounter was strange. At first, I was greeted with an acceptable distance. They let me use a room, where I looked over some records, but then for no obvious reason, I was told to leave."

"I'm sorry to hear that," Murphy responded, feeling in part responsible for Richardson's experience with the plant manager.

"No problem. This happens."

"There seem to be some questionable activities going on, although it may be just how small businesses struggling to survive operate. They cut corners, especially health and safety controls," Dan said.

"But how serious of a health risk do you think it is?"

"Well, if I can be dramatic, death from aplastic anemia or hepatitis."

"I'll talk with the director of our office and get an attorney involved. I think there's enough here for a warrant."

"My name will be kept confidential, correct?"

"Of course."

"Dr. Murphy, I appreciate your diligence. I'll let you know what happens."

Chapter 44

Looking out a window on the twenty-second floor, Barrows worried about the integrity of his plan. Fifteen years old when he left Belfast, Northern Ireland, he had accompanied his parents to Birmingham, England, where his father gained employment as a toolmaker. Educated in England and trained in the British military, he avoided discussion of his Northern Ireland background. In fact, few knew about his heritage. Recent events, however, had caused a profound alteration in Barrows's view of Northern Ireland. The explosion in the London restaurant so disrupted his otherwise charmed life that his attitude changed completely. Old friends were struck by the new personality, which had degenerated from a zest for life's adventures to hostility and anger.

Barrows, frustrated by the Good Friday Agreement and the Brexit terms for Northern Ireland, was furious with the US government's policy toward Northern Ireland. According to the Protestants, or Unionists as they were also known, the Brexit terms would be a detriment to them in many ways, most especially in that they would no longer be a part of the United Kingdom and instead would be merged with the Republic of Ireland. If forsaken by England, they would become a minority in a new Republic of Ireland and lose the benefits to which they were accustomed. The prospects of losing the privileges of the majority held little appeal to Barrows and others who abhorred any peace settlement as the first step to capitulation and a united Ireland.

To Barrows, the Northern Ireland debacle had ruined his life. He had lost not only his wife, but also his pathway to senior leadership in British Military Intelligence. Without a functioning right leg, sedentary assignments became his only option. No longer could he drift underground and be unrecognized as in the past. His clandestine intelligence activities for the British government had provided an excitement that, although filled with danger, motivated him. In its place loomed a zeal for retribution that overwhelmed him and affected virtually all his activities. Beneath the veneer of social grace, so essential to the schmoozing required of him in terms of his business responsibilities, was a man burning in rage. His own plan to exact retribution for his unrelenting misery offered him an outlet that he began to crave.

—

Tony Mesa drove to Jamaica Plain in the same blue Ford pickup truck that he had been using for the past three years. Oblivious and at times hostile to the dictates of fashion, Mesa usually appeared as though he had just worked on the engine of his car. Barrows repeatedly reprimanded him about his unkempt appearance because of the attention that would inevitably be focused on a well-dressed businessman cavorting with a guy garbed in attire unsuitable for a lumberyard. To soften Barrows's ire, Mesa wore a clean work shirt and black pants.

As Mesa drove his truck along Center Street in the Jamaica Plain section of Boston, he caught a glimpse of Barrows, already seated at a booth by the window. A streetcar rumbled by as Mesa pushed open the door to the restaurant.

"Big trouble, mate," Mesa said as he saw Barrows. He took a seat in the booth where Barrows had been waiting for him.

"Do you have to wear that hat?" Barrows asked condescendingly, referring to the blue wool ski hat, a Mesa trademark during the winter. Mesa removed the hat and launched into conversation.

"Something's up! Wilson called. OSHA went over to the plant."

"OSHA. What are you talking about?"

"The feds. The workplace police."

"What were they doing there?"

"I don't know."

"There's a leak," Barrows said.

"Where? Not many people know what we're doin'."

"I have no time for nonsense, Mesa. This matter has gone too far to let it get out of control."

"What makes you think it's out of control?"

"Why would OSHA be there?"

"Periodic check. Who knows?"

"Find out how it happened, then teach somebody a lesson they won't forget. You understand?"

"Right."

"Is anything else falling apart?" Barrows abruptly changed the topic.

A waiter appeared, tentative about interrupting them.

"Gentlemen, can I get you anything?"

"Johnnie Walker black—a double," Barrows replied, the affectation of his accent catching the waiter's attention.

The waiter nodded, then turned to Wilson.

"You have any draft?"

"Yes. What would you like?"

"A pint."

"My pleasure." The waiter turned away.

"What are we gonna to do with all this stuff?" Mesa asked.

"You'll learn in due course. Find out how OSHA was called, and have Wilson do something about it."

"What do you have in mind?"

"Whatever. Make sure they know they're in over their heads."

Moments later, the waiter appeared with their drinks. Barrows rose from the chair, then gulped down his scotch. Mesa looked at him in disbelief. "Aren't you gonna eat?"

"Not hungry," Barrows replied as he put on his coat, then threw a twenty-dollar bill onto the table. "Keep things under control."

Barrows walked away just as the waiter approached the table. "Would you like anything to eat?"

"Yeah! A thick greasy hamburger," Mesa answered.

"You'll have to go elsewhere, sir," the waiter answered snidely.

"Only kidding."

"What's wrong with your pal?" the waiter asked Mesa.

"Nothing. He's just an asshole."

Tony Mesa thought about Barrows, who despite appearing like an arrogant British aristocrat, claimed sympathies with the IRA and those who sought the unification of Ireland. His story of why he had turned against the British interests in Northern Ireland appeared plausible to Mesa. After all, he had lost his wife, his leg, and his career. Mesa never questioned Barrows about how he had lost his leg. He enjoyed the money that Barrows paid and did not need details for the easy, well-funded work he provided.

As Mesa munched on his hamburger, he looked around the room at lots of Irish faces. Raucous conversation filled the restaurant, where the food was known to be great. Not one to question motives, Mesa wondered about Barrows and whether his stated intentions bore any resemblance to the truth.

Chapter 45

The announcer for the soccer match raised his voice in excitement as a goal was scored. Parker Barrows quickly switched the channel. Britain had lost to Germany again.

As Barrows fumbled with his prosthesis, his attention was drawn to the sore that had developed on his stump. Having already undergone two surgical procedures to remove infected bone tissue, he was unenthusiastic about letting the orthopedic surgeon take more of his leg away. On the other hand, the unrelenting ache constantly reminded him of his disability. *Why couldn't these therapists find an artificial leg that wouldn't grind and irritate what little remains of my thigh?* he thought. Now, armed with information provided by his colleague Kerry Butler in London, Barrows grew confident that taking matters into his own hands would rid him of the curse that obsessed him. Only by clearing the world of the scoundrel who had orchestrated the explosion that ruined his life could he avenge his misery. In light of the progress in the Brexit talks on Ireland, he feared that political agreements would interfere with his self-imposed justice. If the current terms were enacted, Barrows feared that his nemesis would get amnesty or some other reprieve from accountability. A similar fate would likely await other Irish criminals, who he felt should rot in eternity in the most abominable jails that the British government could construct. Barrows mused that if he were involved in the peace negotiations, nothing would be given away to the nationalists. *In fact,* the former intelligence officer fumed, *they ought to be pleased to be part of the UK. Ireland would be better served, including the republic to the south, as well as the north, by being part of the United Kingdom. After all, Ireland has only four million citizens. What could it possibly accomplish as a nation?* he thought bitterly.

As he prepared to visit his psychiatrist, Barrows considered what he would tell him. Only by implementing his own solution, namely, exposing IRA support in Boston and disrupting the negotiations, could he achieve the contentment that eluded him. Such an event would draw public attention to the Brexit discussions on Northern Ireland, which the UK government tended to place at a very low priority. Looking at a picture of his wife seated on the horse she loved, Barrows felt the surge of a tear, an emotion that had lain dormant since the accident. Despite the agony of losing his wife to terror, his emotions had been blunted. He never quite dealt with the grief from the tragedy, which ultimately led him to seek out a psychiatrist.

After a short ride from his condominium in Boston's Back Bay to the Longwood medical area, Barrows arrived at Dr. Steven Reed's office.

Shortly, he greeted the psychiatrist. "Some new pictures?" Barrows asked.

"Oh yes," Reed answered, flattered by the attention and anxious to describe another part of his life. "I had them enlarged after a trip to Australia. I just got around to having them framed."

"Why were you in Australia?"

"A psychiatry conference. About our favorite topic—posttraumatic stress disorder."

"That's a nice way to get a tax break," Barrows offered.

Ignoring the barb, Reed went on about his trip. "Sydney has one of the most beautiful harbors in the world, as good as Hong Kong or Rio." He was at ease demonstrating his familiarity with the world's great cities.

Reed then opened Barrows's medical file, a routine associated with the beginning of their sessions. "So, tell me. How have you been?"

"The same."

"The headaches?"

"Yes. And the nightmares are getting worse. I can't get a decent night's sleep."

"Tell me about the nightmares. What do they involve?"

"Anything about the accident. It varies."

"Can you describe them?"

"It's difficult to generalize. I may hear a siren that reminds me of the ambulance, and it'll keep wailing until I wake up."

"Then what? How do you feel?"

"Terrible. I'm breathing heavy, perspiring, wide awake."

"Can you give me an example of a recent dream?"

Barrows reflected momentarily. As he considered his response, he recalled a terrifying dream of a few nights ago.

"Yes. I was sitting in a restaurant, then I heard this wailing police siren, typical in the UK and elsewhere in Europe. Then my leg felt on fire. Then it seemed like a dog was chewing on my stump, until I heard someone yell, 'Rex,' and the dog pulled away. I woke up, and my leg throbbed. I felt palpitations in my chest, and my clothes were drenched with perspiration. I looked at the clock: it was three in the morning."

Dr. Reed nodded to indicate his attention to Barrows's comments and subtly encouraged him to continue.

"Then, I can't get back to sleep. I look at the pitiful condition of my leg and my empty bed and wonder whether I'll be able to get up in the morning. I get out of bed, hobble around, then have a shot of scotch. It helps calm me down," Barrows offered somewhat apologetically.

"I see," Reed responded.

"Sleep should be a refuge," Barrows said. "But for me it's terror."

"What else do you recall dreaming about?"

"Almost anything. It could be my wife. I might see her on a horse, then watch her fall. Then I'll see her mother crying uncontrollably at her funeral. Some other time, I'll see her casket being lowered into the ground and hear her calling out to me."

"Do you have nightmares every night?"

"No. If I drink enough, I can sometimes eliminate them. But then I feel terrible the next day."

"Yes. Of course. Alcohol suppresses REM sleep, which is when people dream. It's the period of sleep that's most critical for restfulness. Alcohol to induce sleep is deceptive. It may make you tired, but it's not a restful sleep."

Dr. Reed guided Barrows through more discussion about the dreams. He hoped to understand activities that provoked the nightmares and troublesome visual images that his patient experienced. Reed also delved into Barrows's background, including his work in Boston and, more important, the reasons why he chose to move to the United States from the UK.

"During our last session," Reed began, "you told me why you came to Boston, saying that you wanted to track down who was responsible for the explosion and that you think you've located him." Reed stopped, hoping for Barrows to respond to the prompt. After a brief pause and no response from his patient, Reed continued. "It would help me understand your situation if I knew more about you so I can appreciate the context in which these nightmares are occurring. So, if you could lead me along."

"Such as?" Barrows's curt response, coupled with his arms firmly folded across his chest, suggested to Reed that his patient had scant interest in opening the gates to his past.

"Let's start with what you do in Boston."

"I work at a consulting firm. We help promote UK business in the States."

"What sort of things do you do?"

"Arrange meetings. Go to socials. Have lunch." Barrows's response reflected his indifference to his working life.

"Do you enjoy it?"

"It's all right. It's not difficult. It gives me something to do."

"And you chose Boston because you thought would find the person responsible for the explosion?"

Barrows nodded in agreement.

"But why? Why would you come to Boston?"

"It's not that complicated. Certain parts of Boston have been supportive of and sympathetic to IRA efforts."

"Interesting." Reed nodded.

"There's a fundraising network. They harbor illegal immigrants. They provide safe havens for people running away."

"I can't imagine this. Wouldn't more people know about it?"

"It's known, certainly in the intelligence community."

"But why Boston? Why would you look here?"

"I can't describe our methods or sources, but I've found the bastard responsible." Barrows raised his voice in anger.

"Are you sure you've found him?"

"Yes."

"Have you turned him in?"

"No."

"Why not?" Reed asked.

"I have my reasons."

"Such as?"

"There's too much uncertainty now with the Northern Ireland situation."

"But why wouldn't you want to turn him in?"

"It won't work."

"Why?"

"I can't get into it," Barrows answered emphatically. He then stared directly at his psychiatrist with an expression that said the topic was off-limits: there would be no further discussion.

The psychiatrist, recognizing that he had reached an impasse through which Barrows would not allow passage, chose to switch topics. "Parker, I realize this is difficult for you, so in the remaining time, I'd like to ask you about the UK."

"Fine."

"Have you gone back to London since this explosion?"

"Once."

"What was it like?"

"I had mixed emotions. It felt different to me. As though I no longer belonged."

"Did you go to the restaurant?"

"Yes."

"Tell me about it."

"I walked to the theater district, and the closer I got, the worse I felt. It was like feeling all of the nightmares at the same time. It was horrible."

"I see," Dr. Reed responded, again hoping Barrows would continue after the gentle prompt. When his patient failed to respond to the cue to continue, Reed said, "Parker, tell me about this person you think was responsible.

"These sessions are confidential?" he asked, not fully trusting the concept.

The psychiatrist answered assuredly, "Most definitely."

"He's actually an American, but he went to Ireland, then London, like some idealist-driven cowboy who thought he was going to save Ireland." Barrows's voice grew angry and loud.

"What did he do? Plant the bomb in the restaurant?"

"No. That was done by one of their sleepers, a stooge of some sort." Barrows's voice grew louder as his speech became faster.

"But why wouldn't you turn him in?"

"Because it won't work. I have to take care of this myself."

"What do you have in mind?"

Once the buzzer to Dr. Reed's office phone alerted the psychiatrist that the session had come to an end, Barrows left the office, showing no interest in telling the psychiatrist his plans. Dr. Reed, however, was struck by Barrows's ominous comments and knew they could not be ignored.

Chapter 46

The OSHA inspector rang the buzzer outside the brown steel door of South Boston Plating. Amazed at how easily he had obtained a warrant, Richardson felt that the plant manager, despite his intransigence, could be handled. Earlier that day, the inspector could not locate records of any air measurements of the chemicals used at the plant. Now, to measure the airborne hazards, he had brought a portable sampling device to the plant. His small pump would draw air through a test-tube-like glass cylinder. The ensuing results would allow Richardson to evaluate how well the plant controlled exposure to the acids, cyanides, and solvents involved in the plating process. Although a more detailed analysis could be conducted later, Richardson was confident that his screening survey would uncover potential problems.

The receptionist greeted him with an indifference similar to that he had encountered during his last visit. "You want to see Mr. Flannagan?" She seemed more interested in the soap opera that was playing on the TV behind her than assisting him.

"Yes, please." Richardson answered politely.

"Just a minute." She then called into the intercom, "Mr. Flannagan!"

Richardson waited in the entry cubicle. Since it didn't seem as though the receptionist would invite him in from the cold, damp entryway, he took the initiative. "You don't mind if I step inside, do you?"

"Just a minute. He'll be right here."

"Do I need to wait here?"

"Like I said, he'll be right here. I can't let you in. Just be patient."

Richardson sensed that his earlier visit had been widely announced to everyone at the plant. Rarely would the OSHA representative need a warrant to conduct a work-site inspection. In his seven years with the federal agency, he had been forced to take that course of action only once or twice a year. In those rare situations, there was rarely frank obstruction, but rather a polite resistance attributed to company policy. On one occasion, he was refused entry even with a warrant—the most tense professional encounter of his career. The actions of an obstreperous plant manager at a small foundry in northern New Hampshire necessitated the security backup of a local sheriff to enable him to conduct the survey.

Richardson, as was customary, strove to be professional by not taking insults personally. His role was to ensure that the plant controlled any potential hazards to the employees. Personal abuse by rude people who were annoyed at his audit was just an unpleasant but inevitable part of the job.

"Richardson. You're back," Flannagan sarcastically greeted the OSHA rep.

"I've followed through as you've suggested, Mr. Flannagan," he answered politely. "Here's the warrant."

Flannagan, his eyebrows raised in surprise, looked over the papers as though he doubted their authenticity. "So, what's this mean?"

"I can review the plant, talk with the workers, and take measurements."

Richardson also carried a camera with his sampling equipment. Taking pictures of various parts of the plant was another option available to him according to OSHA regulations. He had enough savvy, however, not to show the camera or suggest pictures to Flannagan at this time, because it would likely provoke a heated exchange.

Richardson, with no interest in engaging the plant owner in a discussion of the role of OSHA and its regulations, hoped to avoid a tense standoff.

"I'd like to discuss plant operations with you, if you have a few minutes."

"Whaddya wanna know?"

"Can we talk in that room?" Richardson motioned to the office where he had spent time earlier.

"What do you want to know about the plant?"

"I understand you do plating. Could you tell me what types?"

"That's the problem with you regulators. You don't know industry. You never worked in a plant. What kind of a background do you have anyway? How do I know you know what you're doing?"

Richardson quickly recognized that Flannagan was prepared to dig in his heels. Although the warrant would allow him to visit the plant, the OSHA rep anticipated minor indignities along the way. Rather than allow himself to become emotionally entangled with Flannagan, he stepped back from the fray.

"Mr. Flannagan, I understand this is not a pleasant exercise for you. But we ought to be polite about it."

"Polite? You come here for God knows what reason, wanting to look at the plant, talk to my workers, and look at records. Who are you?"

"I assure you that I go about my work with the greatest professional care. You will be treated fairly."

"What kind of education do you have?"

"I have an undergraduate degree in chemistry and a master's in industrial hygiene."

"Industrial hygiene? What's that?" Flannagan asked.

"It's what brings me here. Industrial hygiene is concerned with evaluating chemicals and other workplace hazards. We also recommend control measures, if necessary."

Although Flannagan listened, Richardson had no illusions that he would convert him into an advocate for occupational health.

"Whaddya know about plating?"

"A bit from chemistry courses. I've also been to a few other plating firms. Why don't you tell me about your operation?"

Rising from his chair, Flannagan seemed anxious to demonstrate that he knew more about plating than the OSHA rep.

"Here. It's pretty simple." He pointed to a diagram that included a drawing of a rectangular tank. "In plating, you put a coating on another piece of metal. This is silver plating. The tank holds two metal rods." He pointed to the diagram.

Richardson nodded with interest.

"Each metal rod in the tank is connected to a battery with direct current, like your car battery. Then the metal in solution, the silver nitrate or whatever, gets plated onto the metal."

"You've explained it well," Richardson said, consciously appealing to Flannagan's vanity in an attempt to soften his ire.

"Anything else I can tell you?" *It worked,* Richardson thought. A little stroking and even crusty types like Flannagan could be tolerated.

"Why don't you show me around?" Richardson asked.

"What do you want to see?"

"From start to finish. Where the materials come in, what you do with them, where they go, where you store them."

"You don't want much, do you?" Flannagan answered, his tone lapsing back to disdain.

"It'll be painless. Let's go," the OSHA rep replied. The plant owner led him to the loading area where goods were delivered and where finished products were shipped. Two men drove forklifts. Off to the side stood a few green fifty-five-gallon drums.

"You don't store these here, do you?" Richardson asked, expecting a negative reply.

"Oh no. We have a storage area."

"Can I take a look?"

"Over here." Flannagan led him to a corner of the shipping/receiving area, where he opened a large metal door that led to a room filled with metal and plastic containers of all shapes and sizes.

"You should have these metal cans on a wooden crate, not on the floor," Richardson said, trying not to be argumentative, but wanting to ensure proper precautions were followed. "To reduce the risk of accidents caused by chemicals, you need special storage areas away from production."

"Right," Flannagan answered. *I can't believe I have to put up with this nonsense. How can I get rid of this guy?* he thought.

"Can we see the plating lines?" Richardson asked.

Flannagan led the OSHA official into the production area, where Richardson was immediately struck by a haze hovering over the damp, dark work area. As he walked amid the plating baths, he noticed a worker pulling a rack of metal findings destined for the costume jewelry market from a degreasing tank. Another worker stood to the side, smoking a cigarette, an activity prohibited in nearly all other plating firms that Richardson had visited.

Richardson noticed the local ventilation units over the plating tanks and recognized the effects of casual maintenance. Housekeeping—how well that spills, trash, and materials were handled—appeared abysmal. As the OSHA rep walked on the wooden planks placed between six parallel plating lines, each of which consisted of eight tanks, he recalled how Charles Dickens had written about nineteenth-century British workplaces, thinking that this plating shop would fit some of those descriptions. He then reflected on two modern plating operations at high-tech firms that were a striking contrast to South Boston Plating. They were clean, bright, and open; the workers were well-dressed in protective gear and went about their work with care and precision. At South Boston Plating, spilling acid on the floor was probably not unusual since Richardson noticed workers with burn holes in their pants and shirts.

"Where's your degreaser?" the OSHA rep asked.

"Over there." Flannagan pointed to an area away from the plating lines.

"What do you use?"

"Trichlor."

"Trichloroethylene?"

"Yes. Why?"

"I think there are safer alternatives."

"Trichlor is fine. Nobody complains. It gets the parts clean."

"Do you ever clean the degreasing tank?"

"Once in a while."

"Do you have a confined space policy?"

"Policy? You need a policy to clean a tank? Are you kidding? These regulations get worse all the time."

Richardson was referring to an OSHA standard that requires certain safety procedures for people who work in confined areas, where oxygen levels may be low. Each year, needless deaths occur, often to people in their twenties and thirties, because they went into a confined area without the proper breathing device.

Richardson quickly recognized that South Boston Plating took a casual attitude toward its regulatory responsibilities. Whether the plating firm was making people sick, however, was an entirely different matter. To help answer that question, he would need to conduct air sampling of the chemicals at the plating lines.

"Thanks for acquainting me with your operations," Richardson said. "I'd like to go back to your office and make some notes. Then I'd like to talk to some of your employees and take a few measurements."

"What?" Flannagan asked, unable to conceal his frustration.

"It's routine. No need to be alarmed."

"Why do you wanna talk with the workers? What do they know!"

"It's routine."

"Measurements too!" Flannagan declared. "What do you want to do, give Breathalyzer tests?"

Richardson chuckled, but not in a way to offend Flannagan. "It's a preliminary way to see how well the ventilation system and your other controls are working."

"Go ahead," he said, not hiding his disgust. "Do what you need to do. I'm tired of this," Flannagan said, turning to walk toward the main office.

Richardson removed the sampling device from his equipment bag to prepare for measuring the concentrations of the acids, solvents, and cyanides in the plant. After sampling a number of work areas, he looked over the plant in more detail, then talked with a few workers. After an hour or so, he looked for Flannagan to discuss his impressions of the visit.

Mrs. Johnson, the friend of Dan Murphy's mother, greeted the OSHA agent. "Finished?" she asked.

"Yes. I'd like to talk with Mr. Flannagan. When we conduct a site visit, we usually have a closing conference where I go over the findings."

"I'm sorry. Mr. Flannagan left for the day."

Richardson looked puzzled. "Did he say why?"

"No."

Chapter 47

Why wouldn't you turn him in? What do you have in mind? The voice of Dr. Reed reverberated in Barrows's mind as Barrows readied himself for a meeting with Tony Mesa. After another difficult night of sleep, in which he had gained but a few hours of rest, Barrows thought about gulping the bottle of antidepressant pills that lay on his dresser. *Maybe if I take them with some scotch,* he thought, then reached down to prepare his prosthesis. He continued to obsess about extracting retribution from the man he held responsible for the current state of his life.

Barrows then drove to a restaurant in Cambridge to meet Tony Mesa.

"Parker, my man," Mesa bellowed as Barrows entered the restaurant. "Have a seat."

"It'll be a pleasure," Barrows answered in perfectly enunciated British English. Pulling out a chair to sit, he said to Mesa, "You're looking well. Been boxing lately?"

"As much as I can."

"And you manage to keep your face clean."

"That's 'cause no one can hit me," Mesa said with unflappable self-confidence.

"Let's order," Barrows suggested, changing the topic of conversation.

"Hey, dude!" Mesa hollered to an elderly Chinese man, assiduously carrying five plates full of various meat and rice dishes. The aroma from the freshly cooked dinners distracted Mesa.

"What are you eatin' today, Park?"

"Whatever," he responded agreeably.

"How about we get this dinner number five for two? You'll be my date," Mesa said in obvious jest.

"Fine."

"Good evening, gentlemen. What can I get you?" the waiter asked.

After they made their requests to the waiter, Barrows and Mesa went to work.

"So, what's going on with Wilson?" Barrows abruptly asked. "Anything new?"

"Not sure yet."

"Is he still in contact with Sinn Fein?"

"Yeah."

"They have their own web page," Barrows offered.

"Each week, they publish a newsletter, *Ahn Phlobacht*."

"No shit," Mesa replied in surprise. "IRA has a website?"

"Enough nonsense, Mesa. Will Wilson deliver?"

"As long as I'm involved."

"No more money until the final delivery," Barrows lectured.

"When do we need to be ready?"

"A week or so. Things are moving fast on the diplomatic front. This trip to the US by the negotiators will accelerate everything. It's the perfect time to force the Brits out of their intransigence on Northern Ireland."

"Intransigence? Remember I dropped out of college, Park."

"Resistance. Stubbornness. Unwillingness to change."

"That's what Wilson said. The only way the Brits will do anything is by force."

"You learn quickly."

The waiter approached the table with bowls of fried rice and sweet-and-sour chicken. As Barrows drank Chinese tea, he said, "You'll be paid handsomely. Just follow through on Wilson."

"He's been getting suspicious, Park, about where the money and information's coming from. I don't think he likes the idea of you being a mystery man."

"He'll meet me soon enough—on my terms. Just tell him what I told you—that I'm a wealthy benefactor who is supporting Ireland. Tell him that for business and professional reasons, everything needs to remain confidential." How Ireland was helped, however, was considered differently by Wilson and Barrows.

Barrows continued, saying, "I see no compelling reason to treat Wilson as anything other than as a contractor. Just like a plumber or carpenter or painter, Wilson does work on request. He doesn't need to know the whys and wherefores. He should do what's requested and provide the services for which he's paid. It's that simple."

"So, what should I tell him about our plans?" Mesa asked.

"That he should follow orders, do his job, and be quiet about it. You should have no difficulty keeping him in line. Perhaps we should send him another message. What do you think about having him picked up, mugged, and dropped off in the woods somewhere?" Barrows posed the question in perverse delight.

"Not a good idea. It would only make him more suspicious."

"But it would be nice, though," Barrows responded, whose facial expressions mirrored those of a troubled soul whose unfulfilled sense of justice burned like a cauldron.

"Look, I gotta give my bladder some relief, Park," Mesa said, rising from the table. "Make sure he gives you the Chinese cookies," he said with his typical laugh.

In Mesa's brief absence, Barrows's mind wandered. He thought about Wilson, the Brexit negotiations, and whether he'd be able to pull off his scheme without creating suspicion of his own involvement. For the first time, he realized that Mesa would probably have to go as well. Simply getting rid of Wilson may not offer the protection he needed. Properly executed, the whole episode would appear as a failed

IRA effort that would demonstrate their untrustworthiness, unreliability, and utter unsuitability for participating in Brexit deliberations about Northern Ireland.

Barrows's thoughts reverted to Mesa, whose influence over Wilson had brought them far along in their effort. It was Mesa who had diligently and painlessly extracted details of Wilson's background that persuaded Barrows of his culpability for the London blast attributed to the IRA. Mesa learned that after the explosion, Wilson ducked UK authorities, then went to Germany and the US Virgin Islands, before reaching South Boston, where he found an apartment. Soon thereafter, he resumed his original name of Wilson, which he had ceased using when he first went to Northern Ireland with his ex-girlfriend. She had urged him to use his mother's maiden name of Casey because she feared that a name like Wilson, sounding too English, wouldn't sit well with the locals.

Returning to the United States after three years in Northern Ireland and England, Wilson underwent plastic surgery to correct a nose deformed in a skirmish in a London pub. With his shoulder-length black hair shorn and a remodeled nose and chin, the Jake Wilson of South Boston looked strikingly different from the John Casey who was pursued by British authorities. Mesa, through his bar hopping lifestyle and with his good old boy disposition, eventually tracked down Wilson for Parker Barrows.

Mesa returned to the table and drank his tea, then asked, "How'd you like the sweet and sour, Park?"

"Actually, quite good. Here's what I'd like you to do with Wilson."

Chapter 48

Dan Murphy drove to the Harvard medical area to pick up Anna, who was now scrambling to finish her report for Becker's seminar. They decided that a Steve Martin comedy would be an appealing way to start the weekend. Anna loved movies, and the idea of accompanying Dan motivated her to complete the first draft of her project.

Murphy had spent the early part of the evening catching up on his seemingly endless array of paperwork. As a result, a nine-o'clock movie at his favorite theater loomed as the perfect antidote to a long day.

Dressed in black pants and a red wool turtleneck, Anna greeted Dan at the entrance to her apartment. "Great to see you," she said, stretching up to kiss him on the lips.

"Likewise," Dan responded, as he threw his arms around her. Within minutes, Dan led her to an old Volvo struggling to reach 180,000 miles.

"What did OSHA say about the plant?"

"Not much. I talked with the inspector tonight. He spent the afternoon there."

"Anything unusual?"

"Nothing dramatic. Just a series of minor issues like sloppy housekeeping, bad records, and broken-down ventilation in one area."

"Were there any violations? Will there be any fines?"

"Possibly. He said he'd write up a report and send me a copy."

"Is he going to do anything else?"

"He's not sure. He may need to go back to do more air testing."

"That's encouraging."

"But he didn't seem that enthused. His comments suggested that this was a typical mom-and-pop plating shop."

"What do you mean?"

"Small plating firms aren't appealing places to work. Often they're old and dingy, with all sorts of chemicals around."

Dan pulled his car into a metered spot in Back Bay, a block away from the movie theater.

"So, the OSHA inspection hasn't really helped much, has it?" Anna said with a hint of discouragement.

"No, but the inspector thought the whole exchange was bizarre. The plant manager gave him a hard time, made him get a warrant, then disappeared."

"I keep belaboring you about my journalist hunches, but that plating firm seems suspicious to me. I think we need to look beyond the obvious with them."

"Why?"

"Your brother."

Dan reached the ticket booth. "Two," he said. Dan and the clerk exchanged money and tickets.

As he and Anna walked into the movie theater, she asked, "How's your brother?"

"Not good."

"I'm sorry. What's happening?"

"I'm not sure."

"Why don't we escape for a bit?"

Dan handed the usher the tickets.

"Great idea! I need a few laughs," Anna said, grabbing his hand to lead him into the theater.

Dan and Anna laughed through the exploits of Steve Martin as he bounced around in a romantic comedy filled with clever slapstick and wry humor. As the credits appeared at the end of the film, Anna turned to Dan. "That's just what I needed."

As Dan drove Anna back to Brookline, he asked her, "So, how's the project? Have you finished writing it up?"

"Almost, but I'm having trouble pulling it all together. I really haven't found a specific cause, just this elevation among a few truck drivers. And I haven't been able to make any sense out of their risk. What am I going to say to Becker?"

"Look at the bright side: you've demonstrated a risk for truckers. You've shown how to get some of the environmental information that's out there, and you may be uncovering a real problem at the plating firm."

Anna looked toward Dan as he stopped the car at a traffic light. He gently rubbed his hand across her thigh.

"Don't be so gloomy. Has the movie worn off already?" he asked.

Anna smiled again, then stretched across the seat to kiss him on the cheek.

"Do you think I should refer to the OSHA visit in my report?"

"Yes. At least Becker won't say you didn't pursue the truckers' risk."

"As soon as I get a copy, I'll get one for you."

"You're a sweetheart," she responded.

—

Murphy regretted having passed up Anna's offer to stay at her apartment as he drove away from her Brookline neighborhood. It was much too late, however, and his stint at the health center tomorrow began much too early. If he had not agreed to cover the ambulatory care center for one of his colleagues, he would be in her arms now. Within a few hours, he needed to be at the hospital, prepared to evaluate people with a variety of illnesses and injuries, and work through a twelve-hour shift. Since it was in the midst of a January flu outbreak, the day would likely be busy. Given his decision to leave Anna's, Dan recognized a maturity that he hadn't possessed years earlier. Then, he would surely pursue the pleasure of the moment at the risk of feeling unexcited about going to work in the morning.

As Murphy turned onto Commonwealth Avenue, he noticed a police car pull out of a doughnut shop's parking lot. Moments later, the cruiser's red light flashed behind him. Surprised at the signal, he stopped the car, turned off the engine, and waited for the policeman.

"License and registration," a tall, fit policeman demanded.

Murphy looked at him inquisitively and asked, "What did I do?"

"License and registration. Your taillight's out." Murphy reached into his glove compartment to get the registration papers, but as he opened the door, a small plastic sandwich bag fell to the floor.

"What's that, pal?" the policeman asked suspiciously. He shined the flashlight at the floor in front of the passenger's seat.

Dan reached over to pick up the bag.

"Let me see it," barked the police officer, who looked over the contents and noticed powdered white material. "Get out," he ordered Murphy, who, petrified at the rapid turn of events, readily complied.

"Stand up against the car," the cop ordered in a belligerent tone that suggested any resistance would not be tolerated. The policeman frisked Dan from head to toe, paying particular attention to his legs and back. "You're under arrest." He then placed a pair of handcuffs around Dan's wrists.

"For what?" Dan asked in fright.

"For what? Are you crazy?" the cop answered. "What are you doing with cocaine in your glove compartment?"

"I have no idea. I have no idea how that got there."

"That's what they all say. Just don't be a smart-ass." The police officer led Dan to his cruiser, opened the back door, and directed him to enter. After getting into the driver's seat, the policeman called into his radio.

"This is 542. Got a druggy. Possession and transportation of cocaine. I'm bringing him in."

Murphy, sitting in the back of the cruiser, couldn't believe what was happening. *What's going on?* he thought. The cocaine didn't belong to him.

"You know that's not mine," Dan said, as the policeman pulled away.

Ignoring Dan's comment, he said, "Don't worry about your car. It's being impounded."

"I said that stuff doesn't belong to me. I've been set up."

"Save your alibis for the judge. I've got better things to think about."

The policeman turned up the radio and continued toward the local precinct of the Boston Police Department.

Dan felt powerless. How could he reason with this cop who acted as though he had nabbed a drug suspect whose capture made him look alert to his superiors? As they pulled into the station, Dan said, "Do I really need to wear these handcuffs? They're killing my hands."

"Don't be a candy-ass. You should have thought about that before you put that shit in your glove compartment."

"I told you it's not mine."

"And I told you I don't run the alibi department, so save it."

Dan was struck by the condescending attitude of the police officer. Finding a bag of cocaine in a glove compartment apparently convinced the cop that his suspect deserved no respect.

"Let's go." The cop directed Dan into the police station and into a room with a large desk, behind which sat another policeman.

"What do we have here?" the second officer asked sarcastically. "Another druggy. These guys never learn," he said to the policeman who arrested Dan.

"Stand over here," the cop at the desk said to Murphy. The arresting officer gave the dispatcher Dan's wallet, including his license. As he thumbed through the contents, he came across Dan's hospital identification card.

"Dr. Murphy," he said, emphasizing the word *doctor*.

Murphy looked at him, unclear how, or whether, to respond. "That stuff doesn't belong to me."

"I know. I know. That's what they all say. Everybody we pick up for coke, crack, whatever—it always belongs to someone else."

Murphy looked straight ahead, resigned to the fact that reason would not prevail. Moments later, he was led into another room, where he was fingerprinted and photographed. After taking a Breathalyzer test for alcohol, he handed over all his clothes except his underwear and socks. Even his shoelaces had to be surrendered to the admitting officer.

Murphy was then led to a private cell, where he was told, "Stay here for a while."

"What?" he asked incredulously.

"You heard me. We'll get back to you. No smart talk."

Dan walked into the cell, which was ten feet wide and ten feet long. On each side was a wooden bench. In a corner at the far wall, a toilet without a seat was sitting adjacent to a sink without a towel.

In the background, Dan overheard policemen talking about a car show. Amid the cacophony of sounds and the unpleasant odors that reeked of urine, prisoners could be heard yelling in anger, with obscenities directed at the guards. The word *fuck* was used in every possible form—as noun, adjective, and adverb, and as an expression of surprise, anger, or delight. It reminded Dan of how marginal comedians could always rescue themselves and get a laugh out of teenagers by saying *fuck* in their routine. The clang of cell doors being opened and closed added to the dissonance that amplified Dan's fears of being in jail and the corresponding uncertainties of his fate.

Occasionally, the noise from other prisoners was interrupted by a cop who bellowed, "Sandwiches, sandwiches," as he walked among the jail cells with a plate of cold burnt toast.

"Let me the fuck outta here," someone in another jail cell hollered. The number of jail cells was a mystery to Murphy since those arrested didn't benefit from the courtesy of a tour. From the size of the building, staffed by about six policemen, Dan surmised that there were probably a dozen cells.

"I've been here twelve hours, you motherfuckers," the same voice bellowed shamelessly and stupidly in the background. "Let me outta here."

Dan went to look at his watch, then realized it had been taken when he was admitted to jail. His frustration brewed as he recognized that he had yet to be afforded fundamental rights such as making a phone call or being told how much bail he'd need to post. Seething about his powerlessness and vulnerability, he couldn't understand the need for condescension and rudeness by the police who tended the jail cells. Perhaps years of dealing with hardened criminals and the corresponding risks of physical assault and verbal insult had caused the cops to mistrust everyone. Struck by the outright hostility and belligerence that the police demonstrated without provocation, Murphy adopted a low-key approach.

His cellmates included people charged with crimes ranging from driving while intoxicated, to prostitution, to breaking and entering. Dan fretted about how he fit into the picture and became incensed at his inability to make at least a phone call. Fortunately, his sense of reason had yet to become impaired; he controlled his anger and struggled to maintain his composure.

Eventually, a policeman came to his cell. "Let's go," the cop said as he opened the cell, then placed handcuffs on Dan, who was led to a small office.

"You're charged with possession and transportation of a controlled substance. Bail is five thousand dollars. If you don't have it, you'll have an arraignment on Monday," the desk sergeant said without emotion. Without bail, Dan immediately recognized he'd be spending the weekend in jail.

"Can I make a phone call?"

The desk clerk pointed to the cop who had brought Dan from his jail cell. "Take him over there. No long-winded blabbing sessions."

Gratuitous nastiness, Dan thought. *These guys must watch a lot of bad movies.*

While agonizing in his jail cell about what to do, Dan fretted about whom he would call for help out of the mess. His decision wavered between his brother, Anna, and the chief of medicine at the hospital, but on further reflection, he concluded that the hospital was the last place he wanted to contact. The repercussions of the arrest, regardless of the outcome, would likely prove detrimental to his reputation. Murphy had never been arrested. Aside from a fender bender and a couple of parking tickets, his driving record was impeccable.

Dan dialed Anna's number. After a few rings, he heard her tired but friendly voice saying, "Hello."

"Anna. This is Dan."

"Dan! What's wrong." Immediately sensing a problem, Anna became alert.

"I know this will sound hard to believe, but I've been arrested."

Chapter 49

Jake Wilson lay across the sofa watching an adventure movie. Suddenly, his memory flashed back to a day when he lived in the Ardoyne area of Belfast, where a huge brick wall separated the Catholic neighborhood from the Protestants. Vividly, he recalled his friend's house being searched—floorboards turned up and kitchen equipment tossed about as the Ulster RUC "searched for criminals." Another flash reminded him of their family album with photos of funerals, bombings, and parades, reflecting the terror that had become a fact of life in this working-class area of Belfast. His mind then conjured memories of all sorts of mischief in which he had engaged under the guise of promoting a united Ireland and sending the British back to England—barricaded streets, bombed cars, and gasoline bombs, all done to force the British out.

Although the IRA's campaign of terror had led to an untold number of personal tragedies among the Catholics, the Protestants, and unsuspecting bystanders, Wilson believed that its violent activities kept the hope alive for a united Ireland. Eventually, Wilson, or Casey as he was known in Northern Ireland, had become a "sleeper," an IRA agent in England.

As Wilson's attention was distracted by a commercial, he began to finalize the plans for his work with Tony Mesa. He limited the selection of people for the project to those with whom he held some leverage. Pat Murphy, still hospitalized following his bone marrow transplant, had fallen into debt with Wilson because of his gambling fiascos. Now, Wilson needed to cash in a chit with Murphy. Wilson would not let him off the hook for the final part of their scheme whether Pat was sick or not. He dialed the hospital.

"Hey, Murphy! How the hell are ya?"

"Wilson," Pat answered with palpable annoyance.

"I know you're glad to hear from me."

"It's a gas, Wilson."

"I need you tomorrow night."

"I don't know."

"Do what you need to do to get outta there."

Actually, Pat thought, *it wouldn't be such a bad idea to leave the hospital.* The confinement had hardened his mood. "I don't know," he said, trying to keep Wilson off-balance. Despite his debt to him, Pat enjoyed annoying Wilson for the sport of it.

"Tomorrow night," Wilson answered, showing no hint of compromise. "No nonsense. Just be there."

"I'll do what I can," Pat said, valiantly trying to maintain equal footing in the conversation.

Before Wilson could answer, his apartment door slammed open, and in walked Tony Mesa, who was carrying a case of beer.

"Hey, dude. Gotta a good-lookin' chick on the line?"

Wilson ignored the comment and concluded with Pat.

"This isn't bullshit, Murphy, and I ain't fuckin' around." He hung up the receiver without awaiting a response.

"Got your boys ready?" asked Mesa, whose customarily pale face had blushed a bright red in response to the subzero weather.

"No worries, my man. Everything's under control."

"Then let's get the poker game started. When're the other dudes comin' over?"

"About a half hour from now."

"Let's get drinking. Why wait for them?" Mesa opened two bottles of beer and handed one to Wilson. "We've come a long way, dude."

"We're not there yet. Lots can go sour."

"You've kept it tight, haven't you?"

"Yeah!"

"Do you think any of them have any idea what's going on?"

"No."

"Why?"

"I don't get questions. People like the money, and they know how to keep their mouths shut when they work for me."

"Only you, me, and your mystery moneyman know what's happening," Wilson said sarcastically, referring to Parker Barrows. "I don't know why I can't meet this guy."

"Is your head that thick? He can't risk exposure."

"I still don't know what the hell he wants to do."

"What would you do?" Mesa asked, attempting to extract information to relate later to Barrows.

"I told you: Do it in the US. Let Americans know what's going on in Northern Ireland."

"And how would you do that?"

"Target British interests—embassies, chambers of commerce, businesses. Put them on the defensive."

"But so what! What'll that prove?"

"It'll make people pay attention. The Brits won't do anything unless they're forced."

"What would work?"

"Getting the Brits out of Northern Ireland. That's the first step." Wilson's anger caused the volume of his voice to increase as though he were rousing an audience at a political rally. "Then the Unionists—the Protestants or whatever those fuckin' assholes call themselves—have to negotiate in good faith. Fuck that idea of giving up the arms. Do they think we're stupid?"

"Calm down, dude. You need another beer," Mesa said as he walked to the refrigerator. "Do you think the IRA can bomb the Brits into leaving?" he asked, getting back into the fervor of Wilson's dialogue.

"Definitely. The Protestants won't give up. They'll fight down to hand-to-hand combat. There's so much anger in families that it will take a generation or more to get rid of it. People have lost fathers, sons, brothers."

"What good would more violence do?"

"Keep Northern Ireland in the news. Keep the Brits on the defensive. Motivate the American Irish. Get the message out. The demands are reasonable. Just let everyone on the island of Ireland vote, not just those in the north."

Wilson paused to drink his beer as three consecutive knocks on the door sounded.

"Our buddies," Mesa said. "Good ole Al Struck and his pal are reliable."

"They ain't got no choice in the matter," Wilson replied, rising to greet the people he had blackmailed into working with him and Mesa. Over beer, poker, and cigars, they hoped to iron out the details of their final engagement. They played cards until well past midnight as lively country music played in the background. Along with the poker and beer, they talked about women, football, and how they would spend a lot of money. Wilson and Mesa carefully avoided discussion about Ireland or anything remotely political in front of the others. As far as Struck was concerned, they needed the material for a construction project.

—

The next day, Wilson bought a large white van at a used car lot, then drove it to an auto paint shop. By the end of the afternoon, he was driving a pale green van with STERLING HARBORS emblazoned in bold black letters across all sides. He found it surprisingly easy to buy the truck with cash and have it registered in a phony name. Purchasing a car at the end of the month in an area without much employment was a snap. The dealer seemed willing to bend the rules to make a sale.

That evening, Wilson drove the Sterling Harbors van to the security gate at the manufacturing plant, where he showed the bogus papers and was waved on to the property as planned. Al Struck, as expected, was waiting at the end of the shipping dock, seated in a small cubicle. On recognizing the truck, he guided them into the loading area. Within minutes, the three of them maneuvered a few dozen fifty-five-gallon drums onto the van with the help of forklifts, crates, and raw heavy lifting. Just as they were about to finish, a tall, well-built man in his midthirties approached the loading dock.

"Hey, Al, what's going on?"

"Getting rid of some stuff that's been hanging around back there."

Their exchange caught Wilson and Mesa's attention, each of whom stopped, walking to the front of the van.

"I didn't know this was going out tonight. Are you sure?" the man said to Struck.

"Yeah, it is," Struck answered laconically, hoping he'd go away.

"Where are the shipping papers?"

"Inside."

As the man left the dock, Wilson moved toward Struck in a commanding show of physical superiority. "What the fuck is goin' on here? Who's this asshole?"

"They sent him over today. He's doing some kind of audit."

"No shit!" Wilson exclaimed. "What's he gonna do?"

"Not much after I get him," Mesa offered. Turning to Wilson, he said flatly, "This guy's gotta go."

Moments later, the auditor reappeared. "I can't find any papers," he yelled to Struck. "Where are they?"

"I think they're out here," Wilson yelled. "In the back of the truck."

Wilson jumped into the van, and the supervisor followed. Wilson moved to the back of the van to lift an envelope from a shelf. Just as he was about to hand it over, Mesa punched the man on the back of the head with such resounding force that the man fell instantly. "Let's get out of here," Mesa said, with the nonchalance of a man having just taken out the trash.

"What are we gonna do with him?" Wilson asked. He looked at the man, now unconscious, sandwiched between two large barrels.

"Take him with us," Mesa answered.

"Are you crazy?" Wilson replied.

Al Struck stood on the loading dock, unsure what to do as he looked nervously around.

"Let's go. We'll figure out what to do with this asshole later," Mesa said, referring to the supervisor, now prostrate on the floor of the truck.

Wilson followed the cue and walked toward the truck's cabin. To Struck, Mesa said, "If anybody's looking for this clown, tell them he went home sick."

After driving out of the plant, Wilson turned to Mesa. "What do you want to do with that guy?"

"We need some booze," Mesa said, then turned on the country music station. "Stop at a liquor store."

After driving a few miles to get the whiskey, they had only a short ride to the bar where earlier Wilson, Mesa, and Struck had drunk beer, watched football, and played darts.

Wilson pulled into the parking lot behind the two-story brick building. As he passed an alleyway behind the bar, he stopped the van. Mesa jumped out, opened the back door, then dragged out the auditor, who still showed no signs of reviving.

Wilson asked, startled at the effectiveness of Mesa's stroke to the head.

"He'll have a long nap." Mesa lifted the man onto his shoulders, then laid him on the ground next to the delivery door of the bar. "Where's the booze?"

Wilson handed him a brown bag that held a bottle of whiskey. Mesa opened it and sprayed it over the auditor's jacket and pants, then put the bottle in his left hand.

"That's it," Mesa said, then poked Wilson in the ribs. "Time to go."

Within minutes, Wilson was driving onto the interstate highway that would take them through New York state, and then to Massachusetts, on their way to South Boston.

"So, what happens when he wakes up?" Wilson asked.

"Nothing. Just another drunk who didn't know when to stop."

"But Struck's gonna get hammered."

"So what?! Struck doesn't know shit."

"It's a leak, though."

"Jake, my man. With your combat training, what are you worried about?"

"You can never be too tight."

They drove in silence for a while until they reached a truck stop. After coffee, Mesa was energized for conversation, especially anything related to Wilson's earlier work as an IRA operative. He needed information for Barrows.

"You must be charged up now," Mesa said.

"Yeah! I'd still like to know what your mystery man wants to do," Wilson answered, referring to Barrows.

"Be patient, dude."

"Patience—great quality of the Irish. It's taken centuries to get rid of the fuckin' Brits."

"I could use a good history lesson, man. Tell me about the Irish, their patience, and why you give a shit."

Wilson lost no time in relating his understanding of key features of Irish history, most of which he had learned in Northern Ireland and London as an IRA operative and Sinn Fein member. He emphasized how the Irish voted for full independence as long ago as 1918, but shortly after their fight against the British began, the British government asserted its authority. In 1922 the British carved out six countries in the north of Ireland for the Protestants, who traced their heritage to the late 1600s. At that time, the Orangemen, led by William of Orange, defeated King James in the Battle of the Boyne.

This military campaign, Wilson recounted, gave rise to the Orange parades, which take place each summer throughout Northern Ireland. The marches occasionally provoke civil unrest, protests, and altercations because the Protestants march through Catholic neighborhoods. Wilson emphasized how people resent the inherent superiority and political dominance symbolized by the parades.

"The fuckin' Protestants say it's their culture," Wilson added, referring to the Orange parades.

"What's the big deal?" Mesa asked. "It's a parade, for God's sake."

"It's not that simple. Why do they need to go through Catholic neighborhoods? It's just intimidation."

The sound of a blaring horn distracted them as a huge tractor trailer roared by.

"It's arrogance and superiority of the Brits. Even their prime minister had the guts to say that Northern Ireland is as British as Surrey."

"What's Surrey? Sounds like a lousy French wine," Mesa said.

"It's a high-class area in southern England."

Mesa, too fatigued to listen to any more of Wilson's diatribe, said, "Hey. Boston, twenty miles," as he caught sight of a road sign. Within half an hour, they pulled off the highway, having reached South Boston. Soon, Mesa and Wilson reached a storage warehouse, where they pulled the van onto a parking lot the size of more than three football fields.

—

At the same time, Pat Murphy languished in the embrace of his pregnant wife. Despite the scrutiny given to his decision to prematurely leave the hospital, he found the process easier than he had imagined. It was just a matter of signing a few forms to indicate that he was acting against medical advice, since Dr. Harrington failed to approve his discharge. He had warned Pat that the threat of both infection and graft-versus-host disease had yet to be overcome.

"Patrick, I can't believe you're home. It's fantastic," Maryann said, kissing him profusely on the lips and the cheeks, unable to control her pleasure. "I thought you weren't coming home for a few days. Are you sure it's OK?"

Avoiding a direct answer, he said, "Before long, I'll be back on the truck."

Over the next two hours, they shared homemade lasagna and watched television in bed. Overwhelmingly fatigued from the pregnancy, Maryann quickly fell asleep. Lying beside her, Pat pondered his next move and stole a glance at his wife, now comfortably nestled under a soft bedcover. He cringed thinking she would learn that he had succumbed to gambling again and that he had lost the down payment for the house they hoped to buy. Working with Wilson, however, despite the risk, offered him the chance to come clean on his debts. As he planned to steal away from his home, he ignored the risk to his health and the risk of being caught. Anticipating a final release from Wilson's control over him, Pat rationalized his actions.

Despite feeling sleazy in his deceit, he got out of bed and grabbed the car keys. His dog Felix perked up from his deep sleep , wagged his tail and went out the door with Pat. The buses had stopped operating, and the bars had closed hours earlier. He navigated his car along a few blocks in South Boston, then pulled into a warehouse parking lot.

"Nice of you to make it, Murphy," Wilson quipped, giving Pat a good-natured shove to the shoulder. "Hope you plan to work. We fire malingerers, you know."

Ignoring Wilson's greeting, Pat walked to a platform where about twenty fifty-five-gallon drums had been placed.

"Look," Wilson said to Pat and five other, burly men who were dressed in heavy overcoats, awaiting his direction. "We're gonna do this right and get outta here."

Although the warehouse was not heated, the physical activity of their exploits helped to compensate for the cold Boston night. Pat Murphy began to remove black plastic bags packed in a clear water-like liquid in the fifty-five-gallon drums. He sliced the bags open with a sharp knife, then poured the yellow powder into metal cylinders about a foot high and four inches in diameter. Under pressure from Wilson's annoying gaze and criticism, Pat and the others hurried to complete the job. Dust blew about and easily became airborne because of the carelessness of their work habits. Two of the men coughed intermittently. Working without a break, they drank beer in the process. None wore gloves, masks, or special clothing appropriate for the task.

While Wilson directed his cronies, Parker Barrows sat in the living room of his three-story town house. As usual at this stage of the evening, his hand caressed a glass filled with single-malt scotch. By wreaking fear and terror on US soil, he reasoned, the IRA would be firmly discredited. In Barrows's view, the slippery slope on which Protestant interests lay in the Brexit negotiations would result in Northern Ireland's merging with the republic to the south. Preventing such an unacceptable outcome necessitated swift and creative action to cast the IRA as terrorists, beyond both law and reason and unable to abide by any agreement—especially the terms of Brexit. Confident that his undertaking to discredit the IRA would succeed, Barrows rested easily. The scotch did its part.

Through the quiet assistance of his colleague in the British secret service, he had learned of a high-level diplomatic meeting planned for the upcoming Martin Luther King Jr. holiday. He had learned from his British intelligence colleague in London that a delegation of Foreign Service officials from the United Kingdom planned to visit Boston, ideally outside the immediate scrutiny of the Irish and British press. Fanueil Hall had been selected as the site of the exchange because of its historical significance to the United States.

Barrows had been advised by his UK intelligence colleague that he would eventually learn the names and affiliations of the participants. And perhaps more important to his immediate interests, he would learn the hotel in which the British delegation would be staying. The meeting was promoted as a goodwill gesture to acknowledge the United States for its role in the Northern Ireland peace initiative known as the Good Friday Agreement that was signed in 1998.

They now had to deal with the ramifications of Brexit on Northern Ireland. Barrows, however, along with his colleague back in the UK, viewed the meeting quite differently. His sentiments paralleled those of hard-line Unionists in Northern Ireland at the time of the Troubles, the term used to describe the violence and terrorism that began in the 1970s. The Unionists considered any Anglo–Irish agreement as "a declaration of war on the Unionist people." The Ulster Unionist Party, the largest political group representing Protestants in Northern Ireland, rejected any political agreements that threatened the future of Northern Ireland as part of the United Kingdom.

Barrows had another perspective on the Brexit–Northern Ireland problem. In his view, it was time to stop the diplomatic maneuvering that would lead to a sellout of the North. His plan would expose the United States as a significant site of IRA sympathies, including fund-raising, weapon procurement, and the hiding of fugitives. His planned false flag operation was designed to cause havoc and to attribute the violence to the Northern Ireland Catholics.

For Parker Barrows, the time had finally come to take his revenge against the IRA. What better way to discredit that criminal organization than to orchestrate terror and attribute it to the IRA? Although he hated the French, he liked the premise of a French book that alleged that Israel had fomented the September 11, 2001, tragedy in New York City. Barrows knew that this theory was nonsense, but he would make the same approach work against the IRA and get rid of Wilson at the same time. Barrows considered it ludicrous for the British government to let their Northern Ireland citizens slip into the morass of the Republic of Ireland. Through his ploy to disgrace the IRA and show that Sinn Fein had absolutely no control over its fringe elements, he would disrupt the Brexit negotiations, embarrass the United States, and exact justice for the explosion that had killed his wife and ruined his career.

As Barrows gulped down another scotch, his anger grew as he reflected on diplomatic events related to Northern Ireland. Thinking back to his days in the Special Air Service of the British military, he remembered his enthusiasm for pursuing IRA criminals, even across borders in Europe. At times, he and his associates took justice into their own hands, activities that caused some to surmise that the security service committed numerous crimes, including murder and kidnapping.

While Barrows drank until he passed out, Wilson and his crew finished loading the metal cylinders with the yellow powder, packing them in wooden crates.

"OK. Get it out of here. Perini Construction," Wilson barked to the driver.

"How many times does he have to tell us? Does he think we're idiots?" asked the driver's partner, sitting beside him.

"Yeah, man. We got it," the driver answered.

"Get your asses back here quick so we can make some money off ya at poker."

"Right, Jake! Anything you say," the driver responded.

People dealt with Wilson in a variety of ways. His overbearing personality proved annoying to some, whereas others considered his flamboyance effective in controlling subordinates. Wilson fostered his own reputation as an evasive man of mystery, an image kept alive by how he kept all his charges uninformed about the nature of their work and the source of their pay.

—

At the same time, Anna was pondering how to get Dan Murphy out of jail. Confused and uncertain, but nonetheless motivated to help him, she believed that an aimless late night drive might help her sort out her thoughts. She drove her old Volkswagen Jetta onto Commonwealth Avenue and then into the Back Bay area of Boston past Dan Murphy's condominium.

Where am I going to get five thousand dollars? she wondered. *That's so unfair. He'll spend the whole weekend in that godforsaken place.*

She turned onto the Southeast Expressway and, despite feeling as though in a trance, drove a few miles south to an exit that took her into the quiet streets of South Boston. Her curiosity overcame her judgment, and soon she was driving in the direction of South Boston Plating.

Although the winter sky was illuminated by a full moon, it was still relatively dark out, so Anna found it difficult to see anything but shapes and shadows. Solitary lights shined at various intervals along the street near the harbor. Anna, preoccupied with getting Dan Murphy's bail, was not paying close attention when Wilson's cronies came out of the driveway.

Within a few feet of hitting the truck's driver-side door, Anna jammed on her brakes and was thrust forward. Fortunately, her seat belt prevented her from striking the windshield. At the same time, she heard a large crash as crates fell from the back of the truck onto the street. Wilson ran outside from the warehouse. Anna remained in the car as her heart raced. She stared ahead, frozen in silence. The adrenaline rush had made her numb. It was only when she realized that no contact had occurred and that no one was hurt that she began to calm down. Then, hearing tapping noises on her window, she turned to see a man in his early thirties with shaggy black hair that came over his ears. It was impossible to determine whether the degree of facial hair represented a beard in progress or just a face that hadn't seen a razor for a few days. Whatever the explanation, the gruff look and black wool cap made Jake Wilson appear frightening to Anna.

"You all right, lady?"

Anna, stunned and taken aback, paused before answering. "Yes. I suppose."

"Sorry for the trouble," Wilson said without a hint of sincerity, then turned and walked toward the pickup truck.

Anna started the engine, then drove away in a daze. Wilson watched her drive off and caught notice of her license plate, RNJOUR.

Chapter 50

"Let's party," Wilson bellowed to the four men left behind in the damp, dark warehouse.

A short, bearded fellow, his clothes covered with a yellow dust, called out, "Where's the card table?"

"Over there where it always is, asshole."

"Fuck you, dude. You're out of the first game."

"That's the only way you'd ever win a game." Their good-natured banter, which to the outsider would appear combative, was an important part of the card game.

"Murphy, get your sweet little ass over here," Wilson called out. "You don't think you're gonna leave, do you?"

"I gotta get back, Jake. It's late."

"Ah! Just one card game. With your buddies."

"Yeah! You've been in the hospital too long. You need a little pleasure once in a while."

"Come on, Murphy. Just stay a half hour or so."

The refrains of his companions convinced Pat to stay, especially since it rarely took much prodding to get him to play poker. In the wrong environment, he had little willpower for thwarting his self-destructive urges. Even though he and his pals would only bet small amounts of money, Pat could taste the excitement of gambling. That old feeling was still there. He loved it—but he hated it.

Wilson sat at the table and shuffled the cards. Pat's dog, Felix, ran around the warehouse, chasing anything that people would throw. The room, dusty and dark, resembled a scene from a gangster movie in the 1930s with a solitary light hanging from a high ceiling. The only sound was that of poker chips being tossed around the table. The aroma of cigar smoke filled the air. "Tell me, Jake, what's really going on?" Pat asked.

"We're playing poker."

"Don't fuck with me, Jake. Where's all this stuff going? What's up?"

"When the time comes, my friend. When the time comes."

"I'll take three," one of the players said.

"When will the time come?" Pat asked.

"Who knows!" Wilson answered. "Just play poker."

"That's easy for you to say, Mr. Smoothy, the man with the plan, the ideas, and the deals. But nobody knows what the hell's going on."

Just then a loud noise sounded from a corner of the warehouse. They all turned in the same direction and saw the truck driver and his sidekick come back into the loading area.

"Glad you could make it," one of the players said sarcastically.

"Next time, don't be so quiet. We need a distraction once in a while."

"Hey, fuck you guys. You couldn't even wait for us."

"Jake," Murphy asked again, "why don't you tell us what's up?"

"Yeah, Jake. You think we're stooges?"

"Deal these two jerks in," one of the players said, as the truck driver and his sidekick each pulled up a chair to join the others at the poker table.

Pat threw a tennis ball against a far wall of the warehouse. Felix dashed after it, stirring up a cloud of yellow dust in the process. A few people at the poker table, including Pat, began to cough.

"Let's clean up this shit," Jake yelled out. "Why do you guys have to be such slobs?"

A few hours later, the card game drew to a close, with no one winning or losing much money. Pat Murphy went home with an extra forty bucks. As he walked into the house, he felt lucky to have taken his dog, Felix, to the warehouse. Otherwise, the greeting from his black Labrador would have surely awakened his wife and aroused her suspicion about his absence. Maryann, sound asleep, was nestled comfortably within the sheets and bedcover. Pat removed his dusty jeans and T-shirt, then climbed into bed with her.

—

Penned in his jail cell, Dan found it impossible to rest. The uncertainty about his release and the utter powerlessness of his situation unnerved him. He was unaccustomed to being so totally out of control. The stress provoked an adrenalin rush that resulted in a surge of energy with no opportunity for release. He had no option but to sit in his jail cell and wait, and wait, until a police officer told him about Anna's recent phone call. She was pursuing bail, he was told, but nothing more.

His mind raced purposelessly, never stopping long enough on any topic, until he recalled what he had learned about medical aspects of cocaine abuse in a drug testing seminar. As part of his job at the Occupational Health Center, Murphy reviewed urine tests to determine whether workers used certain illegal drugs. The Reagan administration's War on Drugs in the 1980s had stimulated a rash of initiatives designed to discourage casual drug use. Often with little justification based on experience, some companies implemented drug testing programs and essentially eliminated drug abuse and its effect on transportation-related and some manufacturing jobs. Government mandates soon appeared requiring the testing of employees in certain safety-sensitive positions, a ruling upheld by the US Supreme Court. Murphy, as part of his training to become a medical review officer, a physician qualified to review urinary drug results, learned a considerable amount about cocaine and other drugs that people tended to abuse.

"Sandwiches here, sandwiches here. Get 'em while they last." Dan turned to look at the man who was passing out the burnt toast.

He was dressed in a police uniform that failed to conceal the thirty pounds he had put on since he joined the police force. Slovenliness was his theme—shirt hanging out, shoelace untied, and face in need of a shave. Murphy turned away in sadness at his own predicament. *How am I going to get released?*

The shouts of a drunken inmate down the hall intruded. "Let me out of here. Let me out of here. I've been in this goddamn place forever. Let me the fuck out of here."

"Shut your fuckin' ass up or you'll be here for a fuckin' week," a cop yelled back. The drunken prisoner refrained from responding. As Dan looked through the bars of his cell, he caught the attention of a policeman whose eyes reflected decency.

"Your friend called," he said to Dan.

"When?"

"I don't know." He shrugged. "A short while ago."

"What's up? Can I get out?"

"Not yet. She doesn't have the bail."

"Did she say whether she could get it?"

"I didn't take the message."

Dan looked away and caught a glimpse of the toilet without a seat and the metal bench. The accommodations, purposely spartan, were designed for short-term visits and outfitted to reduce the incidence of violence and suicide.

To Dan's surprise, the cop initiated a conversation. It must have been late in the shift, or perhaps he was bored. "How'd a doctor like you get into cocaine?"

"I'm not. I was set up."

The police officer looked at him blankly as though he had expected Dan's response but did not believe it. "You can face some serious charges, you know."

"But I'm innocent."

"I understand ya gotta do what ya gotta do, but they found a lot of coke in your car. You got a problem, pal, and if you don't know it, wake up and get yourself a good lawyer when you get outta here."

Dan, albeit recognizing the futility of convincing the cop of his innocence, continued to listen politely.

"You may face felony charges. You were busted with over the felony amount. You'll lose your medical license."

Dan knew that criminal sanctions for cocaine possession had changed dramatically in the 1980s. About one out of every six prisoners in the federal system is held for drug offenses.

"Can I make another call?" Dan asked.

"Sorry. You had your call. Relax. She'll call back. They always do."

As the police officer walked away, Dan's mind took him on a chaotic journey of fear and uncertainty, heightened by the potential repercussions of the arrest on his medical career. Murphy held no grand illusions about his importance, but he knew that a doctor being nabbed for cocaine would create a firestorm of gossip, speculation, and media coverage. He dreaded seeing his arrest described in the local paper.

How can I prove I'm innocent? he asked himself. *Would it help to demand a urinary drug test?* On realizing that his test would be negative, he was encouraged, but he quickly became disheartened upon realizing that a negative test would only prove that he hadn't used cocaine in the previous twenty-four hours or so.

Could I really be here till Monday? He was afraid. *If Anna can't come up with the bail, I'll be here all weekend.* Just the thought of such wretched confinement sent a surge of fire through him. The physical sensation resembled that which he experienced when he drank too much coffee. Everything seemed so unfair, as though he were at the mercy of people who considered him guilty, hardly worthy of the most limited civility. He had no idea who had set him up but wondered whether Flannagan from the plating firm was involved. The OSHA rep had advised Dan that the plant manager of the plating firm was furious that OSHA had visited the plant and had even gone to the trouble of getting a warrant to conduct a site visit.

In less than an hour, Dan was expected to staff the Ambulatory Care Center at South Boston Hospital. Would he be released in time?

How would he let his colleagues at the clinic know if he wasn't going to be there? Would they get someone to cover for him? What would he tell people? Thoughts raced through his head as he anticipated a weekend in jail to await arraignment on Monday, that is, if Anna would not come up with the five thousand dollars' cash bail to get him released ahead of time.

After a short Hispanic man sprayed for insects around crevices in the walls, the decent cop made his sandwich rounds again. *Quite the appetizer,* Murphy thought.

"Sandwiches here. Sandwiches here," the cop called, trying to mimic the vendors at baseball games.

This guy must do this every night, Murphy thought, now beginning to dread the routine. Trying to keep their rapport, Murphy answered, "I'll take one."

"Of course, Doctor," the policeman said with a hint of sarcasm.

"Any more news?" he asked. "Did Anna call?"

"I haven't heard anything."

"Would you mind finding out if she called? I'm going crazy in here."

"Let me see what I can do," he answered. "Want another sandwich?"

"No. Thanks. Just a release."

The cop offered a restrained smile, then turned away.

Murphy realized that it was nearly eight o'clock, the time when he was expected at the clinic. The chances of his being on time, however, were remote as the consequences of last night's arrest were only beginning.

After a pleasant pause from the obnoxious yelling of the drunken prisoner, the silence was broken. "Get me out of here." His words, still slurred, had lost their bite. "Get me out of here," he yelled again. Moments later, he hollered a plaintive, "Please," that dragged through the jail.

No one answered.

Chapter 51

Pat Murphy began to feel more at ease in bed than anywhere else. Since he had left the hospital prematurely and helped Wilson at the warehouse, he spent his days sleeping and watching television. On a rare moment, he was motivated to take his dog on a walk through the high school football field. For the most part, his days included talk shows, movies, and the sports page. His thoughts were focused on his predicament and whether he had acted too quickly in leaving the hospital. Although he sensed relief in ridding himself of some of his gambling debt to Wilson, he feared the consequences of his activities with his work friends. On the other hand, he enjoyed seeing his old buddies, playing poker, and winning a few bucks. The irony of gambling while working to pay off gambling debts eluded him.

Murphy listened to his favorite rock station. His hands itched; he felt indescribably tired; and his mind wandered aimlessly in fear of the unknown.

Am I rejecting the transplant? Did I leave the hospital too early? He was afraid. *Maybe Dr. Harrington and Dan were right,* he reluctantly acknowledged. *The hospital environment would clearly reduce complications of the transplant, especially infections, and perhaps graft-versus-host disease.*

As he surfed through daytime television's soap operas, talk shows, and old movies, Pat shook from the fever, which meant his body temperature was continuing to rise. His legs ached as though a belt were tied around them. He could barely keep his eyes open, especially whenever the slightest bit of sunlight entered the room. *Could this be a relapse?* he wondered fearfully. Then, he tried to reassure himself. *It's January. It's just the flu.* His rationalizations, however, failed to assuage his fear of dying from the disease. As fever, pain, and fear consumed him, he envisioned death as a relief. Quickly dispelling such thoughts, he tried to raise the strength of mind and body to recover. *Attitude. It's all attitude.* The words of his school football coach roared in his memory.

Murphy's channel surfing led him to a sports station talk show about the National Football League playoffs. He began to feel the urge to gamble. *It was easier to stop smoking,* he reluctantly admitted to himself.

Despite overwhelming fatigue, Murphy got out of bed to shower. It had been a rough night sleeping, after being awakened repeatedly to accommodate an angry intestinal tract. He tried to recall what he had eaten and how it may have caused him unwelcomed visits to the toilet.

Catching a glimpse of his brightened face in the mirror, he gently rubbed his fingers across his cheek and felt his coarse, scaly skin. Too tired to think about why his hands and face were so red, he went back to bed, returning to sleep.

A few hours later, Pat made another trip to the bathroom. His retching woke his wife.

"Pat, are you OK?"

"I'm fine."

"Are you sure?"

"Sure, I'm sure." Maryann turned over in bed. Her eyes were wide with fear.

When Pat returned to bed, Maryann asked again, "Pat, what's wrong?"

"Nothing. You worry too much, Maryann."

"Pat, why's your face so red?"

"Must be the light."

She stroked her index finger over his forehead.

"It's so coarse."

"Winter weather. I'm a truck driver. I'm outdoors." He snapped.

"Pat, I think you should go to the hospital."

"You're overreacting."

"You know I'm not." Maryann patiently continued, saying, "Let's go to the hospital."

"Later. I wanna sleep now."

"Should I call Dr. Harrington?"

"No. I'd rather talk with Dan first. I don't wanna go back to the hospital."

"Pat, if it helps you improve, it's worth it."

"I'll be fine."

"Have you been taking your medicine?"

"Yes, Mom," he said with a touch of sarcasm.

"You don't forget, do you?" she prodded.

"Would you relax?"

"I don't want to nag. I just don't want to lose you."

"You won't lose me."

"Then why don't you take care of yourself?"

"You want me to get a manicure and a facial?" he quipped.

Maryann looked through the window of their small bedroom and onto a cold, gray winter morning so typical of January in Boston.

"How about if I call Dan?" Before Pat could respond, he leaned over a bucket next to his bed, no longer able to control his vomiting.

"Oh, Pat!" Maryann sympathetically cried.

While struggling to keep his eyes open, he turned his ashen face toward her. His head slumped limply to the side.

"Pat, Pat, Pat." She shook him. He barely opened his eyes in response. "I'm taking you to the hospital," she said empathetically. Then she dialed Dan's telephone number and left a message. "Danny, this is Maryann. Pat's very sick, and he won't do anything before talking to you. Would you call me?"

After hanging up the phone, she looked at the kitchen clock, whose black arms told her it was eight thirty in the morning.

Where's Danny? Maybe he went away for the weekend, she wondered, then recalled Dan mentioning that he planned to work at the hospital today. He had turned down a chance to ski in Vermont.

Maryann then called South Boston Hospital.

"I'd like to speak with Dr. Murphy, please."

"Would you hold just a minute, please?"

During the wait, Maryann heard a taped message about the hospital's new physical fitness training program.

The operator broke in. "Dr. Murphy's not in yet, ma'am. Can I take a message?"

"When do you expect him?"

"No one seems to know. He was supposed to be here at eight."

"What?" Maryann asked, riveted by the possibilities that would account for his absence.

"Like I said, ma'am, I can't tell you more. Maybe you should call ambulatory care. That's where he's supposed to be."

"Would you connect me, please?"

"Just a minute."

An administrative assistant then told her that Dan had not called and no one knew his whereabouts.

Maryann walked back into the bedroom, where Pat was deep in sleep. Although he looked comfortable, she feared that things would get worse. *Where's Danny?* she thought. *He's not home and not at the hospital.*

Chapter 52

The cold jail cell prevented Murphy from getting comfortable. *What a wretched way to spend an all-nighter,* he mused, referring to staying awake throughout the night, something he'd done occasionally during college and medical school to study for exams, drive to Florida, or work at the lab.

Sitting on the wooden bench in his cell, Murphy wondered about who had set him up. The explanation probably centered on the plating firm since he could imagine no other enemy in his life. *OSHA visits, though, are confidential,* he thought, trying to convince himself. *At least the name of the person who blows the whistle is kept secret,* he thought, struggling to believe it, although well aware that OSHA reports eventually became part of the public record.

Murphy was puzzled. How would anyone other than the OSHA rep know that he had requested an inspection of the plating firm? Other than Brenda, his nurse practitioner, only the OSHA official and Anna knew of his request. Tired, sullen, and immobilized, he sat in jail with nothing to read and nothing to do. All he could do was wait, fret, and hope for good news.

While in captivity, Murphy considered the numerous unpleasant consequences of the evening's debacle. The vulnerability associated with his confinement caused him to fear the worst outcomes, especially in terms of a prison sentence. Periodically, he outlined points in his defense, then considered that the absence of his fingerprints on the plastic bag of cocaine would prove his innocence. Immediately, though, he became disheartened upon realizing that he had picked up the package from the floor to handed it to the policeman.

—

Over and over, Dan feared the implications of a prison sentence on his career. He was well aware that the War on Drugs had resulted in more imprisonment of drug offenders. Although he understood certain aspects of the judicial system with respect to sentencing, he feared that his being a physician threw in a wildcard that could hurt him.

"Hey, Doc," he heard the decent cop saying in the background. "Your ship came in."

"What?" Murphy asked with the excitement of a puppy about to be released from a cage at a pet store.

"You're out, man," the guard said, reaching for a key to open the cell door. "This way." The cop pointed to a hallway, then led Murphy into a small office. A man in his late fifties with weathered skin and thin gray hair motioned to Murphy to take a seat. The official thumbed through sheets of paper, initialed a report, then handed a form to Dan.

"Sign this."

Dan, fatigued from his night in jail, lacked the alertness necessary to evaluate the bureaucratic minutiae.

"What's all this mean?"

"You're charged with possession and transportation of an illegal substance. Your bail is five thousand dollars. You'll have a hearing in two weeks. If you jump bail, a warrant will be issued for your arrest and you'll lose the bail. Do you understand?" The official, in no mood for small talk, wanted to make sure Murphy, and others whom he instructed in the same condescending manner, appreciated the gravity of their situations.

Murphy managed a weak affirmative nod to the cop. He knew

that a verbal battle would only inflame a person who seemed poised to explode at the remotest hint of a challenge to his authority. A snide comment or a questionable remark might spark an outbreak of nasty behavior.

"Sign if you want to leave, otherwise you can think it over all you want in your cell."

Murphy, despite his customary reserve in signing any contract or business agreement, immediately reached for the pen.

The cop ripped off one page of the three-sheeted carbonless paper. "Don't lose this," he lectured. Then to his colleague, he said, "Show him where the girl is."

"You mean Anna?" Dan asked.

"Some girl came down here with your bail money. You ought to take her out to a real nice place. Cause you owe her."

Dan nodded, then turned to the cop standing at the door, who was prepared to take him to Anna. After walking down a corridor and around a corner, he recognized the shoulder-length brown locks of the woman with whom he had fallen in love.

On hearing the policeman enter the room, Anna turned.

"Dan," she blurted out, rising from her chair.

"Please, ma'am, just a moment," the official said methodically.

Murphy, too tired to question, and anxious to see Anna, responded as requested.

Shortly, he and Anna departed the police station.

"What a nightmare!" Murphy announced. "Thank you so much," he said, throwing his arms around her in a locking embrace. "How did you ever get me out of Hades?"

"It's a long story, Dan. It's been a real exercise in patience and frustration."

As they drove away in Anna's ten-year-old car he said, "I can't tell you how much this means to me. You've trusted me. I told you that stuff wasn't mine, and you believed me."

"I never doubted you."

He looked at her in earnest, thrilled to know her and anxious to know more. A bond with Anna was forming that he wanted to nurture.

"What was jail like?"

"Horrific. Demeaning. The worst night of my life. You're treated as though you're a guilty criminal not worthy of a decent toilet. There's an unbelievably hostile air about the place."

"Like the movies?" she asked.

"Worse."

"How did you get bail?" Dan asked.

"Oh, I just went to the automatic teller machine and punched in five thousand dollars from my credit card," she said wistfully.

Dan looked back, unsure whether to believe her.

"I'm kidding, of course."

"All right. I'm both intrigued and impressed, as well as grateful. How'd you pull it off?"

"Luck, panache, and a little bit of savvy," she answered.

"I'm listening."

"Your hospital administrator helped."

"How'd he know about this?"

"Through the hospital's security system. Apparently they listen to the police radio routinely, supposedly to prepare for people injured in traffic accidents and violent altercations who may need medical care."

Dan learned that the security office, on hearing that a doctor from their hospital had been arrested on drug charges, notified the hospital administrator.

"So, what did he say?" asked Murphy, now experiencing the worst fears he had while in prison.

"Not much. He seemed helpful and told me he'd arrange bail for you."

Dan looked at Anna, whose facial expression suggested she felt partially responsible for the turn of events in involving the hospital administrator. "I'm disappointed that you don't appreciate what I went through to get you out of jail. It wasn't easy getting five thousand dollars' cash on short notice."

"I'm sorry. This whole situation has me exasperated."

"The administrator called me, Dan. I didn't contact him," she emphasized.

"How did that happen?"

"He called the police department. They told him I called for you," she said, then paused. "Dan, I tried to call you. Do you think I wanted to do this without talking with you?"

Murphy nodded.

"It's not easy getting five thousand dollars at four o'clock on a Friday night. He was nice to me. He said he was sorry to hear what had happened and that he would do whatever he could for you."

"Do you believe him?"

"You're too much. He just got you out of jail and you're questioning his motives?"

"Write me off to sleep deprivation, stress, and overwhelming anxiety. I still can't believe what happened."

"Relax, Dan," Anna counseled.

He reached over the seat to pull her toward him, then rubbed his fingers through her hair. Seconds later, they merged in an embrace that neither wanted to end.

"Did you have anything to eat?"

"Yeah! Lots of sandwiches. At least that's how they describe cold, dry, burnt toast in jail."

"Sounds appetizing," Anna said, then kissed him. "I'll make you some real breakfast," she said enthusiastically.

"Has anyone contacted the clinic?" Dan asked. "I was supposed to be there two hours ago."

"Yes, the administrator took care of it. One of the emergency physicians is covering for you. We can talk about that later," she said. They entered the main hallway of the building and then went into his apartment. Newspapers, magazines, and old coffee cups were scattered about.

As soon as they arrived, Murphy skillfully maneuvered Anna onto his large, soft sofa. Wrapped in her arms, he wanted to lie there forever. *If bad luck were only like an unwanted email,* he mused. *Just delete and move on.* His wishful thinking was jarred when Anna initiated a deep kiss that locked them in the magical bliss of new love.

"Check your messages, and I'll meet you in the bedroom," Anna proposed. "I'd like some more of the lovemaking we had a few days ago."

The voice mail on his phone announced, "Dr. Murphy, this is Richard Jones, the administrator of South Boston General. I trust Anna has taken care of you by now. I need to see you today. Your foray with the law has brought out matters we must address—and promptly. Please call. I'll be in my office."

"What an arrogant, pompous ass," Murphy said to himself.

Anna overheard his comment and called out, "What did you just call me?" good-naturedly ribbing him.

"A luscious babe who should be nestled in my arms," he shot back.

He listened to the remainder of the messages. Although a few calls had been made between nine o'clock and ten o'clock, no messages had been left. Finally, he heard his brother, Pat. "Dan, Maryann wanted me to call you. I feel like shit. Call me when you can." His voice sounded worn out and afraid, as though he couldn't handle another bout of intensive care in the hospital.

Dan walked into the living room, where Anna looked at him in anxious anticipation. "The administrator called. So did my brother."

"I'm sorry, Dan. I forgot to tell you that Jones wants to see you today."

"Why today?"

"Formalities. Plan a strategy to deal with this fiasco."

"Anna, where's this going? Plan a strategy? There's no strategy. I'm innocent, and he can see to it that my hospital privileges and medical license aren't affected by this craziness."

"Dan," she said, putting her hands around his neck, "relax for a few minutes. Come." She drew his hand, then led him into his bedroom. Moments later, they were beneath the sheets and disrobed. Anna loved taking the initiative, and Dan responded in kind to her advances. It wasn't long before Murphy forgot about his travails with the police.

A blissful nap helped recharge both of them, giving them enough energy to get through the rest of the day.

"Do you have any coffee?" Anna asked.

"We even share the same passion for caffeine," Dan said, noticeably relaxed from his interlude with Anna.

"Where is it?"

"Top shelf. I have fresh coffee in the refrigerator if you like."

"Terrific," she said, then bounced out of bed, ready for a shower. Dan marveled at the shape of her posterior, but fixed his gaze at her legs, which were attractively shaped from swimming and doing aerobics. Murphy lay in his bed, unsure of what to do next. His brother so rarely called for help, unless it was a serious matter.

"Anna, would you mind coming with me today?" he asked as she entered the bedroom with two cups of hot coffee. "Moral support," he said to her as she climbed into bed.

About an hour later, Anna and Murphy approached the hospital building where the administrator had his office.

"Look, why don't you go to see Jones, and I'll wait across the street in the coffee shop."

"Are you sure?"

"Yes. You and he need to work this out."

"All right. Wish me luck."

Anna reached up to kiss him on the cheek, then smiled and turned away.

Murphy entered an empty lobby that was inhabited by a lone security guard who asked him to sign a logbook. An elevator took Dan to the administrator's floor. Slowly, he made his way to Jones's enclave at the end of a corridor.

"Dr. Murphy," Jones called out. "Please come in." The office, outfitted in modern wood furniture, seemed to be straight off the cover of *Architectural Digest*. Expense was but a minor consideration in its design. It seemed that health-care administrators had become quite adept at maneuvering funds from managed-care contracts into their own budgets.

"Where's Anna?"

"She's waiting for me downstairs."

"That's disappointing. I was hoping I might get the chance to meet her."

"Some other time," Dan responded. "Thank you for the bail," he said, an effort to change the subject from Anna.

"My pleasure, Dr. Murphy." Jones usually emphasized the word *doctor* when he addressed Dan, in a way that suggested snide condescension.

"Where do we go from here?" Dan asked.

"That depends on a number of factors. First, the director of the medical staff will have to be brought into the discussion," he responded with supercilious flair.

"Why?"

"Why! This drug charge carries substantial ramifications."

"But I've been framed. The cocaine did not belong to me."

"How could we prove that!" Jones quipped as though he relished the fact that Dan was in dire straits with the law.

"Isn't it the other way around? Aren't I innocent until proven guilty?"

"Dr. Murphy, what makes you think logic will prevail in the United States judicial system?" Despite his apparent kindness in having orchestrated Murphy's release from jail, Jones seemed interested in exercising some leverage over him.

"Mr. Jones," Dan responded, "I am indebted to you for your help. I want to assure you of my full cooperation, but I need to make it clear that I am innocent of these trumped-up charges. And I hope I can expect your support and that of the hospital."

"Rather hefty demands from a man facing a suspension of his medical license, among other forms of punishment," Jones replied sarcastically.

Dan, puzzled by the tenor of the conversation, sensed that Jones doubted his innocence. The administrator's reaction was in striking contrast to that of Anna, who upon listening to his explanation of the events surrounding his arrest, immediately believed him.

"Who knows about this?" Dan asked.

"The chief of medicine. The president of the hospital. But I assure you, Dr. Murphy, that I've asked their restraint in informing others."

"Where do you fit in?" Murphy asked.

"I've been asked to oversee efforts to ensure that you are treated fairly. We can arrange legal support. The fees, of course, will be your responsibility."

"Mr. Jones, I appreciate your efforts on my behalf, but I'd prefer to make my own decisions about legal support."

"Do as you may, but when it comes to your hospital privileges and working with the medical staff, that's my purview."

Dan knew that Jones was embellishing his role, but he also doubted the value of debating the finer points of his dilemma with him. The chief of medicine and eventually the Massachusetts Board of Registration in Medicine had authority over his privilege to practice medicine. Dan, struck by the perverse manner in which Jones was treating him, thought, *Why is he taking such an aggressive approach with me? Is there something else going on?*

"Dr. Murphy, there's little reason for you to be combative with me. After all, I hold the keys to your arrest and to getting this monkey off your back, and to facilitating your return to the clinic."

Murphy didn't like what he was hearing. "My return to work?" he asked in disbelief.

"Yes. Until this matter is settled, you're under suspension."

"That's unnecessary, and you know it."

"We feel it's a prudent action to take, Dr. Murphy," Jones said, again sarcastically, emphasizing the professional title. "We can't have a doctor overseeing drug testing programs who himself is facing criminal charges for drug possession. As you well know, a lot of the companies that use your clinic have drug testing programs."

"You know I've been set up."

"I know that's what you told me, but, Dr. Murphy, we have procedures to follow."

"Why?"

"For your own good. Learn to follow directions."

Dan stared blankly ahead, unsure of the proper response.

"Now, I have work to do, if you don't mind." Jones rose from his chair to lead Dan from the office. At the door to the entrance to his office, he said, "I would like to meet Anna. She sounds like a delightful young lady."

Dan offered a half-baked smile, then turned toward the elevator.

"We shall meet on Monday morning. Make that ten o'clock," Jones called after him.

—

Dan couldn't wait to see Anna, who was now buried behind the Saturday edition of the *Boston Globe* at their usual coffee shop. On surveying the customers, most of whom were immersed in reading, holding conversations, or people watching, Murphy noticed Anna off to a corner. *How attractive and intelligent she looks,* he thought, feeling a surge of excitement about the woman whom he was growing fonder.

"Dan." She looked up from the paper with a smile that advertised her pleasure in seeing him. "How did it go?"

Dan shook his head in disgust and frustration. "Not good. Jones wants me on leave—suspension from the hospital."

"What happened?"

"I haven't sorted it out, but somehow Jones has responsibility for taking care of my case, as he says."

"Why?"

"I'm not sure."

A waiter came to their table. "Would you like another cup, ma'am?"

"No, thank you, just a check, please."

"Anna, I have a horrible sense of doom. Between jail, lack of sleep, and the administrator on my case, I'm on a psychological overdrive that's fueled by adrenalin, coffee, and stress."

"Come on. Let's see your brother," Anna said encouragingly, attempting to distract him from his worries.

After navigating their way through the crowds of Saturday shoppers in downtown Boston, Anna and Dan reached the home in South Boston that Pat and Maryann Murphy rented. Neighborhood kids played street hockey as the skyline of Boston's financial district loomed in the background. Finding a parking spot was surprisingly easy, necessitating only a two-block walk.

Maryann greeted them at the door. Dressed in a blue maternity dress, her shape advertised that she was more than halfway through the pregnancy.

"Danny," she said with obvious pleasure at the sight of her brother-in-law.

"Maryann. This is Anna Carlson, a friend of mine."

Anna and Maryann exchanged pleasantries, and soon they were all sitting in the living room.

"Danny, thank you for coming over. Can I get anything for you or Anna?"

Each declined the offer of hospitality, and Dan dove into a discussion about his brother. "How's Pat doing?"

"Awful. He won't eat. He has this rash all over his body, and he's been on and off the toilet all night. And he won't do anything without talking to you."

"Have you called Dr. Harrington?"

"No. Pat would kill me."

"Would you like me to talk with him?" Dan asked.

"I'd love you to. Let me tell him you're here. He's watching a football game."

"Oh yes, the playoffs are on this weekend."

"If you're lucky enough to convince him to go to the hospital, you'll probably have to wait until after the game."

Dan smiled in response, then walked into the bedroom. He wondered whether his brother had bet any money on the game and had fallen back into the gambling habit that had played havoc with his life.

"Get his ass!" Pat yelled at the television, then noticed Dan. "Hey, dude." The words belonged to Pat, but lost was the vigor of his typical greeting to his older brother.

"Pat. What's up?"

"I feel like shit."

"Been taking your meds?"

"Most of the time."

"What do you mean, most of the time?"

"I forget once in a while."

"Does that rash itch?" Dan asked, referring to the red irritated skin on Pat's face and palms. Were Pat to remove his T-shirt, Dan would see blotchy red patches all over his chest and abdomen.

"No, but I feel like some clown who's never been in the sun before and didn't use sunscreen."

Dan grinned, pleased that Pat could take a lighthearted view of himself in the face of illness. Murphy, vaguely familiar with graft-versus-host disease, recognized that the skin rash and intestinal reactions were two of three of its major effects. Whether his brother's liver had abnormalities consistent with the major side effect of bone marrow transplants was unclear. A blood test would settle that issue.

After going through a reasonably thorough medical history with his brother, Dan cautiously concluded, "I think we should get you checked out."

"Why? I'll be all right. What are they going to do at the hospital besides give me lousy food and take blood?"

"Pat, I'm only suggesting that we go to the hospital for an evaluation."

"What do you think it is?"

"I'm not sure. Medical care has become so fine-tuned that I can barely keep up with my own specialty."

"You must have an idea."

"Well, Pat, I do. To be blunt, I think you may be having some sort of reaction to the transplanted marrow."

"You mean I'm rejecting your marrow?"

"No. My marrow may be fighting you. It's called graft-versus-host disease."

"Thanks for the great news. Now what do we do?"

"See Harrington."

"Do I need to be admitted to the hospital again?"

"Most likely."

Pat turned away in silence.

Moments later, Dan emphatically said, "Let's go, Pat."

"All right, all right. I'll see Harrington."

"Today!"

"OK, OK," he said, getting out of bed.

Minutes later, Maryann called 911, and soon thereafter an ambulance arrived. Two emergency medical technicians directed Pat out of the house and onto the vehicle for the short trip to South Boston Hospital.

Later on, blood studies and a skin biopsy confirmed the diagnosis of acute graft-versus-host disease.

Chapter 53

day after Murphy's release from jail, the shock to his psyche persisted. Dan sat across from Anna at a Thai restaurant near the Boston Common.

"Are you going to be able to work?" she asked.

"Yes. The chief of the medical staff told Jones to get off his high horse. It seems he wants me under his control."

"Why?"

"Who knows. Some administrators seem to get a perverse pleasure from managing doctors. Maybe he was rejected after applying to medical school."

"Do you have any thoughts about who set you up?"

"Yeah! It has to be somebody connected with the plating firm. It's the only explanation that makes any sense to me."

"Do you think it's because of the OSHA visit?"

"Probably."

"But didn't you say they didn't find anything significant there?"

"Yeah!"

"Do you think there's a problem at the plant even though the OSHA review was OK?"

"It could be."

"How could you find out? Wouldn't OSHA notice a problem?"

"Not necessarily."

"Why not?"

"OSHA's supposed to make sure that regulations are met. They don't guarantee to determine whether certain health problems may be the result of other issues at the plant."

"Isn't there some other way to get at this, without involving you?" Anna asked.

"Oh, sure. But the plant would have to cooperate, like calling in a consulting firm. They'd have to supply information and be helpful—not too likely with South Boston Plating."

"Aren't there other ways?"

"NIOSH might be able to help."

"You mean the National Institute for Occupational Safety and Health?"

"Yes."

"What could they do?"

"Conduct a health hazard evaluation. But it's complicated to arrange. And they're fairly backed up. I'm not sure it's practical for us. Plus, with this cocaine fiasco, the plant would try to discredit me."

The waiter brought them spicy chicken soup and spring rolls.

"Bon appétit. To better times ahead," Dan said, raising his glass of beer.

"How's your brother?" Anna asked, hoping for an encouraging answer.

"Stable, so to speak."

"Have they reached a diagnosis?"

"Graft-versus-host disease."

"I'm sorry to hear that," Anna answered, her face mirroring the sympathy she felt.

"I spoke with Dr. Harrington. Pat's liver enzymes are elevated. Along with the skin rash and the diarrhea, he has three major organs affected."

"How bad is it?"

"It depends on the stage of the disease."

"What stage is Pat?"

"Harrington wouldn't commit himself, but he did suggest stage two. There are four stages. One is the mildest, and four is the most severe. Nearly everyone with stage four dies!"

"What's the prognosis for Pat's stage?"

"Probably fifty-fifty."

Anna, struck by the sobering odds of Pat's survival, looked at her food, nibbled, then drank some tea.

"What are they going to do for him?"

"The standard: isolation room and drugs that suppress the immune system."

"Wouldn't that make him more susceptible to infections?"

"You haven't forgotten much of your nursing skills," Dan said admiringly. Anna smiled demurely in return, then changed the course of the conversation.

"So, you have a hectic schedule tomorrow?" she asked.

"Yeah! I get to see a lawyer, meet the chief of the medical staff, and keep an eye on Pat. I'll try to get to Dr. Harrington in the afternoon."

"How about Jones, the hospital administrator?"

"He wanted me to meet him at ten."

"Are you going to go?"

"No."

"What do you think he'll do?"

"I have no idea."

Chapter 54

When Dan Murphy arrived at the Occupational Health Center the following morning, Brenda, his nurse practitioner, greeted him warmly. She usually arrived about an hour earlier than he to review paperwork and give immunizations, especially to the health-care workers at South Boston Hospital. Murphy, unsure whether to mention his drug charges, decided to keep the matter to himself. The chief of medicine told him that his arrest would not be made public and that any disciplinary measures would await the outcome of the court proceedings. Murphy worried, however, that the police report would find its way into the newspapers and become common knowledge.

As he sat in his office and planned for the day, his concentration lapsed as his mind wandered to the frustration of being framed on drug charges. Even with an acquittal or perhaps the dropping of the charges, the stain on his reputation would remain. People would raise questions about how he had been arrested in the first place and whether money or his position had enabled him to get off the hook. Murphy decided that only by implicating the plating firm in both the health issue and the drug charges could he rescue himself from a criminal record and thereby salvage his reputation.

As the lunch break approached, Murphy noticed Mrs. Johnson waiting in the examining room. After preliminary greetings, they reached the essence of her concern, namely, whether the plant was making her sick. On her last visit to Murphy, she had given a blood sample for testing.

"Did you get the results of my tests yet?"

"Yes," Murphy replied, then opened her chart. "A few of your liver enzymes are elevated."

"What's that mean?"

"It's difficult to be certain. It may be nothing, or it may be the result of a hazard or medication."

She listened intently, awaiting further comment, then offered her own perspective. "Actually, I think it's my work. Mr. Flannagan had the plant cleaned up right after the OSHA man was sent home."

Unsure of how Mrs. Johnson knew that he was aware of the OSHA visit, Murphy decided to explore her knowledge of the affair. "What did OSHA do?"

"I thought you knew." She continued without awaiting his response. "They came the other day—looked over records, went through the plant, talked with some of the men."

"Why did you think I knew about it?"

"It seemed like something you would do to find out the cause of our health problems."

Dan nodded, gratefully accepting the compliment, but also concerned that she may have served as the leak that had led to the phony cocaine charges.

"Plus, I overheard Mr. Flannagan yelling on the phone, blaming some doctor for having OSHA come over. He was really angry. He went on and on about how he's a credit to the community, giving work to people who can't get jobs anywhere else, just trying to make it, and so forth. I never saw him so upset. He was kinda scary."

Dan recognized that Mrs. Johnson could provide a wealth of information that might help exonerate him and also help him to understand the plating firm's activities. "Does your boss think I had something to do with the OSHA visit?"

"I think so, from the way he was blabbing on the phone. He was furious."

"Mrs. Johnson, why do you think your work is affecting your health?" As Dan became more familiar with the process of evaluating environmental illnesses, he recognized the importance of gaining the perspective of his patients, who often were the first to suspect a link with work.

"Because of the way I feel. I know my body," she answered.

"Why did you come to see me today? Weren't we scheduled for later in the week?"

"Yes, but I thought you might want to see me when I feel terrible like this. The symptoms started this morning again. It seems worse on Monday mornings. I talked with Mr. Shaw, and he thinks it's because the plant shuts off the ventilation system over the weekend to save money. Then they turn it on again, and it stirs up all that dust."

"Did OSHA check the ventilation?" Dan asked.

"I don't think so. I can't imagine he had enough time to really check things out very good."

"Is he coming back?"

"I doubt it. Not the way he was treated. The general manager, Mr. Flannagan, wasn't even there when the OSHA guy left."

"Does Mr. Flannagan know you're seeing me?"

"I hope not."

"Does he handle the company's health insurance?"

"No. Mildred and I do that."

Murphy thought of Mr. Shaw, the custodian in his late fifties who also worked at the plant. The cause of his hepatitis had yet to be confirmed. Now, Mrs. Johnson seemed to have similar, although not as severe, abnormalities in a blood test, suggesting that her liver was not functioning properly.

"Mrs. Johnson," Dan said, "are there other people at work who have similar symptoms?"

"Yes, actually Mildred, the boss's secretary—she's been

complaining about her eyes and her skin being dry, but she would never do anything against Mr. Flannagan. She's worked with him forever."

"Is anyone else sick?"

"I suppose Sally and Mary. I told them I thought something at work was making me sick. They said they felt the same way, but thought it was crazy, so they never said anything. They're afraid too, you know—of losing their jobs. That's why they won't tell Mr. Flannagan about it."

Dan could count on Mrs. Johnson for long explanations, which had therapeutic value for her. Occasionally, nuggets of great diagnostic value emerged.

"I'd like to make a suggestion," Dan said. "I agree that your symptoms are somehow related to your work. The problem we face is proving the diagnosis. It would help if we could show that other people are similarly affected."

"I understand," she responded eagerly, as though hoping for an assignment.

"You might consider asking some of your associates to see me in order to be tested," Murphy said. Then he paused to reflect on the implications if he were found pursuing health-related symptoms linked to the plant. His request for the OSHA visit likely had triggered the fabricated drug charges and the corresponding implications to his career and reputation. By encouraging the testing of other workers, Murphy was inviting further repercussions.

"When should they come over?" Mrs. Johnson asked.

"Why don't you see whether they're interested first? Perhaps you could call me tomorrow and let me know."

"I will … gladly."

"That might help us get to the bottom of this issue."

"Thank you, Dr. Murphy. Is there anything else I should do?"

"I'm still not sure what the cause of the problem is, so the best approach is to reduce the symptoms in the same way you did today with the eye drops."

"Anything else?"

"Call in sick if you're not well enough to work."

"The company doesn't have sick leave. I wouldn't be paid."

"Then try to get as much fresh air as you can, like at breaks and lunch."

"OK. Even though it's winter, I love to take my walks ever since I gave up cigarettes. And you know, it usually makes me feel better."

"Then keep it up. You'll call tomorrow then?"

"Oh yes!" she replied without hesitation and filled with determination.

Through creative scheduling, Dan carved time from his afternoon schedule to meet with an attorney about the drug charges. Selecting an attorney was no easy task since he had never been involved in a criminal matter. Even when negotiating his hospital contract, Murphy had decided against legal support. For the drug charges, he was especially concerned about whom he could trust with such sensitive information. Through an associate at the Massachusetts Medical Society, he had reached a law firm in Boston prepared to offer advice.

The attorney, a man in his early forties of Italian descent, greeted Dan with respect. After brief introductions to their respective backgrounds, Joseph Morelli recommended a general approach to addressing substance abuse charges among physicians. Murphy explained the circumstances of his arrest, then showed the lawyer the paperwork he had received when he was released from jail.

After a brief review of the forms, the lawyer pointed out that the police officer had proper cause to stop his car, namely that Dan's rear taillight was not operating. All other procedures associated with the arrest, including due process, were followed appropriately, Morelli told him.

The attorney suggested that Dan leave the matter in his hands. He would contact the policeman, discuss the arrest, and review the evidence. Murphy, despite the uncertainties of the process that lay ahead, felt more assured that someone else was attending to the drug nightmare.

In closing the meeting, Morelli offered to call Dan later, then asked for a five-thousand-dollar retainer for legal services. *Peace of mind is expensive these days,* Dan thought as he exited the office to visit his brother in the hospital.

—

Dan Murphy felt at home on entering the medical center where his brother, Pat, was hospitalized. Sitting up in bed and watching a television talk show, Pat Murphy gobbled down a bag of crackers. His drawn face, dulled by lifeless eyes, gave him the appearance of someone who had gone without food or sleep for days.

"Hey, dude." Pat extended his right hand to Dan, causing the intravenous pole to fall over. "Just like the frickin' astronauts. My umbilical cord."

"How do you feel, Pat?"

"Worse, man. Worse than yesterday, if you can believe it." He closed his eyes as though in pain.

"Dr. Harrington was in today, wasn't he?"

"Yeah! About an hour ago."

Dan, anxious to hear the hematologist's assessment, listened intently.

"He told me I had a reaction to the transplant. Host-versus-graft disease or something. I know it wasn't the Patriots versus the Cowboys. What was he talking about?"

"It's a condition where my marrow essentially battles some of the organs in your body."

"Gee, thanks. You beat me up when I was a kid, and you're still doing it." Although Pat's wit and humor had pulled him through tough times in the past, this illness promised to stretch his abilities.

The telephone rang, diverting their attention.

"Pizza here, but we don't deliver," Pat said after picking up the receiver. After a pause, he said, "Oh, hi, Maryann! When ya coming over? Dan's here."

For the next few minutes, Pat listened intently to his wife as she described a sad event that would play a role in uncovering the cause of the illness at South Boston Plating.

"Let me talk with Dan. I'll call you back."

After hanging up the phone, he turned to Dan.

"Felix died."

"Felix?"

"My dog."

"I'm sorry to hear that."

"He was a great dog," Pat said, struggling to hold back tears.

"Was he very old?" Dan asked.

"No."

"Sick?"

"No."

"What happened?"

"I don't know. Maryann found him in the kitchen in a pool of red liquid. She thought it looked like wine."

"Was he cut?" Dan asked.

"No. She looked Felix over and couldn't find anything but the red liquid." His grief at losing a pet affected his speech, normally short and crisp, but now laden with emotion. "Why would he die! He was a healthy dog. I just took him to the vet a few weeks ago."

"I'm sorry, Pat. Why don't I go over and help Maryann? She shouldn't be carrying a dog to the vet."

A knock on the door was followed by the entry of a young Latino male dressed in white pants, white shirt, and white shoes who placed the evening's dinner on a table for Pat.

"Thanks, man," Pat called over to him.

As Pat Murphy opened the wrapper housing the plastic knife and fork that would help him attack the chicken breast, Dan couldn't resist taking the chance to probe him about the plating firm.

"Pat, do you know anyone who works at South Boston Plating?"

Pat looked at his brother suspiciously. "Why?"

Trusting his brother to be confidential, Dan discussed his patients from the plating firm and his recent drug arrest. "I think South Boston Plating is responsible," he concluded. "I have no other explanation."

"I knew Liam O'Malley. He used to work at the plant."

Dan recognized the name of the illegal Irish immigrant whose medical records he had reviewed and who just died from aplastic anemia. Liam had worked in the plant's warehouse and also drove a truck for the company.

Shortly, Dan recognized his brother's lapsing alertness and fatigue, which cried out for rest. He left the hospital to see what had happened to Pat's dog, Felix.

Maryann Murphy showed Dan the body of the black dog, part husky, part shepherd, that lay on the kitchen floor in a pool of red liquid. On first inspection, the liquid resembled a fruit drink—a dark red color, light in thickness, similar to water.

"This looks like urine. I don't think it's blood, but we should get it checked."

Maryann nodded.

"Have you called the vet?" Dan asked his sister-in-law.

"No."

"Do you have a vet?"

"Oh yes. Pat just took Felix to the vet a couple of weeks ago for some shots."

"How old is Felix?" Dan wasn't quite ready to use the past tense to refer to the dog that Pat had rescued from an animal shelter.

"Six, I think?" she answered tentatively.

"And he was healthy?"

"Oh yes!" Dan felt awkward inquiring about the health of a dog, although he recognized many of the similarities between human and veterinary medicine. One of his college classmates had become a veterinarian and ultimately an orthopedic surgeon who performed total hip replacements on golden retrievers and other large breeds.

"Was he different over the past few days?"

"No, he's been active, especially since Pat got out of the hospital."

"Where's he spend his day?"

"Here, unless Pat takes him out for a walk or to the playground. Oh, I can't believe he's dead!" Maryann answered.

"Has Pat been taking him anywhere in particular?"

"No. Not that I know about. Why?"

"Well, it seems that Felix died suddenly. If he were healthy, that shouldn't have happened. Think about it, Maryann: why would a healthy dog die with no obvious explanation?"

"Dan, what are you getting at?"

"I'm not sure yet."

A few minutes later, Dan was on the phone talking about Felix to a veterinarian at the New England Veterinary Medical Center. Dan asked, "Do you have a pathology residency program?" After pausing to hear the response, he asked, "Would you be interested in doing an autopsy on a healthy dog that died suddenly?" Murphy hoped to pique the curiosity of a veterinarian in training. It was also a way to have an evaluation performed at no charge if the case were reviewed for its academic and teaching value.

While awaiting a response, Murphy was placed on hold. A tape played a message advising people to curb pet overpopulation.

"I'm Michelle Weinstein, a resident in veterinary pathology. I understand you have an interesting case to review."

Dan, pleased with the favorable response, hoped to persuade her to allow him to bring the animal over for an autopsy. "I don't want to push your academic generosity, but if you could test the urine, it might be helpful in gaining an understanding of what happened."

Dan listened, then replied, "Thank you."

"That was quick," Maryann said. "You're pretty assertive when you need to be."

"We got lucky. The pathology department at the animal medical center was interested."

"Thank you, Danny."

"I suppose I'd better get on with this," he said, taking two large trash disposal bags in which to carry Felix to the animal hospital.

On seeing the bags, Maryann tearfully called to him, "Danny, I can't watch," then went upstairs sobbing.

—

It was a lonely ride to the animal hospital, but everything went as planned. Murphy learned that preliminary results would be available tomorrow afternoon and that he could call the veterinary resident to discuss her findings.

Driving home to the Back Bay section of Boston, Dan reflected on the events of the past few days and attempted to integrate them into a coherent pattern. *OSHA visits the plant; I get arrested on cocaine charges; Pat's readmitted to the hospital, and his dog dies,* he thought, his mind racing uncontrollably. *Is there a common link to all of this? Could the plating firm have thrown me in jail because they exposed people to health hazards and I called OSHA? Where does the dog fit in? Is Mr. Shaw involved? And how about Mrs. Johnson, the plant secretary?* The inconsistencies troubled him. Even though it was plausible for the plating firm to exact retribution for his having called OSHA, it seemed that the cocaine in his glove compartment was overkill. The trumped-up drug charges raised Murphy's suspicions about activities more dangerous than plating.

Murphy pulled into the driveway behind the three-story building in which his town house was located. The winter air, chilled by a light snow, made it an ideal night for reflection in front of the fireplace. He needed to sort out the complexities of the past few days and determine the common thread among the plating firm, Pat, the dog, and the drug charges.

Chapter 55

Parker Barrows enjoyed arriving early for his visits to the psychiatrist, whose office was situated in the midst of the Harvard Medical School hospitals. En route, he immersed himself in the purposeful activity associated with curbing illness and its harmful effects. All sorts of people milled around the streets, shops, and hospital lobbies.

Barrows hoped that his psychiatrist, because of his origins in England, would be more sympathetic to the Protestant perspective in Northern Ireland. *Today,* Barrow reflected, *would be the perfect time to discuss my own plans for retribution for the horrible life-altering effects the IRA explosion in London had on me.*

Dr. Reed's gracious and friendly secretary greeted Barrows on his entry to the office. To Barrows, her smile seemed sincere, ingenuous, and warm—a completely accurate impression.

"Hello, Mr. Barrows. How are you? Dr. Reed will be with you shortly. Would you like some coffee?"

Barrows, flattered by her easy charm, responded gratefully. "That would be wonderful, Marie. I wish British women were as attentive as you to middle-aged men like me," he said with a wry grin. She smiled demurely, then rose from her desk.

Within minutes, Barrows was sipping coffee and reconsidering what he would say to Reed. He knew he needed someone to talk to, a person with whom he could share his fears and plans. Although by nature and disposition, Barrows valued discretion, he also recognized that he needed to rid his life of the consequences of the explosion in London. *Can Reed be trusted?* he wondered. *How secure is the medical confidentiality that psychiatrists so proudly describe as essential to their patient relationships?*

Shortly, Barrows was sitting in Reed's office. The psychiatrist, dressed smartly in a blue suit and bright red tie, seemed alive with energy. His eyes shone with an alertness that promised warmth and understanding. Barrows's doubts about confidentiality vanished.

"How've you been, Mr. Barrows?"

"Terrible."

"I'm sorry. Why don't you tell me about it?"

"There's been no improvement. I continue to get headaches. I have one now, in fact, and I can't get a decent night's sleep. I still get horrible nightmares—even with that medication you prescribed."

"Have you been taking it regularly?"

"Yes, most of the time."

"You need to be a bit more patient. It can take up to six weeks or so for the medication to become effective."

"But I'm not confident that anything will work. I just want to get rid of these headaches and nightmares."

"It takes time. We need to explore more, learn about your background."

"But why? You say I have posttraumatic stress disorder."

Reed nodded. "So, you should have definitive treatment."

"Such as?" Barrows asked.

"A coordinated approach of both medication and psychotherapy. No one form of treatment can necessarily be counted on."

"Then what will work for me?"

"We have to decide as we go along."

"That doesn't sound encouraging."

"Our approach should first control your symptoms while, at the same time, I gain a better understanding about you and the accident."

"That sounds fine, but I feel terrible. That medication hasn't worked at all. I'm not confident that anything will."

"I understand," Reed responded empathetically. "Tell me," he said. "Have you been drinking or using drugs?" The bluntness of Reed's question knocked Barrows off-balance momentarily, but he leaped at the opportunity to talk about his drinking escapades.

"Yes. As a matter of fact," he answered a bit arrogantly, "I have a love affair with scotch. It's become my best friend."

"Tell me about it," Reed said, using his customary way of drawing out thoughts that people otherwise keep well guarded.

"I drink every night."

"Why?"

"It dulls the pain. It makes me feel powerful again—not just a functionary in a ceremonious role."

Reed stared at Barrows.

"What's all this mean? What's going to happen? Will I ever be normal again?" Barrows raised his voice in frustration.

"The outcome of PTSD varies."

"How about me? What can I expect?"

"It's difficult to be certain at this point."

"Will these headaches and nightmares go away?"

"I don't know."

"What do you mean, you don't know?"

"I'm sorry. It could be years. As I mentioned to you earlier, this condition, although present in soldiers in the Civil War and World War I, has only been an official psychiatric diagnosis since 1980. There's a great deal that's unknown about it, including proper treatment and outcome."

"Can you give me some idea of what to expect?"

"It depends."

"Let me be specific then," Barrows said, his frustration at not getting a straight answer from his psychiatrist apparent in the commanding tone of his voice. "Can I go off the deep end with this?"

"What exactly do you mean by off the deep end?"

"Out of control. Beyond reason."

"Such as?"

"That I'd do something out of character."

"It's conceivable." Reed looked puzzled. "But why do you ask?"

"Because of the way that I feel sometimes."

"Could you explain?"

"Yes, if you could explain confidentiality among psychiatrists."

"There's not much to explain. It's quite simple. What you tell me stops here." He pointed to his forehead. "Or here, in this folder. And it can't be released without your permission."

"I can be assured of confidentiality?" Barrows asked.

"Most definitely," Reed replied as though his integrity and truthfulness were beyond reproach. "Please, feel at ease."

Responding to the cue, Barrows began, saying, "Remember, I mentioned that I came to Boston to get the bastard responsible for the sorry state of my life?"

Reed nodded in agreement.

"I've found him. He's both the cause and solution to my problems. If I can get rid of him, I'll be cured."

"How so?"

"Justice, retribution, revenge, and all possible variations on those themes."

"What do you have in mind?"

"Expose him, Jake Wilson, the bastard who killed my wife and made hamburger out of my leg."

"Expose?" the psychiatrist asked.

"Expose him for what he is, a runaway from justice out of the reach of the law, an Irish scum."

Taken aback by the depths of Barrows's anger, so easily provoked by the mention of Jake Wilson, Reed became even more convinced of his diagnosis. The psychiatrist was considerably less confident, however, of the prognosis.

"When you say expose Wilson, Mr. Barrows, what do you have in mind?"

"Make him appear responsible for a terrorist attack."

"What?"

"Pin a tragedy on him, on the IRA, on American influence in Northern Ireland."

Reed, unclear about how to respond, paused to reflect on the significance of Barrows's comment. Startled and frightened by the stark violence in the remark, Reed tried to draw more out of his patient. "Could you elaborate?"

"No. Not now. But it'll be wonderful." His facial expression mirrored self-assurance.

"What do you plan to do?"

"I've not worked out the details, but it'll end Wilson and my nightmares."

"Mr. Barrows," Reed interjected. "You seem an educated man, one of culture. Why do you need to resort to violence, to something that will ruin your life and land you in jail, disgraced?"

"Sounds like my life now, doesn't it? Except for jail," Barrows said sardonically.

"You can do better."

"With what, pills? or talking to a psychiatrist? I'm not convinced you know how wonderful it feels to have control. If I pursue my own approach, I have control. I oversee my own treatment. I don't need pills, psychotherapy, or whatever. I control my own destiny."

"It's a fool's choice," Reed bluntly responded.

"But a fool in control," Barrows rebutted.

"Let me read something that might prove interesting to you," Reed said, as he rose to take a journal from a shelf. As he paged through the contents, he continued, saying, "You said you studied English literature. I presume, then, that you appreciate Shakespeare."

Barrows looked at Reed but was unsure of how to respond.

"You know *Macbeth*. You recall how Lady Macbeth had riveting nightmares about Duncan's death?"

"Vaguely," Barrows answered, still puzzled at the anecdote and its relationship to his own situation.

"This is from an article by McFarlane and his colleagues in Australia who suggest that Lady Macbeth may have had PTSD as well."

"Don't leave me in suspense," Barrows responded.

The psychiatrist read from the journal article, "'*Yet who would have thought the old man to have so much blood in him?* Lady Macbeth thought during her traumatic replaying of the blood-drenched murder scene, which also disgusted Macbeth as he withdrew from Duncan's chamber. Her nightmare continued as she ushered the distressed and guilt-ridden Macbeth to bed. 'What's done cannot be undone; to bed, to bed, to bed.' This is from scene 1, act 5.

"Now I'll read from scene 3, act 5. Macbeth subsequently consults the same doctor about his wife being 'troubled with thick coming fantasies; that keep her from her rest.'

"The doctor replies, 'Therein the patient must minister to himself.'"

Reed put the journal down, then looked at Barrows.

"Macbeth did not readily heed the doctor's advice that the patient must play a primary role in facing and working through the trauma associated with the nightmares. Rather, he seemed to prefer some 'antidote.'"

"But that's precisely my point, Doctor. I am taking matters into my own hands, and here's what I'm going to do. I'm going to kill Wilson and, in the process, expose American sympathies toward the Catholics in Northern Ireland, discredit the IRA, and halt the Brexit negotiations and any agreements that threaten Northern Ireland as a member state of the UK. And walk away clear. And you'll need to keep all of this to yourself."

"How do you plan to accomplish this?"

"You'll see."

Barrows rose from the chair and grabbed his coat to leave the office. As he walked through the door, the secretary called after him, "Goodbye, Mr. Barrows."

He continued walking without responding.

Chapter 56

The following day brought a series of surprises to Dan Murphy. In the afternoon, he received a call from the veterinarian who performed the autopsy on Pat's dog, Felix. The dog's liver was severely damaged, and the kidneys were partially damaged. The vet concluded, "It looks like some toxin caused the dog's death."

"Like what?"

"I can't say for sure. The liver and kidney damage suggest toxic poisoning, but I don't know which hazard may be responsible." The vet had had experience with diagnosing lead poisoning in dogs and, as a result of a publication, had helped convince the public health department to search the homes and apartments of the dog owners for lead hazards, especially dust from chipping paint that may sicken children.

"Is there any way you could find out how Felix died?" Dan asked. "Could you save some serum or plasma or whatever tissue you think is appropriate for testing later?"

"What do you have in mind?" she asked.

"Well, I'm doing an indoor air quality evaluation of sorts. A few people in a certain factory seem to be getting sick from something at work."

"What's that have to do with the dog?"

"I think the dog may have something to do with the plant."

"Why?"

"As I said, I can't get into the details now," Dan answered, wishing he could say "journalist's hunch," Anna's favorite response when available information did not necessarily support her point of view. Dan knew that his brother took Felix everywhere, including local bars, ball games, and especially card games. It wasn't a stretch of the imagination to consider Pat taking Felix to the plating firm as well.

"I don't see why not," the veterinarian answered. "We'll keep it for a week, then if I don't hear from you, we'll need to get rid of it."

"Thanks. I appreciate your help."

Dan, perplexed as to how Felix could have died of poisoning, impulsively reached for the phone to call Pat, who was now in the hospital undergoing treatment for graft-versus-host disease. After an exchange of pleasantries, Dan learned that Pat was improving. He got to the point about the dog.

"What happened with Felix?" he asked sharply.

"I don't know. He died. What do you mean, what happened?"

"Pat, how could Felix be poisoned? Where'd you take him recently? The vet thinks he got poisoned somehow within the past few days."

"I don't know, Dan. I don't know. What does it matter?"

"Because I think if we find out why Felix died, we'll learn why you're sick."

"That's ridiculous."

"Where'd you take him, Pat? Don't bullshit me."

"I took him to play cards the other night."

"When?"

"Friday night."

"Where?" Dan probed.

"Over at the plant."

"What did Felix get into over there?"

"I don't know, Dan. I don't know. Look, can I go? I'm tired." The phone conversation ended abruptly, but it was of sufficient length to arouse further suspicion in Dan Murphy. Why would they have played cards there? It wasn't hard to imagine how Felix could have been poisoned at the plating firm, especially with the acids, solvents, and other hazards lying about. Perhaps the dog entered an area of the plant where chemicals were stored when Pat and his friends weren't watching him.

The rest of Murphy's day flowed routinely and included treating people with back pain and conducting medical exams on workers who had had contact with asbestos and lead. Eventually, Mr. Shaw, the custodian from the plant, appeared.

Shaw, whose liver condition had improved since being out of work from the plating firm, anxiously sought Murphy's approval for going back to work. From Shaw, Dan learned how the plant controlled the airborne hazards generated in the plating of metals. Shaw thoroughly understood how the plant's ventilation system removed hazards and supplied fresh air to the entire facility, including the office area where Mrs. Johnson worked.

Mr. Shaw described his efforts in inspecting and replacing ventilation filters. Although not formally trained in indoor air quality, his grasp of the principles was firm. When Mrs. Johnson had approached him a few weeks earlier about her symptoms at work, Shaw did his own quiet review and found filters heavily clogged with a flaky yellow dust.

"No, I threw them out," he answered Murphy when questioned about the filters and whether they were tested.

Murphy wasn't sure whether Shaw should return to the plating firm. On one hand, Shaw looked and felt well. On the other hand, Murphy recognized his own uncertainties about health risks at the plating firm. Mrs. Johnson, Mr. Shaw, Liam O'Malley, Pat, and Pat's dog all appeared to have become ill as a result of the plant.

"Mr. Shaw, you probably shouldn't go to work yet. I can't be sure, but I think there's something at your work causing you to get sick. If you have repeated contact with whatever hazard is affecting your liver, it could get very serious. I don't mean to be dramatic, but you could get the same type of liver disease that people who abuse alcohol get: cirrhosis."

"I don't drink, Doc."

"It doesn't matter. Chemicals can damage liver cells just like alcohol."

After pausing to reflect on Dan's comment, Shaw asked, "How long do you think I need to stay out?"

"I don't know."

"Mrs. Johnson told me you wanted to do some tests on us."

"Oh. Yes." Dan recognized it was probably safe to discuss his plans with Shaw. After the emotional trauma of his arrest and detainment in jail, Murphy had become extraordinarily hesitant to let anyone learn of his interest in the plating firm. Faced with a serious challenge to his medical career because of the drug charges, and now convinced that the plating firm somehow coordinated the bust, Murphy was charged with a sense of purpose. Rather than passively awaiting the guidance of his attorney, he took on the challenge of pinning down the plant himself as his top priority. Throughout the remainder of the day at the clinic, he assiduously carved out time to devise a strategy to determine whether the plant was causing people to get sick.

After treating a construction worker who had injured his shoulder in a fall, Murphy went back to his office, where a message alerted him to a call from the veterinarian at the animal hospital. "Urine test positive for methemoglobin," his receptionist had written.

Murphy couldn't resist the urge to call back.

The vet explained that the methemoglobin suggested that Pat's dog had come in contact with some type of hazardous material, perhaps an aromatic amine. The veterinarian asked Murphy to share the test results of the plant's workers. She described her interest in how certain pet illnesses can reflect environmental risks to humans, and then described the famous example of how canaries were used in coal mines to indicate when the oxygen level was dropping. When the canary stopped singing, the miners took action. She and a faculty member were investigating lead poisoning in dogs and how it may reflect hazards to children living in the same environment.

Maybe this will be the dog in the plating firm, a variant of the canary in the coal mine, Murphy mused.

Murphy opened his computer to search the term *methemoglobin*, the chemical found in the urine of his brother Pat's dog, Felix. As the director of the Occupational Health Center, he was expected to understand the health implications of exposure to chemicals, even though he had not completed a residency in occupational medicine. Because of the shortage of these specialists, opportunities were available to other physicians like Murphy, who lacked formal training in the field. Recognizing his need for education in the discipline, he had enrolled in the course at Harvard, where he met Anna Carlson. He hoped to apply his new skills in diagnosing an environmental illness.

Murphy wondered why methemoglobin would be in the dog's urine. A review article that he had uncovered in his search gave some clues, although one table listed nearly one hundred compounds, including medications and a variety of chemicals that could result in methemoglobin in the urine. Another table was actually entitled "Methemoglobin-Forming Compounds—in the Dog." Ten substances were listed.

Through the help of the veterinary pathologist, Dan learned that the brownish-red liquid found next to Felix was urine. The coloration was caused by methemoglobin, which was formed when hemoglobin, the oxygen-carrying compound in the red blood cells, was broken down. In humans, high concentrations of methemoglobin in the urine are associated with headaches, tiredness, dizziness, shortness of breath, rapid heart rate, and even impairment in mental ability.

As Murphy scrolled through other articles he identified, Brenda came to the office door. "Mrs. Johnson's here to see you. She doesn't want an evaluation. Just wants to talk with you in the office. Is that OK?"

"Sure. Would you ask her to come in?"

Moments later, the fifty-seven-year-old woman appeared. Dressed smartly in the best selection of bargain store outfits, she excitedly told Murphy, "I have a few people for you for the testing."

"Great. How many?"

"Five. Me, Mary, Sally, George, and Mr. Shaw, our custodian."

"You've been busy," Murphy said in appreciation.

"But I don't want Mildred to know—you know, Mr. Flannagan's secretary."

"Of course."

"Dr. Murphy, we're so happy you're trying to help us. Mr. Shaw, he thinks you're great. Said he'll do whatever you need."

"But you can't tell Flannagan," Dr. Murphy advised her.

"Oh, I never would do that."

The buzzer to his phone rang, alerting Dan to his next patient.

"Mrs. Johnson. I really appreciate your help. I'm not sure when we'll do the testing, but would you call me tomorrow? You don't want me calling the plant."

"Sure. What time?"

"In the morning."

"Fine." She gathered her large black purse and rose from the chair. "I'll call you tomorrow."

The remainder of the day passed routinely for Murphy. Having heard from Mrs. Johnson and the veterinarian, he was convinced that it was worth the risk to pursue the plating firm in order to learn the truth of their activities—a gamble, he recognized, but his unmitigated anger about the cocaine charges drove him to steamroll his hesitation. On leafing through an occupational medicine textbook, he found a section on aplastic anemia that included a list of agents reported as causes: benzene, ionizing radiation (the type associated with nuclear energy and atomic weapons), glues, varnishes, and pesticides. Arsenic, ethylene glycol (a substance used in antifreeze), and trinitrotoluene, used as an explosive and for ammunitions, were also listed.

Murphy looked over an article he uncovered on biological monitoring to address the specific tests for determining whether people had been exposed to any of the hazards listed as causing aplastic anemia. Dan then noted the major hazards used at South Boston Plating, based on the OSHA report. The final list included ten different materials. After calling a local toxicology lab, he was prepared to join Anna for dinner.

Chapter 57

The restaurant, well situated in Boston's theater district, provided the perfect ambience for Dan and Anna. Seated by a window that allowed a view onto streets lined with people leaving work or en route to one of the theaters, Anna said enthusiastically, "It's so good to see you."

"Likewise," Dan replied affectionately.

Dan, tantalized by the emotional, physical, and intellectual attraction he felt toward Anna, allowed himself to be drawn into the web of love and its joys and pitfalls. He resisted yielding to any sense of caution about becoming more involved with her.

"How's your brother?" Anna asked, hoping for an encouraging answer.

"Fairly stable. His fever has dropped."

"How's his mood?"

"Lousy! He's never been known for patience or liking captivity."

A waiter took their orders for drinks—a chardonnay for Anna and a Belgian beer for Dan.

"Pat's dog died yesterday," Dan said.

"I'm so sorry. What happened?"

"I'm not sure. A vet at the animal center said it was probably some type of poisoning," Dan replied.

"How could that happen?"

"I'm not sure, but I hope you'll like my journalist's hunch." Anna grinned in anticipation. "The plating firm's involved somehow."

"Ah! A convert to the value of trusting your gut instincts," Anna said.

"Perhaps we're entering dangerous territory, but I put together a list of chemicals that have been implicated in causing aplastic anemia. Then I looked up how to test for exposure to each one of them."

"What are you looking for?"

"Usually, the chemical itself or some metabolite—one of its breakdown products."

"I know," Anna said playfully, "Remember, I got myself through nursing school. Plus, I'm stuck in a department with a bunch of doctors who only talk medicine."

"OK. OK," he said, then reached across the table to gently kiss her on the lips. "How could I ever underestimate you."

"Now you're talking," she responded with a smile that told him she was thrilled to be with him.

"Back to my story. I cross-referenced the chemicals that cause aplastic anemia with lab tests that can be done to confirm that a person's been exposed to the chemical. Unfortunately, the tests are not available in most hospitals; they have to be done at a separate laboratory."

"What are you going to do?"

"Get urinary and blood samples from the workers who've agreed to be tested."

"When?"

"Ideally, soon after they've been exposed to whatever is causing them to be sick."

"Why?"

"The test results are more likely to be helpful—positive—so to speak, if the person is checked soon after contact with the hazard. The longer a person's away from the hazard, the less likely the toxicology test will be helpful."

"So, what are you going to test them for?"

"About ten different materials."

"Have any of the chemicals at the plating firm ever caused aplastic anemia?"

"No, but maybe we'll find something interesting."

The waiter brought their drinks and took their orders. Both Dan and Anna went for the clam chowder. Dan ordered chicken; Anna requested a Caesar salad.

Anna raised her glass. "To us." They clicked glasses, then drank. Seconds later, Anna reached across the table to plant a kiss on Dan's lips.

"Dan, I'm impressed with your plan for the plating firm."

"I'd like to get decent results before my cocaine hearing next week. If I can show something unscrupulous is going on at the plant, maybe I'll get out of this drug mess."

"What did your lawyer say about the charges?"

"It will be difficult to get acquitted. I probably ought to consider a plea bargain."

"That's ridiculous."

"I agree. Then there's the disruption to my medical practice, the effect on my reputation, and problems with the licensing board. I'm not going to plea to anything. I want full dismissal of the charges."

"How can I help?"

"Tell me what you think of the plan."

"I'm listening," Anna answered eagerly.

"A few workers from the plating firm will come to the clinic to give a urine and blood sample. I'll send the specimens to a toxicology lab north of Boston. One of my colleagues in the occupational medicine class works at a toxicology lab in Burlington. He agreed to analyze everything for nothing!"

"Are the tests expensive?"

"Yes, toxicology tests can be very costly, and health plans usually don't cover them."

"Why?"

"Primarily because when a health adjuster reads that one of these test was performed, they assume it's a work-related problem and that workers' compensation insurance should pay. And, as you might imagine, workers' comp usually denies the claim, at least until a diagnosis can be agreed upon."

The waiter brought their hot dishes to the table.

"So, when is this all going to happen?"

"We haven't decided, but Monday would be good."

"Why?"

"According to Mrs. Johnson, for the past few months, Mondays have been the most severe—at least in terms of her symptoms."

"How can she be so certain?"

"She keeps a diary."

"Have you considered doing air sampling on the same day as the testing?" Anna asked.

"What type of testing do you have in mind?"

"Testing the air, doing wipe samples of dusts, looking over the air-conditioning filters."

"Sounds good, but how could we do it? You know the trouble Flannagan gave the OSHA inspector."

"How about the custodian with hepatitis? Wouldn't he help?"

Dan reflected on Anna's comment but hesitated to agree.

"Access—from within," Anna continued. "Wouldn't our claim be more believable if we could pin something in the work environment to the test results of the workers?"

"You make a good point, Anna, but this is risky business. The plant won't authorize my testing."

"I realize that, but it would help a lot if we could test the air and dust in the plant."

"Any suggestions?"

"Yes, your mother's friend Mrs. Johnson and the custodian."

"Mr. Shaw."

"Have them get us into the plant after hours."

"That's not going to be easy. They're already afraid of losing their jobs."

"They should be more afraid of losing their health."

The waiter approached their table. "Would you like any dessert?"

They looked at each other, then Dan turned to the waiter. "No, thank you. Just a check, please."

"Dan, why don't we pass on the comedy show tonight? I think we should plan how we'll test the workers and go to the plant."

"Should we get a bottle of wine to share?"

"I'd love to."

Over the next few hours, Anna and Dan developed their strategy for a surreptitious on-site assessment of South Boston Plating. Although it seemed obvious to them that the plating firm was responsible for the illnesses, Dan wasn't sure how, since the OSHA evaluation failed to uncover any unusual hazards. Throughout the evening, they discussed the best options for the timing of the tests on the workers and the location at the plant where they should take the air samples. Dan would work with Mrs. Johnson to arrange an after-hours visit under the guidance of the custodian, Mr. Shaw. Anna would collect dust samples and bring the ventilation filters for analysis. By coordinating the medical tests with the air and dust analysis, they knew that their work would have greater credibility.

The plan seemed tight. Trusting the judgment of Mrs. Johnson, they would wait until Monday, unless anything unusual occurred during the rest of the week.

Moments after completing their work, they were nestled beneath soft sheets and wrapped in each other's arms. An explosion of passion followed.

Chapter 58

Caressing a glass filled with scotch, Barrows thought about his last visit to the psychiatrist and the diagnosis of posttraumatic stress disorder. Dr. Reed had assured him that PTSD was responsible for the nightmares and headaches that he was experiencing. The explosion in London served as a trigger, Reed had explained, to all sorts of disturbances in Barrows's life that, given the broad definition, constituted PTSD. What was unclear, however, was the most effective treatment and the outcome of his condition. In some people, Reed told him, PTSD is relentless and refractory to treatment.

Despite his initial hesitation to seek out a psychiatrist for help, Barrows considered Reed's advice valuable. The sessions allowed him to vent his anger and deal with his obsession with Jake Wilson.

While Barrows sipped his scotch, he gazed around his book-lined study. He rolled back in his large desk chair, then grasped the opportunity that solitude allowed him to consider final options for Wilson. It must be done in such a way that Wilson was viewed as the perpetrator of the terror, and it was imperative that he die in the process. A smile slowly crept across Barrows's face as a quiet satisfaction and confidence overcame him.

Assured that his involvement would be virtually impossible to trace, Barrows reviewed the details of his plot. His smile changed to a frown, however, as he pondered the fate of Tony Mesa. It was only Mesa, Barrows assured himself, who had any link to him.

Sipping the scotch that had become both his friend and his poison, Barrows reflected on his plan to derail the Brexit negotiations on Northern Ireland and get his just revenge. As he considered his failed career, amputated leg, and deceased wife, fury overcame him. He rose from his chair, then tripped when throwing his glass of scotch against the wall of his study. He then hobbled to his stereo system to play some of Pavarotti's best arias. Ever since he had trailed a suspect into London's theater district and saw *Rigoletto*, he learned to love opera.

The scotch, music, and solitude allowed him the luxury of unfettered reflection. A montage of images from his past flashed through his mind, including escapades in Argentina, Hong Kong, and Gibraltar, in which he thwarted terrorism and sabotage attempts against British interests. Commendations, promotions, and higher wages followed. Then, he was sent to London and assigned responsibility for assessing IRA activities and plans. His watch was compromised, however, by an unpredictable outbreak of violence. Although he hated to admit it, the IRA had outmaneuvered him in launching a series of car bombings in London. In turn, they had ruined the careers of diplomats and intelligence officials deemed unable to prevent the bloodshed.

British public opinion, less tolerant of the IRA violence, had pressured the government to make changes in its security operations. In fact, Barrows's fate in the service was dubious at the time he had been injured in the IRA-orchestrated blast in London. His declining stature had enabled the government to usher him out of his job more easily. A nice pension, disability payments, and a letter of commendation smoothed the frustration of his unplanned departure from his position in British Military Intelligence—MI5. Barrows, however, had one final score to settle before he could ever hope to gain closure on the past and move on with his life.

Barrows decided on the date and location of the terror he planned to unleash in the name of the IRA. A British delegation for Northern Ireland on the Brexit negotiations was scheduled to visit Boston.

Barrows, in reflecting on his aborted career, kept fixating on Jake Wilson. Although Barrows had been unable to convincingly implicate Wilson in the London explosion, he had no doubt about the IRA fugitive's culpability. As his anger simmered, his attention was broken by a shooting pain racing up his amputated leg.

Barrows sipped the scotch, which assuaged his anger and fueled his confidence. A two-step process, he concluded, would be ideal to exact justice and revenge for his travails. The Irish lowlifes, the working-class scum as he described them to his intelligence colleagues, would be avenged. Their audacity in demanding a separation of British citizens in Northern Ireland was outrageous. Subjecting them further to the rules and customs of Irish Catholics was unbearable to contemplate. As the alcohol fueled Barrows's anger, he drew pleasure from his plan to further discredit the IRA and its sympathizers. The United States government would learn the perils of even casual recognition of a band of lawless working-class thugs who claimed to be peacemakers.

As Pavarotti belted out the lyrics to "La donna è mobile," Barrows prepared another scotch. What had become of his life? What would happen with the Irish Brexit process? Would his work, his suffering, be futile? Then, the confident smile returned. *I can do it all,* he thought, *get Wilson, expose illegal American support for terrorism, and kill the whole Brexit peace process. These negotiations and pending terms of agreement*—he fumed—*are a disgrace to the Unionists of Northern Ireland and the British military, the British police, and other citizens who've lost their lives or been injured by the IRA.* As Barrows drank, the scotch fooled him into a sense of confidence, something he so rarely experienced after the explosion. The alcohol dulled his pain, inflated his powers, and ultimately tricked him about the effectiveness of his plan.

Occasionally during his alcoholic reverie, especially during slow sections of Pavarotti's arias, Barrows entertained doubt. *Should I do this? Am I going mad? Will I get away with it?* Never allowing his apprehension to overcome him, he quickly turned to thinking of the pleasure he'd feel in taking the offensive against Wilson. For years, his professional efforts were focused on terrorism, namely, preventing tragedies and protecting people at risk. Now, armed with information about the time, location, and participants of a political meeting to be held in Boston, Barrows anticipated the pleasure of enacting terror on the terrorists. Based on his experience in New England, the security measures seemed weaker in comparison to those of UK and Northern Europe. He smugly concluded that the United States needed a little taste of the terror, furor, and anger that the Brits had had to endure from the IRA. Americans should disavow themselves of their idealized notions of a united Ireland. Hardened criminals ran the IRA, they should know, not reasoning revolutionaries. Americans, with such little tolerance for outrageous displays of terrorism, would quickly discredit the IRA and its political party, Sinn Fein. Or so Barrows hoped.

With the scotch surging him onward, Barrows took out a pen to sort out his thoughts about what to do with Tony Mesa. *How will he react when he learns that Wilson has to go?* Mesa's importance loomed large to Barrows, who recognized that the former boxer's brute strength and courage were essential to getting rid of Wilson. As Wilson came to mind, Barrows felt light-headed and weak. The room seemed to spin about. Pavarotti sung "O sole mio." The alcohol in Barrows's stomach rumbled, threatening release.

Barrows rose from the chair but was so dizzy that he fell onto the floor. Lifting himself onto the sofa, he rolled into a comfortable position and immersed himself in the music. Feeling a peace that had previously eluded him, he imagined shooting Wilson in the head. He saw his adversary fall backward in shock as Mesa looked on.

Mesa! Mesa! Where are you? he imagined himself yelling as the alcoholic daze enveloped him. Wilson was rising; he hadn't been killed. Where was Mesa? Pavarotti belted out another aria. The soothing lyrics and the comfort of the tenor's voice provided a brief respite from the terror that consumed Barrows. *Mesa,* he thought. *What should I do with Mesa? He's the only link to me. He has to go.*

Chapter 59

Anna, dressed in black slacks and a red silk blouse, sat in Dan Murphy's medical office. Dan, just then completing a telephone conversation, asked, "You'll have the results tomorrow afternoon?" He paused. "That's excellent, Professor," he chided his colleague.

After bidding the caller goodbye, Dan turned to Anna, who said, "Sounds as though you'll be getting the results pretty soon."

"Yeah! With a little bit of luck."

"How'd it go today?"

"Well. Five people from the plant came over, gave urine and blood samples, then went back to work." The phone buzzed in his office. "Would you ask if I could call him back later?" he said to his receptionist.

He continued his explanation to Anna. "Mr. Shaw told me he noticed a messy area in the shipping area of the plant. Lots of yellow dust scattered all over. The same dust he found on the ventilation filters when he changed them last week."

"So, it's tonight then?" she asked.

"I think so, but I still have some hesitation about it."

"Why?"

"Suppose we get caught?"

"It's worth the risk. How else are you going to get out of that cocaine mess? Besides, tonight's the perfect opportunity to coordinate your patients' results with sampling at the plant."

Although Dan knew Anna was correct, he was nonetheless consumed with caution. It was one thing to help people seeking his medical attention, but it was quite another matter to survey a factory for health hazards after work hours and without permission.

"Mrs. Johnson assured me that it would be safe, Anna, but I'm not sure. Suppose somebody like Flannagan comes over. Then what? If these people would frame me with drug charges for calling OSHA, what would they concoct for trespassing?"

"Dan, everyone's at risk. Shaw, Mrs. Johnson—they could lose their jobs. How about me? Do you think Becker will be impressed if I'm arrested? I'm not trying to be the Norma Rae of environmental health. I just want to pin down a problem that seems obvious to me. I've arranged for an industrial hygiene lab to do the wipe samples, and I've been able to get a few Dräger tubes," she continued enthusiastically.

"Teach me. What's all that for?"

"The wipe samples will tell us what kind of dusts are in the plant, and the tubes will give us an idea about the air, at least whether there's anything toxic."

About two hours later, Anna and Dan pulled into a parking area about two businesses down from the warehouse that housed South Boston Plating. They walked along the unlit street beneath the dark, starless sky. On reaching the entrance to the plating shop, they knocked twice. Within seconds, Mr. Shaw, the custodian, answered. Mrs. Johnson stood behind him. After a brief exchange of greetings, Shaw led them onto the shop floor with a flashlight that illuminated the wooden planks that separated the plating baths. The pieces of equipment seemed dated and worn out in comparison to those in modern facilities that Dan had visited.

Shaw pointed out a large metal tank used to remove grease and debris from metals. A special chemical was heated to create a vapor, which then cleansed the material, he explained.

A loud noise, resembling a gunshot, startled them. They stood in silence.

"Turn off your flashlights," Shaw whispered to Dan, Anna, and Mrs. Johnson. As they huddled silently in a corner adjacent to an acid tank, Anna squeezed Murphy's hand. Sounds that they would customarily ignore, such as a car driving by or the distant wail of an ambulance, heightened their alertness and fear.

"Oh my God!" Mrs. Johnson said in surprise upon hearing another loud noise that sounded like a garage door closing. The four of them bent down, unsure of whether to stay put or dash elsewhere. Seconds seemed like hours as they cringed in anticipation of events beyond their control.

"Is there an easy way out of here?" Dan whispered to Mr. Shaw.

"Not from here. We need to go to the far corner of the plant. There's an emergency exit there."

"How far is it?"

"About a hundred yards."

"Oh my God," Mrs. Johnson said in fright. "We'll never make it."

After a tense ten-minute period of watchful waiting, Shaw announced, "I think it's OK. The noise was probably from the business across the street. They work two shifts."

"Are you sure?" Anna asked.

"No, but let's go," Shaw replied in a tone suggestive of a command. "Follow me."

Anna, eager to respond, grabbed Dan's arm as the custodian led them through the darkened plant with the aid of his flashlight. While walking past an acid plating tank, Anna fell onto the wooden floor. The abrupt noise startled Mrs. Johnson.

"What happened?" she screamed.

"Shh," Mr. Shaw admonished.

Dan reached over to help her up. Mrs. Johnson said, "Is she all right?"

"I'm fine," Anna answered. "My mother said I'd never be a ballerina."

Shaw continued to lead them to another area of the shop. After fumbling with his keys, he opened a large metal door that led into a room partially lit by lights outside the warehouse.

"I thought you may want to see this," he said to Dan. "I never knew it was here until I was checking over the ventilation system the other day."

Dan, Anna, and Mrs. Johnson looked over the area, which was cluttered with boxes, wooden crates, and large tables. "Why is it so dirty?"

"What's all this powdery stuff?"

"I don't know," Shaw answered.

"Can we have it sampled?" Dan asked.

"Definitely," Anna answered.

Without hesitation, Anna withdrew a sampling kit from her red canvas shoulder bag and, within minutes, had gathered enough dust for the lab to analyze. Moments later, Dan, Anna, and Mrs. Johnson followed Shaw and his flashlight out to their cars.

Chapter 60

For the first time in months, Barrows felt optimistic. As he looked into the mirror to comb his thinning black hair, relief from his troubles seemed at hand. He gulped down his second scotch, then grabbed his cashmere coat to brave the biting cold that awaited him.

With false confidence fueled by the alcohol, Barrows wandered along Commonwealth Avenue to reflect on his plan. His new well-fitted prosthesis enabled him to savor a stroll to gather his thoughts. It had been months since he designed the scheme that he felt would catapult him out of the psychiatric abyss into which his life had fallen.

Within the past few days, however, as his denouement with Wilson approached, he had momentary doubts about his plans. Was it really necessary to kill him? Would it be just as effective to turn him in?

Turning Wilson in, however, promised too many uncertainties for Barrows. When considering the legal difficulties of convicting Wilson, Barrows grew frustrated. Moreover, the interminable inquiries, depositions, and reports in which he would need to take part made the decision even less appealing. The unpredictability of the judicial system, complicated by the evolving course of the Brexit negotiations, provided further support for his views on how Wilson should be handled.

As he became more confident about his scheme, he felt in control of his life in a way he had not experienced for many years.

A ten-minute taxi ride took him to Harvard Square. He walked to the Chinese restaurant where he had met Mesa earlier. Winter semester had just begun, so the restaurant was filled with students.

Barrows entered. To a casual observer, he appeared to be a college administrator, too dapper for a professor and too casual for a stockbroker. Off in a corner sat Mesa, leaning across a table and talking to a young woman with a ring in her nose. On recognizing Barrows, he called out, "Hey, Park. How ya doin'?"

Barrows nodded, then took a seat at the table.

"Have you met April?" Mesa asked, referring to the woman with whom he was speaking.

"Have not had the pleasure," Barrows answered. The woman smiled in return, but her glassy eyes and slurred speech suggested to Barrows that she was on some kind of drug.

"Tony," Barrows said authoritatively. "It's time."

"What's up?"

"Can we sit over to the side?"

Barrows then led Mesa to a booth in the corner of the restaurant.

"OK. What's up, man?" Mesa began.

"It's the perfect time."

"For what?"

"An explosion or two."

A waiter approached their table to take their orders, while Mesa absorbed Barrows's comment.

"Where?"

"The storage site."

"Why?"

"To take care of Wilson."

"Take care of him? You mean get rid of him?"

"Yes."

"Why? I thought Wilson was working for us!"

"He's working with us to discredit himself, and the IRA, and the bloody Irish nationalists."

Taken aback by Barrows's strident response, Mesa paused before asking, "I thought we were in this together?"

"We are. You and I, that is, but not Wilson. He has to go. He killed my wife and destroyed my leg and my life." He defiantly raised his right leg, then pulled up his trouser leg to tap on the prosthesis."

"But I thought our work was for the IRA?"

"It is. Indirectly. To expose them as the criminals they are. Wilson's a fugitive—a criminal. He deserves what's planned. It's the only way to exact accountability. Jake Wilson is the IRA operative John Casey who orchestrated terrorist attacks in London."

"How do you know Wilson's your guy?"

"Sources in the UK."

"Then why don't you turn his ass in?"

"I don't trust the outcome. It's much too uncertain."

"How sure are you about Wilson?"

"I got a tab on him as long as your boxing career."

"That's not very long," Mesa answered with a laugh that caught the attention of students at an adjacent table. "So, what did Wilson have to do with your explosion?" he asked.

"He directed it. He chose the site. He selected the explosives. He made it happen."

"How'd he get away with it?"

"He didn't, because I'm on to him. His time is up."

"How'd he end up in Boston?"

"He bolted out of the UK after the explosion. Then he went to Germany, the Virgin Islands, and then Boston."

"Where'd he get the money?"

"The same way he always does—with semilegitimate work and living on the edge of the law with petty robbery and an occasional drug deal."

"An impressive résumé," Mesa chimed, "if your career's in crime. But why Boston? How'd he end up here?"

"Contacts here and there. He was told it would be receptive to him, especially South Boston because of the history of Irish immigration."

"South Boston? What's it have to do with the IRA?" Mesa asked in disbelief.

"It's well-known," Barrows replied matter-of-factly.

"Well-known to whom?" Mesa asked.

"FBI, CIA, British Intelligence."

"With all that firepower, why you takin' on Wilson yourself?"

"I have to."

"Why?"

"It's too difficult to describe, but it's the only way out of a quagmire for me."

"A what?"

"A mess, a disaster, a complicated morass of problems with no apparent solution."

"Park, you sound like an English teacher. I told you I dropped out of college. I hated to give up football, but I hated classes even more."

"I need your help, Tony."

"How's Wilson been able to duck all you guys?"

"He's changed his appearance. Had a nose reconstructed and a chin reorganized, and took on a new name. In the UK, he was John Casey. Wilson had himself well covered in London." Barrows continued, saying, "He ran a delivery service. He knew London well. He also knew how to recruit sleepers, so none of them built up a record."

"But what makes you so sure of Wilson?"

"I have excellent sources in London, plus, and most important, I had prints lifted from that glass of his you gave me. They match prints from a flat he rented in East London. I'm convinced it's Wilson. He has to go, and I need your help." Barrows raised his voice sternly as he completed the comment.

"My fees just went up," Mesa said in jest.

"Don't worry about money."

"I'm more worried about jail. Getting rid of a guy is a lot more complicated than dumping him off in a field in the middle of nowhere."

"This will be easier."

"What do you have in mind, boss?" Mesa asked.

"At the storage site. We'll tell him we're taking inventory for his plan."

"How am I supposed to get Wilson to the site? What do I tell him?"

"He wants to meet me. Tell him I want to discuss the plans."

"When?"

"Tomorrow."

"Then what?"

The waiter came to their table. "Finished, gentlemen?"

"Yes. Take it away please," Barrows answered for himself and Mesa. The waiter did as instructed, then left.

"What do I tell him?" Mesa asked.

"That we need to look over the material and prepare to use it."

"When?"

"Friday. When the negotiators meet."

"OK." Mesa nodded.

"Tell him he'll learn more when we meet. Give him something to think about." Barrows felt a surge of anger as he imagined the imminence of his encounter with Wilson.

"Can you give me something specific? Wilson's been suspicious lately."

"Tell him we'll set it off at the hotel where the diplomats are staying in Boston—the Four Seasons."

"When?"

"Early afternoon of the second day, when they will least suspect anything."

The waiter returned with a fresh pot of tea, a bowl of sliced pineapple and a few fortune cookies.

"So, where's Wilson fit in?"

"We get rid of him—at the plant."

"You're serious? You want to kill him?"

Barrows nodded confidently, keeping his eyes firmly directed at Mesa. "A nice little accident. An explosion. An explosion for an explosion. Middle East justice—an eye for an eye." Barrows's facial muscles coiled in a strange sort of way that reminded Mesa of a scoundrel in an old movie.

"What do you want *me* to do?" Mesa asked.

"Take care of Wilson."

"What's that mean, shoot him?" Mesa asked angrily.

"No. I'll have that pleasure. This is fail-safe," Barrows responded, sensing doubt in Mesa.

"Bullshit, pardner. Nothing's fail-safe. How'd your leg get blown off?"

Barrows looked stunned, as though a cold wet cloth had been thrown onto his face. Recognizing his affront, Mesa quickly offered, "Sorry, man. I didn't mean to be so blunt."

"Don't worry about it. Just be there. You'll be well protected and compensated to your liking."

Mesa nodded in halfhearted agreement, then rose to leave the table. "All right. Just don't fuck up yourself, man," he warned, turning to leave the restaurant.

As Parker Barrows sat alone at the table, he speared some sliced pineapple with a toothpick and worried about Mesa's reliability. *Will he deliver? Is* he *a risk?* Then, an unexpected thought overwhelmed him, like a tornado ripping through a prairie town. *Mesa. Oh! It'd be so easy,* he thought, *to get rid of him too. Then, there's no risk of leaks.*

He tried to sip more tea, but his body shook uncontrollably. His hands became sweaty, his head began to swirl, and the contents of his stomach rumbled in discontent. He placed his hand over his forehead, closed his eyes, and forced himself to take slow, deep breaths.

The waiter, noticing Barrows's abrupt change in demeanor, approached the table.

"Are you all right, sir?"

Barrows, appearing dazed as though just awakened from a deep nap, turned in his direction. "No. No." He shook his head as though it would bring his thoughts into focus. "I'm fine. Yes, I'm fine. Thank you."

"Are you sure, sir?" the waiter asked with sincerity.

"I think so. I'll be fine." He rose from his seat, then took a few unsteady steps and left the restaurant.

Chapter 61

Dan Murphy could not concentrate. What had become of his life, he wondered, that he was snooping about an old warehouse?

It was an unusually busy day for him at the clinic. Since the hospital opened the new occupational health facility, its popularity was growing quickly. Early success, however, made the schedule difficult to manage. Today, Murphy had but ten minutes to eat a sandwich before the afternoon's round of patients.

"Dan, at first I couldn't believe the results, but I checked them twice on the GC," his colleague said, referring to the gas chromatograph.

"Are you sure?"

"Absolutely."

"Why would DNAT be in the urine?" Dan asked.

"Only one reason."

"And what's that?"

"TNT. Trinitrotoluene. The explosive—what's used in ammunition."

Dan reflected momentarily, then asked, "Are you sure there's no other reason why DNAT would be in the samples?"

"No. The DNAT in the urine could only be from the TNT, the explosive. There's no other reason why this compound should be detected in the urine."

"Do you know if TNT is used in plating?" Dan asked.

"No. As far as I'm aware, it's only used by the military, at least in the United States. I don't know about elsewhere."

Dan sighed. At once, he felt both relieved and threatened. "Well, John, thanks for your help. Any chance you could fax me a report?"

"No problem."

They bid goodbye, then Dan reached for a few books on his shelf. He quickly learned that the method used to analyze the blood and urine of Mrs. Johnson and the other workers was extremely sensitive and that the corresponding results were valid. In fact, some law enforcement agencies, such as the Israel Police, used a similar technique to detect minute amounts of TNT on people's hands. The methods helped identify the use of explosives.

Murphy, surprised to find numerous entries on TNT in his toxicology text, feverishly took notes to review later with Anna. She, herself, was awaiting results of the filter and dust samples they had collected during their clandestine visit to South Boston Plating.

Dan read that TNT can be a severe irritant to the eyes and the skin, can damage the liver, and can cause aplastic anemia. The assertion appeared so astonishing that Dan repeatedly reviewed the links between his patients' symptoms and the blood results. The situation at the plating shop appeared to fit patterns reported in textbooks.

Murphy also learned that TNT powder could get into the body by breathing it or through skin contact. Unsafe handling practices were reported to have caused serious health problems, including liver disease. Could Shaw's hepatitis be due to TNT? Could contact with ventilation filters contaminated with TNT have led to Shaw's liver disease? Another article that Dan read reported, "Numerous fatalities have occurred in workers exposed to TNT from toxic hepatitis or aplastic anemia." *But how much exposure or contact with TNT is needed to cause the health problems?* he asked himself.

After piling five thick textbooks and a few monographs onto his desk, Dan was advised that his schedule of patients was backed up. His enthusiasm to learn about the health effects of TNT had caused him to lose track of time. At the end of the day, he planned to review as much as he could before he saw Anna. It was clear that a major decision awaited them.

By seven o'clock, Murphy was ready to join Anna for a dinner at a South Boston diner, a type of restaurant fast becoming an endangered species. A few revivals of diners in major cities were bucking the trend.

When Dan arrived, Anna was settled in a booth adjacent to a jukebox. Her smile and embrace, like salve to an open wound, helped distract him from the recent bizarre events in his life: arrested for cocaine charges, workers sick from TNT, and his brother's dog dying of poisoning. Could Felix also have succumbed to TNT?

"Did you get the results?" Dan asked Anna enthusiastically.

"Yes, but they're very strange."

"Tell me. I'm on the edge of my seat!"

"TNT. Trinitrotoluene," Anna told him.

"That's exactly what I found in the workers."

"Dan, this is scary. You get framed on drug charges, then we find TNT in the plant. What's going on?"

"I have no idea, but the whole fiasco's getting more sinister by the day."

"The TNT pulls it all together though, doesn't it?" she said.

"It seems so. The symptoms are consistent with exposure to TNT. Plus the dust samples, the filters—it all fits. The positive urine tests and now your dust results."

"Exactly," Anna said.

"Somehow TNT is at the plant and the workers are getting exposed—and maybe other people as well."

"Like your brother," Anna added.

Dan acknowledged her point with a thoughtful pause. Without necessarily agreeing, he commented, "Aplastic anemia, hepatitis, and all sorts of symptoms like dry skin, headaches, and cough are frequently mentioned in textbooks about TNT."

"But how can we be sure that TNT really caused the illnesses at the plant? Do you think the workers were exposed to the same levels of TNT that you read about?"

"I don't know. How would we ever know? Most of the information in the literature is anecdotal. For example, a report may describe aplastic anemia in a worker who filled ammunition shells, but the amount of TNT to which he was exposed will not be mentioned."

"Isn't there usually an interval between when a person has contact with TNT and when they get sick? My epidemiology lecturer kept talking about latency—how people can get cancer many years after they've been exposed to a hazard like asbestos."

"That interval with TNT seems very short, a matter of weeks, which suggests this TNT operation is fairly recent."

Anna sipped her California chardonnay.

"TNT has an interesting history to it," Dan continued.

"I see you're dying to tell me." Anna grinned.

"It was first used in World War I," Dan continued. "About seventeen thousand people died from either making it or putting it into military shells." He leaned forward. "I think TNT dust got into the ventilation and was spread around. Mr. Shaw probably got hepatitis from the ventilation filters. TNT causes aplastic anemia too. Felix was exposed to it. Those people got sick because they were exposed to TNT at the plating plant!"

Anna gasped. "What are they doing with TNT? That yellow powder was all over the plant!"

"I don't know," Dan said. "But the bigger question is why the plating plant has TNT."

Anna put her cup down and stared at Dan, her eyes wide.

"It's used in explosives, Anna. It's one of the most powerful explosives, and in the United States, only the military has it. They don't use it in plating operations, which is why OSHA didn't find anything in their investigation. If there's TNT at the plant, it's because someone is planning a big explosion."

"Which explains the truck drivers getting sick. They were the ones shipping it to the plant," Anna replied.

Dan drank his beer. "Let me read you more about TNT," he said, thumbing through his articles. "That is, if you don't mind the lecture."

"Just don't give me an exam," Anna replied.

"'When TNT is heated to decomposition, it gives off highly toxic fumes like the oxides of nitrogen from auto exhaust and factories. Health effects clearly occur from low TNT exposures,'" Dan said, quoting from an article. "The author, a former army physician, recommended lowering the safe level of TNT in the workplace."

Anna sipped more wine. The waiter took their orders, then left the table.

"Here's another series of articles," Dan commented, "referring to liver damage from TNT that supposedly is reversible, much like Mr. Shaw, the custodian at the plant, has."

"Good work, Dan. I picked the right partner for my project." She smiled warmly.

"There's more. Most TNT studies involve shell loading. In the past, some shells were loaded with small bags of TNT powder, but the operations resulted in substantial amounts of inhalable dust."

"Interesting," Anna replied in rapt attention. "If they were using TNT at the plating firm, it doesn't surprise me that the men would be heavily exposed. Remember when Shaw showed us that room with the yellow powder all over the floors?"

"Right."

"They probably did everything by hand, rushed to get it done, and were sloppy."

"Very good, Watson," Dan responded in reference to Sherlock Homes.

"Remember! No exams."

"TNT is rapidly absorbed through the skin, and it can cause a reddish discoloration of the urine," Dan continued.

"Pat's dog, Felix?" Anna asked. "Wasn't there a red liquid by him when he was found?"

"Exactly. Later determined to contain methemoglobin, which can be formed after exposure to TNT."

"But why TNT?" Anna asked. "With all the chemical and biological agents out there, why would they use TNT for a terrorist act?"

"It's reliable, and people are unlikely to expect it. TNT's been used in explosives since 1902. The Germans used it then for filling artillery shells. It also doesn't take much of it to fall to detonate. If you drop five pounds from a height of a yard or so, it will explode."

"Why wouldn't they choose something else?" Anna asked.

"TNT has no odor. It's also one of the most powerful high explosives available. Militaries around the world still use it for all types of purposes."

"It all fits, Dan. Now what do we do?"

"I don't know."

Chapter 62

Barrows pulled hard on the bandage, stretching it to give the prosthesis more support. It felt snug, so he stood with assurance, then walked into the kitchen to withdraw a bottle of scotch from his liquor cabinet. Pouring himself a good two ounces, he gulped, then threw his glass into the sink.

In finally coming to terms with Wilson, he felt waves of apprehension and self-doubt amid his confidence and enthusiasm. Hoping the scotch would charge his confidence, which it usually did, at least temporarily, he returned to his living room to watch a late night news program. An announcer read a statement: "The Brexit negotiations move to Boston. Political officials from Ireland, Northern Ireland, and the United Kingdom will be in town shortly to hear the perspective of United States officials." The announcer failed to provide the key information, however, that a select group of British officials would meet two days earlier in a Boston hotel, information Barrows had obtained from his intelligence colleague and former college roommate when he was recently in London.

Barrows finished the scotch, then rose from his chair for more. While he was en route to the liquor cabinet, his cell phone rang. Not too many people called at eleven o'clock in the evening! He couldn't remember the last time he had received a call this late since arriving in the States. On picking up the receiver, he was surprised to hear Dr. Reed's voice.

"I don't mean to startle you by calling so late, but I was thinking about you, wondering how you're doing."

Barrows, taken aback by Reed's call, hesitated to respond. In a matter of seconds, he thought back to his previous session, when he told the psychiatrist that he felt driven to get rid of Wilson. He feared that he had said too much.

"Has the medication taken effect?" Reed asked.

"I don't know. I suppose a bit, but it's difficult to be certain," Barrows answered vaguely. This was not the time to get into detail with Reed. It was more important to get him off the phone. Hesitation could be disastrous. Barrows then garnered his strength to withstand another Reed overture.

"You need to be patient with the treatment, Mr. Barrows. I think we're making progress."

"I don't know. I'm not so sure."

"That's what concerns me," the psychiatrist countered.

"Don't be concerned. I'll be fine."

"I am very concerned about you, Mr. Barrows. What you said in the office worries me. This fellow you described—something about getting him," Reed said, finishing with an inflection that meant he demanded an explanation.

"There's nothing to worry about. I was a bit upset, frustrated. You've encountered people like me before, I'm quite sure, haven't you, Doctor?"

"Yes, of course. But your reaction caused me to be more concerned than I might otherwise be. There was a hostility that I hadn't recognized in you before. So, I just wanted to make sure you're OK."

"Not OK, but not bad either. Look, Doctor, I don't mean to be rude, but it is late. Why don't we continue this during the next visit?"

"You seem troubled, Parker. There's an urgency and agitation in your voice. Is there anything I can do to help you?"

"Dr. Reed, if you don't mind, we'll talk about it later. It can wait. Now, good night." After hearing the psychiatrist's farewell, Barrows filled his glass with more scotch. As he sipped his favorite drink, he began to shake. His hands became sweaty, and his chest felt heavy. Recognizing the potential onset of an attack of dread that Reed attributed to PTSD, he took slow, deep breaths and thought of a beach in the British Virgin Islands. Within moments, the feeling of impending doom vanished as quickly as it had leapt upon him.

Barrows went over to a safe to remove a revolver, which he then placed into a shoulder holster hidden beneath his suit jacket. As he tucked the gun into place, he fine-tuned the specifics of his double-crossing of Wilson. The storage area would be the ideal site—a bullet to his head, followed by a little explosion.

Despite ten years in the British intelligence service, Barrows had never planned to execute anyone. In the line of duty, however, he had seen his share of dangerous gunplay, with one such episode leading to his suffering a wounded left shoulder. After an uneventful recovery, he resumed his career and engaged in foreign assignments. Increasingly convinced of his plan for Wilson, he began to dwell on the final encounter and its orchestration. Would he be able to confront his nemesis? His thoughts then careened to Mesa. *Can he be trusted? Does he know too much? Will he leak anything to Wilson?* Barrows's attention was then attracted to the television, where a talk show host charmed an attractive young actress who reminded Barrows of his wife. As the actress smiled engagingly in animated conversation, his memory served up images of summer days with his wife in Surrey. To Barrows, his wife was vibrant, bright, and alluring, the quintessence of what he valued in a woman. Although his reverie brought momentary bliss, it was soon shattered by thoughts of Wilson, which jarred his mood, causing it to take on an unsettling edge.

—

Anxious to meet the mystery benefactor who both funded their operation and provided key information, Wilson brimmed with self-confidence.

Mesa Wilson usually met in restaurants since business was rarely, if ever, discussed on the telephone and since the apartment in which Wilson lived in South Boston was off-limits. The studio dwelling on the third floor of a triple-decker was situated in a rough neighborhood where one was at high risk of being robbed, mugged, or approached to buy drugs.

En route to tonight's meeting with the man who funded and directed the operation, Wilson was motivated by the possible outcomes of their ploy. He relished the idea that he could both make money and make his mark on Northern Ireland by orchestrating amnesty for Irish political prisoners. Wilson was adamantly opposed to the IRA's surrendering their weapons, a demand insisted upon by British and Protestant factions. In Wilson's view, weapons, violence, and the threat of terrorism had forced the British to finally accede to calls for negotiations.

Soon, Wilson reached an industrial storage site where Mesa awaited him. They immediately began to take heavy wooden crates out of storage and load them onto a truck. They estimated that it would take three trips to carry all of it to South Boston Plating. Unlike their previous escapades, only Wilson and Mesa participated tonight since Barrows, the ringleader, had become obsessed about leaks and insisted that only Mesa and Wilson be present that evening at the storage site.

Although Wilson thought it was strange that Barrows would want to meet where they had stored the crates filled with canisters of TNT, Mesa reassured him. "Bear with the eccentricity," he told Wilson. "It's worth the trouble."

After reaching the plating firm, Wilson used a forklift to take the wooden crates off the truck. Later, Mesa had advised him, they would remove individual cylinders of TNT from the crates for shipment to various locations involving the British delegation. A surprise was the best approach, and tomorrow would be ideal for communicating their demands to the British Embassy: full release of IRA prisoners, no relinquishing of their arms, and a complete withdrawal of British troops from Northern Ireland. They would allow twenty-four hours for the embassy to respond to their demands. To Jake Wilson, the plan appeared sound, even though his surreptitious entry into the delegates' hotel promised to be precarious.

Mesa walked up to Wilson. "One more to go." They got into the truck and drove back to the storage warehouse. Wilson parked the truck, then he and Mesa walked to the storage site entrance.

—

Barrows sat in his car about one hundred fifty yards away and observed them carefully. Reaching into the pocket of his coat to draw out his handgun, he limped into the warehouse and made his way over to the area of the building devoted to storage bins, where Wilson was loading a wooden crate onto a forklift.

"No one will ever suspect TNT, will they?" Barrows chided Wilson, who turned in surprise and faced Barrows.

"Mystery man," Wilson goaded him. "I finally get to meet you."

"Aren't you fortunate?" Barrows responded.

Wilson turned to load another crate onto the forklift.

"TNT will make a terrific explosion. A loud message, indeed, to you and to others," Barrows lectured.

Wilson looked at Barrows in shock. "What the fuck's your problem?" Wilson hollered.

"You, you bastard!" Barrows pulled the gun from his jacket and pointed it at Wilson, who reflexively raised his arms. The steel cage separated Barrows from Wilson, who was now at the mercy of a man on a mission.

"What do you want, dude?" Wilson yelled, the confidence draining from his voice.

"What do you want, Wilson, you crass son of a bitch?!"

"Fuck you," Wilson replied.

"My, what an aggressive remark by a man with a gun pointed at his head."

Barrows smiled condescendingly toward Wilson, who stood motionless, unclear of his next move.

"What do you want from me?" Wilson pleaded.

"Pleasure, Wilson. A pleasure that I've anticipated for some time, ever since you planted the bomb, you bastard—the one in Soho."

Wilson stared at Barrows in fright.

"You killed my wife, you bastard," he screamed, then shot at Wilson's leg, causing Wilson to writhe in pain.

"What do you want, motherfucker?" Wilson wailed.

"Your life, you bastard." Barrows shot at him again, but missed.

"What can I do for you?" Wilson whined, the confidence in his voice having drained beyond recognition.

"What can you do for me! Just turn back the clock and give me my wife and my leg back, you son of a bitch." Barrows again fired the gun, but this time at one of the wooden crates.

"We can deal."

"We cannot deal, Wilson. You fell for my plan, wise guy. There's no way I'd blow up my British colleagues. But I am going to use this stuff to kill any credibility Sinn Fein, the IRA, and the Brexit plan could ever generate."

As Wilson rolled in agony, blood oozed through his blue trousers.

"Yes, Wilson. The IRA and Sinn Fein will take the blame for this. You're going to be portrayed as spineless thugs who can't be trusted."

Wilson writhed in agony.

"But most importantly, Wilson," Barrows said, again with grating condescension, "you're going to pay for this." He lifted up his right leg and removed his prosthesis. Placing his stump through the metal caging, he admonished Wilson. "Kiss it, bastard. Kiss it. You made this happen."

Wilson reached over to grab what remained of Barrows's lower right leg.

"Kiss it. Caress it. Bastard!" Barrows yelled, pointing the gun at Wilson's head.

In a flash, Wilson yanked at Barrows's leg, causing him to fall and drop the gun. Wilson reached after the gun, which now lay outside the metal cage, albeit within his grasp. Both of them grabbed the gun at the same time. A vigorous struggle ensued, until Barrows bit Wilson's hand, causing him to scream and let go of the gun, which Barrows picked up and fired at Wilson, three consecutive shots. The final shot went right into his head, causing Wilson to fall backward to his death.

Having completed the first phase of his plan, Barrows would come back later to detonate the TNT. Wilson would be discovered, his death attributed to a misadventure with military explosives that had been illegally obtained. Barrows did not want to detonate the TNT until hours later, to avoid the risk of calling early attention to his plan. Timing was critical if he was going to prevail.

Chapter 63

"I know this seems hard to believe," Dan said to the attorney. Anna sat adjacent to him in a wood-paneled office in downtown Boston. "But we found TNT—in the workers and at the plating firm—and I think that's why I ended up with the cocaine charges."

"Wait a minute," the lawyer said. "Why would there be TNT? Isn't that used only by the military now?"

"Exactly," Dan answered.

"It explains everything," Anna said enthusiastically.

"This is serious business, Dr. Murphy." Dan's lawyer flipped through some papers in the file and looked up. "Are you sure about the lab that did the testing? As I said, TNT is only used by the military. Why would it be in a plating plant? And you're sure these illnesses are due to TNT and not something else?"

"Yes," Dan said. "The patients' symptoms are consistent with what's in the literature, but the key is that they have DNAT in their urine. Plus, the patient with hepatitis has symptoms that are consistent with TNT exposure."

"Again, this is all very interesting," the lawyer said, "but I'm not sure how we could prove TNT as the culprit."

"Why else would the TNT metabolite be in the urine of the workers? Why would the ventilation filters contain TNT?" Dan recounted.

"I know, but don't you need to be pretty heavily exposed?"

"No."

"We'll need to consider our options carefully," the lawyer responded.

"What do you think we should do?" Anna asked. "My hunch is that Dan's cocaine charge is related to this. He senses a health problem at the plating firm, and they're unresponsive to his overtures to visit the plant. He calls OSHA, then all of a sudden, he's in jail."

"It would be nice if we could tie the drug charges to the plating firm, wouldn't it?" the lawyer responded.

"We need to," Dan said emphatically.

Chapter 64

Barrows looked randomly around his office, then rose from his desk chair and walked toward the full-length glass windows that allowed him a panoramic view of the Boston Harbor. The boat traffic prompted his memory of the *Valhalla*, a ship that set sail from Boston in the 1980s loaded with guns for the IRA. Caught thanks to the combined efforts of the British and Irish security services, the boat had nearly reached Irish soil. Although only a few people knew the details of the operation, investigators traced the *Valhalla*'s origins to Boston.

Barrows would ensure that his current operation was neither leaked nor sabotaged. Disturbed by the dismissive attitude of the British government negotiators toward Brexit and Northern Ireland's future, he thought the Protestants, or as more commonly known, the Unionists, could only lose in any agreement. The privilege of the best economic and political positions would soon be lost to people who were in the Republic of Ireland, to the south. Even though Barrows had left Northern Ireland at age fifteen and was rarely seen in a church, he carefully camouflaged his prejudice against Catholics. They had too many children, drank too much, and couldn't be trusted, not even those who were not sympathetic toward the IRA.

Driven to exact accountability for the loss of his wife, he was sickened by his interpretation of the idealistic views of many

Americans, especially those of Irish nationality, about the Irish Troubles. When Barrows reflected on US support for the Northern Ireland Catholics, especially the prominent displays by US politicians, he felt enraged. By channeling the anger into his own strategy for derailing the peace process, he hoped to achieve justice for his own anguish and also make a mockery of US support for the Catholics in Northern Ireland.

Barrows contemplated his next move, namely, asserting IRA responsibility for last night's explosion at the industrial storage site. The local news reported a horrific blast that authorities attributed to improperly stored construction materials. Barrows, however, realized that it wouldn't be long before the police toxicology report would point out that TNT was involved. As a result, a limited amount of time remained to suggest to the media that a nefarious plan of the IRA had run afoul.

Barrows finished typing a letter to fax to media outlets, especially local television stations and news radio programs. A wide distribution of the demands would heighten the alarm. Sufficiently savvy about media relations, he recognized that the news release should be both authentic and menacing if he wished it to be taken seriously.

As the printer churned out a copy of the letter, Barrows reached for his coat, then opened the lower desk drawer for the scotch that he craved. He took two gulps, grabbed the letter, and left his office.

Timing was an integral part of Barrows's scheme since he knew that once he fingered the IRA for the warehouse explosion, a cascade of criminal justice officials would swing into action. The FBI, politicians, and other self-proclaimed authorities would join the fray in expressing outrage at the IRA's stupidity in orchestrating such a stunt.

He walked into an office supply store located a few blocks from the high-rise building in which he worked. Surveying aisles of business equipment and furniture, he looked for the public fax machine so he could send the message without fear of its being traced back to him. Off in a corner sat the fax that he would use to send television and radio stations the following message:

> The Irish Republican Army regrets the loss of one of its soldiers [Barrow's reference to Wilson] in a tragic mishap last night. Working under the direction of the highest authority, he was preparing for an event to help promote the needs of our people. More destruction will take place to unnamed targets unless the following demands are met within twenty-four hours.
>
> (1) Release of all IRA prisoners.
> (2) Amnesty for all IRA soldiers with criminal charges.
> (3) Recognition of the need for the IRA to maintain arms until all British troops have departed Northern Ireland.
> (4) Full participation in the peace process through Sinn Fein.
>
> A reply tomorrow at noon—announced over the news media—is expected.
>
> —Irish Republican Army

Barrows withdrew an index card from his jacket to review the fax numbers of local television stations and radio news shows. Aware that news programs began at five o'clock, he faxed the press release at half past four so journalists would not have enough time to adequately research the story. Stations would be stumbling over one another to get the scoop on the air and, as a result, would skate the surface in their review. Barrows's condescending attitude toward the media was similar to the view that he held of most people: he was superior from all the important perspectives, but especially in terms of family background, education, and wealth.

While at the fax machine, he said to himself, *Those bastards ruined my life.* Barrows left the office store and entered the fray of people walking along State Street. Having no interest in returning to his office, he wandered along Washington Street amid shoppers, tourists, and businesspeople. He wasn't sure where to go or what to do.

Chapter 65

After the last patient came for an appointment, the receptionist at the Occupational Health Center turned on the television. The reporter seemed unable to control his excitement about the news he was about to deliver. "The IRA has claimed responsibility for an explosion that occurred in South Boston last night. Authorities have found TNT at the site, suggesting that the link with the IRA is plausible. Let's take a look." A view of the damaged warehouse, with the entire side of a two-story wall destroyed, appeared on-screen.

"The material was stored under the name of Perini Construction."

"Any injuries, Jim?" a young blonde-haired woman in her late twenties, sitting next to the newscaster, asked.

"Yes, there was one death, but the body has not yet been identified."

"And I understand there are new threats, Jim."

"Yes, Sue. The IRA has threatened further terror if certain demands aren't met immediately."

"What kind of an effect do you think this will have on the Brexit negotiations?"

"That's unclear. We'll just have to wait and see," he responded.

"Now for a break."

—

Back in his office in the midst of dictating charts, Dan Murphy felt emotionally and physically drained. The morning session with the lawyer had encouraged him about the chances for having the cocaine charges dismissed, but the outcome still remained uncertain.

As he propped his feet on a window ledge, he thought of Anna and how gracefully she had glided into his life. Within a short time, he had grown accustomed to their virtual daily encounters. To Dan, Anna offered the wonderful promise of a bright, loving companion with whom he might be willing to plunge into marriage. As he reflected on the latter, he mentally scolded himself for allowing the lure of romance and its emotional turbulence to cloud his judgment. *But Anna is different,* he reassured himself.

Abruptly, his daydream was interrupted by the nurse practitioner, Brenda, knocking on his door. "You have a visitor," she said.

"Who?"

"Fred Stone." A stocky man in his late forties with a ruddy complexion and thin gray hair stepped in next to Brenda. His jacket, a well-worn British tweed, reflected a casual style unaffected by the dictates of business fashion.

"FBI." He showed his badge.

"What can I do for you?" Dan asked with contained surprise. In a flash, he feared another debacle like the drug episode that had landed him in jail.

"I'd like to ask you a few questions," Stone said. He walked into Dan's office and sat in a chair across from his desk. Demonstrating full authority, he turned to Brenda. "Thank you." The tone of his comment implied that she should disappear.

After quickly mentioning the point of his visit and saying that he had been referred by Dan's attorney, Fred Stone, the agent, launched into an interview.

"I understand you've done some studies on a company here in South Boston. I'm concerned about an explosion at a plant in South Boston. We found TNT, what you detected at the company."

"Yes, that's right."

"Why don't you tell me about it? What's a doctor doing testing workers for TNT?"

Dan described his work with Anna, telling Stone of how they had begun with a cluster of aplastic anemia cases that led to a medical review and eventually pointed them to the plating firm.

"It became clear to us that the plant was the likely cause of the health problems."

"Why?" the agent asked.

"Primarily because of the striking histories that I learned from two of my patients, coupled with some bizarre responses from the company when I asked to visit the plant."

"What do you mean by history?"

"Essentially, the patient's story of when the symptoms occur, what relieves them, and so forth."

"But don't you need more evidence than a history? Isn't that pretty subjective?"

"To make a diagnosis of TNT poisoning, of course. But I only suspected the plant at that point. Anna and I then decided to do some tests."

"How did you decide what to test for?"

"We prepared a list of chemicals that have either caused aplastic anemia or been used in plating shops. Then I selected the tests we would do with the help of a toxicologist."

"If the plant didn't let you on-site, how did you do the sampling?"

"The workers came to the clinic—here!"

"But your lawyer told me something about other tests at the plant."

"We were able to get on-site with the help of the two patients who work there."

"How good is the lab? Do you have official reports?"

Dan reached over to his desk for the lab report that indicated DNAT in the urine of the workers.

"DNAT?" the FBI agent asked.

"Dinitroaminotoluene—it's a breakdown product of TNT."

"Are you sure?"

"Definitely."

"How about the lab? How do you know if the results are reliable?"

Dan, taken aback by the rapidly fired questions, answered, "The lab has an excellent reputation. I'm confident that the results are valid."

"Are you sure?"

"No doubt. Finding five people with a metabolite of a military explosive in their urine is enough to convince me," Dan answered with confidence. "Especially when it shouldn't be present at all."

A knock on the door distracted the agent and Dan from their conversation.

"Anna Carlson is here to see you," the receptionist said.

Dan looked at the agent.

"She did the environmental sampling your attorney discussed?" the agent asked.

"Yes."

"Bring her in."

"Fred Stone, FBI," the agent greeted her, displaying the same badge he had shown to Dan. "I understand you've done some testing at South Boston Plating?"

"Yes," Anna replied.

"Tell me about it."

"We analyzed dust from the plant, and it showed TNT. TNT was also in the ventilation filters."

"So, you both conclude that TNT at the plant caused these people to get sick?"

"Yes," they answered in unison.

"Tell me," the agent said, beginning a request for information with his favorite command, "was there anything suspicious in your dealings with the plant?"

"Yes, the plant management did not want me to come on-site. Now, of course, it makes sense since they were probably up to something illegal."

"Beyond their resistance to you coming to the plant, was there anything else unusual?"

"Yes, I think they somehow set me up on drug charges."

"Your attorney mentioned that as well."

"Doesn't it make sense to you?" Anna asked the agent.

"I don't know, ma'am, I've seen a lot in my career. It wouldn't surprise me."

The agent, seemingly satisfied with the information he had received, rose to leave the office. "Thank you, Dr. Murphy and you—" He hesitated, having forgotten Anna's name.

"Anna Carlson," she said with a wide smile.

"Yes, thank you as well." Then he turned to leave the office.

"What do you think he'll do?" Anna asked Dan.

"I have no idea."

Chapter 66

Not in many years had Parker Barrows felt the adrenalin rush he was now experiencing—perhaps, he reflected, since playing in soccer championships. He drove his rented black Ford to the parking area of South Boston Plating, where Wilson and Mesa had unloaded crates filled with TNT last night. All the material that they had smuggled out of the military base in upstate New York was present. Actually, a bit had been left behind at the storage site for the explosion that killed Wilson. Since Mesa had left the site of the explosion after locking Wilson in the storage bin, Barrows had not been able to get in touch with him. For tonight's finale, he knew he would act alone.

It was Barrows's first visit to the plating firm since he had begun painstakingly avoiding any contact with the business or its operators. Mesa, however, had provided him plenty of information about the plant, especially its layout.

Barrows entered the warehouse, then opened a concealed door that led to a storage area. The room was cleverly separated from the main plating facilities by a floor-to-ceiling metal wall. He shone his flashlight at the wooden crates of metal cylinders that Wilson delivered last night. Observing that the metal cylinders were well protected by the crates and had yet to be removed, he cursed to himself. *I should have had Wilson unload the cylinders too. I killed the bastard too soon.*

Trying to control both his rage and fear, Barrows walked out of the plating firm to his car. From the trunk, he removed a crowbar and two black suitcases, which he brought back to the center of the storage area. The adrenalin rush consumed him. It was hard for him to imagine that he was nearing his goal of not only exacting justice from Wilson, but also protecting the rights of the Protestants in Northern Ireland. With the crowbar, he pried off the wooden planks of the crates, then pulled out the metal cylinders. He opened the suitcases to remove eight dry cell batteries, a similar number of timers, and a radio receiver.

Barrows then picked up a metal pipe and banged off the cap with a hammer. He repeated the process for the remaining seven cylinders filled with TNT. In each open cylinder, he pushed against the yellow powder to pack it firmly. He then inserted a fulminate of mercury blasting cap that he purchased from a construction supply center. After that, he hooked a dry cell battery and some wiring to a blasting cap.

—

Outside the warehouse, a police cruiser idled. A voice came over the police radio. "There's a car parked by itself in the warehouse. Anything funny going on over there?"

"No. Not right now."

"Check the plates."

"Right."

The cop drove the police car into the parking area of the warehouse. The car's headlights startled Barrows, who was not expecting visitors at this time of night. Although Barrows imagined that the plating firm would eventually come under FBI scrutiny, he doubted that it would be the first place they would survey. The momentary fear motivated him to hurry his task, which when completed would further discredit the IRA, embarrass the US government, and destroy the plating firm, which would no longer be able to hire illegal Irish immigrants.

Hastily, Barrows inserted the cap into the TNT powder and hooked a wire to ground the battery and complete the circuit. The TNT, firmly packed in metal pipes, would provide a rocking explosion, especially when placed throughout different areas of the plant. Barrows was confident that little, if anything, of the plant would remain. Although neighboring row houses and a school in South Boston might be damaged, he gave little thought to those potential consequences.

Outside the warehouse, another police car arrived and parked alongside his colleague, who sat in the car with a partner. This time, the light of the second police cruiser troubled Barrows, to the point that he stopped preparing the cylinder, battery, and timer. Since the storage area lacked windows, he walked into the plating area to peer outside at the lights that had attracted his attention. Leaving his handiwork behind, he reached into his pocket to withdraw the same gun that he had used to kill Wilson.

He peeked through a large window onto the parking area but saw neither the police cars nor people. Reassured, albeit falsely, Barrows walked back to the storage area, but on the way he tripped over a metal bucket in an aisle separating the plating tanks.

The noise startled a policeman, who had left his car to walk near the entrance to the warehouse.

Barrows got up then hobbled onward with the aid of a flashlight to set another explosive device. By placing the explosives in strategic areas of the plant and within the range of a radio receiver, he could activate the timers to ensure that the building would crumble beyond recognition. *How different the headlines will be this time!* he mused. "IRA Terror Proves They're Incapable of Peace." "Brexit Plan Backfires."

His rage-filled thoughts continued without letup. *This will crystallize opinion against the IRA. The political leadership will be seen as unable to keep their word. The Protestant response will be predictable and powerful: the IRA cannot control its fanatical wing.*

Barrows prepared another explosive device, which he then carried to a corner of the building where the plating chemicals were stored. Acids and solvents, housed in plastic and metallic circular containers, would enhance the TNT explosion. The anticipation of the firestorm and noise from the action of TNT excited Barrows, causing his mind to race back to the Soho area of London at the time when the IRA attack occurred. Seconds later, he finished assembling the explosive sets.

Outside in the police cruiser, the cop was on the radio again.

"It's a rental car," he said, referring to the black Ford that Barrows had driven to the plant.

"When was it rented?"

"Yesterday."

"To whom?"

"Philip Brown."

"Likely name. How did he pay?"

"Cash."

"You hear anything in there?" the dispatcher asked, referring to the warehouse.

"I thought I heard something a few minutes ago, but I wasn't sure."

"Go in. Find out what the hell is going on."

In the warehouse, Barrows attached a wire to a dry cell battery to provide the spark to detonate the yellow TNT powder, which was tightly packed in the metal pipe. One pipe was positioned at the wall separating the plating shop from the storage area. Another pipe was placed by the acid plating tanks. *My own chemical weapons,* he thought. With his right hand, he stroked the gun hidden in his jacket; in his left hand, he held the timer for the explosives.

A loud crash shocked Barrows, causing him to stop. He heard a door being forcibly opened and then saw a light shining into the plating shop. Barrows froze in place, awaiting the next sound. It seemed too soon for police activity since it had been barely four hours since he faxed the news releases about the IRA blowing up the warehouse. Plus, it was Friday night. Why would anyone from the business be here, especially since it was a one-shift operation that did no work on weekends? *What's gone wrong?* He was afraid, caressing the gun for reassurance. Pondering his next move, he lay on the cold, dank floor. Seconds later, he heard whispers. He scrambled for cover, then hid behind a wooden crate. In the distance, he saw the outline of two male figures, both with a gun drawn in their right hands.

"Police," the cop hollered.

Barrows ignored him.

"Identify yourself immediately."

Barrows remained silent.

The cops shined their flashlights methodically all over the storage area, but Barrows remained hidden behind the crate.

"Police," one of the cops yelled again, the anger in his voice obvious.

Fuck yourself, Barrows said to himself. There was no way he would surrender. How would he ever explain what he was doing in the plating firm, setting up explosives made of TNT? The only chance Barrows had was to kill them, then set the explosives, which would easily account for the deaths of the policemen. Their bodies would be beyond recognition after the TNT detonated, and by that time, Barrows would be safely en route to the airport. The light that scattered from the flashlight of one of the policemen illuminated his partner just long enough to allow Barrows to take aim with his gun. The shot just missed the cop's head and ricocheted off the metal wall.

Barrows fired another shot and hit the partner in the leg. Another shot was fired, but it missed both of the cops.

Barrows ran across the storage area as well as could be expected with his wearing a prosthesis for a right leg. The other cop shot at him but missed.

Barrows reached the dry cell battery and set the timer to activate in five minutes. In the background, he heard one of the cops say, "John, I can't go. My leg's killing me."

"Stay here. Don't move. I'll take care of this."

Barrows thought that his dash across the floor had gone unnoticed, as the injured cop moaned in the background. Now, Barrows stood next to the timer, whose release could destroy all of them. *Should I pull this and make a run? Should I shoot the other cop, then pull the switch?* A bullet shot over his head prompted him to crouch down and fire back.

Instinctively, he activated the timer on the battery. Within minutes, metal pipes packed with TNT would detonate, and then it would all be over—if only he could wait another three minutes before running out from cover. He would need to get into the car and drive away before the explosion occurred. The ensuing chaos of activity would guarantee him a safe departure.

The injured cop lay on the floor agonizing in pain. The blood loss from damage to an artery in his thigh caused him to faint. Barrows caught a glimpse of the policeman's partner stalking him. In the cop's tenacious pursuit of Barrows, he knocked over one of the TNT cylinders. The noise helped Barrows easily pinpoint the location of the cop, in whose direction he fired a shot. Recognizing his opportunity to escape, he fired again in succession at the cop, then hobbled across the storage area, out the door, and into the parking area. As he jumped into his black rented car, three police cruisers drove down the street with their red lights flashing and sirens blaring. They were racing in Barrows's direction.

Ignoring calls to stop, Barrows sped through a traffic light. The chase didn't last long as two other squad cars approached him from the opposite direction. Forced to stop after being surrounded and stared down with threatening police weapons, he surrendered, then was placed in handcuffs and driven back to the police station.

Chapter 67

The stress and drama of the day's events discouraged Anna and Dan from any activity other than watching television, even though it was a Friday night. Lying in bed, they surfed their way through tens of channels until they found a show featuring stand-up comedians. They were shocked when the program was interrupted by a news flash. Then, Dan and Anna viewed a scene of bedlam. Ambulance lights glared and sirens blasted as people milled about police barricades, with the plating firm smoldering in the background.

"Another explosion in South Boston—tonight a plating firm! So far, no one has claimed responsibility," the TV reporter announced.

"Is anyone injured?" her partner asked.

"Two policemen at the plant were taken to the hospital. One injured his leg. Details are still fuzzy."

"Any ideas about what caused the blast?"

"Preliminary results from the fire department's toxicology lab suggest it's TNT."

"Isn't that the same material found at the warehouse that exploded last night?"

"Yes."

"It seems that last night and tonight are related, doesn't it?"

"It certainly does. We'll keep an eye open for further developments."

He turned his gaze away from his partner and looked directly into the camera. "We'll be back for more after this break."

As a commercial pitched a new American pickup truck, Anna turned to Dan. "What do you think happened?"

"We were right about the TNT. I can't see how the explosion can be blamed on anything else, even with acids and solvents and all the other hazards at that place."

"Who do you think's responsible?"

Dan shook his head, then rose from the bed to go into the kitchen. Opening the refrigerator to pull out a bottle of beer, he called to Anna, "Would you like anything?"

"No, just you. Hurry back to bed."

As Dan came back into the bedroom, the news anchor reappeared. "Police have just announced the arrest of Mr. Parker Barrows in connection with the explosion at South Boston Plating. The fifty-two-year-old British native was apprehended two blocks from the plating firm just as the explosion occurred."

The television showed a mug shot of Barrows, taken soon after he had been taken into custody at the police precinct.

"This is incredible," Dan said as he heard the announcer describe the gun found on Barrows.

The newscaster continued, "Police are investigating whether he may have connections with last night's tragedy as well. TNT is only manufactured by the military in this country. It was used in both explosions. Another interesting twist has also surfaced in the death of the man found at the storage warehouse last night."

"How's that?" the partner asked, in an attempt to keep the discussion on course and give him a pause at the same time.

"Mr. Jake Wilson, the man identified at the scene, was initially presumed to have died from the explosion. A coroner's report, however, indicated that a bullet pierced his skull and lodged in the brain, a finding suggesting that he died prior to the firestorm. The circumstances surrounding the shooting—whether at the warehouse or elsewhere—are unclear."

"We'll be looking forward to seeing how all these intriguing events unfold," his partner said.

Another commercial interrupted the newscast.

The news program began again as the young blonde reporter turned to her partner and said, "We have some guests, Ted, to help us understand what happened tonight and what it might mean for Brexit and Northern Ireland."

"Yes, it has been a strange sort of day. This morning we learn of an explosion in a South Boston warehouse that's attributed to a phony construction company, and now we have learned of the arrest of a British citizen in connection with an explosion at a plant known for its sympathy to Irish immigrants."

The partner introduced the guests. "Tonight, we have our political correspondent, Linda Goldman, and our crime reporter, Bob Brenner."

"Bob, do you have any explanation for the bizarre set of events we've witnessed over the past two nights?" the newscaster asked the guest. "And can you tell us anything about these people Parker Barrows and Jake Wilson?"

"Yes. Jake Wilson spent two years or so in and out of London performing IRA work."

"Why would he align himself with someone like Parker Barrows, who I understand does work for the British Trade Office?"

"It may be quite the opposite. That is, Barrows may have sought out Wilson to do the dirty work."

Turning to the other guest, the newscaster asked, "Linda, what effect do you think these events will have on Brexit and Northern Ireland?"

"Unquestionably, there will be some disruptions as these matters are investigated, but it does present an alternative perspective on the Protestants, namely that at least some of them will resort to extreme measures to achieve their objectives. Unionists have voiced strong objections to virtually every proposal related to Brexit."

"Do you think the Unionists were behind this effort?"

"Too soon to tell whether it was simply an extremist acting on his own or whether he was supported by senior officials."

"Do you think the IRA will retaliate?" the newscaster asked the political commentator.

"That's hard to predict. But in light of their adamant denial of the claims attributed to them, they'd be wise to stay calm."

Anna threw her arms around Dan and extended her tongue deep into his mouth. They lingered for minutes as ads pitching soaps, cars, and computers played in the background.

"Do you think the TNT had anything to do with Pat's illness now?" Anna asked.

"It all fits. His recent hospitalization may have been a relapse from reexposure to TNT, but we'll never know for sure."

"How's he doing?"

"Going home Monday, the same day your paper is due for Becker, isn't it?"

"You have a great memory for events I'd like to forget."

Dan continued, "Patrick has done well with the bone marrow transplant and will survive and have a normal life." He reached over to return the kiss that Anna had initiated a few minutes ago. "I'm sure you'll get an excellent grade. How could he pass up piercing blue eyes so full of energy and intelligence?"

"I love the flattery, but don't start writing poetry."

The news show returned to the air. "We have some additional information related to the explosion in South Boston. A fire department hazardous materials team went into the plating firm soon after the fire was under control. An inspection uncovered numerous metal pipes filled with TNT that were not involved in the explosion."

"So, it appears that this tragedy could have been more severe?" the partner quipped. "Especially in such close proximity to homes and that elementary school in South Boston?"

"Indeed. We also learned that, fortunately, the chemical storage area of the plant was unaffected."

"Is there any word on how or why the plating firm was under police review at the time of the explosion?"

"No. Authorities have not given those details."

Dan was pleasantly struck by the integrity of the FBI official who had interviewed him late that afternoon. Apparently, he kept his word in terms of their discussion being confidential.

"And on another encouraging front," the partner said, "hospital officials have released a brief report on the two policemen involved in the event. Each will remain overnight. One is doing well, but unfortunately his colleague is in intensive care."

"I need a break," Dan said, fumbling with the television remote control to shut off the program.

"Are you sorry I twisted your arm to start the study that led to all of this?" Anna asked.

"It would be nice to turn back the clock about two months, but then I wouldn't know you." Dan kissed her again.

"Did you have any idea what you were getting into?" she asked.

"No. And I'm not sure if I want to evaluate any more clusters, but you were worth it."

"What about the cocaine charges? Any news?"

"Yes, they were dropped. The FBI agent we spoke to worked his magic."

Dan reached over to turn off the table light, then rolled onto Anna and thrust his tongue deep into her mouth. She responded rhythmically, and in moments they were immersed in passion, which took them through the night.

About the Author

Dr. Bob McCunney is a specialist in internal medicine and occupational and environmental medicine. He is a practicing physician in the Pulmonary Division of the Brigham and Women's Hospital in Boston, a member of the Harvard Medical School faculty, and a visiting research professor at the Harvard School of Public Health. He is a former director of environmental medicine at the Massachusetts Institute of Technology. Over his career, he has lectured in countries around the world in Europe, Asia, Africa, Australia, North America, including Canada, and Mexico.

Dr. McCunney received a BS in chemical engineering from Drexel University, an MS in environmental health from the University of Minnesota, an MD from the Thomas Jefferson University Medical School, and an MPH from the Harvard School of Public Health. He completed training in internal medicine at Northwestern University Medical Center in Chicago.

He has served as editor in chief of five textbooks and authored or coauthored more than one hundred twenty-five peer-reviewed articles and book chapters. He has also coauthored a book on getting recruited to play college baseball, based on his experience with his son who was recruited to play college baseball at Fordham University. This is his first novel.